A Pride & Prejudice Reimagining

Kitty Bennet's Adventure
Book Seven

NEY MITCH

Dedication & Author's Note

Readers, we're on Book Seven, a little past the middle of the series—and not quite to the end *yet*. Yes, I still haven't embraced the idea that brevity is the soul of wit. Then again, I have never been a wit. Despite one's wishes, we are not all Miss Austen, hard as we try to be. Here is an *important note* for you before you delve into this part of the series.

There will be choices that are made in this tale that will be unexpected. Those sections are inspired by Jane Austen's family, and those parts are me using Miss Austen's characters as a medium where they undergo the similar sentiments her family might have experienced. This will be discussed in the Afterword, which I humbly ask the reader to peruse.

Every now and again, there will be a chapter that deviates from the heroine's perspective, to follow the actions of other characters. This is solely done so that the reader can be given vital information.

Also, this book in the series will have a split narrative and told from two perspectives. It will be told between Kitty's continuing story and rewinding to Jane's tale right after the Bingleys left Netherfield Park after that first ball. It will continue to when Jane met Mary Crawford in Cheapside, London, during the darker times of when Jane thought all was lost. It's to explain how Jane and the Crawfords became friends.

I hope that you like this next installment in the series, but I admit, this one is a little off the beaten path. I hope you will find something about it to enjoy.

Once more, readers, thanks for everything. And a special thanks to Helyn Guy-Roberts, A. Madison, and Laurie Novo for still being there to support me to whatever end.

Prequel

With it having been an exhausting night the evening before, I woke up to see my beloved husband sleeping beside me. I chuckled silently and decided to remain in bed, next to him, until he woke.

Marrying Charles Bingley had been one of the highlights of my life, and one of the first things that I learned about him, when entering the married state, is that he could stay awake and alert during an entire ball...but the day after? Oh, he was asleep and would spend the whole day in bed, if he could.

While my limbs were equally exhausted, my soul was restless though.

Or rather, my imagination was.

Or my memories were.

Looking up at Bingley, I saw the beautiful outline of his face, as he looked there, peacefully.

In that moment, I ought to have been content. Yet with individuals such as I, there is a part of me that is heavily unknown and can only be described as the time-honored maxim: still waters run deep. Within each silent reaction that I give, there are many words that I think, yet do not speak. Many times, I have wished to shout, when I whispered. The voice be serene, but the mind—always awake. Always alive. Always alert.

I should be happy now, and I was. Very much so. But between

the sheets of thought, between the bed of life, we often dwell—or return to times where things were not in a firm state of balance. Of when struggle and folly ruled the day, and not peace and felicity.

And so, my mind chose to dwell, to relive a journey that had long been left alone.

I couldn't help but wonder...so to speak.

My memories drove back to earlier times, more troubling and turbulent times, of when my heart was in a constant state of uncertainty.

Of when, the happy scene that I was amidst, almost did not occur.

Of when everything seemed as if it had fallen apart, months ago...

Sitting down, I opened the letter and smiled when I saw Miss Bingley's familiar handwriting. Immediately I noted the elegant paper and marveled at her skilled handwriting.

And then I began to read the contents of the letter.

By the time I was finished, I cannot honestly recall how I even got to the end of it. Removed from myself even more, I felt as if I was pushed out of my body, someone else had come in, and finished my actions for me.

It was someone else who had re-read the letter.

It was someone else who closed the letter and put it back in the envelope.

It was someone else who stood up, went over to the rest of the company, sat down, and tried—in vain—to ingratiate herself into the party.

It was someone else who was smiling whenever a joke was made—when an anecdote was narrated—when a compliment was offered.

But it was me who was immediately distressed.

It was me who felt as if her world had come undone—had underwent a sudden collapse.

It was I who felt as if a link within me had been severed.

And it was truly me who felt the sudden pangs of heartache, abandonment, and loss.

It was me that was breaking in every way a person could feel broken.

But one thing that *both* of us women had in common was that they both believed that they hid their heartbreak well from the present company.

Both women believed that they did quite well at concealing their agony. Both women were me.

But every minute that I was not allowed to be alone felt like daggers digging into my skin. After what felt like an eternity, the officers took their leave.

At the very moment that they had disappeared down the road, I stole a glance at Elizabeth. She took my meaning and joined me in my room.

With every step we took, the words from the letter weighed me down even more, and the reality of my present became even more real...and even more terrifying to face.

Eventually, we made it to my room, and Elizabeth closed the door behind her.

"Tell me what it is," she urged, "because I could see your disappointment all while you read the letter."

As you know, the two separate women that read the letter: the one who did read it and smiled throughout, and the other woman who cried out in pain...now those women were merging together. Within my form, they united, and we became one.

"You knew that something was wrong?" I asked, heartbroken.

"I saw it in your eyes. Jane, what is it?"

Unfolding the letter, I handed it to her.

"This is from Caroline Bingley." Mentioning it now made everything feel heavier. It made the truth more real, and I could have been knocked down with a feather. "What it contains has surprised me a good deal. The whole party have left Netherfield by this time and are on their way to town—and without any intention of coming back again."

Elizabeth's eyes widened in shock.

"What!" She gasped.

"She tells me that they all are gone. And Mr. Bingley is never coming back."

My whole world had come undone.

All was lost.

With the letter still in my hand, I was motionless.

The shock was real—while also not being so. I felt as if I was not myself, but rather on the outside of myself, watching a woman who looked like me, spoke like me, but was not me. Rather she was someone else, experiencing the pain of the news, undergoing the alarm of knowing that something so certain, so ever-fixed, was all to never come about.

And Lizzy was still there, having heard my announcement. Coming back into myself, I looked at her.

"Jane," she gasped, "I cannot believe it."

"But it is true," I found myself able to utter. Here, you shall hear what she says." Raising up the paper again, I breathed out and in. The page was not more than ten centimeters from my face, and yet the words fell in and out of focus. At last, I steadied myself and continued to read onward.

Resolving to follow after my brother, our entire party has quitted Netherfield Park and returned to town directly. We intend to be dining in Grosvenor Street by the end of the day, where Mr. Hurst has a house.

I do not pretend to regret anything I shall leave in Hertfordshire, except your society, my dearest friend; but we will hope, at some future period, to enjoy many returns of that delightful intercourse we have known, and in the meanwhile may lessen the pain of separation by a very frequent and most unreserved correspondence. I depend on you for that.

I lowered the letter and was surprised to see that Elizabeth was not especially shocked.

"You do not look disturbed by this?" I asked.

"Why should I be?" she responded, "the only surprise there is to the letter is if Miss Bingley truly means what she says."

"Of course, she means it."

"Forgive me, but I am not apt to trust that she intends to remember you or any of us, once she returns to town. Her words are pretty. But that's all they are: pretty. And as for the rest, nothing about it alarms me. I am surprised by the suddenness of their removal, but I see nothing in it to lament. It is not as if their absence from Netherfield will keep their brother from returning. After all, it is *his* home and not *theirs*. Therefore, he can always return without them, which I would find to be a better situation all around."

I bit my lip.

"It is unlucky," she continued, after a short pause, "that you should not be able to see your friends before they leave the country. But may we not hope that the period of future happiness to which Miss Bingley looks forward may arrive earlier than she is aware, and that the delightful intercourse you have known as friends will be renewed with yet greater satisfaction as sisters? Mr. Bingley will not be detained in London by them."

"Caroline decidedly says that none of the party will return into Hertfordshire this winter. I will read it to you."

Taking up the letter again, I continued to read:

'When my brother left us yesterday, he imagined that the business which took him to London might be concluded in three or four days; but as we are certain it cannot be so, and at the same time convinced that when Charles gets to town he will be in no hurry to leave it again, we have determined on following him thither, that he may not be obliged to spend his vacant hours in a comfortless hotel. Many of my acquaintances are already there for the winter; I wish that I could hear that you, my dearest friend, had any intention of making one of the crowd—but of that I despair. I sincerely hope your Christmas in Hertfordshire may abound in the gaieties which that season generally brings, and that your beaux will be so numerous as to prevent your feeling the loss of the three of whom we shall deprive you.'

I felt that surely, Lizzy could decipher, reading between the lines of words and phrases, what Caroline's true meaning was.

"There?" I exuded, "do you not see? It is evident by this that he comes back no more this winter."

Lizzy rolled her eyes.

"It is only evident that Miss Bingley does not mean that he *should*."

She could not see. Heaven and earth! Why could she not see?

"Why will you think so?" I stressed. "It must be his own doing. He is his own master. But you do not know *all*. I *will* read you the passage which particularly hurts me. I will have no reserves from *you*."

My imploring her, willing her to understand was potentially that of a despairing woman who was selfish. Her words were naturally what I should have wished to hear. Yet the news of Mr. Bingley's departure had blinded me to such a degree that my inner voice became quite mad, I was driven to extreme sensibility internally, and I therefore wished for her to feel my wretchedness. She was trying to calm me, to coax me, and that was precisely what I needed. And yet, why did I wish to stress the horror of my situation? In the wake of heartache, we humans are so nonsensical. Looking once more to the letter—the very letter that I should have never read again, but instead clung to like a child touches a hot iron—I continued again.

'Mr. Darcy is impatient to see his sister; and, to confess the truth, we are scarcely less eager to meet her again. I really do not think Georgiana Darcy has her equal for beauty, elegance, and accomplishments; and the affection she inspires in Louisa and myself is heightened into something still more interesting, from the hope we dare entertain of her being hereafter our sister. I do not know whether I ever before mentioned to you my feelings on this subject; but I will not leave the country without confiding them, and I trust you will not esteem them unreasonable. My brother admires her greatly already; he will have frequent opportunity now of seeing her on the most intimate footing; her relations all wish the connection as much as his own; and a sister's partiality is not

misleading me, I think, when I call Charles most capable of engaging any woman's heart. With all these circumstances to favor an attachment, and nothing to prevent it, am I wrong, my dearest Jane, in indulging the hope of an event which will secure the happiness of so many?'

After reading those last words for the second time, then I began to fully feel the effects of it. The implications stung me as I closed the letter, sat back down and stared ahead.

It was moments such as those, in the cold silence of our hearts torn open from shattered dreams, that you become sensitive to every sound and feeling. Reality becomes filtered and you see everything on a finer scale. I felt the softness of the cushion beneath me. I saw the storm clouds outside of the window, threatening rain. I heard the sound of our grandfather clock in the other room. I heard mother's voice in the other room, and Hill's footsteps as she walked around the house. And the vast heaviness of the air around me also felt as if it had developed a heaviness and obscured my vision.

"Jane?" Elizabeth uttered. Her voice pierced through my fevered thoughts and brought me back into her company. "Dearest?"

"Yes," I extolled, breathy. "Yes, I am here."

"You have turned white."

"I am... I am..." I could not find the words, therefore, I shifted back to our main discussion. "Lizzy, you heard the last comments that Caroline made. What do you think of *this* sentence, my dear Lizzy? Is it not clear enough? Does it not expressly declare that Caroline neither expects nor wishes me to be her sister...that she is perfectly convinced of her brother's indifference, and that if she suspects the nature of my feelings for him. She means, most kindly, to put me on my guard. Can there be any other opinion on the subject?"

"Yes, there can. For mine is totally different. Will you hear it?"

I willed myself to be brought back to my senses, and not my sensibilities. Elizabeth had another theory, and it would be to my favor. Therefore, I chose to listen.

"Most willingly," I uttered, awaiting any kind news that she might deliver.

"You shall have it in a few words. Miss Bingley sees that her brother is in love with you and wants him to marry Miss Darcy. She follows him to town in hope of keeping him there and tries to persuade you that he does not care about you."

This news did not satisfy me. As much as I wished that she was correct regarding Mr. Bingley, it contradicted everything that I felt about Caroline. I still believed that I was correct; Caroline was my most devoted friend. She would never hurt me!

"I cannot believe that of her," I denied, shaking my head. Elizabeth stood up, came toward me and sat right down on the sofa, at my side.

"Indeed, Jane," she urged, "you ought to believe me. No one who has ever seen you together can doubt his affection. Miss Bingley, I am sure, cannot. She is not such a simpleton. Could she have seen half as much love in Mr. Darcy for herself, she would have ordered her wedding clothes. But the case is this: we are not rich enough or grand enough for them. And she is more anxious to get Miss Darcy for her brother, from the notion that when there has been *one* intermarriage, she may have less trouble in achieving a second, in which there is certainly some ingenuity. And I dare say it would succeed, if Miss de Bourgh were out of the way. But, my dearest Jane, you cannot seriously imagine that because Miss Bingley tells you her brother greatly admires Miss Darcy, he is in the smallest degree less sensible of *your* merit than when he took leave of you on Tuesday, or that it will be in her power to persuade him that, instead of being in love with you, he is very much in love with her friend."

After considering her words, I carefully gave my reply.

"If we thought alike of Miss Bingley," I pointed out, "your representation of all this might make me quite easy. But I know the foundation is unjust. Caroline is incapable of willfully deceiving anyone. And all that I can hope in this case is that she is deceiving herself."

"That is right," Lizzy supported, leaning back and letting her shoulders slacken, "You could not have started a more happy idea, since you will not take comfort in mine. Believe her to be deceived, by all means. You have now done your duty by her and must fret no longer."

~

In the work of a moment, hope was returned to me. Perhaps Lizzy was correct. For Mr. Bingley made it very evident, before he left, that he was leaving for town for a brief duration. That was all. There was nothing in his tone, manner and habit, that indicated anything otherwise.

All there was for me to worry over, unfortunately, was the matter of his sisters. This alarmed me to such a degree that I felt obliged to mention it.

"But, my dear sister," I compiled, "can I be happy, even supposing the best, in accepting a man whose sisters and friends are all wishing him to marry elsewhere?"

"You must decide for yourself," Elizabeth offered me this ultimatum, "and if, upon mature deliberation, you find that the misery of disobliging his two sisters is more than equivalent to the happiness of being his wife, I advise you by all means to refuse him."

I smiled faintly.

"How can you talk so? You must know that, though I should be exceedingly grieved at their disapprobation, I could not hesitate."

"I did not think you would," Lizzy smirked, "and that being the case, I cannot consider your situation with much compassion."

"But if he returns no more this winter, my choice will never be required. A thousand things may arise in six months!"

"And to that, I find utterly unlikely. Between his continual seeking you out, his inability to attend to anything else when you are present, his eyes so ever-fixed on you that he did not even notice our family's humiliation at the ball, to his dancing with you so often—no! I draw utter contempt at the idea of him not returning. It is Miss Bingley's wishes, and no more. I would say that we ought not to even mention what she wrote in the letter, but I know how we are; we are going to mention it by and by. And even if his family does not look on your match with a favorable eye, I cannot believe that Miss Bingley's wishes carry so great a weight with her brother, that it would influence him to abandon his own will and desires. He is an independent man. Therefore, his heart is independent. Her influence cannot be so very large."

The more she spoke, the more I was convinced that I had no cause for alarm, at present. Her arguments were so logical, and her concern for me too real, for it all to be anything else but the truth.

"I hope you are right, Lizzy."

"I flatter myself that I may be. Unless I am terribly mistaken, I believe that Mr. Bingley will return very soon, to answer every wish that your heart desires of him."

"You write me a happy ending. May reality turn out as you write it."

"If only I was the sort who could control fate, he would be here tomorrow."

Suddenly, another thought struck me! The notion of it was something that I dreaded.

"But what do you think I should tell mother?" I asked. "I'm worried that if I show her this letter, she would be overcome by the news."

"That is an understatement. Her nerves would blow the house down. All that I can suggest is that we tell her the news of the family departing Netherfield. But we should not mention how long he is gone for and merely infer that it is a casual visit to town. We should not give her cause to alarm. If we do, we will regret doing it for the next month."

"I agree. I do not want to make her feel any anxiety needlessly. I'm happy we are of the same mind in this. If we mention that they merely left for a brief time, then she will not be overcome."

~

"What!" our mother cried. "What a horrible thing!"

Lizzy and I had told her the news, thinking it would not trouble her. We were wrong.

"This is exceedingly unlucky!" she wailed, "exceedingly unlucky, and very trying on my poor nerves. What a shocking thing! I said this about Mr. Bingley before, didn't I? You all heard me worry that he was the sort of man to be running here and there quickly and never know how to settle down. You see? I was right. I am always right, but no one listens to me. I'm like a prophet that never gets heard."

Out of the corner of my eye, I saw Lizzy roll her eyes. While our mother's behavior indicated all the signs of becoming hysterical, I sympathized. Truly, I never wished to cause mother any pain, and now here I was, committing the very thing that I attempted to always avoid. I tried to tell myself that it was not my fault, that my mother put too high of expectations on me, but I knew that it would do no good.

"I just cannot believe it!" she continued, arguing with herself. "One minute he is there, and then he is gone. All was going so very charmingly. It all looked promising! And I hope he remembers his promise! Yes, I have not forgotten, you see? For I never forget anything! He promised that he would dine at Longbourn again. We invited him to dinner, and I had planned to two full courses."

"Well, then you have no need for alarm," Lizzy offered. "For if you invited him to dinner, for two courses, and he accepted, then he has no choice to return. After all, Mr. Bingley is not the sort of man to break such an important promise as a dinner with a neighbor."

"Oh, who asked you to speak? Unfeeling, selfish child! At least Jane did everything correctly. You could have been Mr. Collins's wife!"

"But she was right to refuse him," I uttered, defending Lizzy. "They did not love each other and so her actions were correct, and not selfish."

Mama looked away from me, and it was as if she had not heard me.

"Yes, well," she continued, "he did promise. So, he will return.

And when he does, I promise, I shall take care to have two full courses. Yes, for Mr. Bingley, nothing better will do. Two whole courses."

This was the consolation she found at the end. And the belief of Mr. Bingley dining with us eventually was the balm to soothe the wound of him presently leaving Netherfield.

I am Jane Bennet...and my life was unwinding. Now I had to face a world of reactions that I did not wish to endure.

Chapter One

KITTY'S TALE: THE TRIAL BEGINS...

L ife can be much determined by a series of reactions, and the expressions that they cause.

I looked at Colonel Fitzwilliam. He looked at me.

Next, I looked at Elizabeth.

She was looking at Mr. Darcy.

Once he looked at her, he directed his attention to Mr. Bingley.

And Mr. Bingley looked at Jane.

Jane looked at Mary Crawford.

Mary Crawford looked at William Price.

William Price looked at her and held her hand.

Afterwards, I looked at Georgiana.

Georgiana looked at me, then she looked at Arthur Philips.

Arthur looked at Enara.

Then we all finished our expressions and directed our attention back to the chief speaker himself: Mr. Henry Crawford.

His previous words rang out in the corners of my mind: *'It is time that I finally answer for all that I have done. And I tell all, in hopes that one day, I may find forgiveness.'*

And Mr. Darcy's reply: *'For the love of our sisters, who want us to understand each other, I do it for them. Therefore, you may proceed.'*

One was a proper introduction. Henry Crawford was the verbose and charming sort. He could spin words around a person in the same manner that a spider could spin words around its prey. In both regards, the situation was dangerous for the object that both wished to ensnare. But, despite his history, I could not hate Henry, in the same sort of manner that nature could not detest the spider. It was the nature of the predator, and it could not be ignored.

However, Darcy was on the other side of the situation, and his was the proper reaction. He had given Henry Crawford leave to explain himself, but not so much leave that Henry could feel that he was entirely able to be forgiven.

That was the *right* thing to do. Despite my weakness for Henry Crawford's behavior, it made me admire Mr. Darcy all the more. Time had helped me to appreciate him, and this moment was such an instance. He would listen but not be swayed so very easily. Henry Crawford would not be met with a man who gave in so easily, when it came to Mr. Darcy. As a result, he could not pull the proverbial 'wool over Darcy's eyes' but found someone who could not be wooed, charmed, or impressed. Also, Darcy had been courted by 'false' charm before, and now he knew how to see through it. Thus, we could all now delve into the truth of the matter, plunge to the depths of veracity, and see the beauties of sincerity. All is safe from eyes being shut, when there is one among you whose eyes are always wide awake.

"Well," Colonel Fitzwilliam whispered to me. "This ought to be one of the most interesting afternoons that will take place here."

"Yes," I responded, speaking equally low, "I would be upset if it proves otherwise."

He chuckled quietly, and we became attentive.

"When I arrived at Mansfield Park," Henry Crawford began, "you could say that I arrived with no terrible intentions, but I own to having a terrible mind."

"Explain," Darcy said, his tone neither helpful nor cruel. It was merely...strong and impartial.

"You must understand," Henry Crawford began, but Darcy interrupted him.

"I do not *have to* understand anything," Darcy stated, "but you must help me along."

"My husband is correct," Elizabeth supported, "what he wishes to comprehend is entirely up to him, and him alone. You can explain, but he must make up his mind along the way. But never fear, Mr. Crawford, this is encouragement. We will give you allowance to speak, but never to demand."

Henry Crawford chuckled.

"Yes, of course. I have used the wrong words. Rarely do I do that, for I suppose at one point in my life, I once prided myself on saying all the correct things."

"Charm can lead to that," Mary Crawford supported him, "but now, Henry, you are being sincere. Sometimes, sincerity can lead to a person not being as certain as they once were." She looked at us all. "I am not making excuses. But, judging from my brother's history, this is him finding a better way. Naturally, you must all think me to be a little blinded by sibling loyalty."

"When it comes to family," Jane answered, "when it comes to follies and vices, if we don't remain loyal to them, then who will?"

Mary Crawford smiled at her, grateful. No matter what the outcome of this situation, I knew it: Jane would remain steadfast to Mary Crawford forever. Miss Crawford had found her way into Jane's heart, and there, she would hold fast and perhaps forever.

∾

Now that he had his sister's confidence, as well as Elizabeth and Jane's, Mr. Henry Crawford felt his courage rise—or at least, that's how I translated it—and he had the heart to continue.

"I should clarify that my actions might be a blend of nature and nurture. I was born into a world where Mary and I were raised by our aunt and uncle. That was an unhappy marriage, where our uncle's affections were not the best. He didn't think very well of matrimony, and as Mary can tell you, he could have treated our aunt better. I do not lay my private life before you all because I am loose of the tongue, but so that you know the world that Mary and I were in. Besides, much of my life has been in the papers, therefore, what is there left to conceal?"

"I am not so scrupulous when it comes to hiding my family's history," Mary Crawford explained. "That may not be regarded as proper, but I only lay down the history of my life to people who I consider worthy of hearing it. I trust Jane and Kitty, and I know, by extension, that I therefore can trust you all. I appreciate the efforts of my uncle, in that he financially supported us. But that, perhaps, could have come about through the simple expected devotion to family, as well as from our aunt's imploring him to. However, it doesn't change the fact that he did not respect us women that were in his life. He did not love my aunt—or if he did, he did not respect her. His disrespect went so far that, all throughout their marriage, our uncle kept a mistress."

My eyes widened in shock, but not in the traditional manner. A man having a mistress was not uncommon. What was uncommon was that Mary and Henry knew of this woman.

"Then..." I began, "you knew this? Even when you were children?"

"Yes, we did," Mary Crawford explained. "Even going that far back in our history, I cannot recall a time that we lived there, and we were ignorant of the matter."

"Monstrous," Enara commented. "You were exposed to such immorality at too young an age."

"And that is the fact of the matter," Henry Crawford said. "You see, when you are given rotten fruit to eat, since your child-hood, immorality becomes commonplace."

"You become used to the idea of immorality and vice being acceptable," I put in.

"Precisely. Thus, Mary and I were nursed on this doctrine, this jaded perspective on marriage being something that is taken for granted entirely on the gentleman's side, and it being something that the wife must endure. Perhaps, I clung to that message too well—but it's hard to overcome a lesson that you were taught since you were children."

"We shall take that into consideration," Mr. Darcy responded, "but at some point, a man is like a woman. When reaching the very peak of our manhood, we must eventually stop blaming others and eventually learn to blame ourselves."

"I do blame myself now, I assure you. For where does the negativity of influence end and the negativity of one's own independent iniquity begin? I am certain that I do not know anymore. If I ever knew to begin with. I just say this so that you know my history, and how my sordid past is a blend of being given the worst of influences from the very beginning, and I was left to enhance my negative qualities with the independence of being a wealthy young man, who could practice his nefarious habits without the ability to yield to a more principled way. For, you see, my uncle loved me. I was a boy, who he could mold into being another version of himself. He raised me to be quite like him, and I, in my love for him, indulged and learned every lesson that he was willing to expose to me. I loved my aunt, but I also admired my uncle for having a mistress. After all, my uncle trained me to love her and consider him right to have her."

Once more, I looked at Georgiana and Colonel Fitzwilliam.

In Georgiana's eyes was alarm at such confessions on the horrid uncle.

In Colonel Fitzwilliam's eyes was resignation. Leaning into him, I could not help but whisper.

"You look upset but not disturbed."

"Because this is common. And you don't look upset about this either."

"Because I am like you. This is common, but we seldom speak about such things. That's what makes it even more horrible: that I am not surprised—though a young lady ought to be."

Colonel Fitzwilliam took my hand, to show camaraderie, and quickly released it. I was grateful to him.

"When I reached proper age," Henry Crawford continued, "I stood to inherit Everingham, as well as a sizeable fortune that made me free of all restraint. Mix this independence, of being given everything in life, with the education that I was raised on, and then also with an uncanny ability to endear myself to the female sex. You see, when I was very young, I realized that I was very ugly."

All us ladies looked in between ourselves, and we all had the same thought: *'he knows this about himself? Surely, a man of such winning ways with women would be ignorant of his own physical inadequacy? It seemed like it was something that one would think that he was completely unaware of.'*

"But I also am a man who is very much enticed by the joys of the female sex," Henry Crawford continued. "One could even say that I was quite obsessed with them. Therefore, being the ugly mortal that I am, I thought it wise to correct my natural defects by learning how to speak well. At first, this was a study of mine, and I began to kneel before the great goddess that is 'Charm'. And that was where I discovered the penultimate lesson of my life."

"What?" Elizabeth asked.

"I learned that I was quite good at it. Imagine, Mrs. Darcy, to discover that you can make a woman forget that you are nothing worth admiring. You can make her forget that you are hideous, that you are unworthy of her—and make her believe that you are worthy. That you are the handsomest man she has ever met. God gave me the natural grace for all to look past the beast and see the beauty of myself. This was my skill. And I prided myself on it. After all, it is a common thing to pride oneself on one quality that we have, be it real or imaginary. Well, my skill was real."

"But what has this to do with your past actions?" Georgiana asked.

"It's the beginning of it all," Arthur Philips summed up, to which we all turned to him. "You see, Miss Darcy, when you discover that you can lure people in, and that there will be no consequences to your actions, no fear of being censured or despised for any moral misgivings, you can easily make a sport of it. Or am I wrong?"

Henry Crawford chuckled sadly.

"No, you are not wrong. On the contrary, Mr. Philips, you could not be more correct. From my childhood, I had two perspectives of marriage rolling around within me. First, there was the idea that one should not go into marriage lightly, or I would be miserable in the way that my aunt and uncle were not happy with each other. Therefore, I never wanted to go into marriage lightly, or indiscriminately. If I were to marry, it had to be something that I deliberated over and would not go into it unless I was very certain that I had chosen the right sort of woman for it."

I leaned back and looked at Mrs. Grant. The poor woman. She had two siblings who would forever throw her into the path of emotional crises, but she also could not turn away from them.

"But there was the second part of it," Henry Crawford said, "and that I also loved women, as well as I loved to entice them. Draw them in and make them love me. But not to marry. Oh no. Like I said, I would not enter it lightly, or for a passing pretty face, or goodness of character on the woman's part. I found pleasure in making a woman love me and then moving on."

"You're a siren," I noted, "is that it? I do not say this to harm you, but to clarify. As a siren, you call to women, lure then in, break their hearts, then wait for the next one to come along?"

Henry sighed.

"Yes, I do that."

"But Kitty," Mary Crawford said, "very few young ladies have broken hearts that mean a great deal."

I blinked, surprised at her saying such.

"Miss Crawford," I responded, "what do you mean by that? Do our hearts mean nothing? Why should we not be equal in that way?"

"Mary?" Jane asked. "Surely, you do not mean that."

"Actually, I do," Mary Crawford said.

"Are you so severe and coldhearted to your own sex?" Colonel Fitzwilliam asked.

"On the contrary, I do it as an endearment to my sex."

We all looked at her, confused.

"How so, beloved?" William Price asked, hoping that Miss Crawford would say something to contradict her cold statement.

Mary Crawford looked on us all, completely unafraid, and not intimidated in the slightest. Even Mr. Darcy could not scare her.

"I speak from the perspective of a woman who has had her heart broken," Mary Crawford began, "believe it or not, tragedy gives a young woman perspective, as I am certain that it might do for a young man. While it is bewitching to meet one's first love and that be the greatest love of all, what of all the other lessons in life? Also, the world speaks of us women as if we all have the sad story of coming undone because we had our heart broken, at one time or another. Well, I tell you now, that is not true. There is life after heartbreak. There is still so much more for the woman to experi-ence—to do, and even to be. That is why I said very few young ladies have hearts worth caring about if they are broken...because I believe that we can recover from it. And if we can't—if we give into this notion that we cannot fall from the wagon of loves labors lost, dust off our petticoats and continue, then what are we? We give into every single generalization that we ladies are too delicate. Let's be broken for a time, have our cry out, write some sad entries in our journal, then we recover, learn from our experiences, and move on. Call me what you wish...but that is how I feel. A broken heart is not the end of our lives. Sometimes," and here she looked at William Price, "it can lead to a better tomorrow."

"Yes, but Miss Crawford," Elizabeth countered, "one should never set out to deceive or not care for another person's heart. It is ill to toy with the affections of either sex."

Mary sighed.

"Well, that is very true. I am not even going to pretend that you are not correct, for you are. No one should set out to deliber-ately break a heart. I have told Henry this. But I still cannot believe that a woman ought to fall apart due to one romantic misfortune."

"On that score, you are correct. Giving way to one's sensibil-ity, to the point of ruining one's own life, is never wise."

"Precisely, Mrs. Darcy. And it is that sort of creature that you shall become acquainted with very soon. Love can cause destruc-tion in two ways, but there is one more prevalent than the other."

"And what way is that?" Colonel Fitzwilliam asked.

"That, sometimes, when it comes to romantic disasters, it takes two people to cause an accident. In this case, both parties were at fault. My brother, and the other woman."

"You refer to Miss Maria Bertram, don't you?" I asked.

"Yes, I do. But we are getting ahead of ourselves. Henry, you may continue."

"My sister's words deserve no rebuke," Henry Crawford uttered. "She speaks from the perspective of someone who cares for me, and wants me to be given a fair hearing, and not spoken through a perverse corruption. Though, perhaps, too much credit has often been given to me. Yes, I did have a habit of setting out to entice every young lady who I had a passing fondness for, but I never pursued it to such depths as I did until I arrived at Mansfield Park. When arriving there, I was met with three ladies: Miss Maria Bertram, Miss Julia Bertram, and their cousin, Fanny Price. Being a cousin from a lowlier side of the family, she was initially not someone I regarded highly of, because she was the Right Hand to Lady Bertram. I suppose that was where my chief mischief lay."

"She was the woman who you eventually proposed to," I voiced.

"Yes, she was." Mr. Crawford turned to his sister, Mary. "You were right, as you often were. I was the one who was taken in by the end. But it was myself that put me into that mess." He looked at Mrs. Grant. "You were right, as well, in that I was a wicked sort of creature."

"I wanted to believe that you had it in you to be better," Mrs. Grant said, "I thought Mansfield Park would cure you of your wandering ways."

"In another life, I would have been as good as you, I suppose." Next, he turned to the rest of us and continued. "Well, when I arrived at Mansfield Park, it was to the scene of the eldest Miss Bertram being engaged to another gentleman, named Mr. Rushworth of Sotherton. This is the one, and only quality of my character that I could attest to being lacking in malignance. I showed more preference toward Miss Bertram than I did the single sister, Miss Julia."

"Why?" I asked, without fear. "Why would you do that?"

"Because I firmly believed that it was the better path. I liked Maria the better for her engagement. For an engaged lady is always more agreeable than a disengaged lady. Her cares are over, and she can bestow all her powers of pleasing without suspicion. All is safe with an engaged woman, and no harm can be done."

"Wait," Mr. Darcy said, "you mean to tell me that, initially, your plan was to charm Miss Bertram, because you believed that it was the safer avenue to ensnare? After all, if she is engaged, then her heart could not seriously entertain many thoughts of you."

"Yes. I liked the idea of being charming with her, primarily, because she was ultimately going to marry someone else. Of course, I could not ignore Julia, and I did make myself very agreeable to her. But I also did things to display that I did not prefer her. Therefore, Miss Julia escaped my attentions, overall unscathed, because I did not offer her too much encouragement. All this my two sisters can attest to. They have heard me voice such viewpoints often."

"It's true," Mrs. Grant said, "I am not making excuses, but I can verify that Henry did approach Miss Bertram under the belief that he could bestow all his powers of being pleasing and not have to worry of her heart being bruised. He thought her engagement was a safety—a barrier that could keep her removed from falling prey to his attentions."

"And then came the first tragedy of it," Mr. Crawford continued, "and that was where I should have refrained...but now, I wonder, even if I had, would it have mattered?"

"How so?" Mr. Darcy asked.

"Because, soon into my coming, I discovered very quickly that Miss Bertram did not love her fiancé at all. In fact, she despised him. That should have been the first sign that I had taken a step too far."

Mr. Darcy leaned back, detecting his meaning.

"She did not love her fiancé, and therefore, her heart was still open to choosing another. And you were the perfect candidate."

Mr. Crawford sighed.

"Yes, I was."

～

Suddenly becoming thirsty, Mr. Crawford took a drink from his tea.

"How heavy confessions can be," Mr. Crawford uttered, "I suppose that I am not used to giving them. There are few times I have ever needed to explain things in my life."

"What happened next?" Mr. Bingley asked. "This story may have been told to me before, but your own perspective allows more to the tale. What is there to it?"

"I should have removed my pleasing words from Miss Bertram's ears, but I did not. I should have run, but I did not do that either. No. It was more pleasurable for me to draw her in, as it were. Along with her sister. The only one that I did not pay any heed to was Miss Fanny Price—but she was safe from me. Soon into meeting her, we deduced that she was not out, therefore, there was no point in noticing her. Very quickly I gained the affections of both sisters, but soon I put an end to that with Miss Julia, who escaped my charms, and grew to care very little for me. By the end of it all, I was nothing more than a common acquaintance to her. But, with Miss Bertram, it was another matter entirely. Very soon, she grew to despise her fiancé, and when her desire for me reached its peak, I withdrew from her company."

"You left her broken-hearted," I noted.

"Yes, I did."

"But...all things considered, she was engaged to another. Therefore, technically, her heart was not yours to break."

"That is what I mean," Mary Crawford uttered. "That is why I say that her heart didn't have much to be broken over. Henry was wrong to engage her affections."

"But she had no right to give them away."

"Precisely," Jane uttered. "I will never subscribe to Mr. Crawford's way of thinking, but in this circumstance, Miss Bertram must own to her own actions. I feel for her, but she had no right to attach herself to a man, when she was attached to another. If the roles were reversed, and a man did as she did, then I would not condone him either."

"Also," Enara pointed out, "there is the other matter, which is that if this Miss Bertram realized that she no longer loved this Mr. Rushworth, then why did she not break off the match? Many engagements don't lead to marriage. Someone has a change of heart eventually. It makes no sense why she went through with it."

"I think I know why," Elizabeth deduced.

"Why?"

"First I must know," Elizabeth asked Mary Crawford and Mrs. Grant, "were either of you still present at Mansfield Park when your brother left?"

"Yes," Mrs. Grant answered, "we were."

"Did this Miss Maria Bertram display any signs of inner disquiet, heartache, or contempt?"

"Yes," Mary Crawford answered, "she did. But it was not in a very public way. Her anger was concealed with the subtlety that we ladies are often told to display to rein in our sensibilities. But every now and again, I saw it. When she was with Mr. Rushworth, her hatred towards him was definite, it grew, but she also became more desperate to speed up the wedding—it was as if..." Mary Crawford's eyes widened at the revelation, "she was trying to prove something."

"Precisely!" Elizabeth declared. "She was trying to put on a brave face. That is what occurs to many of us, when our heart is broken. We don't all learn how to quietly leave the table when love is no longer being served. Many of us don't know how to confront shame. Rather, when our hearts are broken, we don't want anyone to think that we have been shattered. Our pride cannot afford that. Therefore, we must put on a strong face. I think Miss Bertram's sudden choice to go along with the wedding, even rushing to the event, was her way of putting on a brave face. Mr. Crawford, you must have really broken her heart. By doing so, her reaction was to rush into an attachment that she knew would make her look strong."

"But that's foolish," I noted, "it would only lead to her utter misery and undoing. After all, she would only bask in her triumph briefly before she realized that she resigned herself to her own version of hell." I leaned back, answering my own quandary. "But she didn't see that at the time. All she saw was her way of looking victorious and not defeated. After all, that's what happens when your heart is crying out. You make a hasty decision, and you damn yourself."

"I did the right thing of staying away from Mansfield Park until both sisters had left, for Miss Julia attended Mrs. Rushworth on her honeymoon," Mr. Crawford continued. "Once I was aware of their departure, I viewed it as the perfect time for me to return to Mansfield Park and visit my sisters again. I know it may be hard to believe, but my coming was done expressly to see how my sisters were faring. When I arrived there, the cousins' absence put me in the place of indulging my traditional idle behavior. I was a charmer with no woman to charm. Or at least, I had thought so at the time."

"And that was when you set your sights on Fanny Price," Jane deduced.

"Yes, I did. And that was the beginning of my ultimate wickedness. Fanny Price was different than other women. Having witnessed how I flirted shamelessly with her cousins, she wanted nothing to do with me. This led to my ego being affected, my passions being ignited. She did not want me."

"And as a result, you wanted her," Arthur Philips deduced. "I am right, aren't I? The classic 'wanting what one does not have' motif."

"Yes, it is such. I confess to that act as swiftly as I confess to everything else. She was determined to not look upon me with admiration, and I was determined that she ought to. It was in this place that Mary chastised me."

"I advised against it," Mary Crawford explained, "and rather, I advised Henry to be satisfied that he had secured the hearts of the Bertram sisters, and that was enough. But I was unsuccessful."

Out of the side of my eye, I watched William Price, who was Fanny's brother. He shifted in his seat, uncomfortably. He probably wanted to say so many things but didn't know how to approach the subject—especially so publicly perhaps.

"It didn't matter what you would have said," Henry continued. "You know as well as I that I would always have gone my own way. And I did. Initially, I set my sights on snatching Miss Price's heart from her and leaving her in the same anxious state that I had secured of many other women. But Mary was correct; I was the one taken in at last. Miss Price's demure nature, her serene countenance, her refusal to be drawn in by me, were all very proper inducements, were natural attractions, and I fell in love with her. I proposed marriage to her, but she would not have me. In fact, she was against every prospect of being my wife...and perhaps, that made me want her even more. I had never had a woman run away from me before."

Within Mr. Crawford's eye was a strange exhilaration that I could not make out. All that I could deduce was that he was recalling his past with this Miss Price woman, of better moments, of perhaps an age where she did not despise him as she perhaps did so now. I knew that look. It was of a man pretending that life had not turned out the way that it did, that he had not taken a step too far in the wrong direction.

Yet, he had, and he had no choice but to fall back to the reality that he had placed around himself.

"I was determined to win her heart," Mr. Crawford elaborated, "and I went so far as to begin to find a way into the recesses of her tenderness. However, one day, I received an invitation to attend a dinner party that Mr. and Mrs. Rushworth had given at their townhouse in Wimpole Street."

"And you went?" Mr. Bingley asked. "What possessed you to do such a thing?"

"Perverse curiosity, I suppose. When knowing that I had

obtained her affections, I also was aware that her attitude toward me had soured. Unable to bear the idea of a woman being alive in the world, and thinking ill of me, I could not rest till I secured her good opinion once more. It was vanity, pure and simple. And then, when I did meet her once more, I was met with utter coldness. Well, I could not have that. I was not used to being wholly unable to make any woman my enemy, so I set out to find my way into her affections once more."

"Sir," Darcy uttered, "that was monstrous."

~

Monstrous.

That was the ultimate judgement that would be placed on Mr. Crawford's actions. Even before the full testimony had been concluded, the label had been cast.

Henry sighed.

"I know. Believe me, initially, I only had done it to improve my opinion in Miss Bertram's eyes. After all, who here, in this room, does not wish to be universally loved?"

"That argument is shared by many of us," Jane said, "but it will not work for your hosts, Henry."

"Very much so, Mr. Crawford," Elizabeth said, still very interested in what Mr. Crawford had to say. "Mr. Darcy is the sort to understand that a person has a right to have a few enemies here and there. For if a person does not have an enemy, then it is a strong indication that *that* person doesn't feel strongly about anything."

"Precisely," Mr. Darcy stated. "My wife and sisters-in-law understand me, sir. Strength of positive feeling and moral sincerity often breeds enemies, because there is always someone out there who is quick to be offended. You speak prettily, and I do understand the root of your thinking, but that's as far as it goes. It would have been better for you to have allowed Miss Bertram to think what she would of you, allowed her contempt to remain steadfast, because it would have been the strongest indication that you had relinquished any aims at her, entirely. She is also guilty in the matter—as such, the last thing that you ought to give such characters is encouragement. As it has proven true because I know the rest of the history. You did your best to convince her that you still cared, she took advantage of your intentions, acted on them, and left her husband to chase after you. Am I correct?"

"You give my history in a quicker fashion than I could have given."

"It has been my constant study, that being brief is the best way of making summations. You will grow accustomed to my manner over time. Or you might not, for which I could not care less."

We all turned to Darcy, who did not flinch. Rather, he leaned forward, his eyes bearing a unique hue and expression that we could not read. But it was strong; he meant to exert his influence.

"There," Darcy declared. "You see what I did there? You must despise me, in this moment."

"I am in your home, at the mercy of your hospitality," Mr. Crawford responded, "I have no right to hold you in contempt."

"Then you are not used to being offended. And because you are not accustomed to it, you do not feel it. Or you do feel it, and you are not telling me the whole truth. Well, I want you to feel it. Look into my eyes, sir."

Henry Crawford had no choice. He had to look into the eyes of this formidable host. It was undoubtable that he had not encountered such a gentleman as Mr. Darcy before and might never do so again. Darcy towered over Mr. Crawford, and his handsome mien rendered Mr. Crawford's charm as dwarfish. Therefore, he had no choice but to bend to his host's will. Mr. Henry Crawford stared into the eyes of Pemberley's master.

"Do you feel me judging you, of me not yielding? Tell me, do you feel anything from it?"

"Yes, I do. I feel upset."

Darcy blinked, his eyes relaxed and he leaned back in his chair.

"Good," he stated, "if a man does not feel anything, when he is being labelled and judged, then I fear for such a character.

Because his ultimate crime is indifference, and I can't help indifference. None of us here can. For us to help you, I need to know that you feel something other than the love that others pour into you. For if you prove to be the reverse, and are nothing more than an empty vessel, who is obsessed with absorbing what you are very much lacking in your life, there is the possibility that you are beyond our assistance." Darcy leaned back. "Do you know this about yourself?"

"I would not describe myself as an empty vessel."

"It's hard to see it when one is such a way." Darcy's eyes no longer were penetrating, but they shifted to deductive. Almost sleuth-like. "I have seen your kind before, sir. You are not alone. Right now, I'm not asking you to blame yourself, nor condemn yourself. I am simply asking you to know yourself. We've all blinded ourselves to our true natures so very often. You know your ways, habits, and means... I do not need to correct your acknowledgement of your past mistakes. But what I do need to do is help you discover the source of them. If you didn't live off the praise and adoration of others, if no woman cared for you, what would you do?"

Henry Crawford blinked. For the first time in his life, I saw all drippings of confidence quite escape him. Even when Mr. Darcy and the rest of us were questioning him, Mr. Crawford never lost his charisma, nor his self-assurance. He was above being knocked down. But when Darcy asked him that question, that very simple question, Mr. Crawford buckled.

"I suppose..." he uttered, "I would not be upset."

"You answered me slowly there, and without your traditional smoothness of tone," Darcy penetrated, "come man, it was a simple question that does not have to have a simple answer. Tell me the truth. What would it be like for you if no woman cared for you, and no man laughed at your jokes, marveled at your words—what if no woman ever wanted to hear you speak again, nor wished to sit beside you, to mold your words around, and validate your existence? What if no one loved you...can you love yourself?"

Within Henry's eyes was something I had never seen before: he was almost about to cry.

No, not almost.

There was one solitary tear in each pupil...he was holding in emotion. He was holding in the ultimate tragedy of his life: he was uncertain...

Chapter Two

JANE BENNET'S TALE: THE KNIFE OF LOOKING DOWN

I was uncertain. About everything.

The days rolled on, and still I received no letter from Caroline Bingley. Soon after they arrived in London, I wrote to her to maintain our friendship, but I was met with silence. Too much of my hopes seemed to fall on the side of being in vain.

Therefore, with the rise and fall of each week, it brought closer the shadow of Mr. Collins but presented no sign of Mr. Bingley himself.

Elizabeth never said anything to me about it. But her silence came at the comprehension of my character. She knew that it would make me unhappy.

Then the dreaded rumor spread throughout Meryton that Mr. Bingley was not to return for the whole winter. This report was proved true when the servants were reported to cover all the furniture in the house to keep dust from settling and the house being closed.

The evidence was proof enough, but mama, who was so against confronting the truth of this, denied it all, proclaiming it to be a scandalous falsehood.

One day, her constant remarks and complaints on the subject drove me to become unnerved. Until then, I was mostly quiet, letting her speak as she would.

Yet something within me was not as strong at withstanding

the constant talk of a man who left. And there was another discovery that I had made of this all.

For, in one moment, Mr. Bingley was dancing with me at Netherfield Park. Then soon after, he was gone. In the eyes of everyone, how would that look?

"Mama," I cut in, soon after she was referring to the news of his staying away from the country, "you must excuse me for a moment. I just realized that I forgot something in the shrubbery."

"What, pray tell?"

"I shall go out with you," Elizabeth offered.

"Thank you, but it is a simple task," I responded, "Besides, I do not know where I placed it. It shall take some time, and I do not wish to make someone take time to look with me. Leaving the tool out there was a foolishness that only I should suffer for."

Turning away before anyone could object, I went to the hall, hastily put my bonnet on, as well as my cloak, and left quickly. Going out into the yard, I walked past the side of the house, towards the shrubbery, and stood there. Turning back, I looked back at the windows and saw that no one was watching me. Now that there were no eyes upon me, I moved toward the side of the greenery where there were some pretty woods.

Losing myself in the wilderness was precisely what I needed. Moving more hastily, I approached the trees and lost myself under the cover of the branches.

The day had proven windy, and I welcomed it. There was something about the windiness, the overcast of clouds, and the darkness of the branches and shade, that matched my mood.

Giving way to sensibility, I began to twirl around the tree trunks, pulling at the branches, and allowing myself to become dizzy. The feeling of my vision falling into disarray gave me a rush. My body and spirit were now exhaling, and I was able to release my inner frustrations.

But more was brought to the surface of my mind.

I thought of the first time

that I met Mr. Bingley
at the assembly.

I twirled around a tree.

I remembered what it felt like to
Touch his hand when we first danced.

The wind swept around me.

I recalled the look on his face
When he saw me sick at Netherfield.

I ducked under a branch.
Then I twirled around another tree.

The look on his face when
he danced with me at the
Netherfield Ball.

I twirled around a tree once more.
My vision now was fully blurred.
The wind picked up.

And now the reality had come to me!
I was still heartbroken.
Rushing forward, while stumbling
Due to being disorientated,
I keeled over, clutching my stomach.

I wept.

So very much, I wept. Under the cover
Of the trees, hidden from the world,

I let all my frustrations give way.

And then I realized...that I was not alone.

Turning around suddenly, with my tearstained eyes, I saw Mr. Atkins, our uncle's clerk, standing there.

~

"Mr. Atkins!" I gasped, utterly shocked.

"Miss Bennet!" he intoned, frozen where he stood. Removing his hat, his face was wonderfully empathetic. "My apologies. I was walking to visit Mr. Long and I just thought I would walk this way. I didn't mean to intrude."

Turning from him, I began to wipe my eyes.

"No," he uttered, moving forward slowly, "don't do that."

"Do what?" I asked, still looking away from him.

"Wipe the emotion from your eyes," he clarified. "Do not do that. That is the mind's way of telling you that something is wrong."

"It is improper of me to show such a display of emotion to anyone."

"What is necessary is not improper," he assured me. There was something in his tone that was soft, inviting, and familiar. Mr. Atkins always appeared to be a kind man, but now I felt as if something was safe about him. "If it will help, Miss Bennet, do you not think us friends enough that I would run because you express some sadness. Miss Bennet...won't you turn around and look at me?"

Immediately, I felt myself grow comfortable. My sense of reserve gave way, and I turned toward him, my eyes, and cheeks still red.

"I must look affright," I apologized, "forgive me."

"There is nothing to forgive. I would hold you, but that is incorrect."

"Yes, it is. But I understand your meaning. I should return home."

"So soon?" he asked. "But you are not well."

"I am being improper letting you see me like this."

"And why?" he asked, blurting it out with strength. This question made me look up at him, surprised. "Why?" he continued, still with strength in his voice. "Miss Bennet, why is it improper for you to tell me what you are feeling?"

"Because it does not follow decorum, sir."

"And who is here to condemn you, to laugh at you and scoff at your sincerity? And more importantly, when have you ever known me to be made of such weak stuff that I run from any display of sensibility? Come now, will you not look at me?"

I looked at him again. Seeing his eyes, and his well-meaning look of kindness, I gave way and let my heart reveal itself.

"Mr. Atkins," I confessed, "I am so very miserable."

Now seeing my eyes getting wet again, he removed his handkerchief from his pocket, approached me and handed me the cloth.

"Thank you," I said, taking it and drying my eyes.

"You're welcome," he assured me. "Now tell me, what is making you miserable?"

"I should not say."

"Because it is improper?"

"Because it is also not your burden to bear."

"And we are friends, are we not? I'd be a pretty poor one if I was afraid of you taking me into your confidence. Miss Bennet, are we friends?"

"Yes, I think of us as such."

"As do I. You are not well, but the remedy for it is not that you need to return home, is it? If home was your desired place, then you would not have been weeping among the trees but rather would be crying in your bedroom."

"That was where I should have done it, if I had been wise."

"But you didn't. If I were to make an assumption, I would say that you found it safer or healthier to release your true feelings out here. Am I correct?"

I looked down at the ground but didn't respond.

"If you are afraid to answer that question, I will deduce that I am correct. Especially since you are not the first person to have this idea."

Hearing that he was familiar with my plight, I looked up, surprised.

"I'm not?"

"No, you are not. Does that knowledge comfort you?"

"I suppose that it might."

"Many people seek the cover of the woods to hide their grief from the world. Dense trees are good for that."

I chuckled through my sadness. Seeing my spirit change, Mr. Atkins sat down on a rock that was right under a tree.

"Now," he began, "tell me what is troubling you."

"I cannot tell you."

"Are you saying that because you mean it, or are you saying you are obliged to? For I have found that, very rarely, people want to hide feelings such as the one that you were displaying. Often, they want to talk to someone about it, but they are not allowed to."

"You know what I feel?"

"It is what everyone feels. We are living in strange times; we praise sense and logic but never understand the importance of discussing our own sensibilities. Humanity now leans toward a divine imbalance that I have found doesn't work as well as everyone considers."

"I feel stifled," I voiced, happy that he understood me.

"We all do, from time to time. And I tell you now, it helps to talk about it. Would you sit down with me?"

I looked at the ground and saw some tree roots that were nearby.

"If it would help," he assured me, "whatever you wish to talk about, I give you my complete confidence."

"You do? If I am to speak, you must promise me that you will never reveal anything that I say. That is all that I shall ever ask of you."

"And I shall hold to it. Whatever you say now shall never leave this spot, and these woods."

This invitation had come to me at such a vulnerable time that

I could not fight at all. Giving in, I sat down on the tree roots that were near him and began to confess everything.

~

"I feel as if... I am in a cage." I began.

"And as if you cannot get out?" he furthered.

My eyes widened, amazed that he knew what I meant.

"Yes!" I gasped, "precisely."

"And what inspired this feeling of confinement and suffocation?"

I looked down at the ground, digging my left foot into the earth.

"Miss Bennet," he pressed, "I promised you that everything would be said in confidence. And, also, without judgement. You are safe here."

Looking up at him, I studied his face. Mr. Atkins was a man who you can easily see but is hard to describe. He was neither handsome nor ugly. His face, however, was distinct, and ageless. I got the sense that, how he looked when in his teens, to his twenties or forties, his face would always remain the same. Yet, either way, he always gave a person a feeling that you could trust him...or that, when near him, nothing bad would ever happen. He would keep you safe.

"I do trust you," I assured him. "It is just that this is all so very difficult to confess."

"Could it be possible...that your sorrow has something to do with Mr. Bingley's departure?"

I wiped my eyes with his handkerchief again.

"Perhaps," I admitted.

"Are you upset about his leaving?"

"Yes, very."

"He shall return."

"But, Mr. Atkins," I blurted out, "we do not know that. And it's worse. Much worse."

"How so? Are you talking about Mr. Collins's engagement to Miss Lucas?"

"That does add to my woes."

"That, I do not deny, is a cold set of events. I do not judge Miss Lucas, *but* many of us cannot help but feel that the Lucases are boasting too much about it."

"They are."

"Yes. And your cousin's immediate transference of affection from Miss Elizabeth to Charlotte was not as prudent a step as he considers it to be. I know your sister, and I presume that she was the one who rejected him. But to transfer his feelings—which are founded solely on wounded pride—from one direction to another so quickly, smells strongly of a vain choice. No man of sense is fooled; we know his intentions. And no woman of sense is fooled either. So, does that make you feel better?"

"A little." I smiled.

"And now, let us return to the other subject of Mr. Bingley."

"Yes. That humiliation."

"Humiliation?"

"Yes. And heartache."

"By heartache, you mean that his leaving you has broken your heart."

"Yes, very much. And I have a hard time trying to recover. I walk here and there, from day to day, always pretending like I am like I have always been. But I am not. I feel lost, broken, shattered, and deceived. He has done nothing to deceive me, I know."

"Yes, he has."

I looked at him, surprised.

"He has?" I asked.

"Yes. He came here, charmed you a great deal, paid particular attention to you, and then left. That savors strongly of inconsistency and inability to consider the woman's feelings."

I chuckled sadly again and then dabbed my eyes once more.

"Either way," I continued, "I cannot forget him, Mr. Atkins. I try and I cannot forget him."

He placed his hand in mine, to coax me. I did not recoil or stop him.

"And you never will," he announced. "The truth is, when it comes to falling in love, losing it will never be something that you recover from. I do not say this to give you pain. I say this to show you that you are not alone, many have been where you have been, and many recovered from it. But their recovery did not come from one day ceasing to love the one that did not return their affections. They often continued to love the one who broke their heart. They recovered because time was their friend. Every day, they decided to wake up, put on their clothing, eat their meals, and live out the day. Each day, the heartbreak they experienced lessened and lessened. They never forgot that lost love of theirs. Time just taught them how to deal with it. And besides, it is a good thing to fall in love every now and again and then feel pain when it ends. Do you know why?"

"Why?" I asked, enthralled.

"Because it lets you know that your heart is still working. That is a good thing. A happy thing. Many people spend their lives being too afraid to fall in love. They go from day to day, never risking their hearts, or listening to what their heart is saying. You had the courage to listen. And that will always be an encouraging thought."

"But what about what others might think of me?"

"What do others think of you?"

"I can only assume that they noticed that one day, Mr. Bingley was dancing with me, and then he was gone. What if people think that I drove him away? Or that I was so inadequate, that I could not get him to make me an offer of marriage?"

"First, I have heard no one say that. Also, if they did, no one would give credit to it. Thirdly, even if they did, what are we here for, but to make talk and sport for our neighbors sometimes?"

This observation made me smile.

"Neighbors always talk about other neighbors. That is the fact of life."

"Yes, I daresay that it is."

"Yes. There, do you feel better now?"

"Mr. Atkins..."

"Yes?"

"Of all the people that I spoke to, you are the first person to lift my spirits, help me recover, and bring me back to life again."

He smiled. "My good deed for the day."

Taking my hand, he helped me stand up again.

~

To maintain decorum, we left the woods and walked towards the road, to ensure that no one had the wrong impression of us.

Eventually, we reached Longbourn, and we stood in front of it.

"There," he said with a smile, "I return you safely to your home."

"Yes, you did. Thank you, Mr. Atkins."

"You are very welcome."

I curtsied and began to walk to our door. Coming upon an idea, I turned to him.

"Promise me that these moments will be something you try to forget," I pressed.

"I promise. Everything we spoke of will die inside of me."

"Good. Then that leaves me to say this: I don't know which of us Bennet sisters that you are in love with. But whichever one of us that you are in love with, I am sorry if our mother has given the impression that her permission will only be given to men who have some wealth."

This sudden acknowledgement clearly disconcerted him. I could tell that not only did he not know that I was going to say that, but he didn't know that I knew the secrets in his heart.

"Have I troubled you by saying that?" I asked.

"No," he responded, "you only surprised me. In truth, I cannot tell you which of you that I have felt the most for, because it has varied from sister to sister over the years. I admit, I am fickle in that way. But I have recently discovered a preference for one of you, but that secret must remain my own for a little while longer. Either way, it does not matter. I have given up hope that your parents would ever approve of any of you attaching yourselves to your uncle's clerk. Oh well, I was never good enough for any of you anyway."

"You are good enough. Mr. Atkins, you very much are."

We were interrupted when Mary exited from the house.

"Oh," she said, "Jane. And good day, Mr. Atkins."

"Good day, Miss Mary," he said, removing his hat and bowing to her. "I was on my way to Mr. Long's home, and I happened to come upon your sister on the road. Therefore, I thought it my duty to deliver her safely to her home."

"I was just on my way to Mr. Long's home as well," Mary piped up. "I was told that Mrs. Long has a book that I was hoping to borrow."

Mr. Atkins smiled.

"Then would you oblige me and allow me to be your walking companion for the day?"

"I would be glad of the company," she said. "A good companion can always make a journey feel shorter."

"Sound judgement, Miss Mary. As always."

She smiled, he offered her his arm, she took it, and they turned to me.

"I shall return in an hour or two," Mary said to me.

"Tell your mother and sisters that I asked after them," Mr. Atkins said.

"I shall," I smiled.

Together, they both walked down the road to Mr. and Mrs. Long's estate.

Going into the house again, I heard my mother's voice, calling after me. Gathering my resolve, I walked in, now with my strength to fortify me.

As my name is Jane, I shall sojourn. Despite all the uncertainty that lay ahead...

Chapter Three

KITTY'S TALE: MARY CRAWFORD TAKES THE STAND

Uncertainty!

Such a simple word. But such a potent one.

It is the most humbling word ever, for it has the power to make us strip off every veneer that we place around ourselves, tear down every deception, and bring about the ultimate revelation about our lives. It renders us with the power to make us better than we have ever been. While also making us ultimately boring. For uncertainty also can be our great undoing. It makes us question every decision we make, makes us think, think some more, and then ultimately overthink, to the point where we result in making *no* decision at all.

Henry Crawford was a creature of action, but as Darcy was showing us, why was he? What drove Henry to not care about the feelings of others and instead be like that of a siren: calling to anyone, luring them in and then dashing them against the rocky terrain and sending them to their death.

Darcy called him an empty vessel that needed to be filled. And now, when hearing a supposed world, where Henry Crawford would have to walk the earth, with no woman to fawn over him, to cherish him, or to even listen to him...it made Mr. Crawford grow cold. He looked ill, and as if he had lost everything that was important to him. Was it so? Was Mr. Crawford a creature that needed others obsessed with him, because there was a void within him that was lacking? If so, could it be filled? Could he be cured?

"Mr. Crawford," Mr. Darcy stated, "you have to entertain that your past actions are not behind you, until you see what you are in the days ahead. Confront why you need to capture every woman's heart that you take a fancy toward, and confront what inside of you is a monster, who desperately needs to capture the identity of others to fulfill yourself. You are scared now, and that's good. Because something tells me that it is the truest emotion that you have ever had."

～

Seeing that Mr. Crawford was uniquely quiet, I thought it was the proper time to direct my attention to Mary Crawford.

"And what of you, Miss Crawford?" I asked. "Jane has told us your history. So far, the only crime that has been accredited to your faults is that you desperately tried to persuade your brother to marry Maria Bertram. Is that all that there was?"

"I admit, there was a little more to it than that," Mary Crawford admitted, "but I have suffered my penance enough, therefore, I feel that I have faced the darker elements of myself."

"We shall determine so," Elizabeth said, to which Mary Crawford looked at her, equally defiant.

"Only to an extent," Mary retaliated, "but I will not live my life based on the good opinion of others. I would die if that were the case. At the end of the day, I develop in my own way, and habit. I do not speak out of disrespect, Mrs. Darcy, for I do respect you. I just ask for the same sort of respect: the respect to still not be lorded over or reigned over. I value my independence of thought. I cannot have that taken from me, just as I cannot live under the judgements of others."

"Dearest," William Price was about to censure, but Elizabeth cut him off.

"No, she is correct," Elizabeth responded, "I will judge as I may, and as I find, but I know what it is like to be reigned over by the thoughts of those around you. It is not a happy place to dwell.

Perhaps I spoke hastily, for Miss Crawford, you are right. You do have the right not to live suffering under the judgements of others. If we humans did that, we could not say that we were living properly all the time. Our words would never be our own, but an echo of everyone else's. But it must be rightly understood between us, we both can speak as we wish. I may say something that you may not like, and you may say something that I might object to. But it does not mean that difference of opinion means difference of values. We can disagree peacefully. Do you understand this?"

"I do. Most readily."

"And you must promise to respect my wife while you remain here," Mr. Darcy said, stoically.

"I will. Believe me, Mrs. Darcy, I always wish to hold you in high esteem. But I must have my freedom. As Mrs. Bingley knows, without it, I am not Mary Crawford."

"And I would not be Elizabeth Bennet. Yes, I do see the turn of your mind. Now, what is your history?"

Mary Crawford tapped her hands against a nearby table, and she looked as if she was delving into a deep thought.

"I suppose, my largest sin was that I would not marry a life that I did not want."

"You would not marry a clergyman," I recalled.

"No, I would not. It was the worst sort of life that I could consider for myself. I know the sort of woman that I am, and a life for the church is not something that I was made for. I knew that, and I don't apologize for knowing that. And that is where it all comes down to: I know what I am. This knowledge has often gotten me into trouble, as well as the fact that my principles are neither puritanical nor prudish. I do not run or cry in the face of opposition. I firmly believe it is our moral duty, to always continue on, you see? I don't believe in rolling over and giving way to feminine delicacy when problems face one. No, it is not my way. I believe in taking action—I believe in the right to recover. If that's what makes me a villain, then so be it. When Henry and Maria Bertram ran off together, I was upset, unsettled, and irate. I was in an irrational state. I blamed Henry for giving in. I blamed Maria Bertram for being so damned foolish. Like a harpy, I blamed Fanny Price for not accepting my brother's hand immediately, which I believed was the cause of his wandering ways."

"How could that be?" Georgiana voiced. "Surely, you could not blame Miss Price for other people's actions."

"Like I said, I was not in the best frame of mind." She took William's hand. "Mr. Price is aware of my foolishness, and I have confronted that part of myself. But at the time—I just... I thought that Fanny's rejection led to Henry feeling as if he had been missing something. That feeling would lead to him wishing to turn to a heart that he knew would accept him eventually. If Fanny had accepted Henry, then he would not have cared a fig for regaining Miss Bertram's good opinion."

"Oh," I acknowledged, "I see."

This reaction led to many in my family looking on me critically.

"I do not judge Miss Price," I clarified, unwilling to give way to feelings of shame for speaking. "What I am saying is that I merely understand such an assumption. After all, can't one entertain an idea, without fully accepting it? Don't I have the right to empathize with a train of thought, even if I don't agree with it?"

"She is correct," Colonel Fitzwilliam said, supporting me, "it's not wrong to understand where Miss Crawford's feelings originated from, even if not adapting it into our ways of thinking. Two opinions on this matter can live without disregarding the other."

"Thank you," Mary Crawford said to us, "I am happy that you understand my viewpoint. It was not a correct one, but I should not be condemned for it. I was just heartbroken with how circumstances had turned out, and I was unleashing my frustrations on whoever I could. I don't hate Fanny, and I realize that she was correct. I just wished that things had turned out differently, for quite some time."

"And they were right to not be any other way," Mr. Crawford said. "I thought that, by marrying Fanny Price, I would have been anchoring myself down to a dear, sincere, and pure sort of woman. Our attachment would be the makings of me into a better man."

"I am happy that you thought that," I said, "but still that would have been a terrible marriage."

"Kitty..." Elizabeth said to me, about to begin her reprimands.

"Never fear, Mrs. Darcy," Henry Crawford said, "let her speak her mind. I am not afraid."

"Thank you," I said. "Mr. Crawford and Miss Crawford, you know that I can never despise you. So, this is not spoken out of malice, but mere observation. But the fact of the matter is that, if you enter a marriage, expecting that the other person will enhance your own character, then you only present that your goodness is external. And not internal. What I mean is that you ought to never come to a match expecting the other person to bring out the very best in you. When you do that, you eventually start using that other person as your tourniquet, and then you eventually tire of them. And the wrongs start all over again. You have to enter a match as complete as a person can be and not broken. If you do that, you break the other person that you promised to love, honor, and obey. You cause destruction, while the whole time, you had thought you were going to save yourself. I know that I am not married, but I've been observing unequal matches my entire life, as well as equal ones. And the one problem that the miserable alliances had in common was that both spouses entered the match with incorrect pictures of each other, but also incomplete images of themselves."

I was prepared for Henry Crawford to behold me in utter confusion and alarm. I was prepared to be cast down by everyone in the room. Therefore, imagine my surprise when Mr. Crawford's eyes lit up.

"And that's precisely what I am," he declared.

~

We all looked at him in wonder, but Mr. Crawford sojourned onward, with no apprehensions or feelings of discomfort.

"For so long," he uttered, "I did not know myself, except to rely on my own confidence, pride and conceit. I felt that, even when others called me wicked, I knew what I was about. I ignored any wrongdoing that I caused, under the guise that my actions would not cause any lasting damage—and then it did. Maria Bertram and I were like two faulty carriages that crashed into each other. And the damage was extreme. And then, after all the smoke had cleared away, I realized something. I never cared a thing for her. There she was, this destroyed creature, and I didn't care what happened to her at all. I had gained what I wanted and still felt nothing. Fanny Price, who I once claimed to care desperately for, soon became a longing desire of mine. A flame... but why? She rejected me, I didn't notice her for so long, we barely had anything in common, she seldom spoke to me, she lacked the charisma that I liked in a woman—so why? Why did I still care? Now I know. I needed to feel for her, because that feeling gave me a sense of fulfillment—a fulfillment that I am naturally lacking. There is nothing in me. That's why I pursue women, drawing them in with my arts and allurements. It is because I need their love—because there is something in me that is missing. I use their love for me, as a mirror, and I reflect myself on them. I cannot explain why I do that, but it just... is me."

"A wise deduction, and what of you, Miss Crawford?" Colonel Fitzwilliam asked. "Besides being occasionally incongruous and indelicate with your speech, you have committed no action that makes you worthy of condemnation."

"But I have, in the eyes of some. I tried to persuade Mr. Bertram, Maria's brother, that we had to convince Henry to marry Maria, and from there, we would hold good dinners and large parties to help restore her reputation."

"So, you were trying to save your siblings from being exiled from society," Enara summed up.

"Yes."

"But what's wrong with that? After all, it would make sense for you to try and save your sibling and Miss Bertram from a life of constant rejection."

"It's what many families have had to do, in such circumstances when two people have been living together, unmarried," Elizabeth determined. "There is nothing else to be done, most of the time."

"But, in a world where people go to church to practice mercy on Sundays and then forget it entirely by Mondays," Mary Crawford declared, "I was considered indelicate and coldhearted."

"For trying to solve the problem," Jane summed up.

"This has led to me also being rejected by the Bertram family."

"Though I do not deny that my sisters have been jilted, due to their association with me," Henry said, "for the Bertram family to pretend otherwise is them deceiving themselves. I know that they are incapable of being people who believe that one fallen sibling is not injurious to the others."

"A traditional superior-religious belief," Arthur Philips declared.

"And it has led to the family not accepting our engagement," William Price announced. "Down in Portsmouth, my parents and my other siblings do not care very much at all for my fiancée's affiliations—then again, they also consider her pocketbook more than my affections. However, at Mansfield Park, the hammer has come down the hardest. The Bertrams will not receive Miss Crawford, nor offer me their blessing. Two of my sisters reside there. One is Susan, who does not share the other's disdain for my choice. Yet, my other sister, Fanny, has both raised and lowered my heart. She says that she is sorry for the reception that my engagement has caused and wishes me well, but she is also apprehensive about my choice. Fanny is delicate and less robust in body and mind than Susan. Her dislike of the idea is perhaps augmented by the rest of the family's disdain for the Crawfords. After all, I know my sister. If there was no other influence on her, she would accept my choice. She loves me dearly, but she might be a victim of over-persuasion."

"Either way," I deduced, remembering the torment that I received for Lydia's plight with Wickham, "no sibling should be blamed for what the other sibling has done. Each person's reputation is their own."

"As logical as that sounds," Colonel Fitzwilliam said, "sadly, the rest of the world is not that logical."

"That proves me more correct than ever," Jane added. "Mary, you and Mr. Price have every right to be well-received."

"Very true," Darcy said, "and that only leaves us with one verdict to distribute." Here, he looked at Henry Crawford. "Mr. Crawford, you have been heard clearly, and your confession is well-meaning."

"I am of the deduction," Mr. Crawford uttered, "that you are about to say something awful."

"Not awful, Mr. Crawford, but something that might antagonize you. I am taking my time."

"Your time?"

"Yes. Time to deliberate on what is the best thought process to be done. For that, I need to consult my wife. She is best at seeing the truth of things, and we need to make the decision together."

Ah, another wonderment in the winter's light! When hearing that her husband was not going to make any rash decisions until he consulted her first, Elizabeth's eyes lit up in admiration. The joys of having a husband who listened, who considered, who thought of her as well as himself—was this often the case? Was this the result of true love? If so, I knew to wait longer, to take my time, for what was the price of a voice if you forfeited it to the will of one who claimed to care for you but really didn't.

"I understand," Henry Crawford said, "and I thank you just for receiving me, my sisters, and my soon to be brother-in-law into your home. However, if there is one thing that I may say to prove my veracity."

"By all means. Whatever your past, this has proven to be a very entertaining afternoon."

Henry Crawford chuckled to himself, and then he turned serious again.

"As you all have deduced, I am charming. I charmed two sisters into loving me. Many women in the London aristocracy, who both mother and daughter wished me to make up my mind. I have endeared myself into the good graces of men who wanted me to wed their daughters, sisters, and nieces. I have charmed almost every person that I have met, making it hard for them to ever despise me, until they have felt spurned in some way. What I mean is that... I could charm you all now. I could wrap words around you to make you sympathize with me, accept that I have been cruelly judged, and am the victim of Maria Bertram's inability to leave me alone. I could do all these things. For it is well within my power. But I have not. And I never will. Perhaps—hopefully—my willingness to avoid the deceptive sides of myself is proof that I have improved."

Mr. Darcy leaned back, his face still unchanged.

"A wise thing to utter. However, there is one flaw to that."

"And what would that be?"

"Yes, perhaps you abandoning your alluring nature and tone is evidence at your changed character—if it were not for one realization. You are a smart man, Mr. Crawford, and you were aware, very soon into meeting me, that your charming demeanor would not work. Not in the slightest. Therefore, dropping your charade was the only way that you could appeal to me. I'm not wrong, am I?"

"No, I suppose you are not. I knew the sort of man that you were from the very first. But I promise, I do mean what I say."

"My wife and I need time to deliberate. Till then, I do believe that you, your sisters, and Mr. Price, need time to be able to enjoy each other's company. Perhaps, you need time away from us. I don't want to force you to stand on ceremony when it will be awkward for everyone. Besides, my wife and I need time ourselves."

Mr. Darcy turned to Jane.

"Sister," he said, "would you be willing to take a turn about the grounds with our new company? I gather the sense that you are the only one that can make them feel at ease."

Jane was overjoyed by this.

"Thank you. There were things that I did wish to discuss with them." Jane turned to them. "Pemberley is a large estate, and by the time I show you only an eighth of it, it will be time to dress for dinner."

"That is precisely what I would have wished for," Mary Crawford said, elated. "We have much to discuss and find our own joy over."

"I am glad that you feel the same."

Soon, the company split, and it gave me time to approach Georgiana.

"Well," she said, flustered, "what do you think? This is altogether shocking."

"I know. Exciting, isn't it?"

Georgiana gave me a 'Kitty, really?' look.

I stood by my assessment...

Chapter Four

JANE BENNET'S TALE: ON THE OPEN ROAD

Despite Lizzy's feelings toward Caroline Bingley, I stood by my assessment.

Yet each day did not bring forth a letter from Caroline. Every day brought further silence on the matter, and further confirmation that Mr. Bingley would not return for months. If he returned at all.

Even Elizabeth began to fear that Mr. Bingley's sisters would be successful in keeping him away. I still disbelieved that his sisters had anything to do with influencing Bingley from coming back to the country. But she was not to be persuaded.

What we agreed upon, however, was that the best thing for me was to never let the subject arise between us.

My mother still spoke about it almost every hour that she was awake, informing me that I ought to feel ill-used because of it. It took a lot to forbear her constant attacks on the subject, but Mr. Atkins's advice helped me withstand it all.

What was even more arduous to endure was that Mr. Collins had returned for his wedding to Charlotte Lucas. This threw mother into even greater agonies, and I felt the pressure of her pain even more heavily enforced on my mind.

Internally, I was falling apart, while externally, I was maintaining my composure. And yet, I worried that it was only a matter of time before I felt as if I would fully come undone. How long did I have before the inevitable break, the darkness at the end of this journey, the last resort to where it all would conclude?

But I had to smile. I must smile! For indeed, my smile was all that I had left.

And Miss Bingley still had not written.

❧

This whole situation cast mama into a state of perpetual wretchedness. And the more wretched she became, the more hostile her tone could be to Lizzy. For, by seeing the one man who could have saved us from destitution constantly in the throes of love with another woman gave her no end of peace, and tormenting Lizzy was her only solace. It was altogether a terrible business. I felt terrible for what mama was going through, yes, but my pity extended only so far. It did not then, or ever, extend to the point where I condoned how she treated Lizzy, or Mary and Kitty, for that matter.

Also, if I had the gift or desire to list all the events that led up to the inevitable wedding day of Mr. Collins to Charlotte, then I would tell you all. Yet I lack the talent of telling it in an interesting manner. And I lack desire to narrate it, for the memory of it alone reminds me of my mama and sister's grief.

Therefore, I shall tell you only this.

The days leading up to the wedding were arduous for mama to hear about. The sight of Miss Lucas was odious to her. As her successor in that house, she regarded her with jealous abhorrence.

Charlotte would come to visit, but there was a marked change in how we all greeted her. Even Lizzy felt that there was a rift between them that could never be fully salvaged.

❧

The next day, I found myself hastily running up the steps. Just a few seconds ago, Hill approached me, informing me that I had a letter.

After thanking her, I took the letter and read the front.

It was from Caroline Bingley!

That moment brought me more excitement than I'd had for weeks. Eager to read its contents in private, I rushed to my room, opened it, and began to read through it.

She briefly inquired about my family and my health, wishing that both were good. How much I had hoped that she would get to the matter at hand, telling me when they would return...and then I was not left to wait for long. She came upon the subject very quickly...

> *My dear Jane, how happy I am to be returned to a civilized company and to know that it will be permanent! With you, I must be entirely open. We are all settled here in London for the entire winter. It is what I always wanted.*
>
> *Also, Charles wishes for me to express his most sincere apologies for not having had time to pay his respects to you and all his other friends before he left Hertfordshire.*
>
> *But you must understand, his eagerness to see Miss Darcy again overpowered him to such a degree that all other thoughts left his head. I've never seen him so happy...and so much in love!*
>
> *And now that we are to remain in London for the winter—in truth, Charles is hinting at never returning to the country again, for his love of town has been rekindled—I am certain that a most desirable event may take place.*
>
> *Jane, I fear that we shall never meet again. Well, the memory of our friendship will remain intact, at least.*
>
> *Goodbye, my friend, for what I fear may be forever...*

I lowered the letter to the floor, sitting down gently on my bed.

Hope was once something I held within me.

Hope was a fire that kept my soul warm.

Now...hope was over.

Entirely so!

They were never coming back. And so... I would never see Mr. Bingley again.

He had been the first man that I loved since my first...disappointment. It would take me sitting in quiet reflection for a while before I could attend to the rest of the letter's contents. Caroline was still affectionate to me in her writing, but there was nothing in it to give me any sort of comfort. She continued to list all of Miss Darcy's accomplishments, praising her every action, and furthering the belief that soon a desirable event would take place, uniting Miss Darcy with her brother. And I was made to feel so little and so poorly made with each bit of praise given to this woman who I had never met.

Very soon, I heard familiar footsteps and Lizzy's voice.

"Jane," she called, "may I enter?"

"Come in."

She entered and it took only a few seconds of seeing my pain and the letter in my hand for her to read my mind.

"You had a letter from Miss Bingley again?" she asked.

"I have."

Slight pause.

"How bad are her venomous words this time?"

"She is no snake."

"You may believe that, if it gives you comfort. But I sense that I am not wrong, am I? She sent bad tidings."

I handed her the letter.

"Read it, I don't mind," I stressed.

Taking the letter, she sat down and read it. When she was done, she looked at me.

"This is ridiculous," she scoffed.

"What part of it is?" I asked.

"All of it. I do not argue with his remaining in town all winter. That all seems likely. I still do not pay any credit to Miss Bingley's assertions to her brother liking Miss Darcy. Her report is too stressed, too forced, and too pointed for it to be anything else but a vicious pursuit on her own ends. Believe me, when she wrote these words, she was as much trying to convince herself as she was of convincing you." She tossed the letter on the bed and plopped down into my rocking chair. "I declare, when it comes to love, there are too many parties involved, too many people who have their hand in the dealings of it. It is like the two people, who the love chiefly concerns, have little to say in the matter at all!"

"Caroline means well," I excused, "I am sure of it."

"But there is more to it," she continued, "I admit, that I am not proud of Mr. Bingley in this moment either."

"Lizzy," I gasped, "why would you be?"

"Because, if he remains away because others are pressuring him to do so, then what does that say about his own strength? It means that he has little of it, that he does not stand by his own principles, and respect for you. After all, he is breaking your heart, by remaining away, and is not taking that into consideration. Had his own happiness, however, been the only sacrifice, he might have been allowed to sport with it in whatever manner he thought best, but your happiness is involved."

"His friends' and family's opinion are important to him," I argued, coming to Mr. Bingley's defense. "I respect that about him."

"And I do not, if that respect leads to him disrespecting you." She stood up and began to pace. "No, Jane, I am resigned. And my opinion of him has fallen, shrunk under the weight of how he has behaved. It doesn't matter if he stays away because his affection has faded, or he is being pressured by his friends. This is abominable."

"Whatever his reasons," I responded, still willing to keep my pain hidden, "I am sure they are correct, in his eyes. I can ask no more of that. Therefore, Lizzy, do not trouble yourself on my behalf. I am not worth it."

"Yes, you are."

"Then be happy around me. Help me be cheery."

She gave me a sad smile, and that was the end of it.

For the moment.

How happy I was for the end of the year to come. For now...it was December, and the time of Christmas had come.

Good news at last!

After a week, Mr. Collins was called away, having to return back to his parsonage.

With his departure brought the arrival of another. He was gone on Saturday.

And happier relatives came to us on Monday.

"Oh," mama cried as we prepared for the visitors, "finally, some relatives who *I* actually *want* to see! I feel as if it has been ages since I saw my beloved brother. I shall grow nervous from being quite distracted."

"I hope they brought us presents!" Lydia wailed, while mother fluttered here and there, ordering the servants. Lizzy and I were putting away all our sewing and needlework, while Mary practiced on the pianoforte.

"They brought presents for us the last time, so I don't think there will be any change to worry over," Kitty remarked. "I hope Aunt Gardiner has much news to tell us of town. She always makes us happy again. Aren't you happy to see her again, Lizzy?"

"You know that I am," Lizzy said. "I'm not that much of a fool that I would feel otherwise."

Leaning over Mary, I touched her shoulder.

"Mary, Aunt and Uncle Gardiner will be here any minute. Go upstairs and put on that bracelet that they brought you a couple of years ago."

"It is a very fine bracelet," she answered, "I feel as if I give off the appearance of vanity if I wear it."

"If you wear it, you will make them feel happy to see you cherish it."

"Jane is right," Kitty groaned, "Mary, there is nothing wrong with looking pretty every now and again. Go and put it on."

"Fine," Mary extolled, rolling her eyes. "If it will make you happy. Besides, there is sense in what you say. If there wasn't, then I would never have allowed myself to be influenced by it."

She went upstairs, got the bracelet, and came back down just in time.

"I hear their carriage!" Lydia cried.

"I do as well," Elizabeth supported. We all rushed outside, and sure enough, our uncle's carriage was coming down the road.

"They are here!" Mama cried, waving at them with her hand-kerchief. "They are here! I was so worried about their lateness in coming."

Their carriage reached the house, stopped, their footman opened it, and our Uncle Gardiner jumped down to meet us.

"Well met, and happy as ever!" He cried when seeing us.

"Happy to see that you are not stuck in a ditch somewhere or attacked by highwaymen!" Mama cried. "You both are late, and I was worried that you had been set upon."

"Sister, that is nonsense. We have arrived at very good time."

He reached in, took his wife's hand, and helped her down.

"Oh, we are so glad to see you all again," Elizabeth said.

"Family is always a happy sight at this time of year," Mary remarked.

"And I can translate Mary's speech," Kitty pointed out. "It means that she is happy to see you."

"And you did bring us presents!" Lydia wailed.

"You all spoke precisely as we thought you would," Aunt Gardiner said, "now, who wishes to let me embrace them first?"

All five of us Bennet sisters hugged her, while mama hugged her brother.

And Longbourn really did feel happier, I think. Our aunt and uncle's arrival did make things feel all the merrier.

"Now, come inside to see Mr. Bennet," mama ushered them in. "And get yourselves in from out of the cold. You shall not be disappointed in your coming. No indeed! You shall not. We have a list of parties this time of year, as you well know from last year."

"That is why we always come here for Christmastime," Uncle Gardiner said. "I can find no place better to spend the holidays than Hertfordshire. What say you, my dear?"

"I say amen to that, dearest," Aunt Gardiner replied, "and the first thing that it is my duty to dispense with...presents!"

Lydia and Kitty laughed, Mary smiled gently, Lizzy and I were content.

"It is more than just presents," mama urged, "I rely upon you to tell us of all the latest fashions in London. I can tell, by the way that you are dressed, that you still do very well at looking remark-ably well and smart."

"Mrs. Bennet," Aunt Gardiner smiled, "you and I both know that when we become mothers, we have less interest in remaining fashionable ourselves. But I knew that my office was to satisfy your curiosity, so even though I am not the most fashionable person myself, I brought all the latest catalogues and designs from the best shops in London. And I daresay that there are some new designs that will suit all five of you."

Her contributions to our party were well-received and Uncle Gardiner was the epitome of paternal excellence. He was not only our uncle but felt as if he was another father. He was kind, pleas-ant, and a man of information.

"It is always unfair," Lizzy whispered to me. "That our mother will never be anything like our aunt, and our parents' marriage will never arrive at anything like our aunt and uncle's."

As much as I wished to find some way of disagreeing with her, I found no answer. For, despite it all, she was correct.

Once our aunt and uncle finished telling us news from town, our mother felt it only proper to give news in return. Soon, she began to regale them with my history with Mr. Bingley and Mr. Collins's proposal to Elizabeth. For since two of her girls had been upon the point of marriage, and after all there was nothing in it, these disappointments had to be uttered.

Moving away from them when mama began this speech, I went over to Lizzy and Kitty and offered to play a game of horse-shoes. Despite the cold, they agreed, and we were off to leave mama and our aunt to talk about us now that we were gone.

"You leave because they are talking about you both," Kitty suggested as we exited the house, wearing scarves and coats.

"Nonsense," Elizabeth denied.

"We are alone. Therefore, there is no reason to lie to me."

"Oh, very well. You may possibly be right."

Kitty smiled.

"Yes, I might be right. Yes, yes, I might."

We went outside and played horseshoes for twenty minutes, before finally considering returning into the house. Thinking that surely mama must have tired of speaking about us, we thought all would be safe. Only for us to enter and still hear mama talking about it.

While removing our bonnets and pelisses, we heard the end of the discussion. Elizabeth rolled her eyes, and we entered again.

At that point, Uncle Gardiner had returned to sit with us, and it felt as if we all could now be very merry.

~

That night, I had just got done washing my hair and preparing for bed, when Elizabeth knocked.

"Come in, Lizzy."

She opened the door.

"How did you know that it was me?" she asked.

"You are the only one who ever knocks on my door at this hour," I pointed out, still putting curling paper in my hair. "If it were someone else, the surprise might've killed me."

"Jane," she burst out, closing the door behind her, "I have the most wonderful thing to tell you. You might be free of hearing Mr. Bingley's name very soon!"

Abruptly I stopped tending to my hair and turned to her.

"Lizzy, what are you talking about?"

She walked over to my bed and sat down on it.

"It was Aunt Gardiner's suggestion. She knows about what happened between you and Mr. Bingley. Indeed, after our mother spent the day talking about it, I would not be surprised if people in Germany knew. After mama told her everything, Aunt Gardiner came to me. At first, she theorized that Mr. Bingley's actions were that of a mercurial kind. And a popular one. She believed it was simply the case of another young man falling in love with a woman for a few weeks, and then easily forgetting her when they are separated. Apparently, she's seen this happen very often. But I set all that to right and assured her that Mr. Bingley's behavior was different."

"But Lizzy, we don't know that he was different. What if he truly is as our aunt says?"

"You know that you do not believe that."

"At this point," I admitted, uncertain, "One does not know what to think."

"Begging your pardon," she overrode me, "but one knows *exactly* what to think."

Willing to let her override me, I continued to listen.

"Aunt Gardiner has invited you to stay with them in London."

When hearing this, I brightened immediately.

"She really plans to invite me?"

"She believes that change of scenery might be refreshing for you, and I agreed. Also, we both believe that a little relief from home may be useful in recovering."

I leaned forward, truly happy.

"Lizzy, this is perfect!" I gasped. "This is the precise thing that I would have hoped for. If I go to Cheapside, no one there will ever mention Mr. Bingley's name. There can be the chance of finally recovering."

"For let us not lie to ourselves... there is no way of you recovering from your disappointment here."

"Yes, I do agree with you. How is one to recover from a heartache when one is always being reminded of it?" Suddenly, I felt myself grow cold under the revelation of a possibility. "But Lizzy, I cannot go to London!"

"And why ever not?"

"What if... I was to accidentally see Mr. Bingley. I would be devastated."

"Aunt Gardiner assured me of that not being a factor. Since they live in so different a part of town, with all their connections being so different, and, as you well know, they go out so little, that it is very improbable that you should meet him."

I exhaled happily.

"Good," I sighed, "And since Caroline is not living in the same house as her brother, I do not need to worry about calling on her. So, all is safe. Lizzy, I cannot explain it, but there is something so very hard about seeing someone who you once...held in such high esteem."

"I've been told that is a natural reaction. I am not jealous of your state."

"But then that means that I will leave you again."

"Do not worry about me!" She assured me. "I will be fine."

"Are you certain?" I asked, truly worried about her. "Mama is still a little...cold toward you. I don't want you to be alone during it all."

"I can bear the cruel remarks very cheerfully," she pressed. "It has reached a point where, if mama does *not* find fault with me, only then will I get worried. For I learned a long time ago, that if mama tells me to do something, sometimes the right thing to do is the *opposite of that*."

I smiled...I was going to go to London!

And forgive me, but perhaps I did not tell the entire truth. Pray, would I be happy if I saw Mr. Bingley again? Perhaps, deep within, I would be.

~

When I told the Gardiners that I accepted their invitation, they were excited. I wrote a letter about it to Caroline, so that she would know when I would arrive. To see Caroline again, would bring me some happiness.

After remaining with us for a week, the Gardiners visit had come to an end, and soon they were back in their carriage, with one addition: me.

With my luggage packed, and my best clothing, I was now kissing my family goodbye and looking to the future.

They all offered us good wishes, good weather, safe roads, and to not be attacked by highwaymen—mama said that last prayer.

I gave them all one last look, before the carriage set off and I was leaving Longbourn with my aunt and uncle.

"The rest of your Christmas holidays will now be spent in town," Uncle Gardiner announced.

"And I could not have wanted a better gift," I commented, "and of that, I can assure you."

And I meant it. For Lizzy would eventually write to me that

soon after I had departed, Mr. Collins came to marry Charlotte. Perhaps I did not have the strength to see mama during that crisis.

Looking out of the carriage, I saw the road ahead, and the skies were clear. I took all this for being a good omen.

I was Jane Bennet, I had my whole life in front of me... and so, I would ride along and find out where I ought to end up.

But for the rest of the journey there, what was I to think?

Chapter Five

KITTY'S TALE: VARIOUS VIEWS ABOUT THE UPCOMING VERDICT

"Well," Elizabeth asked us, "what do you all think?"

After the company had dispersed, Jane did go to tend to Mary Crawford and the rest of our guests.

That gave the rest of us ladies time to converse with each other.

Lizzy, Enara, Georgiana and I were in Georgiana's room. We had removed our shoes and were laying on the bed, staring up at the ceiling.

"What do we all think?" I repeated. "That is the dilemma."

"He ran away with another man's wife," Georgiana announced. "It is distressing, that one does not know what to think."

"Begging your pardon, but one knows exactly what to think," Enara said. "He did something awful, but so did the woman. She chose to marry a man that she did not love, then doomed herself to her fate. We have two villains here."

"But that is the problem," Elizabeth said, "Maria Bertram is not here to speak for herself. In many ways, I am happy that she is not present."

"Yet one thing is quite clear," I stated. "Mary Crawford has every right to not be judged by her brother's actions. She should not be condemned for any rash words she might have said. Any woman or man might have said something similar, in such a circumstance. Besides, if all us humans are set down as villains, forever, because we said some selfish or misguided words a couple times, then we'd all be perpetually cast out of paradise. Sometimes Mary Crawford does speak callously, yes. However, I will not forever be chastising her. I'm sorry, but excepting Jane, I have never met a woman or man who was dissimilar to Miss Crawford."

Elizabeth looked at me and then she looked away.

"Yes," she admitted, "that is quite true. Miss Crawford suffers from a very strong sense of pride in her powers of deduction."

"But Elizabeth, haven't you and I been the same way quite often?"

"Yes, and that's why I cannot despise her at all. The question is not whether we should accept her but accept the brother. What if Mr. Crawford is deceiving us? What if he merely wishes to improve his character, for the sake of vanity, and not out of any true or sincere feeling? We've seen such characters before."

"True," Enara said, "it is a frightful thing to give such a person a second chance and then to have them deceive you...yes, I can see how frightening that is."

"I am happy that my brother knows to consult you on the matter before he decided himself," Georgiana inferred, "it was very well meant."

"Yes, it was," Elizabeth responded, her eyes gentle. "I think I might have accidentally stumbled on one of the few greatest men in England."

"Oh, I don't know," I smirked, "I daresay that I have met some great ones as well, though I admit their last name is not Darcy, and maybe that is not so much in their favor."

They all laughed.

"But again," Elizabeth gathered, still staring at the ceiling, "what to do? Our mistakes are, after all, our mistakes, but when they are in the past, does one forgive, or does one deduce that such a character cannot be changed? Henry Crawford may be a plain sort of man, but he is alluring. Even when watching his confession, he has a way about him, where he draws sympathy and affection from his company. He's an actor who doesn't need a stage, and his fellow acquaintances are not as much fellow people to him but rather are always an audience. How do you deal with an actor who might always be acting and never drops the persona that he has established so well? Especially, when that role is something that was instilled in him since he was a child."

"That's the other issue," Georgiana considered, "all those bad influences that he has had! At some point, where does a person garner sympathy from the horrible history that they were drenched in, and then where do we declare that they are responsible for their own actions? After all, we all must grow up, and not blame others for the choices that we make."

"Yes," Elizabeth said, "yes."

After a moment's silence, Elizabeth came to a decision. Jumping up, she put her shoes back on.

"Where are you going?" I asked.

"I am going to do what I ought to do best: be the mistress of Pemberley. I walk away and discuss matters to everyone else but to the people who this all centers around."

"You are going to seek out the Crawfords, aren't you?" Enara asked.

"Yes, I am." Elizabeth blinked. "No one stop me."

"I am not even going to try."

With that, Elizabeth left, perhaps to walk down a path of intense truth, or at the very least, the seeking out of it.

"Good lord, she's a brave one," Enara commented.

"I know," I said, "where does she get the energy for it?"

"So," Mr. Bingley asked, "what do you think, Darcy, Arthur, and Colonel?"

While the ladies were in Georgiana's room, speaking about the recent developments, the gentlemen were similarly occupied.

Rather, they were in the billiards room, each with a stick in their hand as they tried to knock the balls into the pockets. Arthur's right hand had been hurting him, so he sat down and did not partake in the game. Rather, he poured himself a glass of wine and watched them all.

"I think that Mrs. Grant is the most innocent of the lot," Colonel Fitzwilliam said, "she has suffered the most from her brother's actions. As for Miss Crawford, she is flawed, yes. But her only crime is that she is unafraid to speak her mind and does not fit into the standard that is placed on young women of a certain dowry. She has the right to marry Mr. Price and that be an end of that part of it."

"On that we agree," Mr. Darcy said, shooting a ball into the pocket.

"Then, it appears that the only dilemma we have is on the brother," Mr. Bingley said. "I confess that I am quite at a loss of how to proceed in that way. A pity. I thought that I had grown to be more perceptive over time. I lament that I was wrong on something that I prided myself on."

He shot at a ball, but it missed the pocket.

"It's not your fault, Charles," Colonel Fitzwilliam responded, "this is one of those subjects that cannot be entered into lightly. In fact, the true answer seems to be hidden behind some storm clouds."

He too missed the ball he was aiming to shoot into a pocket.

"And therein is the problem," Darcy stated. "My first impulse is to reject Mr. Crawford forever. Any man whose initial reaction to charm women and then offer them nothing but his changeable ways, only to ensnare a married woman, is the last thing I would like to receive in my home. But nevertheless, he is here now." He looked at the balls on the table. "By George!" He swore. "I have no good shot anywhere." He aimed the ball, but it went wide, off the mark, with no chance of achieving a point.

"It would upset Jane for us to reject him outright," Bingley pointed out, "her happiness means much to me. And she has had a longer acquaintance with them."

Bingley scored a point.

"I know," Darcy said, "but your wife has a goodness that she often sees in others, even when they don't deserve it. However, I have been wrong about people before."

"And the company has touched on one proper observation," Colonel Fitzwilliam said, scoring a point, "we go to church every Sunday, are taught to forgive imperfect people, and then we forget about that the very next day. Does it stand that we can condemn those that we are supposed to have more faith in?"

Darcy laid his billiards stick on a nearby table savagely.

~

When a man, of slow movements, makes a sharp movement, it always is followed by a surprised reaction.

Darcy's slamming down his stick, made the others flinch, except for Arthur Philips, who had been silent all the while. Darcy sat down, folding his hands over his shoulders, his brow furrowed.

Arthur poured a glass of wine and handed it to him.

Darcy looked at the glass and then looked up at Arthur.

"Sometimes, things become clearer after a little bit of vino and courage," Arthur offered.

"Thank you," Darcy said, taking the wine and drinking a little bit of it.

Arthur sat back down and looked at him, shrewd.

"You are worried about what to do," Arthur noted, "aren't you? You are scared that whatever decision you make, it might be the wrong one."

"Yes," Darcy confessed.

"Elizabeth will know what to do," Colonel Fitzwilliam coaxed him. "Things will be clearer by tomorrow morning."

"And that is the woe and wonder of it," Darcy noted, "before I married her, I was determined, and everything felt definite. Now I need her. Tell me, you three—surely, I won't be offended if you tell me—do I abandon my mental independence and depend on her too much?"

"No," all three men said in unison. They all looked at each other, surprised by that. This unified negative relieved Darcy.

"Well," he uttered, "that is the best 'no' that I have ever received in my life."

"It's wise to always be on the same level with the person you marry, Darcy," Bingley suggested. "I defer to Jane on many subjects."

"And when it comes to domestic issues," Arthur said, "I don't even care to be invited into the conversation. I just want Enara to do everything."

Colonel Fitzwilliam chuckled at this.

"Well, as the only unmarried man, I also defer to Kitty on some matters as well."

Darcy looked at him, sympathetic.

"How does your inner peace do, Richard?"

"Oh, I'm in hell," Colonel Fitzwilliam said, shooting a ball and missing it. "Pure hell."

Bingley pat him on the shoulder.

"It's not fair," Colonel Fitzwilliam said, "in one way, I am jealous of Henry Crawford very much. He has the wealth and house to marry a woman like Kitty but would perhaps just whisper nice words in her ear before he goes off and starts flattering another woman. I don't hate him but only find that life has been very hard on me. I have the steadiness to choose the right sort of woman, and the wealth is not distributed in equal proportions. Then again, no one said that life would ever be fair. But I just can't help but stop and reflect on just how unfair it all is. When a man in love cannot have the means to support a woman, but an inconstant man has all the wealth to support her, it is too much. Maybe that is what is getting in the way of me caring to pardon Mr. Crawford. Perhaps I am jealous."

Darcy, Bingley, and Arthur gave each other a look.

Darcy picked up his stick again, walked up to the table, shot a ball and it went straight into the pocket.

"Thank you, Richard. You have helped me a little on how to proceed."

"Well, I am glad that I helped in some way."

He turned and was distracted by seeing a lone rider coming down the lane.

Recognizing the person's figure, Colonel Fitzwilliam sighed. He walked up to the window and watched Lieutenant Finlay riding down the road, to pay a visit to Kitty.

"Pure hell," he whispered to himself.

"Is that Finlay?" Darcy asked, barely looking out of the window.

"Yes. Coming to call on the woman that we both love."

"I could tell him to call tomorrow," Darcy said, caring for his cousin's feelings.

"Thank you, but I must ask you to let me talk to him and receive him myself in the front parlor?" Colonel Fitzwilliam requested. "There is something that I have to ask him. It's a conversation between two men, and I will not be able to ask it in company. And, whether I like it or not, Kitty has a right to see him."

Darcy nodded.

"Very well. Promise me that you both will not resort to blows of any kind."

"You know me. I always step outside before I decide to settle things as a man. Never in the house. It would hurt the furniture."

With that, he left the room, to tell Mrs. Reynolds that he would await Lieutenant Finlay in the main parlor.

∼

"Oh," Mrs. Grant said as she saw Lieutenant Finlay riding toward the house from a distance away, "you are expecting an officer?"

When the company had dispersed, Jane escorted the visitors along the grounds of Pemberley. Despite that it was winter, and the weather was cold, it was a sunny day and there was no harsh wind. Therefore, they were able to traverse the grounds without feeling any intense biting weather.

Jane looked in the direction that Mrs. Grant was gesturing. The rider was still a distance away, but Jane had sharp and perfect eyesight. Therefore, she was able to see Finlay's outline with clarity.

"Oh, that's one of our friends from Colonel Forster's regiment," Jane explained, "it would be best not to return to the house. He comes because he wishes to see my younger sister, Kitty."

"Oh," Mrs. Grant cooed, "is there love in the air on that score?"

"I cannot tell you for certain," Jane lied, "all that I can say is that he comes for her friendship."

"Of that, I can determine," Mary Crawford says, "Kitty is one young lady who does not need to get married currently."

"Mary, the things you say!" Mrs. Grant said.

"What do you mean by that?" Jane asked, not offended, but merely curious. Ever since Mary Crawford had come to Pemberley, Jane had wanted a private word with her. A desire to return to the friends they used to be, always in each other's confidence. Now was her chance. She drew closer to Mary Crawford and took her arm. "You do not think so of Kitty?"

"Naturally, not so," Mary Crawford said, "you know me, Jane. I believe that everyone ought to marry as soon as they can with advantage. But with Kitty, I don't see the word 'wife' being attached to her. At least not at present. She is too much of a younger sister, too much of a woman who is seeking some sort of direction, though I cannot say that I know what that direction is. But what I do know, is that Kitty seems like a woman who is everything else but prepared for matrimony."

"You think so?" William Price asked her.

"I know so, Mr. Price," Mary cooed, pressing her nose against his, "I know so."

William Price chuckled.

"Well, you were once the same way," William Price acknowledged, "so, I suppose that you shouldn't be surprised if you see it in others."

"Me?"

William Price turned to his fiancée, with a knowing look in his eyes.

"Mrs. Bingley, I trust you had as much deductive powers as I. Did you ever wonder, when you first met my fiancée here, that she was so much her own woman, that it seemed like no love was prepared to touch her just yet? Some people need more time to live and lust after life before they can let an honest love come to them."

"In that respect, Mr. Price," Jane said, "I quite agree with you."

Mary Crawford's eyes widened.

"You do?"

"Oh, yes," Jane said, "I felt that about you from the start. You are so much your own woman, that I couldn't see your hand secured by anyone just yet—except for Mr. Price, but that's because his eyes speak of new horizons, good nature and general cheer."

William's cheeks reddened, feeling the weight of the flattery.

"But as for the rest of it, Mary, your verbosity, and freedom of speech was more your friend than your enemy, in this case. It took you away from the wrong sort of suitor and drove you to the right sort. Now you are ready to be a wife. And, no matter what happens, I support your wedding."

Mary Crawford chuckled.

"One can always rely upon Jane Bennet to always do the right thing, can't we?"

"You tease me, Mary."

"Nay, I do not tease you." Mary Crawford lowered her voice so that they could speak more in confidence. "Jane, no matter what, I cannot fully change my nature. I will always say something uncivil every now and again. But believe me when I tell you this. I will always be a true friend to you. Call for me, and I will come."

Jane's heart felt light.

"I know you will," she whispered, "that is why, I thank god, that you never married that Edmund Bertram character."

Mary chuckled.

"Still feel that I escaped a drear fate there?"

"Yes, I do. You both would never have made each other happy. And he would have limited all the experiences that you needed to undergo to enhance yourself. You needed more time to live, Mary. Now you have it, and no sooner or later than the time came for you to experience it."

Henry Crawford leaned against them, his lips close to Jane's cheek.

"The ladies whisper. I feel left out."

~

"Oh, Henry," Mrs. Grant countered, "authority must not always be given to you to learn every woman's secrets."

"Time has shown me that it must not be," Mr. Crawford said, whimsical, "but a tiger cannot change his stripes. Sadly, there will always be something wanting, something anxious to know what ladies talk off, when I stand here alone." Henry Crawford looked at Jane, his eyes sparkling with charm. "And must I be alone, Mrs. Bingley? No, Henry Crawford must not be so."

With any other woman, Henry's eyes would have proven captivating. The turn of his countenance was always the proper pose, the perfect posture, and it could make one begin to realize that they had encountered a misunderstood hero. But with Jane, it was the reverse. She only felt a casual interest in him, and a general belief in his innocence, that was no different than how she would have believed in anyone else.

"You cannot rely upon my secrets to fill up your curiosity," Jane responded to him, pleasantly. "For what interesting secrets might I have?"

"You are the lady to a wealthy man." His eyes turned keener. "There is always a secret there somewhere. To plummet to the depths of a woman's true character is to swim the deepest oceans and find the most compelling creatures there. And Mrs. Bingley should be no different."

"Well, I thank you for finding me special, but that will not do, Mr. Crawford."

"And why not?"

Jane suddenly became introspective.

"How do you do this?" she asked, putting an end to pretense and intense flattery.

"Do what, pray?"

"Come to Pemberley, knowing that you are being judged, your fate is uncertain, and yet you still flatter us ladies?"

"You think your brother-in-law will chop off my head and it would roll on the floor like the savages from our history?" He joked.

"No, of course not. But you don't need to charm me, Mr. Crawford." She looked at him with gentle sincerity. "Put aside your allurements for a moment and speak innocent truth with me. Do you still have the impulse to fill your confidence through drawing ladies in? Is that impulse still there?"

Henry Crawford looked ahead, just at the time that Lieutenant Finlay arrived at Pemberley's front steps, and the footman took his horse's reins as Finlay dismounted.

"I cannot help it, Mrs. Bingley. There will be something about me that will always be fascinated with women. I find you all to be the ultimate pleasure in life."

"I suspected as much. I think that, inwardly, you do need us to justify your own self-importance. And that's because I think you do admire us, to the point where it is easy to become a libertine. I cannot tell you to ignore the company of ladies, because you are pleasant to be around, and your desire to be around us shows that you value us. However, Mr. Crawford, please, I need you to do this for me."

"Whatever Mrs. Bingley needs from me, I will desire to oblige her," he implored.

"Do be serious, Mr. Crawford. Never charm other men's wives. Let her sins be her own, but do not contribute to them. And when you do set your sights on ladies' company, be honest with them. Let them know that your intentions are not to seek any wife, but merely to enjoy their company. Be sincere and give them the right to choose how they feel. Please, Mr. Crawford. I believe in you. I believe you have it in you to be a good man. It would hurt to know that I was wrong. You claim to care for me. If so, then please, sir. Do not hurt me. Let me be right in this manner. I have been wrong before, and it would devastate me to be so wrong again. Give me a reason to believe that I placed my faith in the right place. Give me that."

Inwardly, Henry Crawford could not deny that he secretly regretted that he could never make Jane Bennet fall in love with him. After all, no sinner could fully reform so quickly. But a part of him also cried out that it was the wrong thing to do. And that maybe... it would hurt his own pride to let Jane Bennet down.

Sometimes, the human spirit cannot grow, but lays forever squalid and stunted, unable to learn. Whatever his flaws, Mr. Crawford was now finding ways to change. It was a conscious decision, because his vain side might ignore the pleadings of this eternally good woman who was begging him to become a better man. He realized that it would really hurt him to not live up to Jane's belief in him.

Taking Jane's hand, he shook it.

"Mrs. Bingley. Just for you." He bit his lip, altogether perturbed.

"What is it, Henry?" William Price asked.

"I suppose, I feel something now. It is a strange sensation."

"What is it?" Mrs. Grant asked.

"I feel...ashamed."

He smiled.

"I don't know why. But for some reason, it makes me happy."

None of them spoke. Yet it was not done out of confusion. Rather, they seemed to understand him in that moment, and they didn't want to speak, because they feared that it would break the spell.

Soon, they were interrupted. Behind them, they heard footsteps. They turned to see Elizabeth approaching them, walking across the field.

Chapter Six

KITTY'S TALE: TWO INDEPENDENT WOMEN

Elizabeth had never lost sight of where Jane and the visitors had walked. Therefore, she emerged from the house even before Finlay had ridden down the lane and was waited upon.

With her warm coat, bonnet, wearing two scarves and fitted gloves, Elizabeth approached the group.

"Mrs. Darcy," William Price said, "you do us an honor by joining us along our walk."

"I was curious to see how much superior my sister was at being a tour guide than I am," Elizabeth responded, "and I can see, by your glowing faces braving against the cold, that she outstrips me by leaps and bounds."

"Nonsense, Lizzy," Jane said, "I am quite abysmal at it."

"And that is more nonsense on top of the nonsense that was already presented," Mr. Crawford commented. "There is not a chance, in the stars, that Mrs. Bingley could be a better guide, just as there is no way that you, Mrs. Darcy, could be anything short of as being equal. I can admire humility, but I cannot allow it to get that far."

"You presume to know me very well, sir," Elizabeth observed.

"I know you little enough to not presume to know the recesses of your mind. However, what I am not entirely ignorant on is your abilities as a hostess. Give me no more and less than that, and I will be a model guest."

"I'll give you a meter today, Mr. Crawford. Then, tomorrow, I shall see if I am willing to give you an eighth of a mile. Who knows? Maybe one day, I'll give you a whole mile entirely."

He laughed.

"You find the wisdom in wit," he observed. "A woman after my own heart."

"And what of you, Miss Crawford," Elizabeth said, directing her attention to the sister. "Do you believe in wit?"

"I do, when I can find a way to bend it to my will," Mary Crawford said, "wit can be like any other great creature: it can be tied down and tethered eventually. Now the question is, does the world accept my wit?"

"An interesting question that you and I will spend our lives wondering about. I came to escort you this way, to a small little bridge that we have run over the streams. I think you shall like the prospect."

"Thank you, that would be a pleasure."

Without thinking, Elizabeth took Mary Crawford's arm in hers and led her onward.

This sudden direct action of physical contact did not escape Miss Crawford's notice, who could not resist casting a glance at Jane's way.

This reaction was not alone, however, because Elizabeth also gave Jane a look.

Miss Crawford's reaction said, 'Your sister is deliberately leading me away from you all, for reasons of her own'.

Elizabeth's reaction said, 'Yes, I am taking Miss Crawford away from you all deliberately. Do not interrupt me'."

Jane, having been the sort to discern and dissemble both ladies very easily, read their expressions correctly, and turned to Mrs. Grant and Mr. Crawford.

"Did I recollect to tell you how we shall be celebrating our holiday this Christmas?" Jane asked, distracting them as her dear sister and close friend would either come to an agreement, or distress and vex the other one.

"No," Mrs. Grant said, "Is it exciting?"

"It is interesting. I shall leave it to you to determine if it is exciting."

~

Now that Elizabeth had safely steered Miss Crawford far enough away from the group, Miss Crawford knew that it would do well not to be silent.

"Well," Miss Crawford said, "I congratulate you on your choice of husband as well as the beautiful grounds that Pemberley holds. I never saw an estate of such magnitude in my life."

"I had the same reaction when I first visited Pemberley."

"Yes, Jane told me. You were touring Derbyshire with your aunt and uncle Gardiner at the time, you visited Pemberley and that was when you re-met your old acquaintance, Mr. Darcy."

Elizabeth raised an eyebrow, and Mary Crawford could see that this news did not flatter her host but only unnerved her.

"You are worried that Jane has told me too much about your life," she observed. "You have no cause for alarm, I can assure you. Jane often tells me about her sisters in her letters, but she never reveals anything that ought to be kept between the family. Your sister understands discretion and family loyalty."

"She does. I suppose, perhaps, I was being too prickly."

"Well, I hope I did nothing to get stung. Besides, even if she did, she knows that I can be trusted, in turn."

"She does?"

"Yes. Our relationship began in a way where I had to lay down my whole history when we first met. After that sort of exposure, it is difficult for secrets to always be kept."

"You are intelligent, Miss Crawford."

"Thank you."

"But in a more particular way. You are also shrewd and discerning, and you know that we don't have much time before propriety demands us to return to the company."

"Yes, I suppose my powers of deduction do go that far." Mary's eyes shifted from animation to a keener look, and the change began. "You do not mince words, Mrs. Darcy, and you would prefer to get to the heart of the matter."

"I trust that you have the strength to endure it, as I do. Besides, life is filled with fluffy words, and we are not delicate creatures. Are we?"

"No, I don't suppose that we are."

"I shall be candid, but also kind. Miss Crawford, whatever flaws you have to your nature, are neither damning, nor uncommon. You speak about marriage and fortune, the way that many of us are taught to and are trained to take into consideration. We have been brought both high and low based on the effects of our education. I want you to know, whatever happens tomorrow, that I bear no ill will toward you, and I wish you joy in marriage. The same joy that I have found in my match."

Mary Crawford's brow transformed from being creased to relaxed.

"And for a moment, I thought that you were about to bring my image down with a hammer and was about to say something frightful."

"When in such circumstances, it does seem like all news must be bleak. Whatever you have said in the past, was of a woman who was trying to survive a tense situation."

"I thank you. That is very kind."

"It's not kind, but rather, it's objective. I have been the one in the room that everyone criticized for not saying the correct thing or because they would suffer no argument. I have also been the one who prided myself on my own judgement and needed to be set down a little. I know what it feels like to reject a clergyman, who I knew would not suit me. I don't condemn clergymen, but time has taught me that I am not the sort to be an ideal wife to them. I also believe in being agreeable and considerate, but I still often will go my own way, much to the dissatisfaction to some characters who weren't worth my concern. I have laughed at the follies and failings of others. I even once callously asked a man how much he needed from a wife's dowry to support them both, unless if his brother proved to be sickly. I have also been the one who has seen a person have to accept that their child ought to marry someone that their child ran away with. In those circumstances, I understand that those matters are complicated. I have also been in tense situations where I hated how helpless I felt and wanted to help the way that you did. Put simply, I cannot cast aside a woman who I am so much like."

"You see a similarity when it comes to the turn of our minds?" Mary Crawford asked. "Yes, I was wondering when you would discover that."

Elizabeth's eyes widened in surprise and slight disappointment.

"You are not surprised? Well, that is a blow to my revelations and sense of triumph. Truly, there is something so very vexing about having a realization and someone else uttering it first."

"I have no superiority when it comes to mental faculties, I assure you. I have had the luxury of a longer acquaintance with knowing of your nature. Jane has described her friendship and bond with you ever since I met her. I have long been aware that, perhaps, the reason she formed a friendly attachment to me, was because she already felt she knew me. Because she already was sisters with you." Mary Crawford leaned into Elizabeth, speaking lower so that no one would overhear. "Please, do not tell Jane. I don't want her to assume that her reasons for befriending me are simply because I am a substitute for whenever you are not present in her life. I want her to always believe that her kindness toward me is purely out of her general goodness."

This remark stirred Elizabeth's reassurance that she had been right all along. Her posture stood more erect, and she continued freely.

"You want to protect her from that innocent truth, don't you?"

"Of course, I do. I have a natural instinct to protect Jane from things. I do not know why I am like that."

"It makes sense to me."

"Of course, it does. After all, you were the one who walked three miles to tend to her when she had a cold. We both, perhaps, have a natural inclination to be better in her presence. It's Jane's special ability, if you will. If Jane were to discover that her friendship to me might originate from a selfish desire on her part, it might hurt her inner compassion. I have always been of the opinion that selfishness must always be forgiven, you know."

"Because there is no hope of a cure," Elizabeth stated.

Mary Crawford's eyes widened.

"Oh, Jane told you that I like to say that line about my philosophy."

"No," Elizabeth said, a little shakily, "she never did."

Both women looked at each other, in slight alarm. Now their similarities were becoming a little too in alignment with each other.

"We can never become truly good friends, can we?" Mary Crawford asked.

"No, I don't think we can. For we are too much alike. But we have Jane."

"Yes, we do have Jane. That is good enough for us both."

"And we must always try to be worthy of her respect."

"Yes, we must."

~

They reached the small bridge that overlooked the stream, and it truly did render a beautiful sight.

"Oh, that is so lovely!" Mrs. Grant said, "and—"

They were all interrupted when they began to feel snowflakes along their skin. They looked up and the sky's cloudiness gave way to a beautiful, but gradual snowfall.

"Snow! It is snowing!" Mrs. Grant laughed.

"Well now," Mr. Crawford observed, "I have a tendency to view snow as a good omen. For it to begin when I have come, I view it as mother nature's encouraging me that there is hope somewhere."

Elizabeth took this as the last chance to speak in confidence with Mary Crawford.

"Miss Crawford, one more thing before we enjoy the turn of the weather change."

"I am all ears and curiosities."

"Tell me the truth. Please, for a second, abandon the deceptions that we siblings place upon each other. I know that you love your brother, as a sister should. I know that you will never turn your back upon him because he is your brother. I understand that because that is what true family is for. But I must think of my husband now, and I don't want to see Jane be deceived. Please, try your best to be honest with me. Does your brother really mean that he has reformed? Does he have a desire to be a better man?"

Mary Crawford's eyes lost their twinkle and morphed into slight apprehension.

"What is that look for?" Lizzy asked.

"It's a look of ignorance, much to surprise you there, I daresay."

"Ignorance in what way?"

"Before I begin, I want it to be rightly understood—truly, I cannot stress this enough. I *love* my brother. I am loyal to him, and I will never abandon him. No matter what his flaws or mistakes are, he is my brother. I know that you understand."

"I do. That is why I am begging you to do your best to be impartial, no matter how hard it is. But I know that you love him, and ought to never do otherwise."

"Thank you. Mrs. Darcy, I want to believe that I know my brother. He has always been honest with me, even when he was being wicked. But here's the thing. Through all his wickedness, I never foresaw him running off with Maria Bertram. And when I did see my brother potentially improve, he reverted to his traditional manner. He is changeable and inconstant sometimes. Even when he sets it down by resolution. I think he wants to be a good man, but the bad influences he has had—mingled with viewing love in a narcissistic manner—sometimes will always win out. That's why I can say, with good authority, that I don't know if he is sincere. Because, sometimes, even he doesn't know when he is. With my brother, what you have is an actor, who is so good at speaking, that sometimes, he deceives himself. But what must be understood is that he has done something that he has never done before."

"And what is that?"

"Abandoned his charm, arts and allurement. I have never seen him do that before. And he has admitted to his own faults and does not make excuses for them. I want to believe that *that* is progress. Therefore, I want to believe that he means what he says. But I would be lying to you if I said that I was certain. I do not fully know."

"Thank you for telling me the truth."

"But there is one thing that I can assure you of."

"And what is that?"

"He will never hurt this family."

"Why not?"

"Because he actually likes all you Bennet sisters, and Miss Darcy by extension. There is something different about you all to any other women that he has encountered. With Jane and yourself, I think it would hurt him to feel like he has lost your good opinion."

"Why would he care for mine?"

Mary Crawford gave her a look.

"Oh, that's right," Elizabeth said, rolling her eyes, "I remind him of you."

"Yes. With Jane, her goodness startles him into being better than usual. With Miss Darcy, she feels like Kitty's second self, and he would never want to hurt Kitty either."

"Why not Kitty?"

Mary Crawford looked ahead, considering the best way to put it into words.

"I cannot determine why, so very clearly, but I think it's because he knows, that he might actually hurt her. And for some reason, he knows that she does not deserve that. Or maybe, he knows that she is the last of you all to still be seeking the road to her own happiness. And he knows that he should not get in the way of her finding it. But I have been wrong before."

Chapter Seven

I worried that going into town would not change my happiness too greatly, but I had been wrong before. And I was now!

Riding into London always made my eyes widen, made my heart stir in amazement, and helped me rise out of anything that I was feeling.

"You clearly are happy to be back in town," Uncle Gardiner noted, reading my expression.

"That is the strange thing about London," I observed, "every time that I visit, much looks the same, and yet each time, it still feels like I am coming to a different city."

"Often I have said," Aunt Gardiner boasted, "that London is the city that refuses to ever stay the same."

"Yes, I quite agree."

Eventually we reached Gracechurch Street and were finally at their home. Once we arrived, their children rushed out to meet us, while a couple of servants exited, to bring down the luggage.

My aunt and uncle had four children. They had two girls and two boys. The eldest was Isabella, who was thirteen years old, the second was Isaac, who was ten, the third was Ruth, who was eight and the fourth was Daniel, who was four. All four were delightful children and I was very glad to see them. The only strange aspect was Daniel, who didn't like to speak.

"Did you bring us presents?" Ruth asked me.

"Ruth, we must wait till she offers to give us them," Isabella corrected her.

"Very good," Uncle Gardiner said, "Ruth, Isabella is correct."

"It is all right, and I took no offense," I assured them. "Yes, you four musketeers, I come bearing gifts for you all."

They all cheered. I kissed them all on the cheek, with Isabella being the last.

"Isabella," I observed, "you are turning into quite the beautiful young woman."

"I'll never be as beautiful as you, I fear," she said as we all entered. "And I wish I would be."

"You are much lovelier, I assure you," I said, removing my pelisse and bonnet when we entered. Looking around, I was secretly joyous that everything still looked the same. There were some things in my life that needed to remain constant, and the Gardiners' residence needed to remain a consistent sanctuary.

Turning around to them all, I smiled.

"I feel as if I have finally come home."

The next day I wrote another letter to Caroline Bingley, informing her that I had arrived safely in London and that I wished to call on her. However, I still was slightly alarmed that I had not received any return letter from when I first had written to her. Yet, the mail service can always have gone astray, and my letter could easily have never been sent to its recipient.

I was not left to consider it for long, because while I was sitting down on the floor in the sitting room, working on a puzzle with Ruth, Uncle Gardiner entered.

"How was your day at the factory, dear?" Aunt Gardiner asked when he entered.

"No machine broke, no worker was lazy, and we finished our orders for the day," he said, entering with a letter in his hand. "But you know what I always say."

This next sentence, they said in unison, because Aunt Gardiner was so used to hearing her husband say this.

"No machine broken, no worker lazy, and finished orders is always a good day."

"Yes, yes, yes," Uncle Gardiner said, sitting down. "And I am just about to make the day even better. That is, unless you don't like news and an invitation."

"An invitation?" Isabella perked up.

"I am sorry, Isa," Aunt Gardiner said, pinching her cheek, "but it is sadly the sort of invitation for us boring older folk."

"Just as you will," Isabella responded.

"It is better that it is just for grownups, Isa," Isaac inferred, "Because older people only do boring things. So be happy that it doesn't include us."

"Isaac, the things you say!" Aunt Gardiner responded. "You must not talk that way again."

"He only speaks the truth," Ruth added, "doesn't he, Jane?"

"Obey your mother, you both," I supported my aunt, "but yes, I can see how, from a child's perspective, we adults are such boring little things." Here I made a face at them, and they laughed.

"Well," Aunt Gardiner advised uncle, "begin with the news and then tell us who has invited us where."

"I knew that was what you were going to request," Uncle Gardiner said, removing his jacket and rolling up his shirtsleeves.

"Did you?"

"Yes, because you have a wonderful tendency to enjoy saving the best news for last."

"I like things to end well, in case the beginning ends terribly."

In that second, I marked them both. The scene between my aunt and uncle was placed in stark contrast to that of my parents. On one side, there were two individuals who married for both love and sense. And on the other, there was the scene of two people who married without fulling understanding each other's temper and mind and were forever each other's mutual torment. I loved our parents, but I always secretly admitted to myself what they were. If I were to marry, I would want to have a relationship like that of my aunt and uncle. Such marital bliss was possible... despite my parents showing me the reverse. Never would I utter it, but I believed it:

I did NOT want to end up like my parents. To be in a relationship where one party did not love or respect the other, could never be agreeable.

"Very true," Uncle Gardiner added, "and now we shall have a wedding to attend."

"Ah," Aunt Gardiner smiled, then she turned to me to explain. "Mr. Gardiner has a custom; we always attend his employees' weddings. If they marry, we attend and give them a gift for their house."

"That is delightful," I grinned.

"So, Jane, would you be willing to join our party? One of my employees, a Miss Diana Caldwell, is marrying a naval captain by the name of Thorpe."

"I think my white muslin gown would be delighted that I had something to do with it," I accepted. Then I turned to Ruth and Isaac. "Take heart. We adults don't always do boring things."

"Weddings are boring to me," Isabella admitted.

Uncle Gardiner laughed and Aunt Gardiner chided her.

"My apologies mama, but they are," Isabella said, "there is nothing truly exciting about them. It never seems like anyone is happier at them than any other church service. It is the day that you marry the person you love. So why not celebrate it with more decorations, and not wearing your Sunday gown, and having no laughter?"

"You speak sense, Isa," Uncle Gardiner said, "because often the merriment of the event is in direct proportion to how the two people getting married feel about each other."

"Father, do you mean that the more or less the wedding is merry is directly linked to the more or less the two people who are marrying feel for one another?"

"Precisely. When your mother and I married, we were all smiles and your mother's parents succeeded at getting the parson to let us decorate the church. They were a popular family, so there were many who attended."

"And mama and I worked so very hard to make a new gown that your father had never seen before," Aunt Gardiner added. "I did not want him to see me in something he had seen me in so many times already."

"Her gown was a lovely pink," Uncle Gardiner recalled. "And it was like I was marrying the most beautiful flower in the town. And I really was. So, Isabella, be happy! Your parents made sure to never have a dull wedding ourselves."

Isabella laughed.

~

"Now that the news is done with," Uncle Gardiner continued, "it is time for the invitation. Jane, I promised you a time in town where we would all be quiet and comfortable. And here I am doing the reverse."

"I am willing to open myself to anything," I assured them. "For I am not so foolish that I came to London and am quick to be afraid of noise."

"Well, good. Because we have been invited to a ball."

Everyone in the room became filled with animation—except for Isaac.

"A ball?" Aunt Gardiner repeated. "Really?"

"Yes, it is from one of my business investors, a Mr. Weston. He is holding a ball at his home on Wimpole Street, and he has most expressly wished to invite us there."

"Wimpole Street?" Aunt Gardiner's face shifted to a look of uncertainty. "Wimpole Street is filled with the aristocracy. Did he really wish to request our company?"

Uncle Gardiner noted the dubious tone of her voice, and he interpreted her meaning.

"Marianne, I see what you are feeling. But you need not worry. Mr. Weston is a gentleman whose father was in trade himself, and there are many gentlemen in his circle who... due to their excessive lifestyle, find themselves needing us men of trade in their circles. Also, Mr. Weston's wife comes from a family who were in trade originally as well. Due to their parents' success, their children have been raised into society, but they manage to maintain an open temper and they lack any snobbery. When we are there, we shall not be met with any coldness or contempt. I believe that Mr. Weston would not stand for it. Also, if we do not go, I feel as if we shall be slighting him. And if I do go, this might be good for the factory. Any new connections that I might have can help. Therefore, what say my ladies? Are we of one mind?"

Aunt Gardiner turned to me and grinned.

"What say you, Jane? Can you humor your uncle?"

I smiled.

"I believe that we can."

"Well, Isabella," Aunt Gardiner said to her, "is a ball dull?"

"I say that it greatly depends on the people who are there, and if they all like each other," Isabella responded.

"Very wisely said."

~

The next day, I expected to receive a letter from Miss Bingley, but no letter came. Nor did any letter come the days after. Naturally, I felt disappointed, but I did not show it. Besides, the news of the ball and the gown fittings were enough to distract me from not hearing any news.

Eventually, Saturday arrived. Isabella took a glimpse of my gown before we set off, approved of it, and I took her kind wishes as good luck. Little Daniel didn't say anything, but his smile was confirmation enough.

Soon we were in the carriage, riding through London and eventually we arrived at Mr. Weston's home on Wimpole street.

When we entered, we were announced, and we waited in line to greet the family.

As we did so, I looked around, but not for Mr. Bingley. Rather I was set on enjoying the look of the home. It was lovely and still had holiday decorations everywhere. I was so occupied with admiring everything that I didn't notice that we had approached Mr. and Mrs. Weston in the line.

"Staring at my home, I see?" Mr. Weston asked. His words woke me up from my observations.

"Forgive me," I apologized, "I was just admiring the general splendor."

"You are amazed by our home," Mrs. Weston said, smiling. "That means that we have succeeded."

"Yes, you have indeed," Aunt Gardiner agreed, "your home looks beautiful."

"Mr. Gardiner," Mr. Weston said, "you bring a young lady with you who appears to be lovely and agreeable. My nephew is here, and he has little acquaintance in town." Then Mr. Weston turned to me. "But he loves to dance. Can I introduce you all to him so that he feels like he shall not be alone the entire evening?"

"We should be delighted," Uncle Gardiner said. Next, we moved along the line and looked around. As we did so, I noticed that Aunt Gardiner was scrutinizing me.

"What?" I asked.

"You look happy," she noticed. "Happier than you have looked for quite some time."

"You are concerned about my happiness," I deduced, taking her hand. "That means a great deal to me, I assure you. But for tonight, you need have no worry of me ever imposing my feelings on anyone. I am determined to be nothing else except for truly agreeable. Even if no one talks to us tonight but the Westons, I will still think I am the most fortunate woman in the world."

"That is delightful to hear." She patted my hand. "You are a sweet girl, and I know that I never need worry that you might display yourself inappropriately, but I was just worried that your heart might be sore. I am happy to be wrong now."

"And, as inadmissible as it is to contradict a lady," Uncle Gardiner refuted, "I do not think you are correct, Jane. I believe that many people will talk to us. The Westons set the tone for our evening with their amiable nature. Hopefully, other kindness shall follow."

Mr. and Mrs. Weston proved to be the most amiable hosts that there could ever be. Faith, I declared that they might have even rivalled Sir William Lucas with their cordial manners.

There were others who were invited, who were already acquainted with my aunt and uncle. They met us eagerly, I made new acquaintances who were all very friendly, and the evening seemed to be going perfectly well. After the Westons greeted every person that had arrived, they finally came to us and introduced us to their nephew.

His name was Mr. Guy Weston, he was perhaps four inches taller than me, had a pleasant face—though not particularly strong or handsome. He had blonde hair that was parted properly and framed his face well. Clearly, he was nervous when we met, but when I smiled at him, he smiled back in turn.

"Guy loves to dance," Mrs. Weston said, "but he never has the courage to ask women if they wish to agree."

"Aunt," Mr. Guy Weston said, looking down at his hands, "you reveal my secret shame."

"It is a popular tendency, I can assure you, sir," Uncle Gardiner said, "when I was your age, I was mortified to ask any woman to dance, despite loving the activity myself."

"When he first asked me," Aunt Gardiner said, "his cheeks were red with blushing."

This announcement seemed to make Mr. Guy Weston raise his eyes from the floor.

"There, you see?" Mr. Weston said to his nephew, "A common tendency of us men."

"I am merely worried about asking a woman and she might not want to dance with me," Mr. Guy responded.

"Well, even if that be so," Mrs. Weston assured him, "I can cheer your insecurity; even if she does not want to dance with you in particular, she will enjoy the dance for the sake of the attention, and the dance might lead to her having more partners later. Either way, she benefits from your request."

Mr. Guy Weston looked at them, then at myself, and his eyes twinkled.

"Does it seem like they want us to dance?" he asked me.

I chuckled, but didn't respond. For I didn't know what to say.

"Yes, they do," Mr. Guy answered his own question, "and I am perfectly happy to oblige. Miss Bennet, if you are not engaged for the first dance, might I request your hand?"

"I am not engaged, sir," I informed him, "And so, yes, you may."

In that moment, I thought of when I first had danced with Mr. Bingley. Yet I tried to dismiss him from my mind as soon as I could.

~

As I began to attempt conversing with others in the company, often I found my eye wandering to one corner of the room. Do you know how, every now and again, there is that one person in the room who is so very striking? You cannot explain why they are, or what about them has more natural appeal than anyone else. Yet, they are the most appealing people anyhow.

However, as I remained in other people's company, there was something about this one woman who often drew my notice. She was sitting in a corner, with three other women. They were talking animatedly. But the woman in the center—though it could be argued that she was no more handsome than Lizzy, Kitty and Lydia, I still couldn't help but find something electric about her appearance. And, from how she was centered between her friends, it was evident that she was the main one amongst them—the leader of the fashionable. In short, I found her to be one of the handsomest women in the room, but it wasn't her looks that gave her that title. It just seemed that whatever us women had, she had more of it.

Later in life, I would learn what it was that she had: gusto.

But for the moment, she was a curiosity—and an even larger one when I noticed that no men were taking any pains to engage her for a dance. That left me to only assume that she was not a woman of wealth, and perhaps men in the London ton were often obliged to consider that before anything else.

Very soon, Mr. Guy Weston met me for the first dance. The music was struck up and we began. To my utter surprise, Mr. Weston was a remarkable dancer. At first, we said nothing.

"I do not know what to say," I admitted.

"Why ever not?" he asked.

"Because I do not know where to begin."

"Fortunately, the dance can speak for us. You dance remarkably well, Miss Bennet."

"Thank you, sir," I smiled, "you are very kind."

"You smile a great deal."

Immediately, my smile left my face.

"I know," he rushed out, "I did not mean that by way of a censure. It was merely an observation. You smile because you appear to be genuinely happy. That is remarkable. I find little to smile about in the manner which you do."

"I promise that I only smile because I feel it."

"I can see that, for your smiles are real. Often, I see smiles be things of artifice."

"I find that I cannot act, even if my life depended on it." I just realized that he complimented my dancing, but I had never returned the praise. "Forgive me, I realized that I never praised your dancing as well. I am happy that your aunt and uncle persuaded you to think yourself worthy of the dance. You do the act successfully."

"I am happy that they pushed me into being courageous as well. And thank you. I love dancing! But my apprehensions are founded on more than just because of fear for myself, but fear for the woman."

"And how so?"

"Well, it is the custom that if a man requests your hand, then you have to accept us. If you refuse, then you can't accept any more offers for the rest of the evening. Normally, I like all the power being on my side, but in this case, if a woman dances with me because she has no choice, that is not fair. Have you ever noticed this?"

"I confess that I have," I admitted. "I never thought any other men had—except for one."

"One?"

"I once knew a man who believed that a woman could reject a

man's offer to dance and still have the right to dance the rest of the evening. He was a rarity. You remind me of him now."

"That is nice to know that we are two in number. But I am happy that you appear to be enjoying my company. When I first saw you, you were the precise sort of girl that I wanted to dance with."

"Was I?"

"Yes. There were two women that I felt such a strong pull toward when they first entered the room. I got the sense that you both were kindred spirits. And you were one of those two."

"That is very kind. And who was the other woman?"

"She is the woman who is sitting in the corner in the pink gown, surrounded by her friends. There," he directed, but I didn't need to look where he gestured to know who he spoke of. "She is the other." Quickly, I glimpsed the other woman, who had been the exact woman that I found so very compelling before. When I turned back to him, I saw him look worried.

"But what is wrong?" I asked. "Have I done something to offend you?"

"No, quite the contrary. I realize that I have offended you."

"How so?"

"Because, here I am, dancing with one of the most elegant women that I have ever had the pleasure to dance with, and I speak of another woman."

"I can assure you," I stressed, "I am not offended, nor have you offended me. I have not met the woman that you speak of, but I saw her when I first entered. Your placing me on the same level as her is the most flattering thing. For even I found her to be striking. Besides, we have just become acquainted. I do not have the right to be the main object of your attention."

"I just cannot help but desire to dance with such superior women," he continued. "And you have made me very happy. I wish that I can dance with you for the entire evening, if it were proper. For, I suspect, that you would make me feel comfortable, and would be the best company in the place."

"I fear that I would not live up to your expectations. They are too high, and I do not deserve your praise."

"I believe that you do."

I smiled and hoped that I could think of something to say. If Elizabeth were here, she would know how to reply. So, what would she say now? Indeed, what would she say!

"Well," I continued, "I shall do the best I can to live up to your faith in me. And I shall start doing it by encouraging you. Be brave, sir, and dance the entire evening. It appears that you have the stamina for it. And dance with that other woman as well. She seems to be of my mind and enjoys to smile."

"I cannot ask her to dance," he stated flatly.

My brow furrowed.

"Why? It is evident that she is pleasant. Or does she not prefer to dance for the evening?" He was silent at my questions, and I wondered if maybe I should gather my courage and deduce why that would be. I came up with one theory. "Oh, are you afraid that she will accept your hand because she is obliged? Are you upset that she has no choice in the matter? Because if so, then that is very considerate of you, but I believe that she will find your company stimulating."

"It is not that. I just realized that you do not know about her."

"What of her?"

"She comes from a dubious family."

"Dubious?"

"Yes. Her brother ran off and had a tryst with a married woman."

My eyes widened in shock.

"What?" I gasped.

"Yes. Her brother, a Mr. Henry Crawford, had an affair with a married woman named Mrs. Maria Rushworth. Mrs. Rushworth was married to a Mr. Rushworth, who lives here on Wimpole Street. Well, what do you think? One moment, she is married to her husband, and then a week later, she has run off with Mr. Henry Crawford."

This news almost made me lose my footing in the dance.

"I see the shock etched across your features," Mr. Weston noticed.

"Because right now, you could knock me down with a feather. That is horrid. It cannot be true."

"But it is."

"I just cannot fathom that such a thing did occur. Perhaps these are rumors that people have driven out of proportion. And that there were some great mistake and slander. Sometimes the world paints things as being worse than they are. Maybe this Mrs. Rushworth's crimes were exaggerated."

"You are kind for suggesting it, but sadly, it is all very true."

"But this Mrs. Rushworth did that? Without any consideration of how it would hurt her husband? It is too frightful to consider. And what became of Mr. Crawford and Mrs. Rushworth? Did they get married?"

"Nothing so clean and neat. They did not get married, and Mr. Rushworth divorced his wife, naturally! And Mr. Crawford disentangled himself from the whole affair."

"And what became of the lady?"

"When last I heard, she was living in the country, separate from her family. Some may regard it as seclusion, but I know an exile when I see one. And her divorced husband can't stand to hear the mention of her name."

"My heart goes out to them both. He suffers from heartbreak and her life is ruined by her own hands. That being said, I shall wish to make allowances for distortion of tale. I have met neither person, so it is my duty to reserve judgement."

We were separated by the dance, and that gave me a moment to look back at the lovely woman in the corner. Her brother had run off with a married woman? How shocking! But now that I thought further on the matter, the question still had not been answered.

When Mr. Weston and I came back together again, I continued the conversation. This discussion was quite fascinating to me.

"But I am still confused. What does her brother's affair have to do with you being afraid to dance with the lady?"

Mr. Weston looked at me, perplexed.

"Well, due to her brother's mistake," he explained, "she is not the most desirable person to dance with."

I began to understand his meaning. The implications horrified me.

"Are you saying that you do not wish to dance with her, because you find her guilty by association? You mean to say, that because her brother did something, she is tainted in your eyes? Despite that she never committed the deed herself?"

Mr. Weston's resolve dropped at my questions.

"Well...it is the proper thing to do."

His remark had a strange effect on me. The very concept of it was baffling to my sensibilities and I could not believe he was like that. Despite that I had never met the woman before, for some reason, I found myself caring for her. I could not account for it; but I just... believed in her. It was irrational to say the least. But until the woman did something untoward, I felt inclined to defend her.

"I do not understand," I acknowledged, "How is it proper? After all, why would she, or any of us, be guilty for the actions of another?"

Mr. Weston did not know how to respond to my inquiries. Immediately, I felt sorry for my rashness.

"Forgive me," I added hastily, "I can see that my words have caused you pain. Please do not believe me to be always like this. In that moment...well, I was not myself. I do not take pleasure in being contrary."

"You mistake my silence," Mr. Weston overrode me, "it is not done out of being unhappy with you. But rather, your words are correct. And they have shamed me. The young lady looks charming to me, and I suppose that I was being a coward just now. I heard about her family, noted how others regarded her as being finished, and allowed myself to be influenced by such persons."

"I can understand a desire to go with the words of the crowd," I supported, "so your cowardice is not cowardice, but a desire to be in agreement with others and to be peaceful. Either way, I cannot help but feel for anyone who is belittled just because they are guilty by association. After all, they are being blamed for something that is not their fault. If such a thing were to happen to me, I would think it was unfair. And if you were disrespected in such a way, would you not want me to still be kind to you?"

"You have quite converted my mind," he said, "and your advice will not fall on deaf ears."

"You flatter me."

"I would not say such if I did not mean it."

I blushed.

"It is now me that owes you something," I said, "for never before have I had my opinion valued in such a way. Thank you for listening. That is a rare talent in itself."

"You are most welcome."

The dance soon came to an end.

Mr. Weston went off to get us some punch, and we were near the 'infamous lady' and her friends. Every now and again, I couldn't help looking at her from the corner of my eye. I could still not explain why I found her so fascinating. Yet like I said, she seemed to have more womanhood about her than the rest of us did.

Eventually, after my third time of stealing a glance at her, her eyes fell upon mine, and I felt so embarrassed. I was about to look away from her when she smiled at me.

For a second, I was worried that she was smiling at someone else, so I looked around myself. But as I saw that there was no one else that she would be looking at, I was left to assume that it was me she was smiling at. Turning back to her, I smiled back and curtsied to her.

"You dance very well," she called out to me.

"Thank you," I replied, my voice faltering a little, nervous. "I was worried that I would be nothing compared to you London ladies."

Her friends next to her laughed, but she ignored them.

"Your modesty does you credit," she added, "I admire modesty, because it's something I find too expensive to have myself."

"Thank you. When I first came here, I felt like a square peg..."

"...in a round wotsit," she said with me. I laughed at her ability to read my thoughts.

She was witty! How was I ever to make her still interested in talking to me? I had nothing to recommend myself to her company.

"Am I to assume that you are from the country then?" she asked.

Without even thinking, I walked up to her.

"Yes, I am from Hertfordshire. My father's estate is Long-bourn. Forgive me, I have not introduced myself. My name is Miss Jane Bennet."

"Well, Jane," she said, "I am half like you. A part of me is of the city, but another part of my soul once rested in the country. I am Miss Mary Crawford. My brother owns a prettyish estate of his own in the country as well. It is called Norfolk, in Evering-ham. Yet I live here in London, with my sister, Mrs. Grant." She curtsied to me, then she turned to her friends. "And I think we have a new lady to be happy to meet, don't you all think?" Her friends gave in to her influence, they smiled and curtsied. Their names were Miss Wainwright and Miss Higgins.

"And while we look forward to your company," Miss Crawford said to me, "your company seems to be desired elsewhere." She gestured behind me. I turned and saw Mr. Weston approach with a cup of punch for me. I smiled at him, and he followed my eyes. Seeing Miss Crawford with me, he thought it wise to approach us. "Miss Crawford, Miss Wainwright and Miss Higgins, can I intro-duce you to a friend of mine?"

"If it's the man who is coming up with your punch," Mary Craw-ford noted, "then he looks amiable enough. We shall not eat him!"

I laughed. Mr. Weston, having just come up to us, had over-heard her last comment.

"Eat me?" he repeated, "That is very good. For I doubt that my taste would suit anyone's palate."

Mary Crawford laughed.

"Miss Bennet," Mary Crawford said, "you had better introduce us quickly. The sooner that you do, the sooner that we can speak to him."

I introduced them all to Mr. Weston. With him being the only man amongst us, he felt special immediately. Handing me my punch, I began to drink it as all the women began to talk. Very soon, I worried about feeling as if I was going to fall to the wayside, but Mary Crawford proved to be striking for a reason. She spoke to me as much as she spoke to Mr. Weston.

"And you are a man who loves to dance?" Mary Crawford said, responding to Mr. Weston, "now that is a rarity. Is it not, ladies?"

Miss Wainwright and Miss Higgins agreed.

"But I wonder," Mary Crawford continued, "do you like to dance because of the activity, or because you had just been dancing with the lovely Miss Bennet?"

"Both were equally enticing of their own accord, and having a pleasant partner adds to it. Miss Bennet was kind enough to be one of the best partners that I ever had."

"Thank you, sir," I answered. "But I believe that all three of these ladies shall prove to be the best partners that you have yet."

"I shall never know unless I have the pleasure of dancing with all of them. Miss Bennet believes that I am worthy of dancing with you three, but only you can choose. Miss Crawford, Miss Wainwright, and Miss Higgins, would you all be so kind as to let me secure your hand for the next three dances?"

They all agreed readily. Despite their doing so, Mr. Weston still wished to enhance his gallantry. Leaning into them closely, he lowered his voice to a whisper.

"Of course, I did not mean to press you. I wish to dance with you all, but if you do not wish to dance with me, you can refuse me, think no more of it, and still dance with other men. I do not wish for you to be troubled with a man you do not wish to dance with for half an hour."

"I agree readily!" Mary Crawford laughed.

"Then may I secure your hand now? And if Miss Wainwright and Miss Higgins can reserve the third and fourth dance for me?"

"We are still delighted," Miss Wainwright said.

"And Miss Bennet?" Mr. Weston requested, "might I have the pleasure of dancing the fifth with you?"

"You may," I agreed.

Taking Miss Crawford's hand, they began to walk to the dance floor. Having a second thought, Mary Crawford turned to me.

"Miss Bennet, before the evening is out, I shall wish to know more about you. You helped me get a dance partner, therefore I owe you the right to become more acquainted."

She walked to the dance floor and immediately I felt as if there was a bit of a social void. Miss Wainwright, Miss Higgins, and I all looked at each other, immediately trying to entertain each other. Despite our efforts, none of us felt fully comfortable now that Miss Crawford was not in the party. Fortunately, Miss Wainwright and Miss Higgins had gentlemen who came for the dance they had already secured from them. As a result, I was not left to try at a conversation that I was going to be a little awkward at. Once the women departed, I was left to return to my aunt and uncle and immediately felt comfortable in not speaking much.

I danced once more with Mr. Guy Weston, developed a wider acquaintance with the Westons as a whole, danced with a few more gentlemen, and found myself not slighted in the least; Miss Mary Crawford had not forgotten me.

In between dances, she came up to me and we spoke small trivialities—but I liked those small trivialities. I discovered that her sister was a widow who did not like coming to balls but was very amiable in every other respect. Her sister's late husband had been a clergyman, she was raised partly by an Admiral Crawford, her brother was charming, but she warned me not to give in to his charms, and that she loved to laugh.

I told her all about my family and found my words coming freely out of my mouth. There was something about her that was very disarming, and I couldn't help talking. When I mentioned that my uncles were in trade, she showed no signs of being perturbed on that score.

"I love not having to suffer the lot of having a profession," she said, "but therein is the irony of me. I was given 20,000 pounds in my dowry, but if I was allowed to work, I could make my fortune instead of having to worry about marrying into it to keep my lifestyle."

"That is what my sister, Lizzy, says," I supported her. "She enjoys the freedom of being a gentleman's daughter, regarding not having to toil, but then she also realizes that perhaps a bit of hardship is worth the pain, if one can always supply a room of one's own and a living."

"I flatter myself, that I think your sister is correct," she laughed. Soon, we were to be interrupted because our dance partners came to claim us. "After this dance, I promised my sister that I would return home at 10 o'clock, so I must leave afterwards. Before I go, might I call on you at Cheapside? Or do you wish to never see my face again?"

"I would love for you to visit us. Whenever you write to come, I shall make myself available. And I can safely say that my aunt and uncle would enjoy for us all to become better acquainted."

Soon we parted.

Eventually, the evening came to an end, and I was riding back to Cheapside with my aunt and Uncle Gardiner.

"That was more successful than I thought it would be," Aunt Gardiner exclaimed. "We were met with such affability and such openness."

"Yes, my dear," Uncle Gardiner said, yawning from exhaustion. "I trust your faith in me is as justified as ever; for I would never take you to a place that would make you feel disrespected."

"Yes, my faith will never be shaken," Aunt Gardiner chuckled as they squeezed each other's hand.

"No one should ever have to feel disrespected for anything so small as their station in life," I gathered, "we are oft too quick to hurt others for no reason. Why must life be so complicated?"

"These are delightful questions that you must wait till the morning to ask," Uncle Gardiner said, "because I am too tired to be smart at all."

"And this night seemed to be such a success for you," Aunt Gardiner pointed out, "you were the beauty of the ball."

"Thank you, aunt. But there were many lovely women there who I cannot claim to be their equal."

"You have every right to be modest," Aunt Gardiner intoned, "for modesty, I have always believed, is a definite virtue. Don't ever lose it. Besides, this entire evening, it seemed as if you had truly lost yourself into the comforts of it all. I am glad of this."

"Now all we have is a wedding on the rise, and then our lives will go back to being dull."

"I welcome dullness," I offered. "Sometimes too much excitement can have unfortunate endings. But thankfully, this evening was not one of that."

I looked out of the window, and for the first time in a few hours, I had thought of Mr. Bingley.

BUT—that had been the first time that I had thought of him *in* hours, and that was not usually the case. Even when I pretended to be disinterested, and spoke of other things, he was always in my mind. Never had I usually gone a moment without him being tied to my thoughts, and I would sit and relive a flashback of him and I dancing together.

And yet, I had not thought of him until then. I knew that I was still heartbroken, but I truly did believe that I was recovering. Hopefully tomorrow would bring a continuance of my progress.

But, of course, it didn't.

I thought of him still. How the heart can often never leave us alone...

Chapter Eight

KITTY'S TALE: TWO ROMANTIC MEN

T ruly, how the heart can never leave us alone!

When Lieutenant Finlay had arrived in front of Pemberley, with the express desire to call on Kitty, he was ushered inside immediately.

"You will find Colonel Fitzwilliam in the parlor, sir," Mrs. Reynolds said, when he entered.

Astonishment!

This was the last thing that he expected when he entered. After all, Colonel Fitzwilliam and himself had a silent agreement to see each other as little as possible. But now, his friendly rival was seeking him out.

"Yes, thank you," was all that Finlay could respond, because to object would be most objectionable. Instead, he followed Mrs. Reynolds to the parlor and breathed in deeply.

She led him inside, and it was to see Colonel Fitzwilliam standing by the window, with his back to him.

"Colonel," Mrs. Reynolds said, "Lieutenant Finlay, sir."

"Yes, bring him in, Mrs. Reynolds."

When she did, Finlay braced himself and bowed to his superior.

"Colonel," Finlay said, "how kind of you to receive me."

"Not at all, sir. Are you in good health?"

"At this time of year, I doubt anyone is."

When Mrs. Reynolds was finally out of earshot, both men relaxed.

"Well," Colonel Fitzwilliam said, "I am sure that this is a very unpleasant surprise for you."

"Surprise, yes. But it's not entirely unpleasant. As far as romantic rivals go, you are definitely one of the best ones that I have encountered. I just don't see why you want to see me. If I were you, Colonel, I would wish to never be in my company."

"I needed to talk to you about something."

This last sentence made the hair along Finlay's neck stand on end. What was the Colonel about to ask? Was he intending to propose to Kitty? Was he about to tell Finlay that he wished to never have Finlay speak to Kitty again? When it came to love, the mind often had the habit of turning to the negative.

Both men sat down.

"It's about my time here," Colonel Fitzwilliam began.

Finlay's brow furrowed, not understanding.

"Your time?"

"Yes. I can only remain in Pemberley for another week before duty calls me away. I... I need a favor from you."

Now that all seemed to be leaning more toward a gentle discussion between them, Finlay's body grew loose, and he relaxed as coffee was brought in.

Both men drank the cup that was offered them, Colonel Fitzwilliam dismissed the servant, and both men were alone again.

"A favor?" Finlay asked.

"Yes."

"I never knew that I was in the way of being able to offer you anything of any value, Colonel. You have taken me quite by surprise."

"Well, it won't be an unpleasant one. Or perhaps it might be, but the pain will be temporary."

"How so?"

"Because I am staying for only seven more days, I would...I would like to spend as much time with Kitty as I can. We have managed to be very good at keeping her all to ourselves at different times. But this is the one time where I would like to ask you to not visit Pemberley until I am gone. I would like to have as much time with her before I leave. And when I am gone, you can return to her company solely belonging to you."

"Seven days without seeing her?"

"I know it may be difficult. That is why I am asking for this favor."

"Did you speak to Kitty about this before asking me?"

"No, I did not. I did not expect you to come today. I thought it best if I discussed it with you while we had time alone."

"Well, I can see why you wish for this, and I am not so callous as to not consider your feelings. Would you mind, however, if I see her during this visit? After all, I am already here. Would it not look strange for me to visit and not pay my respects to her?"

"Of course," Colonel Fitzwilliam said, clapping his hands. "I understand that, at least. But, other than that, I request of you to give me these next seven days. I simply..."

"Need her now more than ever," Lieutenant Finlay finished his sentence.

"Yes. Soon I will have to say farewell to her again. And it's a miserable sort of business. I do not like saying goodbyes. Or at least, not where women that I love are involved."

"Yes, it was never easy for me either. Do you ever wonder?"

"What?"

"With the way we shuffle Miss Bennet about so... it is as if we rent her out to the other."

"Yes, I have noticed. We are terrible."

"Yes, we are. And yet I cannot help myself."

"No, I cannot help myself either. Sometimes, I wonder if we really do hurt her, and she merely hides it."

"Perhaps we do hurt her a little, but not to a terrible amount. If we still hurt her heart, she would have told us already. She is a woman who knows what she is about—why do you think we are so much in love with her?"

"Yes, I suppose that is it. Besides, she probably still would not know which of us to choose."

Colonel Fitzwilliam thought of this harder.

"Perhaps we are going about this the wrong way," Colonel Fitzwilliam proposed. "We presume to know a great deal about what Kitty is thinking before we even consult her on the matter."

"Precisely," Finlay agreed. "We are not consulting the primary person. Would it be disagreeable to you if I asked her about this when seeing her today? And then, when I leave, you can discuss this all that you choose with her."

"It would be best if we did. When you leave, I can gather what you both have decided on. Perhaps, you will have done me two favors."

"How so?" Finlay asked, lowering his teacup on the table.

"You begin the discussion. Therefore, you bear the brunt of the first part of conversation, and I undertake it after Kitty has already gotten introduced to the matter."

Finlay groaned.

"I walked into that, didn't I?"

"Like a blind man, lieutenant. Like a blind man."

Chapter Nine

KITTY'S TALE: SISTERS-IN-LAW

After Elizabeth left us, Enara said that she needed to take a moment alone, because a sudden headache came upon her. Excusing herself, it was only Georgiana and I who were left in Georgie's room.

When alone, we would not have wanted it any other way.

"Well," Georgiana said, as we both removed our stockings and propped our feet up by the fire, "this has been an interesting day."

"Not has been, Georgie," I said, "but still is. After all, with how the whims of chance constantly seem to puff us about, we don't even know what can happen next."

Georgiana and I both looked at each other, and smirked.

"I wish it were summertime."

"So do I. Let's imagine it is. Things were simpler at that time. The trees had leaves, and the sun was kind."

"And we knew what we were about."

"Yes, we did. Would that it was a midsummer's eve, where all is at its most romantic."

For a second, I imagined us in that oasis, before I decided to continue.

"I am happy," I said.

"Happy. Why?"

"Because this is a situation that is all quite out of my hands. I am not the lord or lady of Pemberley, therefore, it is not my place to decide whether to allow the Crawfords to still be received here. And I am merely an observer of the situation. As such I can enjoy this all as something where I can watch human nature unfold and be a study of character. Sometimes, as much as I hate to admit this, but there is something comforting about when situations are out of your hands and beyond your control. It gives a certain liberty to a person."

"That's really what you are feeling?"

"Yes. You are upset with me, aren't you?"

"Well, yes, I might be. But not in the way you think."

"Oh, dear, I've made my friend unhappy. Go on, you can call me any sort of name that you like. Perhaps, I do deserve it."

"No, I am not here to hurt you for being honest with me. Besides, I was not clear with what I said. Naturally, you would think that I was reprimanding you, when I was merely astonished with you. Yes, we do not have the power to do anything about it, but that does not mean that we cannot determine things for ourselves. We can have our own judgements about things."

How interestingly provocative things can be when your dear friend does not understand you! I could scarcely contain my laughter.

"Georgie, you really don't know me by now? Yes, I feel the comfort of freedom from not being the ultimate judge. However," I leaned forward, placing my hands on my lap. "I always have an opinion on everything."

"Good," Georgiana said, feeling better, "I was worried that you were getting too reserved for me, at present. And that might very well be the last thing that is needed at this time. I want to know what you feel."

"First, before I tell you what I feel, I need you to understand that my judgements are not as severe as some would expect."

"I suspected as much, but why?"

"Because it's hard to judge others for having the same flaws that I have."

"You never ran off with another person's spouse."

"Yes, but it doesn't stop the fact that I am in love with two men at the same time."

"First, that is not your fault."

"But I have said things that have raised eyebrows."

"And I once accepted an elopement with a man who was using me for my money."

"That was not your fault. Wickham was a childhood friend who preyed upon your trust, and you were only fifteen years old. No woman at that age ever knows what they are about."

"Well, that is true. I still regret my foolishness, but there is much truth to the circumstances."

"And that is why I am confused of what to fully think. You see how we are making excuses for our behavior? We believe that there are reasons for why we took a step too far somewhere. And we are right to. With us, it was complicated. Maybe, there was something complicated with this situation as well. As we learned, Henry Crawford was rejected by Miss Price. Maybe that rejection affected him more than he thinks. Especially since we have just discovered that Mr. Crawford suffers from a character that depends upon the appreciation of others, and always feels like he needs to be loved, as opposed to having true feelings. Maybe he needs to be adored, and when he's not, he gives into the baser sides of his character. But that's no excuse."

"And then, there is the main problem with this situation: this Miss Maria Bertram. She married a man that she did not love, it obviously made her miserable, and then it led to her running off with the man who once spurned her, in a way that rendered him almost obliged to marry her in turn. Which he did not do. But that originated from the fact that she had a broken heart, that Mr. Crawford initially caused."

"Precisely. When you dig deep enough, everyone has an excuse behind why they are villains, at one time or another."

"But then, as we discussed earlier," Georgiana recalled, "at some point, you have to grow up and take responsibility for your own actions."

"Yes. Mr. Crawford is doing that now. It will never be known if Maria Bertram is doing that in her exile—oh, to not be received by one's own family!"

"Yes, that is a severe punishment of its own kind. Maybe she deserves it, but she shouldn't suffer for it forever."

"True. Punishment is important."

"It's a great learning tool. I learned my lesson when Wickham abandoned me soon after it was evident that he would not receive my dowry. The look on his face when he abandoned me was punishment enough. But no punishment should last for an eternity when it comes to errors of judgement. This Maria Bertram was an adult—she chose all the wrong paths to make. And then she expected no punishment for it. It was good of her to be humbled."

"Yes, humility is important, in the end," I said, looking into the flames. They danced along the logs. I watched the smoke rise into the fireplace, suspected the journey it had to fly up through the chimney and into the skyway. I cannot explain why I marveled at so small an event, but in that moment, I was dazed at the ways of man and woman to always sojourn forth and make life a little easier for the rest of us. Perhaps, each invention, each new path that humanity takes to make life a little easier is done because of knowing that each of us have to deal with our own complications.

The conveniences of life are done from a general understanding that we are all going to seek out ways to make our lives difficult. So, humanity tries, repeatedly, to make life a little less stressful, because of the clear understanding that sometimes we all invent our own heavens and our own hells. Maria Bertram created her own inferno, and then she was flung into it. I wondered if she was appreciating a warm fire, or if she was sitting around, wallowing in her own despair, and never confronting her own mistakes. After all, there will always be the sorts who always believe that their misfortunes are always everyone else's fault.

And the fire was beautiful.

"But we have one thing that makes our flaws so very forgivable," I declared.

"And what is that?"

"Everything we did, was done out of an act of love. Maria Bertram's downfall was because she married someone she did not love. It drove her into an abyss. Mr. Crawford's mistake was that he enthralled a woman that he had no true love for. All of this happened because of people not loving those that they sought after."

"True," Georgiana uttered, "what we did was an act of love. That is the one reason that makes all our missteps perfectly respectable. We care. We love. And so, I am now more resolved than ever. If and when we do marry, it must be from the greatest love of all. Nothing less will do for us now. Especially since we have seen the misfortunes that arise when a person does not love and respect their spouse."

"And what of Miss Crawford," Georgiana said, "what do you think of her?"

"She is honest, for better or for worse. I cannot help but admire her for that. She says things that are indelicate, I admit, but she also is aware that she has vices, yet is harmless, in every respect. Her flaws are those of the everywoman, not the malicious woman."

"A part of me is happy that I am not her. And then another part of me is quite jealous of her."

"And why so?"

"She is courageous. She is fierce, for better or worse, as you put it. And as a result, she evidently did find a man who loved her."

"Even though it is the last sort of man that she expected."

"Many people fall in love with the last sort of people that they expected. It's a common practice."

"True, it is. But above all, she is striking to look at. Often, I find that I cannot look away from her. I think that it may be because she believes in herself. Or at least, she sounds like she does."

"I wish that I did."

"You have the right to. You have so many virtues."

"As do you. But you do not always believe in yourself either."

I looked at her, surprised. At one point did Georgiana begin to pry into the secret part of my soul and see everything with a sharp clarity that was akin to the angels who know the truth about our inner demons? She was correct, and I was curious as to how far she would be so. Choosing my words carefully, I spoke slowly.

"How did you know?" I asked her. "How did you know that I still do not fully believe in myself?"

Georgiana drank some of her chocolate and then set it back down. Avoiding my gaze, she continued to look into the fire.

"I love a good fire," she said.

"Yes, it is. Nothing is better than a comfortable room, a lovely fire, and company who you can confess to the most sordid of desires and no one will judge you."

"All too true."

We sat there for a moment before Georgiana found her courage again.

"I don't avoid your question because I am afraid, but because it is a very bland answer that I have. I would like to say it is because I am perceptive. But that's not it. I would also like to say that it has been from my ability to observe others better. But that's not it either. Then I would like to say it's because I saw a bit of myself in you, but that's also not true."

"Then what is the answer? How did you know?"

"I just guessed. I assumed it was so and merely leant my voice to it."

I smiled.

"Lucky guess. We want the confidence that Miss Crawford has. That's why we find her striking. Perhaps she has something that we want."

A startling revelation then came to me. It was almost disconcerting.

"What if we never find it?" I asked. "What if we never know how to believe in ourselves?"

Georgiana looked back into the fire.

"This is a lovely fire."

"Yes, it is. It keeps us warm, for the moment."

In that moment, we both didn't want to voice it, but we might as well had done so.

We didn't know the answer to that question.

We were interrupted by a knock on the door...

Chapter Ten

JANE BENNET'S TALE: OLD FRIENDS IN NEW PLACES

O nce more, I was not interrupted by a knock on the door.

The next day brought no letter from Caroline Bingley, and this weighed heavily on me. Yet, I was still resolved to travel to her home to pay her a visit.

Despite the minor disappointment of still not receiving any word from her, I was not left low in spirits for long at all.

For fortune decided to help compensate: I had not received a letter from Miss Bingley, but I had received a letter from Miss Mary Crawford. She had written to ask if she could call on me on Thursday. After getting permission from Aunt Gardiner, I sent a confirmation and was excited that I might make a new friend.

The rest of the day was spent with me writing in my journal of the ball, and what I felt of who.

While I tried not to think of Mr. Bingley at all, I was not so fortunate. The solace of my constant thoughts toward him might have been to have received word from Caroline, but I could only surmise that perhaps my letters to Caroline had been lost in the mail. After all, such things were known to happen.

But I had another announcement that cheered me, compiled with Miss Crawford's letter. Aunt Gardiner had informed me that she was going to the area of town tomorrow, where Caroline was staying. She had to go for some form of domestic business, and therefore it would give me the chance to call on Miss Bingley.

Happy to finally have some good news to inform Lizzy, I wrote her this information at the beginning of a letter. Yet I thought it wise to not send the letter yet but wait till after my visit to tell her what it was like to see my good friend again. Never did I understand why Lizzy thought so ill of her.

～

The next day, I had gone with Aunt Gardiner to Grosvenor Street, and we parted ways at Miss Bingley's residence. After ringing the bell, I fixed my bonnet and clothes to make certain that I looked presentable. A servant opened the door, I was granted entry, and I waited while I was being announced.

It was strange, for now I was seeing Caroline in a place that I was not accustomed to. Looking around myself, at this lovely home, the foreign setting made me feel a little... uncertain of myself. Passing this all off as some sort of folly, I allowed another servant to take my cloak and bonnet and wait till I was presented. Eventually, the steward entered and escorted me into the sitting room.

Upon entering, *finally* I came face to face with Caroline and Mrs. Hurst again. Taking in a sharp breath, I smiled warmly. There they were! My dear friends.

"Miss Bennet, ma'ams," the servant said, and I curtsied.

"Miss Bingley and Mrs. Hurst," I cried merrily as they curtsied in return, "it is a great pleasure to see you both again."

"And we feel the same," Miss Bingley responded, "for this is a surprise indeed."

"Is it?"

"Yes," Mrs. Hurst proclaimed, "for one moment, we think you are in Hertfordshire and then here you are on our doorstep. The surprise was quite disarming for us."

"Indeed," Miss Bingley supported, "for we have not received one word from you about you being in town. Why did you not write?"

I closed my eyes in relief. I had been right all along!

"That is so good to hear," I said, "for when I received no word back from you, I wondered what happened to thwart our connection. Miss Bingley and Mrs. Hurst, pray believe that I never forgot you or how much I enjoyed your company. I had sent you a letter about my coming to London and precisely when I would arrive."

Mrs. Hurst and Miss Bingley gave each other a look.

"Ah," Miss Bingley said, "did you?"

"Yes, I did," I continued. "Therefore, it seems that we both have been at the mercy of the postal service. I can clearly see how, now, it was my letter that had gone astray, and you both have not received it."

"Ah," Mrs. Hurst said, "well now it is all explained."

There was a sudden pause in our conversation, where both sisters looked at me and then looked at each other. An awkwardness seemed on the verge of creeping in upon us, and I felt urged to fill it. But truly, what could I say?

"Well," Miss Bingley offered, "you have come and have remedied the confusion. Truly, it is delightful to see you, Jane."

"And I with you," I echoed, and then I looked around the room. Suddenly, I felt compelled to unveil the apprehension that I was feeling. "I confess that I was ever so startled when I entered."

"Startled?" Miss Bingley and Mrs. Hurst gave each other a look. "But why should you have been?"

"Because it had just occurred to me that I had never seen you both in any other setting than a home or street in Hertfordshire. Therefore, when coming in and seeing you both here, it all felt so strange. I suppose that I was just used to seeing you in our part of the country, that to see you anywhere else is altogether so overpowering to me."

"Now you see us in our more natural environment," Mrs. Hurst declared, "we live, breathe, and thrive in the city. Don't we, Caroline?"

"Oh, truly!" Caroline smiled. "Nothing is superior to town and the urban ton. There could be no better company than London aristocracy."

I just realized that *that* was the first time that she had smiled since I had arrived. And when she expressed her glee, it was at the expense of us provincial folk. Yet I should not have been surprised; I always knew that she preferred town to the country.

"So, you must be happy to be back amongst your more common acquaintance," I gathered, "and now I see that our places are quite switched. When we met, you had come to the neighborhood where I was raised, and now here I come to the city that you are accustomed to. I daresay that I now understand what you were feeling when you first entered the assembly on the evening that we met. It was perhaps the same way that I felt when I entered this residence."

"Quite," Miss Bingley agreed. "And since our places are reversed, now you understand our desire to return. It is no slight against you, but it is merely..."

"That the comforts of home and what feels familiar are **always** preferable," Mrs. Hurst added.

"No matter where that home is," I confirmed, "yes, home is home, I suppose."

"And speaking of home," Miss Bingley added, "how is your family?"

"They are quite well. They have been enjoying the Christmas season—indeed, it is our favorite time of year. Oh, and I have news! Our cousin, Mr. Collins, is engaged to be married to Miss Charlotte Lucas."

Their eyes widened at this announcement.

"What?" Mrs. Hurst gasped.

"Your cousin, Mr. Collins?" Miss Bingley echoed. "Engaged to Miss Lucas! That is shocking news indeed."

I felt my spirits rise. Up until this point, both women had seemed to be a little out of spirits, and not exerting themselves in ways that they used to.

"Yes, I know," I responded, "I hope that they shall be very happy."

"Jane," Mrs. Hurst gasped, truly surprised, "this is altogether very shocking news indeed. I thought...well, I thought your cousin's marital interest lay elsewhere."

I could not mistake her meaning; she was thinking of Mr. Collins' somewhat-courtship with Lizzy.

"Yes," I acknowledged, "they did seem to be headed in one direction. Then things altered, and he transferred his affections to Miss Lucas."

Miss Bingley and Mrs. Hurst smiled at each other, and I felt as if they were about to suppress a laugh. I then got the impression that they might have thought that my cousin had thrown Lizzy away, and that the embarrassment was entirely on her side.

"As for the original direction that he appeared interested," I piped up, "the main source of his seeking his choice at Lucas Lodge was because... his original choice desired to find her happiness elsewhere."

My implications were obvious, and I could see that they understood my meaning.

"And so," I reaffirmed, "I do believe that Mr. Collins's current choice is best for him. He and Miss Lucas seem to have been made for each other."

"Yes," Miss Bingley grinned, "quite so. Quite so. Well, I wish them all the happiness in the world and that you all enjoy the *addition* to your family. After all, I recall that Miss Lucas and your sister were close friends. Now, they shall be family. That must make your sister, Miss Elizabeth, very happy."

"Very soon after hearing of it, she realized that it was for the good of all."

"But I would recommend, my dear Jane, for you to encourage your sister to not reject every offer that is made to her. She is not sure to receive another offer."

I blinked. I did not agree with her there and would never encourage Lizzy to marry just for the sake of saving herself or our family. In the end, every man and woman had the right to marry wherever they wished—or did not marry wherever they wished.

Thus, desiring to change the subject, I directed my attention to their family.

"But what of you all and your family? How do you both do? And how is your brother?"

Once more, Mrs. Hurst and Caroline gave each other a look.

"We are perfectly well," Mrs. Hurst said, "and are happy as ever, for we are in town. As for our brother, we see little of *him*. And that is precisely as it should be! For, as you saw, Miss Bennet, our brother, is very popular. And he is more popular with a certain young lady."

"Ah, Louisa," Caroline added, chuckling, "we need not be concealing it. In my last letter to her, I informed her of the fortunate woman." Turning to me, Caroline elaborated. "He is doing very well on that score! He is so much often engaged with Mr. Darcy, that we scarcely see him. And we can easily suppose why. For Miss Darcy is still in town, and he is so often delighted in her company, that we never wonder why he does not desire to see us often. In fact, we even expect Miss Darcy for dinner today. You would love her, Jane! She is the most accomplished woman that Louisa and I have ever seen. Even your sister, Miss Elizabeth, would have to admit that she is the epitome of being a true lady."

I smiled during all this, but I could not help feeling hurt. I lacked all the accomplishments Miss Darcy was said to have...and I felt so small in that moment. So—this was what jealousy felt like? I admit to being ashamed to feel it.

Suddenly, Mrs. Hurst and Caroline stood up.

"Forgive us, Jane," Miss Bingley said, "for I just noticed the hour. We had plans of going out, so I apologize for our brief discussion."

"I understand," I said, standing up as well, "for naturally, you must have so much to do."

We made our farewells, with Miss Bingley promising to call on me one day.

On the day that Caroline would knock on my uncle's front door, I looked forward to.

Chapter Eleven

KITTY'S TALE: FINLAY, THE INFORMED

K nock! Knock! Knock!

The sudden noise made Georgiana, and I flinch. We both jumped up, remembering what we were about, and rushed to get our shoes on and make ourselves presentable.

"Just a moment," Georgiana cried.

We managed to get on our stockings and shoes, throw off our shawls, make sure that our hair was proper and then we sat down, acting as if we were the most unoccupied ladies in the world.

"Come in."

The door opened and it was Colonel Fitzwilliam. When seeing him, our posture slackened, and we felt how much we did not need to stand on ceremony.

Seeing our shoulders relax, Colonel Fitzwilliam grinned.

"Presentable ladies of Pemberley. I cannot help but wonder what you had looked like two minutes ago."

"We didn't even need to remove our shoes." I groaned. "The Colonel would not have cared."

"Oh," Colonel Fitzwilliam said, "now I am getting the proper picture of what I missed out on."

"You sound wicked, cousin," Georgiana said.

"You are just noticing now?"

"No, she has known it all along," I said, "she is just now

putting words to it. So, who needs us? Do you come as a herald of woe or a herald of happiness?"

"I come to show you that we have another addition to our party. But this will be a much shorter visit."

"Who else arrives?" Georgiana asked. "Pemberley is slowly running out of room."

"This house could store an army. Either way, an officer comes."

"An officer?" I asked.

When looking at me, Colonel Fitzwilliam's face grew heavier.

"Yes. Lieutenant Finlay has come to call."

Well, can the heart be both light and heavy all at once?

I stood up, eager to see Finlay as soon as able.

But my eagerness was immediately dampened at Colonel Fitzwilliam seeing my zealous behavior. I hated myself in that moment.

Georgiana looked between us both and decided to ease the tension—or perhaps throw it out the window entirely.

"Well," Georgiana said, "this is a very difficult situation, isn't it?" Colonel Fitzwilliam looked at her. "I don't see the intelligence of us pretending that this subject does not exist. We must receive him, and Kitty will need chaperones. Therefore, the sooner we approach the subject, the better. Since Elizabeth is occupied, I shall go to him first. I expect you both to follow me soon behind."

"Yes," I said, as she left the room, while I slowly walked up to the Colonel. I raised out my hand and he smiled as he took it. I covered his fingers with my other hand, to show solidarity and affection. "How you bear this all shows me just how much you are the man I thought you were, and more."

"Finlay and I have come to an agreement."

"Never pretend that this situation does not cause you pain. It probably does."

"Yes, it does."

"I would take any burdens from your heart if I could. Now come, and I will do my best to make certain that I do not cause you any pain during this all."

We followed Georgiana and went to the parlor.

Breathing out and in, I gathered my resolve as we entered and faced the visit that would cause pain to both men that I had come to care for.

When we entered, Finlay stood up, bowed, and Georgiana received him with all civility and was the proper hostess.

Colonel Fitzwilliam informed us that Finlay was already given refreshment. However, Georgiana had some cakes brought in with some tea, just in case he wanted some more.

Soon into seeing him, Georgiana wondered if Colonel Fitzwilliam would do her the honor of choosing music that he thought would be best for her to take to Rosings Park for the holidays.

This gave me the opportunity to invite Finlay to join me by the window so that we could have a private discussion and be as far away from Colonel Fitzwilliam as we could.

He agreed to this, and we walked to the window on the other side of the parlor and watched as I saw a marvelous sight.

"It's snowing!" I cried.

"What?" Georgiana cried. From their side of the room, Colonel Fitzwilliam and she went to the window, and they saw it as well.

"By Saint George," Colonel Fitzwilliam laughed, "it really is."

I moved the curtains aside, then looked up at Finlay.

"Beautiful, isn't it?"

He looked at me, as opposed to the snowfall.

"Yes, it is. Very beautiful."

I blushed and looked down at the floor.

"Now she blushes," he continued.

"Yes," I said, looking up at him, "yes, she does. Whatever will you do with her? Surely, a blushing woman is not the sort that an officer would prefer."

"What? We prefer the blushing ones most of all. For, her beauty is the kind that we wish to see at all times. In our hearts. In our heads. And beside us, as we lay her down and husband and wife become one."

"You make me wonder if I can stand, for I might fall to the floor, shriveling up under the weight of your words."

"I am being very wicked now."

"No, you are being Finlay. And I would not want it any other way. By the way, I have much to acquaint you with."

"Before you do, I must tell you that the Colonel and I have been talking."

"I am happy that you both can bear to be in the same room with each other."

"I marvel at it as well. Though, sometimes I wonder if maybe it would not be better if him and I were to engage in a fight with our fists."

"Why?"

"Some men resolve their arguments better when they have a good fight. I cannot explain why that is so, but I wonder if we are such men."

"You both are behaving like reasonable gentlemen," I said, smirking, "enjoy it and do not feel like barbarism has to be the order of the day. Now, a little savagery is understandable, here or there, but it must not do for the likes of men named Lieutenant Finlay or Colonel Fitzwilliam. You know that it is not so."

"Recall that I am a proud Irishman."

"Very well, I shall let you joke about yourself for the moment. And then I shall laugh with you. Afterwards, I will declare that you ought not to place generalizations on your nation."

"But for the moment..."

"Yes, Finlay, for the moment..."

"We shall laugh at my joke."

"Yes, we shall laugh at your joke. After all, it's the British thing to do."

"Oh, is it?"

"Actually, I'm not certain at all. Some of us don't always know a good joke when we hear it. But I do, and I'm English enough for the both of us right now."

We chuckled.

"I miss you whenever you are not near me," Finlay said.

"You had better, or I would be very upset with you. Now, what is it that you and the Colonel wish for me to know of?"

His tone shifted to serious.

"It is something that we should have spoken to you about first."

"Yes, yes, yes," I said, dismissively, "I know that you respect me. Now do get on with it."

Finlay then told me about how Colonel Fitzwilliam was to leave in seven days, so Finlay agreed to keep his distance. Then he would pay more visits when the Colonel was gone.

When he finished, I expressed that it was a very good plan, and I thanked him for caring for the Colonel's feelings.

"You are not upset with us for not consulting you first?" he asked. "Truly, we didn't do it out of lack of concern for your own will to decide."

My heart warmed at the prospect that both men felt that I had a right to rule my own life.

"I know that you both didn't," I assured him, "and that is the one thing that makes your actions very honorable. Besides, it is not as if you were ordering my life for me. The Colonel had a request, you saw the logic of it, and now you are consulting me. It all seemed to happen organically and not out of a deliberate desire to omit me from the plan. And you tell me now, which is suitable, and it gives me the choice rather than thinking that my female mind is not strong enough to be correct in this case. There is nothing wrong with a gentleman making decisions as long as the lady can make them as well."

He looked at me in marvel.

"I wonder how I found such a logical person to fall in love with."

"I am an Englishwoman who feels madly for an Irishman who initially didn't care for her at all: I am the epitome of illogical. Which is good. Knowing one is illogical is the greatest step to obtaining true knowledge. That does not make sense, but it is nevertheless, very true."

"Yes, it just might be a new sort of wisdom."

"Wise? Me? Now that is a good title. A fleeting title, but a good title, nevertheless."

"No more despising yourself. If we ever get married, you can do plenty of that, because I will fight to have you forgive yourself. Now, what is this other news that you have to acquaint me with?"

I told him everything about what had transpired this afternoon. As I narrated, Finlay remained engaged. And I could see why. Tales of romantic upheaval, wrong steps taken, corrupt paths that were walked down, is the stuff of true interest.

When I finished, I felt that I couldn't help but address this strange tendency of ours.

"You look so engaged, it's almost comical," I noted.

"Well, I cannot help it. This tale is so very intriguing, in a repulsive sort of manner."

"And thus, adding credence to my philosophy that we mortals can preach morality all that we want, but without tales and news of immorality, our lives would be a blank. We love adventures that are filled with gruesome actions and selfish archetypes."

"Well, it does give us something to talk about."

"Oh, I believe that it's more than that."

"How so?"

"I think we like tales of evil deeds being done, because, in some ways, we live it through the villain. After all, there are few humans alive who spend every day being a saint. Therefore, we need some way to exorcise the demons in us. What better way than to watch a theatre performance where the villain is the lead, read a book of evil men and women committing evil deeds, or reading about a scandal committed by the crème de la crème of our supposedly superior society? We gasp about it, but we are drawn to it all, like a moth to a flame. We live through them, our evil actions were committed by someone other than ourselves, we feel pure once more, we scoff at their malignant nature, and then we are able to be ourselves again. As long as the villains get their comeuppance, of course, and gets properly punished."

"You paint a bleak picture, where evil must exist, so that it serves as a foil for our good actions to act off of."

"Do you know what is really frightening?"

"What?"

"That I might be correct."

"I think you just might be."

"Oh, well," I sighed, "it is all out of my hands, so there's an end to it."

Finlay raised an eyebrow.

"What do you mean that it's out of your hands?"

"I merely live here, Finlay, and I am not the lord or mistress of the manner. I am merely a bystander to how this is all going to unfold."

"Kitty, I don't know whether you are now thinking so meanly of yourself or so indifferently. You forget that you have a voice. Or are you now the sort to retire in leisure and say that the world will turn as it will, and there is nothing that you can do?"

Oh, the shackles and chains of feeling offended. Especially by the one that you care deeply for. Honesty is what all perpetually request to have in our lives. Sincerity, dignity, and self-awareness. But when feeling offended, all three of those things come into question. AFTERWARDS. Those things are often taken into account, after one's initial reaction. But beforehand, you just are angry.

"I beg your pardon?"

When it comes to speaking to a woman that you feel a deep affection for, those are the four scariest words in the English language. It's enough to make one nervous, doubt oneself, and feel as if that is the beginning of the man and woman being at odds with each other. '*I beg your pardon*'.

Finlay flinched.

"You are about to be upset with me," he deduced.

"Perhaps I am. It all depends upon the next thing that you are intending to say."

"Kitty, I am not here to offend."

"Go on," I relented, "If you don't tell me, I will spend the entire day wondering what you were going to say. And you will spend the entire day hating yourself for suppressing your speech."

"But you might be angry with me."

"I probably will. On the other hand, I will spend the day

angry, and you will spend the day knowing that you have made me so. Well, if we are to choose which purgatory that we both are going to be in, it might as well be the one where we are more enlightened. So, spit it out. I am prepared."

He sat down next to me, in a way that our legs were touching. Looking over my shoulder, he made certain that Colonel Fitzwilliam and Georgiana were not observing us. Then he offered me his hand to take. At first, I did not take it.

"Kitty," he said, "please..."

Giving in, I placed my hand in his.

"I love you," he said, "but sometimes we are going to disagree with each other. We have before. We have argued, and we have weathered. You know you have it in yourself to adore me even after I give you a lecture."

"And you say this because you want me to pardon anything that you might say that will lead to me getting a most definite scolding."

"I do not scold. I advise."

I groaned inwardly. No one likes a lecture, even if that is the best thing they need to be given.

"Very well. Proceed."

"From history down to my own personal experience," he began, "I have seen the mistakes of those who say 'I do not need to do anything, because it is out of my hands'. Many horrible acts of indifference occurred because someone stood by and let it happen, because they said they were powerless to do anything."

I allowed myself to grow numb as I listened. It was the only way that I could sit through this experience and not lose my temper.

"You are saying that I am wrong because I accept the fact that I am not the one responsible for determining who is right in the Crawford's case," I said, "even when it is the truth."

"In this case, perhaps I am being too harsh. But I do not want you to spend your life with that philosophy. The second that you tell yourself that you have no power to do anything, or the right to determine anything, you forfeit your voice. And nothing will ever improve in your life. That's how progress occurs: by someone saying that they have the power to stop something that kills. You forfeit your right to choose something, then you forfeit everything."

"You are exaggerating. This is not a life-changing event, but a family with a dilemma. Besides, if we were to be speaking of something that affects the globe, you cannot lecture me on the matter that I really never have the right to have a say over. You are a man, Finlay. You have the right to go out in the world and are given the right to do more. I am a woman and am not given the same liberties and rights to ever make the final judgement on anything."

"There is credence to that, but you forget, yes, I am a man. But I'm also poor in a world where much is against me. I might as well be a woman. But do I roll over and give in, or do I keep believing that I can rule my life and affect everything around me? Also, yes, the world does hold you down in many ways, but that's the thing about freedom: sometimes it's not going to be given to you. If you want to have a say, then have one. If the world will come down on you for it, then stand in its way and say, 'I am here, and that is the end of it'. Or roll over and say, 'it's out of my hands'. Yes, we men have quite ruined your chances of equality in many ways...but by not fighting back, by not saying that you will not be moved, how are you helping yourself? I treat you equally, don't I? Well, don't I?"

"Yes, you do."

"Of course, I do. It's because you were not afraid to stand up to me. And you were right to. You want me to believe in you. Believe in yourself first."

Chapter Twelve

KITTY'S TALE: TRUE VICE

At first, I opened my mouth to respond, and then I closed it.

A part of me was filled with a sense of resignation to his viewpoint. The other half of me wanted to cry out that he was being too severe, and too much taking a wider view of a small circumstance.

"Finlay," I began, "forgive me, but you don't know what it's like to be a woman... who just wants to be allowed to be as she wishes to be. The world is pulling me this way and that, telling me how to and how not to be, and quite frankly, if I begin the fight, then I will have to be fighting my entire life. Why must I have to always be fighting? And why must the world always ask this of us? I should not have to fight for something I ought to be naturally given. I should not have to be ridiculed or set down because I don't want to be judge as well as jury."

"No, believe me, I—"

"I know why you said it, and I also know that there is sense in what you say."

I stood up, and he grabbed my arm.

"Lieutenant!" Colonel Fitzwilliam called from the other side of the room. Finlay and Fitzwilliam stared at each other. Whether the Colonel did it out of general compassion for me, or because he could not abide Finlay touching me, I did not know. Nor did I care to know. "You most remember yourself, sir."

"Yes, Colonel," Finlay said, releasing me. "Pray forgive me. I forgot myself, for a moment."

He looked ashamed.

"Kitty," Finlay whispered to me, "please, pity me. Do not abandon me."

Not looking at him, I steadied myself. Closing my eyes, I evened out my breathing as I tried to remain composed.

'Kitty,' I said to myself, 'what are you doing? This is an overreaction to say the least. Besides, Georgiana said something similar, and she was correct.'

When I opened my eyes again, it was to the sight of Colonel Fitzwilliam looking at me most decidedly. In his eyes was a 'do you want me to put an end to this visit, because I should like to', expression. Another time, I would thank him for his chivalry. Yet, for the moment, I needed to not run away.

I nodded to him with a 'I am well. Continue on as you were' look and then I sat down again, beside Finlay.

"No," I said, "I will not abandon you."

"Thank you," he said. "I didn't say any of those things to harm you or break your resolve. I just... don't want to have to see you conform to a practice of perpetual passivity. When that happens, a woman can lose her voice."

"Yes, I suppose we might. Georgiana said the same thing to me. It is just... I don't want to spend my whole life fighting for something that I ought to naturally be given."

"Neither do I, but I must. For if I do not, nothing in my life will ever change. I fight for you, even against all odds. I know that there is something so very taxing about always having to brace yourself for another emotional battle...it's just..."

"What?"

"If you stop fighting for things in your life, and for your own willpower, then I suppose that I am afraid that you will soon stop fighting for me. I have a lot going against me when it comes to having you in my life. I suppose that is why I don't want you going off into that good night. I need your warrior-side, because if not, then what do I have to continue holding on for?"

When hearing his last speech, I softened at every word. His love for me was like a rock on which I would place the foundation of many of the stronger aspects of my character. How he had become such a vital aspect to my inner resolve, I would never know. But his words rested in their proper place, and that meant that all was worthy of respect. Despite these tender feelings toward his confession, I was not wholly blind and was aware at the real intention behind his effusions of joy.

"Finlay," I sighed, "why must you say the perfect thing, after so much strife? Must you always tear my heart in every direction that is always the right one?"

His eyes softened.

"I shall always care. No matter what."

I rolled my eyes.

"Very well. We shall not part ways as enemies. That would be most objectionable, wouldn't it?"

"Yes, it would."

I laughed.

"And the Bertrams' think that Miss Crawford speaks evil. If we were at Mansfield Park, that family would think that we were the most malignant things in the world."

Finlay's laughter slowly faded and was replaced by a perturbed look.

"Mansfield Park?"

"Yes. What of it?"

"Why did you say Mansfield Park? Wait, the Bertram family that you are speaking of...is this the family of Sir Thomas Bertram?"

"Yes, it is."

Finlay leaned back, disturbed.

"What is it?"

"Perhaps it's nothing."

"Oh, no," I declared, "no, no, no, you don't get to do that."

"Do what?"

"Have an intense thought and then not tell me. Finlay, that is not fair. And you just told me that I have the right to stake my claim like a woman of spirit. Therefore, you reap what you sew. Now, spill the truth behind your unsettled state, or I will ask the Colonel to ask you to leave."

Finlay raised an eyebrow.

"That's extreme, don't you think?"

"Yes. You taught me so well."

He smirked.

"Our love is not going to be an easy one, will it?"

"It never was."

"No, it never was. I am proud of you."

I didn't smile, but I felt my eyes twinkle.

"I know."

"Well," Finlay said, "I could be wrong, so I must know the facts. The woman that Mr. Crawford ran away with is definitely the daughter of Sir Thomas Bertram of Mansfield Park? And the man who spurned Mary Crawford is definitely the son, Mr. Edmund Bertram."

"Yes."

"And just to be doubly certain—for I do not want to begin causing confusion and misinterpretation for a family who is wholly innocent of any wrongdoing—but is the estate, Mansfield Park, located in Northampton?"

"Yes, it is."

Finlay's inquisitive look transitioned to one of disturbance and utter resentment. He was angry, and I wanted to know why.

"Hypocrisy, thy name is Bertram!"

This exclamation led to a widening of my interest and astonishment. Immediately, I abandoned my passive posture and leaned forward, aching to know the instinct behind that bitter reply.

"What do you mean, sir?"

"That family," Finlay said to himself, grinding his teeth. "How dare they banish anyone for being impure when they are the epitome of aristocratic ugliness? It is suitable to commit the basest of crimes, but as long as it is out of sight and does not get an article in the newspapers, then it does not matter. A crime is only a crime if it gets exposed. But everything else..."

"Finlay, you are still not being forthcoming."

"Kitty, I need you to help me now. I need you to support me. The Bertrams have no right to turn away from Miss Crawford's and Mr. Price's marriage. No right at all. I need Mr. Darcy to grant me an audience, along with the Crawfords. I need to speak with them immediately. It might be the only way to end this. Sometimes if you can't appeal to someone's better sides, you appeal to their guiltier sides."

"Finlay, I must know."

"Yes, you should. Kitty, what I am about to tell you now is something that will disturb you. But you need to know the horrors behind it. Because if I don't tell you, then I will look like the sort of man who shields you, under the pretense of feminine delicacy."

I gathered my courage and was prepared.

"I don't fear anything."

"I know. Here is the truth."

Finlay then unfolded the horrid truth about the Bertram family to me. With each fact displayed, I grew internally sicker. I didn't want to believe it, but Finlay's experience with other lands, of other lives, was vaster than mine. It must be true. It was despicable, but it *must be true*. When he finished, I was silent for a moment.

"Was I wrong to tell you?" he asked.

"No. I just hope it's not them."

"It is most likely to be. But I have to know for certain. Kitty, will you help me?"

"I like Miss Crawford, Mrs. Grant, and Mr. Price. I can't even say that I fully despise Mr. Crawford—as long as he is a better man. If there is the slight bit of chance that you are right, then we have to try."

I stood up and approached my cousins-in-law.

"Colonel and Georgie," I said, "I need you both to help me and Finlay. I need you to ask Darcy to gather the whole family before supper, as well as the Crawfords, for we must arrange to give Finlay an audience."

"Why?" Colonel Fitzwilliam said.

"He has something very important to reveal. But to do that, he must speak to the Crawfords first."

"I need to be absolutely certain of my facts before I proceed," Finlay said, to assist me. "I don't want to say any more until I know for sure."

"Good god, what is the matter?" Georgiana asked me.

"I am not at liberty to say it, Miss Darcy," Finlay said, "for I must ask your brother if he wishes for you to hear it. I do not want to disrespect his authority in his own house."

"Remember when you did that before?" I sniggered quietly.

"Yes," he said, rolling his eyes. "That was not a pleasant experience. And I do not want to repeat that incident." Finlay directed his attention to the Colonel. "Colonel, please, now it's me who needs the favor. Believe me, I am not wasting your time, but this just might be of upmost importance."

Colonel Fitzwilliam squinted and then he came to a decision.

"Very well. You will have your audience."

Colonel Fitzwilliam stood up.

"I'm depending upon you to not embarrass me by creating puffs of smoke. Whatever audience that you present, remember that you represent the uniform, our dignity, and our sovereign. Put simply, Lieutenant, it better be good."

"If I am right, it is."

"Then I suppose, I have a family to call forth. Come along, Georgie and Kitty." Colonel Fitzwilliam turned to Finlay. "Forgive me, but it is inadmissible for me leave Miss Bennet alone with you."

Finlay's face grew heavy from regret.

"Yes, I am aware, sir. I prefer otherwise, but I understand."

"I'm sure that you do."

We all three left together and Colonel Fitzwilliam immediately took the authoritative position.

"I never saw Finlay to be so determined, therefore, it must be urgent. Georgie, the Crawfords are along the grounds with Mrs.

Darcy. Fetch them and have them brought to the music room. It's the most private of the public rooms in the house. Kitty, go and fetch the Philipses. I will get the rest of the gentlemen and then have Mrs. Reynolds escort Lieutenant Finlay to that room."

"Yes," Georgiana obeyed, then she looked at me, "How interesting is this day going to get?"

"I think we have no idea," I answered as she went to see to the Crawfords. When I did not move, Colonel Fitzwilliam turned to me.

"What is it?" he asked.

"I just...if something does get uncovered, then I am proud of him. But the way that you have handled this all, I am terribly proud of you."

His eyes softened and they even began to get misty. I wanted to hold him.

"Thank you," was all he could muster. Turning my heel, I did as he bade and brought the Philipses to the music room. When we arrived, Darcy, Colonel Fitzwilliam, Finlay, and Mr. Bingley were already there.

"Well," Arthur said, "we just have to await the plaintiffs."

"Don't let them hear you call them that," Enara replied to him, jokingly.

When I entered, I beheld Finlay and Fitzwilliam were standing on two opposite sides of the room. With a quick glance at them both, I knew the worse thing to do would be to sit too near either of them, because it would display partiality. That was the last thing that I wished to show. Therefore, I sat down next to Enara, and we gave each other a look. Yes, she knew. Enara always had a way of knowing.

"What's it like?" I asked. "To be comfortably married."

"I don't want to hurt you," Enara whispered back.

"You won't."

"If you find the right partner, it is delightful."

"Just like if you do not find the right partner, it is a downward abyss."

"Precisely." She looked between the Colonel and Finlay. "Find the right partner, Kitty. Find the right one."

"That's the problem. Excepting finances, they are both right."

I looked between both men.

They were so beautiful. Like two walking works of art, dressed in military garb. The uniforms spoke true about the person who was within. They both were gallant, as well as warriors. I felt so utterly sorry for the state they both were in, but also sorry for the fate that often awaited them on the battlefield. Both men did risk their lives. Both men had no choice but to, physically and emotionally, be throwing themselves in harm's way. For England, for Britain, and by extension... the world. For what is a man, as what is a woman, who does not care?

As we sat down, we were not left to wait for very long at all. A couple minutes later, Jane and Elizabeth entered, followed by the Crawfords, Mrs. Grant, and William Price.

"Well," Mary Crawford announced, "this is quite...oh dear, I think I am quite frightened now."

"Not at all," I said. "You shall not be cooked and eaten."

Mary Crawford smiled at me.

"Kitty, your wit gives me leave to not cower."

"And it should not," Colonel Fitzwilliam uttered. "Actually, you were brought here for information."

"Information?" Mrs. Grant asked. "How can we assist you?"

"This is Lieutenant Finlay," Mr. Darcy announced, gesturing to the Lieutenant, "Finlay, this is Mr. and Miss Crawford, of Everingham, and their sister, Mrs. Grant. Mr. William Price is Miss Crawford's fiancé."

"Yes," Miss Crawford said, "he is the unfortunate soul who I tricked into falling in love with me."

"My fiancée jests," Mr. William Price said, bowing to us, "Sir."

Introductions were quickly made, and Lieutenant Finlay decided to get to the heart of the matter.

"Mr. Darcy and the rest of the household have been so kind as to hold this meeting, so that I might ask you a question. It is concerning the Bertram family that you are well acquainted with. This is not done to cause you any pain at all, but merely informational. I am aware of your history with that household, and this is important to know. It has to do with the Bertram family's professional affiliations."

"Professional?" Henry Crawford repeated.

"Yes. The Bertrams are a wealthy family, belonging to older money, but do they still acquire new income? What I mean is have you ever heard of them gathering more financial returns through an establishment in Antigua?"

"Yes," Miss Crawford said, "I recall hearing about them having property there and that's where Sir Thomas and his eldest son, Mr. Thomas Bertram, went because it received little profit. And... if I recall..."

"Yes, Miss Crawford," Lieutenant Finlay added, "I'll finish your sentence for you. And thank you for answering my question and putting an end to any confusion that I had on that score."

"Well then," Mary Crawford uttered, "I am so blind. How did I not see the underhanded dealings of this situation before?"

"It's not your fault. You didn't see it, because you are of a position where you are never told to see it—and it has been kept out of your sight for so long that you never got the chance to see the real truth of that."

"I confess to still being ignorant of the matter," Elizabeth inferred, "to what are you referring to?"

"Antigua," Mr. Darcy uttered, covering his mouth. "Dear god, I didn't think either."

Lieutenant Finlay turned to the rest of us and delivered the truth that the rest now ached to know of.

"The Bertrams cannot attack anyone for moral missteps because they have taken the worst sorts, that was the most egregious. Sir Thomas Bertram, and his sons, who stand to inherit, are owners of an estate in Antigua. It's a plantation."

Everyone's eyes widened when they realized where this was all headed.

"The Bertrams of Mansfield Park, of past generations and recent ones, make their fortune from enslaved people that they have collected from the Trade."

When hearing that, the rest of our company had grown quiet, but not from ignorance. No. It was from shock.

"You mean to tell me," Elizabeth declared, "that the Bertrams, the family that cast out Miss Crawford for her wishing to solve a solution to their problem, have alienated Mrs. Grant just by being associated, Mr. William Price for choosing the woman he loves, and Mr. Crawford for a moral disturbance that their daughter also was a culprit for, dares to play judge and jury, when all the while, they are committing to the acts of human bondage?"

"I can guarantee it."

"He is correct," Mr. Crawford said, "Mr. Bertram, the eldest son of Sir Thomas Bertram, had told me some events that took place when he joined his father at Antigua. He did not go into many details, but it can be verified that Antigua was a plantation of slaves, born into their situation, from the generations of enslaved people who came before them."

"And they dare think they have the right to judge anyone?" Arthur Philips pointed out.

"There is no surprise that they think so," Colonel Fitzwilliam asserted, "you must have never encountered a master over men and women. They never associate their actions as being incorrect. They pass moral judgements all the time, while never being reprimanded themselves, because what they do is legal."

"It is more than that," Finlay added. "What they do is granted permissible, not only because it profits this country, but also because of a timeless truth: when something is out of sight, it is also out of mind. These great men and women who hold mastership over other unfortunates have been wise. They place their evil and underhanded dealings outside of polished society. They place them on an island where most of Britain cannot see it, and therefore, the evil becomes invisible. But one thing is certain. Sir Thomas Bertram's plantation is the most disgusting of all of them."

"How do you know this?" Mary Crawford asked. "You speak by someone who is not ignorant of the scene."

"Because I've been there."

"You have?" I asked, surprised.

"Yes. I have been to Antigua. And it was quite possibly one of the most horrid experiences in my life."

"Finlay," I asked, amazed, "what brought you there?"

"Before I enlisted in the army, I very briefly tried my hand at the more nautical profession. It took me to all parts of the kingdom. Very soon, that's when I began to learn the pains of being born different. Many sailors did not take to me. I suppose that was where my spirit crippled a little." I closed my eyes and looked down. That was where it must have all began with him. When I first met Finlay, I was meeting a man burdened with a darker history. No wonder he was so taciturn when we first met. How I wished that I had learned of that before. "Well, when being a sailor, we eventually were hired to make berth at Antigua. Most of us were given shore leave, decided to take a visit and tour the island. And that was when we saw it."

"The plantations," Enara clarified.

"More than just the plantations, Mrs. Philips. We saw everything. We saw the horrors, how ugly it all was, and how those people were forced to live. We saw the squalor, the degradation, the torment, and the torture." Finlay turned to Mr. Darcy. "Sir, what I am about to reveal now is what is being hidden from almost all of England, Wales and Scotland. I'm about to tell you the truth of what really happens on those plantations. I know that Miss Bennet has the strength to bear it, but I am not certain that it is suitable for the ears of other ladies. If you like, you may dismiss them."

"Thank you, sir," Mr. Darcy said.

"Oh, that is just quite archaic," Elizabeth interrupted, to which we all turned to her. When she noted that maybe she had spoken too hastily, Elizabeth cooled her words. "Forgive me. Lieutenant, thank you for your consideration of our feelings. It was chivalrous. But what I mean is that we ladies are not always meant to be fine and fancy creatures who are incapable of hearing the seedy sides of the human experience. What I imply is that we none of us wish to be in calm waters all our lives. We have the ability to endure many truths. Or at least, that is so in my case. Kitty will not be alone. I shall stay with her. Every other lady that is present can do as they wish."

Naturally, all other ladies in the room did have a sense of

pride. When knowing that Lizzy and I were staying behind to listen, they were not willing to look the role of a coward and quietly leave. They all declared that they would stay. The only husband to implore his wife to leave was Bingley, but he did it in so gentle a manner that it was more of a quiet appeal than a demand.

"Dearest," Bingley requested, "are you absolutely certain that you wish to remain? I have had some experience with hearing about these situations. They are gruesome images that can only be explained by gruesome words."

"Thank you, Mr. Bingley," Jane replied, "however, I have come this far. I do believe that whatever lies ahead, I can bear it. Besides, my sisters and cousins are here. I would be ashamed if I did not set a better example. I will remain."

"Are you certain?"

"Yes, I am."

Mr. Bingley was forced to see his wife about to endure a discussion that he worried would disconcert her—and leave her forever changed. He was right to worry. Our lives would never fully be the same again.

"Very well," Lieutenant Finlay said, "here is what occurred on Antigua when I was there. And from every report that I heard of that dreadful and doomed place, it has not changed at all. But above all, I am about to reveal that Sir Thomas Bertram is not honorable and is another who hides his failures away from the rest of respectable British society. Antigua is where shame and torture lives."

From his memory, Finlay told us every evil that he saw over there, and all the evils that we have been shielded from had been unveiled. Every secret that was safely tucked away in the islands was exposed. Graphic images were brought forth and with each detail given, I felt my stomach shrink.

What was the use of being angry over not having the proper ribbon? Of not going to Brighton or Bath? Such simple problems made me quite ashamed of myself, when in the face of true tragedy.

After Finlay finished his tale, we all sat there, in horror.

"And this is all true?" Jane asked, greatly unsettled, with her hand on her chest. "All of it?"

"Yes," Finlay concluded, "I am afraid it is."

"Lieutenant Finlay speaks true," Mr. Bingley confirmed, which led to us all looking at him. Seeing that he spoke with some authority, Bingley realized that an explanation was needed. "It was my father. He found his fortune through manufacturing trade in the North because he wanted to turn me into a gentleman in an honest sort of manner. This was a reaction to his exposure to images he saw when he visited Antigua as a young man. After being exposed to every situation that Finlay described, he abandoned everyone's advice and did not go into the Trade. Then, one day, when I was thirteen, I was caught dipping a girl's hair into some ink. Her parents were furious, and so was my father. Then he told me something that shielded me from ever getting into trouble again. He told me everything he had seen in Antigua and said 'remember, your punishment is no dinner for this evening. If you were on Antigua, you would never have a decent meal for your entire life. And sometimes, your dinner was a whipping across your back and chains on your wrist in the morning'."

Overwhelmed, Jane covered her mouth and then placed her hand over his.

"Dearest, that must have been awful."

"On the contrary, that was precisely what I needed to hear. It might even account for my cheery disposition, especially since I was quite the bashful child once. When you learn of loss and horror, everything becomes more beautiful, you become more agreeable, the food tastes better, the wine, shrub and coffee quench your thirst—everything becomes more lovely, because you have a proper contrast to set it off as."

Bingley turned to Finlay.

"It must have been a horrible thing to actually witness it."

"And I am glad of it," William Price declared. Well, this was a sudden and interesting declaration. "I say this, merely because it is the proper and just way to consider the matter. I owe Sir Thomas Bertram some things, for he has assisted me in the past, and he took in my sister, Fanny, to ease the burdens off my parents' shoulders. But to belittle the importance of my future bride, when all the while, this is the man that he was?"

William Price stood up and began to pace back and forth. "And Mr. Thomas Bertram and Mr. Edmund Bertram, surely they must know about this."

"They do know about it," Mr. Crawford informed us, "they have always known about it."

"I am not informing you all about their true natures as an excuse to justify the wrong actions of ourselves, or anyone in this room," Finlay said.

"True," Mr. Darcy inferred, "one should never justify one's own flaws to those of others, or we will spend the whole day justifying the wrongs we commit to others, just because there are even greater wrongs out there. However, when one party censures another for a breach in propriety and moral standing, when all the while committing worse deeds, then it stands to reason that they are hypocrites of the highest order."

"Again," William Price said, "I am grateful for what they have given me."

"But that does not mean that they are above censure and correction," Finlay finalized. "Especially when they have committed worse crimes than any scandal that the Crawford family may have done."

"And it doesn't matter that the Trade is not illegal yet," Elizabeth finalized, "there are enough people in Britain who want to eliminate that aspect of our habits forever." She stood up. "That gives me an idea."

Chapter Thirteen

KITTY'S TALE: PASSION PASSING THROUGH

F inlay had stayed for dinner and then I saw him off to his horse.

While I escorted him, I saw Colonel Fitzwilliam watching us from a window.

"Do you think that the Bertrams will accept this idea?" he asked.

"I wish that I could say, due to the sense of humility or perverse curiosity, that it will work," I said, "but I am not sure. There are some people in this world who, due to a laxness of temper, feel no desire to move from their parlors, and would let the world wash over them. However, if Sir Thomas Bertram, his sons, or this Miss Fanny Price, have any ounce of familial respect, any sense of obligation to respect Mr. Darcy's and Elizabeth's appeal, then they will come. If they do, would you like to be here when they arrive?"

"I should like that. If I'm going to be the one who informed these people for what they were, then I had best do it to their face, rather than being the sort to discredit them behind their backs and then expect other people to utter my words for me."

He mounted his horse and offered me his hand, which I took.

"If it weren't for you," I said, "the real problem would have never arisen, and we would have been sitting there, in a dilemma that we had to judge."

He smirked.

"I guess that means one thing only."

"And what would that be, pray tell?"

"That I am vital to being in your life."

He egged his horse onward and rode down the lane, back to Lambton.

Behind me, I heard footsteps. Turning, I saw Colonel Fitzwilliam exit. Taking a look in his eyes, I saw the desire for a sense of ownership. He needed me to possess him. Or for him to possess me.

"How can I make you happy?" I asked.

He blinked.

"How did you know?"

"I had a suspicion."

"I just..."

"What?"

"If all goes according to plan, then the Bertrams might either send a letter, giving their blessing to the happy couple, or the Bertrams will come to Pemberley themselves. But none of this was my doing. It was his."

"You cannot blame yourself for not having the same knowledge as Finlay."

"But I am aware that they had some dealings in Antigua. The Fitzwilliam clan and the Bertram clan cannot go their entire lives being entirely ignorant of the other. I may never have met them, but I was aware that they had something to do with owning property there. I suppose, I just never made the deduction."

"You are afraid that you have been turning a blind eye?" I asked, walking up to him.

"Yes, maybe I was."

"Even if so, you turned a blind eye to a family that you never met and hardly knew the history of. You had no ability to know how far their destructive habits were, and also nothing is comparable to the witnessing of things. You have never been to Antigua, have you?"

"No, I haven't. I've never set foot on a plantation in my life."

"Of course, you have not. Because I daresay that your parents would never let you. Like we discussed, this sad side of our culture has been shielded away from us, away from inquisitive eyes. If it were not so hidden, so shut away from the casual observer, I am certain that the Trade would have ended long ago. Too much of Britain would have known the truth, seen it for their own eyes, and saw the horrors of it. When it comes to those who pretend to be one thing, and blind us to their uglier aspects, we are also the victims."

"I just..."

"Wanted to be the hero here," I deduced.

He sighed.

"You must stop doing that."

"Finishing your sentences?"

"Not only that," he said, taking my hand and pulling me with him. Instead of taking me into the house, he pulled me along the grounds, and we stood under a window and behind a bush.

Almost no one could see us.

I could not understand why I was not afraid. All I knew was that I trusted him beyond reason. When it comes to those you love, they can come poor, plain, torn apart, broken, and tired... and you will not be afraid. You never feel the fear because you cannot look away.

What plainness was in Colonel Fitzwilliam?

What more was he but another exceptional road that a person can walk down in life, always being a temporary slice of elegance that you are meant to travel along, but never stay amongst?

Him and Finlay—always teetering on the verge of men coming apart, then patching themselves together, and then becoming entangled in a situation that they never had foreseen.

Pushing the boundaries of masculine beauty—manly excellence. I defy all that did not look upon them and marvel at the events that they were. Placing myself between wave of satisfaction and dissatisfaction, and still I would not have it any other way. The joys are worth all the other moments in between.

And Colonel Fitzwilliam still had me, beside him, along the bushes of Pemberley, under a window where no one could see us, with no other soul in sight, excepting mother nature, who looked on, but dared not judge. After all, were we not just another set of beasts who moved along her terrain, merely existing? Merely living.

"I am being rash," he uttered.

"I know," I said, "and it is my fault."

"No, it's not."

"Perhaps not. Perhaps it's no one's fault."

"And once more, you speak as I feel. What does fate and fortune want from me?" He cried, aggravated and bitter. "Do you know what I cannot stand?"

"You are angry with me."

"Yes," he hissed, "I am."

"Tell me what makes you angry."

His eyes tensed up even more.

"You are not afraid of me," he said, but not by way of surprise. He more-so was stating the obvious.

"No, I am not. Because I know that nothing you say will truly hurt me."

"Of course, it won't. We are bound to each other, whether we like it or not."

"What makes you angry? Tell me," I implored him. "Tell me and be done with it."

He sighed out, his words harsh from the passion that stirred within him.

"I am angry that you know what I am thinking even before I am thinking it. I am angry that you know the last words in my sentence and see into my heart. I am angry that I love you. I am angry that I am in pain often, and I put myself through this. I am angry that the world must always find its way into our lives, and tangle its web around us, forcing its ugly grimace over our joy. But more than anything, more than my heart being torn in two—even more than the evils and strife affecting your happiness, and my time with you, I am angry with myself."

"It does not do to hate yourself, Richard."

"It does. For I am angry that I am not the hero now. He is. He is the hero."

"And it tears away at you."

"Yes, it does. I try not to hate Finlay."

"I know you try. And you succeed, Richard. No man can do it better than you."

"But I cannot stand the idea of his image being higher than mine in your eyes. He brought the truth to light. He cast the gleam of hope onto the Crawfords' situation, and I just sat there. Ignorant and useless."

"You did not," I cried. "And don't you ever tell yourself that again. When Finlay needed you to hear him, you answered the plea. You brought the family together and gave him the audience that was his due. You DID that. What other man, rivalling for the heart of a woman, would do so much for his rival?"

Slowly, I placed my hand on his cheek. The effect was immediate. That simple touch relaxed him, his cheeks swelled with pride, and I felt the balm that was acceptance wash all over him. He was cured of his emotional wounds.

"No other man would. Do not ever think yourself poorly-made and wrongly-done, Richard," I ordered him. "The world could scoff at you, cast you out, and you would be a hero of mine. Never more or less than that."

He looked down at me.

"Tell me you adore me," he whispered, harshly. "Whether you love us both or not, I must hear it. Kitty, tell me you adore me."

It was an order I was all too happy to give. Demands are not something that anyone favors to suffer under. Yet, this time, I felt the immediacy of that order, the desire for it—the very need for it! Obsession is dangerous, but obsession also reminds us just how much our heart is working. How much it still yearns for something and believes that it has the right to obtain. But obsession only works when it is welcome, on both ends. I did not fear his rashness now, because I welcomed it. This was not intimidation or allowing oneself to be ordered about. This was about holding the one who deserved your adoration the most.

"Beyond reason," I said, "I adore you beyond reason."

When I told him so, Colonel Fitzwilliam closed his eyes, only to open them soon after.

Next, he raised his hand and placed it on my cheek.

"You will never be lovelier than you are now," I added.

"I must look affright."

"You just needed to tell me that," I said, "because if you didn't, your heart would burst."

"And you know how my heart works. How do you know me?"

"Because we have no choice. We will walk along the world, having no choice but to always understand the other."

He ran his hands along my cheek and down my neck. The touch of his fingers was intoxicating, and for the second time that day, did I feel the exhilaration of a man's skin alongside mine. I should have ordered him to cease, but moments such as those almost compel someone to lose all of one's control. Passion is too powerful an emotion, at times, and the will gives way.

"Kitty," he sighed, running his hands further down the nape of my neck and then slowly, he lowered his fingers down to my chest, and cupped his hands around my breasts.

A breath escaped me, and I almost cried out. The joy of it. The unparalleled ecstasy of the feeling was too much to bear. I could almost deny him nothing as I felt his fingers slowly begin to move under the top of my gown, winding its way under my shift and getting nearer to my nipples.

Then suddenly, sense rushed back in. All logic returned to me in the most provocative manner.

What was I doing to be so giving of my affections? I was neither wed, nor engaged.

Like a burst of lightning across the clear blue sky, Lieutenant Finlay's face emerged.

'Kitty,' he urged, 'do you hurt me so?'

I had to awake from this blissful dream that was also a stale nightmare all in one. It was time to wake up.

"Colonel," I implored. "You must stop."

"Be mine," he uttered, "and damn the rest of it."

"Richard..." I sighed, but then I felt his hands dig even deeper within my bodice and cusp my breasts in full. It was, and would go on to be, one of the happiest moments in my life. How I dreaded and welcomed my new wave of self-control. We were on the grounds of Pemberley. Our family was inside. We owed them a better moment than this.

With every fiber of my strength, I pulled Colonel Fitzwilliam's hand from under my bodice, feeling the lingering effects of his hands on the softness of my skin.

"Richard, I will not let you hurt yourself," I whispered harshly.

No more reprimand was needed. We heard some movement to our left and jumped away from each other just in time to see the gardener approach from across the green. He did not see us, initially, and that gave us time to appear as if we had been quietly walking along together. We evenly fell into line with each other, nodded to the gardener and walked back to the front steps.

Avoiding each other's gaze, we entered the house.

"I must go to my room," I said, "to change for supper. Please offer my apologies to anyone who feels that I am being missed."

I went to the steps, but Colonel Fitzwilliam stopped at the bottom of them.

"Kitty," he said urgently.

"Yes?" I replied, my voice equally as low as his.

"Lord knows what you must think about me now."

"I don't hate you, and don't think I ever will," I insisted. "You had a moment of weakness, and I will not have you walking the halls, weeping from your mistake."

"You are determined to forgive me for my behavior? Why?"

"Because it is you. If it were any other man besides the men that I care for, then I would banish you from my company forever. But Colonel Fitzwilliam must never feel abandoned or unwanted. Never from Kitty's presence. Come now, Richard, I am an imperfect woman. What makes you think I would turn my back on an imperfect man?"

"Then you still cherish me."

"Yes. No matter what tomorrow brings, you must never feel unwanted again. But as for your actions, please remember this: Lydia has caused one scandal in our family. I didn't want to be one to do the same. We must try to control ourselves. And I must protect you now. If you are caught with me, you will have to marry me. If you marry me, you marry a woman who brings you no income. I will not be your undoing, Richard. No matter what, I will NOT destroy you."

"I know. Even when I destroy yourself."

"Life was unkind to you. You destroy nothing."

With one last longing look, I went upstairs to my room.

There, in the quiet confinement of my living quarters, I felt the solitude fold its arms around me.

I collapsed onto the bed and roared out into the pillows.

All I ever wanted was a simple thing, a simple kind of life.

When did I start making everything so very difficult for myself?

Therefore, I did all that I could do.

I dressed for supper.

Chapter Fourteen

JANE BENNET'S TALE: NEW FRIENDS IN OLD PLACES

When getting dressed in the morning, all that you can say to your reflections is: 'I did all that I could do.'

While we were eating breakfast at the Gardiners, the post arrived, and I had a letter from Lizzy.

"As I sent a letter only yesterday, it is delightful that I receive one so quickly when arriving," I said, then I looked to my aunt and uncle. "Do you mind if I...?"

"Yes, you may read it," Aunt Gardiner allowed.

While eating, I opened the letter.

"It is from Lizzy!"

"Oh," Isaac cried, "what does Lizzy say?"

"She writes about the wedding. Well, it is now done. Mr. Collins and Miss Charlotte Lucas have gotten married. He arrived in Hertfordshire soon after I left it. They were married on Thursday."

"Isn't it true that now Mr. Collins and Miss Lucas will get Longbourn once your father passes away?" Isabella asked.

"Yes, well, everything will be different, I suppose," I admitted, "including that we no longer can call her Miss Lucas. Now, she is Mrs. Collins. Oh, and Lizzy now writes that Charlotte has invited her to come and stay with her at Hunsford Parsonage. Her father and her sister, Maria, are going to visit Charlotte in March. She wishes for Elizabeth to join them."

"Has cousin Elizabeth agreed?" Ruth asked.

"Yes, she has. In March, Elizabeth is going into Kent."

"I have heard wonderful things about that part of the country," Aunt Gardiner said. "It is said to be beautiful."

"I believe she shall be happy to see Charlotte again. I do not believe that either of them has been so long away from each other, now that I think of it. For friends to be so separate from each other, after being able to see each other every day, will be difficult. But Lizzy is sure that they will write to each other. I believe they will."

"I do so wish that we all were able to receive letters faster," Isabella noted. "Imagine if you sent a message to someone, and you never had to wait more than a few minutes to receive it. Now wouldn't that be something?"

"Yes," I smiled, "it would, Isa."

"If I were allowed, I would invent such a system myself. If only we were allowed more to our education."

"I believe that you shall," Uncle Gardiner said, "times are changing, little Isa."

"Yes," I said, "perhaps you will be the one to save us all."

"They think I can save them all," Isabella smiled, looking at their mother. Then she looked down at her food, continuing to eat. "I like being told that. I like it."

"After the couple were wed, they set off to Kent from the church door," I elaborated.

"And I believe that everyone is still talking about it, aren't they?" Aunt Gardiner asked. "If there is one thing that I know, it is the country."

"Yes, I believe that people shall speak about it for many days at least," I said. "Nothing makes people more voluble than a wedding."

"I'm certain," Uncle Gardiner said, "that wherever my sister is, it will be a topic that she will speak much on."

I smiled. Perhaps, in time, mama would find it in her to accept Charlotte as Mrs. Collins. Yes, perhaps so.

❧

Sewing in the sitting room, I wondered if Caroline would call on me. Yet if she did not, then I had something else to look forward to—and I was not left waiting long at all.

At the appointed time, the bell rang, and Miss Mary Crawford entered, with an elegance that only she contained.

"Miss Bennet," she laughed while she approached, curtsying.

"Miss Crawford," I smiled, truly happy to see her. "It is a pleasure to see you again."

"The pleasure is all mine. For I come to visit the most beautiful girl at the ball."

"You must be referring to yourself," I retorted. "When I first saw you, I felt as if I was so small in comparison."

"Not at all, and that will not do," she responded, then she turned to Aunt Gardiner, "Mrs. Gardiner, she may not be your daughter, but I see your elegance in her."

"You are very kind, Miss Crawford," Aunt Gardiner greeted her warmly, "And welcome to our home."

"And a lovely home it is."

"Please, do sit down. Compared to what you must be accustomed to, I know that our home must pale in comparison."

"Oh, not at all," she said, sitting down as we did so. "I live with my sister, Mrs. Grant. I do hope that I may have the pleasure of introducing you to her, one day. My sister is the dearest woman in the world. I suppose that I see a bit of you in her, Miss Bennet. When I first saw you, I thought to myself 'she has the same kind face as my sister'. When it comes to us younger sisters, having a lovely older one is a blessing."

"I am happy that you and she have a delightful relationship," I said, as Aunt Gardiner ordered tea for us, "for sisterly affection is the best thing."

"Especially since we are living in a world where sisters do not always get along," Miss Crawford said. "Therefore, when you are so fortunate as to have an affectionate bond with yours, it is a blessing."

"I agree entirely."

"Oh, but I shifted away from my original point," she corrected as the tea was brought. "Mrs. Gardiner, we were talking about homes, weren't we? First, I find your home to be the epitome of comfort, and that is the first thing that a home should be. Also, my sister is a widow, and we live modestly, as well as without artifice. And while her husband was still alive, they resided in Northampton, in a parsonage that belonged to the great estate, Mansfield Park. And...have you heard of it?"

"I confess that my knowledge of other counties is limited," I said, even though Mr. Weston told me some of her history.

"Neither have I, I confess," Aunt Gardiner added.

Our ignorance did not set us down in her judgement. On the contrary, when she discovered that we were completely ignorant of it, she only seemed more pleased by it.

"No matter," she continued, "you have every reason and right to not know of Mansfield Park. It is a lovely place, but great homes do not have to be important to everyone. Especially if you have never seen it. Besides, this is merely to explain my previous living conditions. While my sister lived at the parsonage, I had extended visits there, and the parsonage was not as large as this. Therefore, no! I am not one to turn my nose up at a house because it is not the size of a museum! This house is as lovely as my brother's home in Everingham. For after all, home is home."

"That is precisely what I often say," I supported, happy to know that we were of the same mind on that score. The tea was prepared, and we all drank and ate casually.

Eventually the children were brought down, and Mary Crawford made each of their acquaintances. She spoke with all four of them (well, little Daniel didn't say anything), and, unless I was mistaken, Isaac might have begun to fancy her.

We spoke more, getting better acquainted, and we learned more about each other.

"Since you have enjoyed the delights of both," I asked her, "what did you prefer? Did you like living in the parsonage in the country, or do you prefer living in town?"

"It is altogether strange," she admitted, "but both have such benefits and drawbacks, that I can never fully decide. The country had much appeal to it. It seemed to bring a freshness and purity to oneself. Yet, the city provides many diversions and sometimes I find the noise of constant crowds to actually be comforting. I suppose that there is a part of the country that makes me always happy to be there, but there is a part of my spirit that is attached to town. Do I make any sense now?"

"Yes, you do. And I very well comprehend you. In the country, I enjoy our manners, but there is something about town that is very invigorating."

"Yes, truly. I like the peace, tranquility, and sincerity of provincial people. But every now and again, I feel...restless. As if, if I did not move or act, I would fade. I was not meant for cold prudence, even though prudence offers peace. I was not meant to sit still and do nothing. But I see that you have it better. Your nature seems to possess that happiness that comes from serenity."

"Thank you, but I do not sneer at those who are more active. There is use for women such as you in the world, Miss Crawford. I believe so."

"You are very kind. Besides, when it comes to the idea of town versus country, both have another benefit. Sometimes, a person needs a change of scenery to feel as if they are made anew. Sometimes, something can occur in town that is so overpowering that you feel as if you need to get away—retreat to the country to recover. And sometimes, well... the reverse can happen. Sometimes, something can happen in the country that hurts to remember, and so you need town to retreat to, so that it can give you a chance to recover."

"As if a change of location can help you feel born again?" I hinted.

"Precisely!"

I smiled, happy that we understood each other once more. How quickly our spirits found a kindred way. It was as if, within my very soul, she saw what I was feeling, and she voiced it. And by voicing it herself, I did not have to. It was the perfect sort of arrangement.

"And so it presents the strange conundrum," Aunt Gardiner gathered, "that if one desires to be in town as well as in the country, then perhaps we humans are never fully happy. For we are always wishing to be where we are, while also wishing to be somewhere else. Wherever that 'somewhere' else would be."

"You therefore present a portrait of restlessness," Miss Crawford determined, "and that restlessness is the very essence of the human soul. Mrs. Gardiner, perhaps you are right. But I enjoy us all the more for it. Perhaps we are all meant to always want more and be seeking some form of utopia, in one form or another. Perhaps it's the pursuit of it that gives us a drive to go ever onward and face new things. That is why I suppose I can never remain locked into stasis. By doing so, I feel as if I am never moving. And if I am never moving, then where am I going?"

"These are very philosophical questions," Aunt Gardiner said, "and we poor women here at Gracechurch Street can never give you an answer that will make you happy."

"But I like that you make us ask the questions," I encouraged, "even though I could never answer them myself, you make me wonder about them."

Mary Crawford stayed for a little longer, then her visit came to an end. I requested if we could visit her, so that we could meet her sister, or requested Aunt Gardiner if we could invite them again. Aunt Gardiner offered that she would gladly welcome them visiting. I acknowledged that if I ever called on them at her home, it would have to be a dinner visit, because I had to keep my mornings free to await my visit from Miss Bingley.

Miss Crawford accepted these conditions, and promised that she would write to me soon, once she spoke with Mrs. Grant. Thus, she left, and I felt very much in the best of spirits.

For while she was there, there was not one moment that I thought of Mr. Bingley.

When she was gone, Aunt Gardiner looked kindly toward me.

"Well, I daresay that you have made a friend."

"I hope so," I sighed, happy. "I cannot help but feel drawn toward her. I cannot understand why I was so, even before meeting her. But there it was. I just feel that she is different."

"Of course, you were drawn toward her; after all, she is similar to Lizzy."

This revelation made my eyes widen as I accepted the connection.

"Do you think so?" I asked.

"Yes. There is something about her disposition and air that is similar to Elizabeth's, so it has affected you."

"I had not thought of that before. But now that I think of it, yes, you are correct. There is something about their countenance that is remarkably alike. Oh dear! You don't think that I am foolishly transferring my feelings from one person to another, and therefore projecting Lizzy's character onto Miss Crawford's? If I am, then you must tell me at once. For it would be most unkind to Miss Crawford. She does not deserve that."

"It is not unkind at all to admire a person because they have similar attributes to someone that you admire. Besides, if you need to ask that question, then you know that you have the presence of mind not to mishandle your relationship with your new friend. Just remember not to ever get angry at Miss Crawford for not living up to Elizabeth's shadow. Very few friends are perfect in this world. And, judging by her speeches about herself, I deduce that Miss Crawford is aware that she is not perfect. But I know that you will be kind towards whatever side of her that she presents. No, I believe that you both shall be good for each other."

Either way, I had made a new acquaintance who made me immediately feel comfortable and felt like something... new. While also feeling like something... old. I just met her recently, and yet I felt as if I had known her already. And that was all that mattered.

Especially since Caroline Bingley didn't call on me that day. Assuming that she was just engaged elsewhere, I made my excuses for her and chose to think no more about it.

~

Two days came and fell, and still Caroline did not call. My spirits were lifted when Miss Mary Crawford came again, but she was not joined by her sister.

"My sister begs your leave and apologizes for being unable to attend," Mary said as she removed her spencer. "Yesterday, she felt a sore throat and cold coming on and hoped it would be well the next day. But she is worse than before and neither of us wished for her to venture out for anything."

"Oh, then you need not have held your engagement with me," I augmented, "I am not as important as her. Believe me, I would not have been offended if you did not come."

"But I would have offended myself by sending a note the day of canceling a visit. Besides, my coming shows no lack of sisterly regard, but a kindness. When my sister is sick, she prefers to sleep and only be tended to by our trusty servant, Sofia. By having me come today, this will give her the chance to not hear my pattering about the house for a little. She shall therefore have time away from me."

"I'm sure that she is always happy to see you."

"Oh, we love each other, but like it always is with people we love, sometimes we need time away from them. Sometimes you can love each other so much, and your affection can reach such a pitch that you might proceed to kick and throw each other out the window at the slightest provocation!"

"You would never do that." I laughed.

"Always believe that everyone in this world is capable of almost anything," she laughed as well, "even me. And it is a pleasure to see you as well, Mrs. Gardiner."

"Welcome back into my home, Miss Crawford," Aunt Gardiner greeted, "Jane has been looking forward to seeing you ever since your last visit."

Miss Crawford arched her eyebrow and gave me a quizzical look.

"Is this true, Miss Bennet? Have you been waiting to see me?"

"I confess that I have," I admitted, "and it is not just me, but Isaac has been asking about you as well."

"And where is little Isaac?"

"I shall bring them down," Aunt Gardiner said, having the servant send for the children.

"Miss Crawford!" Isaac called.

"Hello Mr. Gardiner," Mary smiled at him. "And Miss Gardiner, Miss Ruth, and Mr. Daniel, you all are looking very smart today."

"Thank you," Isabella said, curtsying, "I think your gown is very fine."

"I was able to choose what gown I wear today," Ruth said.

"And you are already showing yourself to be a woman of superior fashion," Miss Crawford complimented, "You and Miss Isabella are clearly going to grow up to be true ladies. And Mr. Isaac, when they grow up, it shall be your duty to defend them against the many suitors that shall be knocking on their door."

"Suitors?" Isaac responded, his face scrunching up, "I do not like the sound of them."

"No proper brother does."

Aunt Gardiner ordered the tea and cakes to be immediately brought in. Once we sat down, we all found ourselves looking at Mary Crawford. Realizing that all eyes were upon her, I felt a little embarrassed, but she rallied very quickly.

"While two days is not enough for me to tell you anything you have not heard before, I still felt it my social duty to have news, and I do!" Miss Crawford announced, filled with ease and confidence.

"Is it good news or bad?" Isaac asked.

"The news that stirs more conversation than the movement of armies. On Friday, there is to be a wedding of two people who have found happiness with each other."

"Someone is going to get married," Isabella grinned.

"Yes. And even better; the couple in question even like each other."

"Oh, who is the happy couple who are to be wed?" I asked.

"A naval captain by the name of Mr. Thorpe, and a friend of mine, a Miss Diana Caldwell."

Aunt Gardiner and I both quietly exclaimed at the same time.

"Well, that is a delightful coincidence," I remarked. "Aunt Gardiner, is this not the same Captain Thorpe and Miss Caldwell who's wedding we are to attend?"

"Depends if there are two couples of the same name. But I shall confirm for us both. Miss Crawford, are the Captain Thorpe and Miss Caldwell getting married at St. John's church?"

"And also are the same couple that have chosen to hold a ball immediately after the ceremony takes place?"

"Yes!"

"Then we do speak of the same couple. Now this is a fine coincidence indeed! I have been invited to the wedding as well. Not only since Miss Diana and I are well acquainted, but also because Mr. Thorpe is a Captain in his Majesty's Navy. My uncle is Admiral Crawford, so they are in the same service together. And you all are going to be a part of the company."

"Often it is said that the world is smaller than one thinks," Aunt Gardiner observed, "and never has it been proven truer than now."

"And it is all so exciting," Miss Crawford continued, "for them to have a ball *after* the wedding. What a delightful idea! Have you ever noticed, quite often, that wedding ceremonies are rarely ever grand affairs? The couple go to the church, wearing their best clothing, the wedding ceremony is solemn and lacks any joy, and it is all so simple, over and done with. Then the couple departs from the church, we wave and go about our day."

"I admit that I have always been a woman who leaned more towards simplicity," I confessed.

"Ah, then you are a better woman than I. My soul is too active, too always movable to always be giving into prudence."

"Oh, no I am not better than you. For while I would prefer the simple act of a wedding myself, I am very far from objecting to others who wish to do more to celebrate the most wonderful day of their life. This idea of having a ball and banquet after a wedding is both novel and appealing. I do so love to dance."

"So do I," Mary smiled.

"Therefore, I am happy that this Captain Thorpe and Miss Caldwell are allowing us an opportunity to be a part of their most joyous day."

A servant entered, for a couple letters arrived for Aunt Gardiner. Begging leave to read it, and sending the children to the nursery room, Miss Crawford and I were left in the parlor to talk alone.

"Since we both enjoy to dance," I voiced, "I do so hope that there will be some there who think me worthy enough to ask for my hand. I have such little acquaintances in town. Yet I am certain that you shall dance every dance, being so fine as you are."

When saying this, Mary's eyes shifted, and she looked downcast.

"No," she retorted, "I daresay that you will be the belle of the ball, and I shall fade into obscurity."

"You have no reason or right to be so unkind to yourself," I chided her.

"Pray, I do not say this out of false modesty, and unkindness toward myself. But rather, I say this out of acceptance of the reality. And now that I think about it, perhaps we are fortunate that your aunt had to read her letters, and we are left alone."

"Miss Crawford," I asked, somewhat alarmed by the sudden change of her tone. "What could you mean by that?"

Standing up, she moved away from me and began to pace around the room. Even though she was in movement, there was a stillness and stiffness to her posture that felt very unlike her. At last, she moved to the window and began to look out of it.

"Forgive me if I alarm you now," she began, "and believe that what I speak of is something that I must tell you. First, I say it because I do not want you to hear about it from anyone else first. And second, I wish to tell it to you because I want to believe, Miss Bennet, that you are kind. And that you are not the sort to blame someone for being guilty by association. And I need a true friend now. Tell me, Miss Bennet? Am I wrong about you? Are you that sort of person?"

Intrigued and immediately wishing to make her feel as if she could confide in me, I reassured her. After all, she was not already telling me about things that I hadn't heard already. Now I was able to hear her side of the story.

"I believe that I am not the sort of person who will throw anyone to the wayside for actions that they are not guilty over. And even if you were guilty of something, I can assure you that I would attempt to understand what occurred at the time before passing any judgement. Would it help, Miss Crawford, if I were to tell you that you may confide in me, and tell me anything, and I shall let your tellings die within me?"

She breathed out a sigh of relief.

"I knew you were such a person. When I first saw you, I believed you to be truly compassionate and not quick to ridicule or censor. I am happy that I was right."

Turning back to me, she began to narrate her tale of misfortune.

"As you recall, I have told you about my brother, Mr. Henry Crawford, of Everingham, in Norfolk."

"Yes, I remember him."

"Well, do you also remember when I mentioned how my sister's late husband had his living at the parsonage on the estate, Mansfield Park, in Northampton."

"Yes. I take it that both those items will be connected."

"Oh, they are connected indeed, in the most deplorable way. Miss Bennet, I confess that what drew me toward your company was the obviousness of you being entirely ignorant of the scandal that rocked the tranquility of that estate, and of the part my family played in it."

Immediately my heart reached out to her. I was prepared to hear something awful...because I already knew part of the tale. But I was prepared to feign ignorance and allow her to believe that she was giving me the truth for the first time.

"What scandal happened? Again, I shall not judge you."

"Well, my sister and her husband took up residence at Mansfield Park parsonage, and her husband was the reverend there. She is Henry and my half-sister, on our mother's side. Despite this, we were quite close, and she doted on us. Upon her residence there, she invited Henry and I to come and visit her. I was apprehensive, because I was not accustomed to living in the country, but I was happy to see her. I was happy to fall somewhere with comfortable family because my relationship with Admiral Crawford was always strenuous. Our Uncle favored Henry, but not me. When going to the parsonage, Henry and I immediately became acquainted with the Mansfield residents. They were the Bertram family. The patriarch, Sir Thomas Bertram, had four children there. The eldest was his namesake, Mr. Thomas Bertram. Then there was the second. His name was... Mr. Edmund Bertram."

When she said the second name, I marked a change in her expression. In her eyes, I felt I saw a sort of—pain.

"And there were the daughters, Miss Maria Bertram, and Miss Julia Bertram. It is with the eldest daughter that the chief pain occurred. And that brings me to my brother, Henry. He's my brother and I love him very much so. It's not in my nature to abandon my sibling just because of the things he does. That's family for you, I suppose. But I never denied to myself what he was, and what I label him now is what I have already labeled him to his face. My brother was a shameless flatterer and flirt. Indeed, he made quite an art of it. He was very good at engaging a woman's heart and then, once obtaining it, he was satisfied and would cease giving her any attention. I always labelled him as a rattle, but he would prove to be quite the rake. Well, the eldest Bertram daughter, Maria, was already engaged to be married to a Mr. Rushworth, of Sotherton. My brother met them all, along with Mr. Rushworth and even befriended him. Yet that did not stop my brother from paying particular attention to Miss Maria Bertram, obtaining her affections, and she was in a right way of falling in love with him."

The story was still only partly told, and I was already shocked at hearing the particulars!

"Your brother attached himself to a woman who was already engaged to another?"

"Oh, he did not attach himself at all. No. That was not his aim. Henry had a love for winning hearts and then letting them go once he obtained his goal: to make them violently in love with him. And he succeeded; she did fall in love with him—while still engaged to Mr. Rushworth."

"She did that? I cannot believe it."

"I was there. Believe me, I speak the truth."

"Even though the idea of her doing such a thing is too horrible for me to believe, I do not know what to think. Perhaps there has been some terrible mistake, and she simply was slandered. Do we have any evidence to the particulars?"

"I wish that were all that it was. But soon I shall present you with intangible proof behind it all. Soon after winning her heart, he relinquished any attention to her on that score and he quitted Mansfield Park. Miss Bertram was bitter, and in her affected state, she threw herself headlong into her wedding with Mr. Rushworth, married a man she did not love or even like, and triumphed by putting herself into a state of marital misery. The triumph of marrying Mr. Rushworth did not last long in her eyes, and she felt the tragedy of the very fate that she placed on herself. Then, upon seeing my brother again one day, my brother found her determined to ignore and forget about him. Dear Henry, to this day, I wish he had not done this! Always in a pursuit of winning the heart of any woman who was determined to be indifferent to him, he set out to win her affections again. It was not out of any initial desire to actually get her to leave her husband. No. It was all vanity. He was determined to make her like him again, just to satisfy his own self-gratification."

"Then," I whispered, "what happened next?"

"He succeeded. She became violently in love with him again, and his pride was satisfied. That is what so many mistakes in the world boil down to: pride! And vanity as well! At that point, I do not know the extent to which their flirtation... went. I never cared to ask Henry. But I didn't need to. I know the truth. I just don't care to speak about it. But however deep their intimacy was, it led to so large a folly on Mrs. Rushworth's part. She left her husband's home, sought out my brother and was adamant to go with him. My brother, wholly giving in to immediate temptations and her whim, took her with him. This was immediately followed by Mr. Rushworth filing for a divorce, which was quickly granted."

"So, your brother married this Miss Bertram after it all? And so you speak of the scandal of her heartbreaking actions and the divorce?"

"They never got married."

"What?" I asked, shocked.

"Henry chose not to marry Maria Bertram. Nor did her family wish to have her at home."

"Then what became of this lady?"

"A small home was set up for her in another county and she lives out her life there—from what I have heard. And you were smart to ask for proof. When this scandal erupted, it was much the talk of the ton, and it was in newspapers. My family's scandal, connected with Mansfield Park, was laid bare, on the front pages of the columns. It talked of how Mrs. Rushworth had quitted her husband's house with my brother, who was a close friend to the Bertram family. Ask any person in the ton and they can tell you, it is true and written about. Now you know the story of the horror of my family's past."

~

When she finished her narration, I sat there, dumbfounded. But she referred to newspapers and public documentation. What person would do that... unless they spoke the truth. Besides, what did Mary have to gain by lying? Not a thing. In fact, she had everything to lose by telling me this. So, now that I got her side of the story, all had been confirmed, and I had not been given vicious and erroneous gossip before.

"This is so shocking," I said at last, "how you must have suffered while this all occurred. It must have broken your heart."

"I refused to allow myself to break under the weight of the circumstances, and I am not trying to be immodest, I assure you. My instinct was to repair the damage that my brother had done. But all my schemes fell to the wayside and came to nothing."

"And what has happened to your brother?"

"He is a man and therefore is naturally able to recover from such incidents than we women cannot. But even if that was not the case, he was unattached when he committed the misdeed, but Maria Rushworth was not. So, I suppose it does make sense that the hammerstroke fell hardest upon her. By refusing to marry her, my brother untangled himself from the worst of it. He also untangled himself from a woman he was selfish enough to seduce, but he was not foolish enough to love. He can move about the world, free and able to immerse himself everywhere, due to his winning charm. But what one does not speak of—what is often forgotten about...are the scars."

"Scars?" I repeated.

"The scars that begin to form from the incident. Or shall we call them the after-effects. Yes, my sister and her late husband are not to blame for my brother's actions, but they were connected to it. They could not remain at Mansfield Park, but had to leave, out of embarrassment. His actions caused a chain reaction, and the Bertram family severed all ties to us. We were all guilty by association, and that even found its way to me. Many people once knew me as Miss Mary Crawford, the niece to the Admiral and sister to the owner of Everingham. Now I am Mary Crawford, the sister of a man who ran off with another man's wife. And that's why you didn't see any man dance with me when we first met. They do not know how to approach me. Women snigger behind my back, and I now live in a permanent state of gray. Whatever respectability I once had is now called into question. After all, if the brother once acted so abominably, then people assume the sister will as well."

"Oh, good god," I gasped, "you mean to say that many people see you through the lens of your brother's misconduct."

"Yes. I have encountered such."

"Miss Crawford! I am so sorry for what you have undergone due to the folly of others. You deserve better."

"Thank you," she sighed. "So, you do not judge me then? You do not look on me differently than you did before?"

"Not at all. You are not to blame or be viewed differently for whatever your brother or this Mrs. Rushworth has done. No one should be guilty because of the actions of another."

"Thank you. But you are not saying that out of pity either, are you? Because I cannot suffer being pitied as much as I cannot suffer being despised for no reason."

"No," I assured her, taking her hands in mine, "I do not pity you. I merely empathize, no more and no less. And I will not view you as any different than I viewed you before."

"Oh, Miss Bennet!" She rushed to me and instinctively, we embraced.

"Never fear, Miss Crawford," I assured her, "all will be well. I promise. This horror will pass. And now I have something that I must confess."

"What? You have not been damned in the same manner once, have you?"

"No, and I hope that I will not have to suffer under the folly of a foolish sibling, but actually, I did know a little bit about your brother's history."

"You did?"

"I learned of it when I was at the ball. Someone informed me of it."

"And you didn't judge me even then?"

"It didn't seem like the logical thing to do."

Soon her visit came to an end, for she did not want to be too long away from Mrs. Grant. Upon our parting, she expressed a great desire for me to call her Mary, and I returned it by saying she could call me Jane.

We parted ways with much affection on both sides. Her confession only enriched the camaraderie that I felt for her, and I exited that day with a feeling of contentment.

For it was another day where her very words helped me not think of Mr. Bingley once more.

Never would she know the service that she rendered me, for her company somehow was helping me to recover. For here, I was in a place where I did not have to hear his name constantly mentioned, nor suffer the looks of people who knew that he did not wish to marry me. Here I was my aunt and uncle's niece, their children's cousin, another woman in London...and Miss Crawford's new friend.

I thought to write about her in a letter to Elizabeth but quickly decided against it. After all, just because we never heard of Mr. Henry Crawford's scandal at Longbourn, didn't mean that it was unheard of by anyone else in Hertfordshire. And if, by mere chance, they knew of it, then Mary's story would circulate all over the countryside. Therefore, for the sake of Miss Crawford's happiness, I decided for my friendship to her to be something that remained in town.

Chapter Fifteen

KITTY'S TALE: ELIZABETH'S PLAN

How we still lived during Jane's pursuit of friendship.

After supper, we all met in the sitting room. Initially, Elizabeth had intended there to be a game of cards played. Yet before that, she and Mr. Darcy had an announcement, which was the first step of her plan.

"My wife and I composed the letter that we shall have sent to Mansfield Park, by express, tomorrow morning. With any luck, it will reach Northampton in no more than two days, and I informed them that we shall anticipate a response by the end of the week."

"Why the urgency?" William Price asked.

"Because we are due in Kent a few days before Christmas. That gives us little time to get all our affairs in order."

"What I have suggested," Elizabeth said, "is for me to read the letter aloud, so all are aware of what steps will be taken, to ensure the best outcome to this situation. We feel it is right for you all to know everything before it is sent," Elizabeth said to the Crawfords. "You may object, but personally, I would find that most objectionable. The rest of our company has the right to know how everything might unfold. For, ironically, we might all be in this together."

"Well," Miss Crawford said, "I, for one, do not object. I prefer that we all are on the same level with every step that is taken."

"I agree with my sister," Henry Crawford said, "and I confess, I am a little curious. Therefore, I eagerly await your reading, Mrs. Darcy."

Elizabeth cleared her throat, raised up the missive and began to read:

To Mr. and Mrs. Thomas Bertram, of Mansfield Park estate,

Our present circumstances have never lent us to being acquainted, yet after reading this letter, we hope you can forgive the oversight that nature has led to us never meeting before.

First, we wish you a happy time during this festive part of the year, and hope that you enjoy the holiday season.

I write in concern of acquaintances that we do share: the Crawfords of Everingham, Norfolk, Mrs. Grant, and Mr. William Price from Portsmouth.

As we understand it, Miss Crawford and Mr. Price have formed an attachment and wish to marry. However, they have not been bestowed with the blessing from your family, due to the history that the Crawfords share with your own.

We shall be forthright and tell you now that while your decision is your own, we have accepted the match and will help these two marry.

They will be married at Kympton, the church along Pemberley's estate, and we shall celebrate their union.

Yet that puts you into a difficult state, we imagine, due to the repercussions of knowing that Mr. Price's marriage was accepted along the Pemberley estate, and by extension, a significant portion of the aristocracy will be aware of these developments. As well as that none of Mr. Price's relatives were in attendance.

You may choose how to distribute news of his family's absence as you see fit. However, both of these individuals are blameless, guiltless and have caused no offense against your family. There ought to be no guilt by association, even though, if one were to be fair, whatever guilt they have is no lesser than the guilt that your own family exudes by your own actions and history.

And if you do not wish to yield any breach caused with this happy event, and still will further condemn it, you do so at your own risk. For, whatever is the horrid history between both families, half of that mistake belongs to your own kin. We do not demand but recommend a softer approach. A blend of correction, but also forgiveness. How you treat your own daughter is your affair, and we cannot judge. But after proper punishment, at some point, your child is still your child. And you must ask yourself if their true crime is their own folly, or your own misdirection as a parent?

But what is known, here at Pemberley, is that no one is guilty for the crimes of another. Mr. Price's marriage to Miss Crawford is well within the respect of both.

How you behave after their wedding is your affair, yet we ask for no slander to be bestowed upon their match.

For remember the holy words: why do you look at the spec in your brother's eye, but fail to notice the beam in your own eye?

In the scope of one's life, when summing up all of one's actions done in England, and outside of Britain, when considering how all your fellow man and woman is treated under your power, regardless of their look, national background, or history, can you say that you are always guiltless, and pure? I am certain that none of us can declare that. Therefore, I find it best to examine your conscience, and see if forsaking these two—one of who is your beloved nephew who bene-fited from your kindness toward himself and his sister—worth such strict measures? Or maybe, by accepting their union, you may bring about an even greater thing—acceptance bestowed after judgement has been passed. Forgiveness.

For as our Redeemer has often declared: religion is made for sinners. Therefore, it is made for them, and for yourself.

This letter comes to you, by way of express. If you have changed your mind, and views, and realize that maybe you wish to wed these both yourselves, on the Mansfield Park estate, and bring about an end to discord between the Crawfords and the Bertrams, we would very much prefer a reply as soon as possible.

However, if you find it to be impossible in your power to allow these two into your society, then we shall proceed as follows.

And if you find it erroneous of us to wed two people who love each other, based on their affiliations with your family, then we must respectfully acknowledge that we have taken everything into perspec-tive: not just their connection to Miss Maria Bertram, but also the attitude of England that is shifting more in favor of the freedom for all. And for those who continue with their belief that there is no error on their judgements and never reform from such heinous acts, that is questionable.

All things will be taken into account, under the shades of Pemberley.

I want to believe that you are a good man, and that your family is respectable, but times are changing. And what is regarded as respectable is changing alongside it.

We look forward to hearing a favorable and express response, where you welcome an attachment to Miss Crawford, Mr. Price, and you welcome Mrs. Grant into your society—and can find it within you to forgive the follies of your own kin, as well as Miss Crawford's.

If you do not wish to take part in their happy union, then Pemberley shall suffice to fulfilling that happiness, and not by our will, rumor and news will spread that Mr. Price's uncle and family opposed the match. I cannot guarantee that your eldest daughter's history will not resurface, and you will have to confront that problem all over again. But your silence will guarantee that it will.

If anything that I have written displeases you, or offends you, then I request no letter from you as a reply. On the contrary, I would welcome your company here at Pemberley, so the matter can be discussed in person. Write to me before the holiday season fully begins that you shall arrive forthwith—but understand, we shall be away on December 21st, therefore, please write by way of express, that you shall visit before then. If you do come, I would prefer that you at least travel with your two sons, and any ladies of the house that you might see fit. For, I believe that they also have a role in this situation.

If we are to exchange insults, then we ought to do it as gentlemen: to our faces.

Whatever disrespect you feel now, it is done for the express desire to remind you all, at Mansfield Park, that you are better than you are now.

F.D.

When Elizabeth finished reading, she lowered the letter.

"This is the letter that shall be sent tomorrow morning," she announced, then she turned to the Crawfords, "is there anything else that you wish for us to add?"

"None at all," Miss Crawford said, amazed, "you are truly fearless. Is there anything that you are afraid of?"

Elizabeth smirked.

"Very little. Very little at all."

"Well, this is interesting," Arthur Philips said, "I guarantee that Sir Thomas will be angry. And because he is a gentleman, we hope he will have no choice but to come to Pemberley."

"Oh," Darcy smirked. "I'm counting on it."

Chapter Sixteen

KITTY'S TALE: TORN IN TWO

I was walking through a glade of lovely woods, smelling the freshness of the air, the warmth of the sun on my face. Gone forever were dark and bleak days of winter, but the welcoming heat of a warm summer's eve.

The trees and flowers were in full bloom, from the green above and the brown of the dirt below. Yet there was a foreign quality to it.

This is not England.

Nor is it Wales.

What land had I fallen into that brought on such a blissful sensation? No, this land could not belong to anything that was real but was of the fantastical sort. A magic exuded from the place, as if it was a haven, shielding me from any grim days ahead or behind. No. I was at peace. I was unafraid and unfettered. Unshackled from everything that had ever brought me downward, into a state of misery.

All earthly cares were over.

I was alone.

And yet...why was I happy?

Is not singularity of existence the most haunting thing in the world? The fear of loneliness and as if there is no other creature in the world.

But I was not frightened. I moved among the tree and bush,

finally arriving at a rocky precipice, and I looked out. Before me was a swift sunrise on a beautiful land.

I suppose I didn't fear being alone, because I wasn't. The rocks, the trees, the rivers, the waterfall—and the mountains in the vast distance, all had life. Spirit. They were alive.

And so, I could begin.

Placing one foot in front of the other, I moved along the grass and wound my way through the underbrush. With each step, I felt a certain liberty.

As did Prometheus when he could finally be unbound, I saw my way, and my chance.

I walked on and on.

But I was not done. No, my feet were not tired but only challenged me to go onward. So onward I would go...

My eyes opened, and I awoke. It had all been a dream. Rubbing my eyes, I squinted, trying to capture every moment of it. However, as is the way with dreams, they begin to slip from you. As such, I willed my thoughts onward, making sure to grasp at every image of this magical bit of nature that I had found.

The memory was there. But the feeling was gone.

Rolling over, I looked out the window and saw how the sky was changing from black to a dark blue. It was not yet dawn, but soon, the sun was preparing its rise within an hour.

There was no point in falling back asleep, therefore, what was I to do but lay there in my bed and stare up at the ceiling. I was safe in this room, but for how long?

When the sunrise came, the day would begin. What did it have in store for me?

~

The next day, Colonel Fitzwilliam was giving me another lesson in the stables. He was teaching me how to clean the horse's hooves and how to properly insert a horseshoe.

"Did Mr. Darcy really send the letter to Mansfield Park?" I asked him as we worked away.

"Oh, yes he did," Colonel Fitzwilliam said. "He is most determined."

"I wonder what it's like for him, to have to be in this situation?"

"Oh, it's both difficult and easy for him."

"How so? Those are two polar opposite mental states. How can he be so much in irony?"

"Darcy loves a life of leisure, but he also is a man of action. I know it seems strange, but that is who he is. He's not an easy man to confine one or two traits to. Then again, many of us are that way."

"Yes, we all do seem to consistently suffer under being mislabeled, don't we?"

Colonel Fitzwilliam laughed.

"Precisely. Then again, there is such a duality even in that regard. For, with all of us, there is the one side of us that everyone sees, and then there is the person that we all want to be—or know that we really are."

"And woe betide when that side of us emerges," I joked.

"Yes. Everyone will die of shock if we do that. I never got the chance to ask, how is your family doing back in Hertfordshire?"

"The last letter that we received was a couple weeks ago. Mother and father are still in excellent health. Same with my aunt and uncle Philips. I hope nothing happens to them for so long. Not just because it will smite Mr. Collins's dreams of getting Longbourn, but also because home represents stability. Besides, my parents are getting better at seeing me for what I am. Even though it's been quite a while before I saw them, I know that they are improving in that regard. Whether or not they find their love for each other again, only time will tell."

"I doubt it might happen, but miracles have been known to happen in the South every now and again. Perhaps it will with them. But, with some marriages, times make things stale. When you are married for so long, it can lead to three outcomes: 1) you become so comfortable with that other person, that you are forever linked together. 2) the bloom wears off and you fall into a state of subtle indifference. And 3) you grow to hate the very sight of the other person."

"With my parents, it was the second. When they first married, I knew that they were once very much in love. Then they realized just how much they did not know each other enough before they did. Or they only knew the better sides of themselves."

"Well, when one gets married, there will always be a little taking-in done. We all hide our worst habits from our spouse until we have trapped them in some way."

"That is often true. Sometimes, I wonder how, in god's name, royal marriages don't end in both parties wanting to smite each other down."

"Well, historically, that did occur a few times."

We both looked at each other and read each other's minds.

"Henry VIII!" we said in unison.

"God, that man!" I declared.

"We got divorce out of that situation, and that was the ONLY good thing his reign brought about," Colonel Fitzwilliam sighed.

"I wonder what Miss Maria Bertram feels," I said, "to be divorced. Then again, if she despised Mr. Rushworth that much, she might prefer exile, rather than to remain living with him. After all, it must be a very unhappy arrangement to prompt lechery."

"And sometimes, not even the case. Some people have been known to be happy in a match and still be unfaithful."

I looked at him, surprised.

"Really?"

"Yes. Some people are just born with the wrong sort of way of thinking. And others are spoiled."

"Maria Bertram was probably spoiled."

"Yes, she probably was."

≈

Suddenly, a thought came to me, and I froze in my duties. This did not escape Colonel Fitzwilliam's notice.

"Kitty?" he asked. "What is it?"

"You know how you have a thought. It's something that you never thought of before. And it's a frightening one. It's one that won't change anything, but maybe it does have the power to change everything?"

"Yes. Why? What thought struck you that way?"

"I just wondered. I know that my mother has never fallen in that way, but with men, who have more exposure to the world, there is the chance for more opportunity. I wonder if my father ever wandered?"

"Mr. Bennet?"

"Yes."

Suddenly, Colonel Fitzwilliam let out a hearty laugh. For some reason, I found that to be very provoking.

"And why do you laugh, Richard?" I asked, with malice in my words.

"Because it's funny."

"You think my father having a potential affair is funny?"

"No. But that you should entertain the fact that he might is. Kitty, how long has your father been the sort of man who always retreats to his library whenever he wishes to escape?"

"Ever since I can remember." Then I realized my foolishness. "Oh."

"Yes, 'oh' indeed! Where was he going to meet these other women? As you said, when you were younger, your mother was a great beauty. They were obviously romantically attached, because they had five daughters quite successfully and eagerly. And that's probably not counting any miscarriages that your mother might have had. Therefore, by the time that your mother lost her looks, and their attachment to each other died out, he was no longer interested in the sensual side of humanity's cravings, and he retreated into the world of books. Between the hallway and his library, where are these hordes of women that he would have enticed?"

He laughed some more, and I acknowledged that he might

have been right. Rather than fully give into his superior way of thinking, however, I merely shoved him backwards, he fell gently on some hay, and I went over to retrieve a horseshoe.

"Very well. Make fun of me all that you like."

"I can and I just did," he said. Giving into the spirit of the moment, I began to laugh as well, causing my stomach such pain that I fell over and collapsed on the hay next to the Colonel.

~

When I ceased laughing, I looked up at the stables' ceiling.

"I haven't laughed like that in ages," I said.

"Because we have been living in serious times in these last couple of days. There wasn't much time for levity."

"But even more than that," I said. "My laugh has not been that hearty since I was back home, in Hertfordshire. My two friends there, Diana Long and Maria Lucas. Sometimes we used to laugh like that. I miss them."

I looked at the Colonel, who watched me on the other side of the hay.

"Do you ever wonder how that is, that bosom friends can suddenly become so distant from each other?"

"Distance helps it. Besides, it's the way of life to fall away from comrades every now and again. But, when you go back home, I am confident that you will fall back into your previous ways and you three will be as you once were."

"Unless I return, and they are married. Then no. Everything will be different."

"How so?" he asked.

"Marriage always changes a family circle. It's the most beautiful divider that there is."

"Yes, I can see how that is."

"Is it like that with men? Did being married to Lizzy affect your relationship with Mr. Darcy?"

"Yes, it did. But I never had much time to even notice."

"Why not?"

"I met you soon after."

"Yes, you did. And all the indecisions and complications set in. I suppose that it didn't give you time to feel the weight of the shift in your friendship with your cousin."

"No, because I had other cares to distract me."

"Well, I am happy that I helped in that way, at least."

"It will be the same with you," Colonel Fitzwilliam coaxed me, "whenever Miss Long or Miss Lucas marry—or Georgiana—you will have other events in your life that will not make you feel the shift so terribly in your circle."

I squinted.

"Georgiana?"

"What about her?"

"You mentioned Georgiana. Why did you mention her?"

"Well, I thought it was obvious. You and she are very close friends, and when the time comes for her to choose a husband, the relationship would shift between you both. I was just trying to assure you that your friendship would not suffer just because she would become a wife."

Disturbance! That's what my confidence felt when he related this frightful prospect. I felt disturbed, in a similar way that I had when I felt threatened by Emma Watson at the Osbourne's ball.

"Yes," I whispered, hardly knowing myself, "I suppose it would change."

"You never thought of that before, did you?" Colonel Fitzwilliam asked.

"No, I did not. Or perhaps I did, but then I belittled the event in my mind and chose to forget about it. I don't like losing friends, I suppose. I'm just realizing that now."

"She really does cherish your friendship," he assured me.

"Thank you. I know she does. I'm just... oh, I don't know what I am feeling now."

"You are afraid of losing one of your best friends."

"Yes, I suppose that I am. I'm utterly sick of losing friends. But I will be happy for her when the time comes."

"You will be. And then your life will turn over and you will find another path to take. I just realized that I am giving offense, by implying that Georgiana would marry before you."

"No, none of that," I assured him, "put it out of your mind. You were not being offensive but being realistic. Georgiana is most likely to marry first."

He smiled sadly.

"Why are you always so determined to forgive me for anything and everything?"

"Because that's what friends do with each other. Besides, you wouldn't have it any other way."

"No, I would not," he said, looking deeply into my eyes. I returned his gaze of affection with one that was full of strong feeling—however ambiguous that it might appear as.

"We must not become affectionate," I said, "temptation becomes us not."

"It becomes us well. But yes, you are correct."

We were interrupted when we heard footsteps. We both stood up and maintained our duties.

"Soon our luck will run out entirely," I whispered.

"I know," he mouthed when a stableman named Harkins approached us.

"Beggin' your pardon, Colonel and Miss Bennet, but Colonel Fitzwilliam, we've got a spot of bother, sir."

"How large is this worrisome spot, Harkins?"

"It's the new horse that Mr. Darcy purchased, sir. She's gone berserk, and we were wonderin' if maybe she needs to see a more familiar face."

"That's the brown mare that Darcy purchased from the Ibsen residence, correct?"

"Yes, sir."

"That's the one that Darcy bought for Lizzy?" I asked.

"Yes, it is," Colonel Fitzwilliam said, rolling up his shirtsleeves even more. "I'll return soon."

Colonel Fitzwilliam left me in the stable, where I retrieved some more hay for Horace, the horse that I was assisting.

When I finished placing it in front of him, I looked at Horace.

"Any chance you will help me sort out which horseshoes best fits you?" I asked him. He gave me a look and went back to eating. "Ah, the strong and silent type, eh?" I patted his neck. "It's not as good of a look as you would think, Horace."

"What a lovely horse."

I jumped when I heard the voice. Turning around quickly, to the point where I felt my neck ache, I saw Mr. William Price standing in the stable door.

"Sorry," Mr. Price exclaimed, immediately shirking away from the doorway, "I didn't mean to frighten you!"

Placing my hand on my chest, as if that would help my heartbeat lessen, I assured him that I was well.

"You are very light-footed, I declare," I noted, "I didn't hear you at all."

"It's probably the stables," Mr. Price said, "the hay and dirt along the floors makes it easy for my footsteps to go unheard. Sorry, I was walking about the grounds and was directed to see the stables. Miss Crawford has a headache and needed solitude to recover. I thought that I'd take this opportunity."

"Oh, I understand." Immediately, I felt self-conscious. With the dirty, plain clothes that I was wearing, I was not fit to be seen by anyone. "I'm afraid that you do not catch me at my best."

"Your looks are not dampened by your activity. Besides, I would not expect, nor intend for you to be wearing your fanciest gowns when tending to horses."

"Do you like the look of a good horse, sir?" I asked, minding the horseshoes while I spoke with him.

"Visually, yes. But in truth, I know little to nothing about horses. Being a sailor, I wouldn't know a prize stallion from a breeder. This one is named Horace?"

"Yes."

"Good day, Horace," Mr. Price said, bowing, "you are a handsome sort."

"He knows that he is," I said, putting my nose against Horace's. "I am learning about horses myself."

"It might be a lesson that I might have to forego. Besides, in Portsmouth, one does not have to own a horse. No one even has the space to put one."

"And that's where you were born and raised?"

"Yes. Portsmouth is heavily reliant on being a harbor city. Being a sailor was a natural reaction."

"If you don't mind me asking, what does your family in Portsmouth think about Miss Crawford?"

"I haven't fully taken Miss Crawford to see them, but not out of shame for her. Rather, it's the contrary. My father is—well, he means well, but he loves a bottle of whiskey and gin more than is his share."

I put down a horseshoe.

"You are afraid that Miss Crawford would see your background and reconsider choosing you?"

He looked at me, surprised by my inquisitiveness.

"It's a natural fear, Mr. Price."

"Yes," he said, evidently feeling more exposed. "That is the truth."

"Forgive me if I am impertinent."

"No, it is not that. You are perfectly right to ask me. I suppose we all want to show the better sides of ourselves to the person that we love."

"What was it like when you and Miss Crawford first met?"

"For me, it was like being hit by a thunderbolt. Of course, it was different for her. When she first met me, she had a prejudice against the Navy. It was very much NOT her favorite profession."

"And she said that to you?"

"Yes, she was very vocal about her apprehensions toward it."

I sat down on a stool that was against the wall and gave him my undivided attention.

"Perhaps it was because of her experience with her uncle. The Admiral was not the best parent to her, as well as being a terrible influence for her brother, and a difficult husband to his wife."

"That was precisely the reason that she had a disdain for my vocation," he agreed. "I was aware of it soon into making her acquaintance. The delightful thing about my fiancée, besides her beauty and vivacity, is that one always knows how one stands with her. She communicates all to you. Perhaps it was loneliness. Where I came from, women would never stand up with me for a simple dance, because I wasn't even a midshipman. But when going to Mansfield Park, Miss Crawford always talked to me. Even when she did not show love for the Navy, she still found me respectable and was gentle in her criticisms. After all, at least a woman was talking to me, and a handsome one at that. Even though I was a stodgy sailor who was beneath her, I still couldn't help it. I fell in love with her."

"Time has taught me that men can still love women even after disagreements."

"Oh, yes. Some men even have been known to like a challenge." William Price smiled, and his eyes twinkled. "Perhaps I am like that myself. Either way, I fell madly in love with her. Of course, I never told her—I felt that she was just so far above me. In truth, she is. But when I left Mansfield Park, I knew to never voice my feelings. Especially since it was so heavily implied that Mr. Edmund Bertram was also in love with her."

"Mr. Bertram? The one who is now married to your sister?"

"Yes. Fanny."

I leaned back and felt the wonder crawl all over my face.

"Oh, what a tangled web that we weave!"

"I know. Love does make wandering fools of us, doesn't it?"

"Yes, it does. You were in love with a woman, who at the time was being indirectly courted by a man who would go on to marry your sister and is now your brother-in-law. And I suspect does not support your attachment to her?"

William Price's eyes widened at the revelation of this. That was when I think he had considered that for the first time.

William Price rubbed his face, his cheeks becoming a whiter shade of pale.

"I had never thought of that," he noted. "I am, indeed, marrying the woman who my brother-in-law once favored. Naturally, he would take this as a personal attack. But he shouldn't. After all, he was the one to reject Miss Crawford because she tried to resolve the crisis that their siblings incited and didn't weep in a corner."

"Perhaps that doesn't mean anything," I said, "even when we are the ones who do the rejecting, we still feel betrayed when someone chooses the one that we loved. It's vain, selfish and illogical, but true, nonetheless."

"I suppose I never had that thought because Mr. Bertram is happy with Fanny. Besides, my brother-in-law is a clergyman. Such resentment is not something that he should harbor."

His ideal words were quickly done away with, as I saw his expression shift to one that doubted his own words.

"Historically speaking, Mr. Price, clergymen have been known to do things that were a lot worse. They are no more or less human than the rest of us. They are capable of resentment, jealousies, vanity, selfishness, cruelty, and other things. Think of it this way: how often have the ones who spoke the most about love, are the quickest to hate? The ones who preach about acceptance are the first to commit to acts of prejudice and segregation? They are filled with stuffed-up pride with their own words, that they never notice how hypocritical they are. And the whole world is in love with them because they cannot look past the words, the veneer, and see the gorgon that lies underneath. I don't know Mr. Edmund Bertram, but until I meet him, I don't know what manner of man he is. I am determined to believe that he is as human as the rest of us. He simply doesn't know that he is."

Mr. Price chuckled.

"What?" I asked.

"You remind me of my dear Mary now."

"I remind you of Miss Crawford? Me?"

"Yes. That is how she talks about clergymen. She has had too many negative encounters with them to unsee what she had learned of them. Her tone has softened as she has grown, and she understands that it is never good to make mass generalizations. However, I would never censor her right to observe the obvious and comment on the follies of the world."

I clapped for him, and this made him laugh again.

"Good," I said.

"Really?"

"Yes. You don't censor your fiancée's right to see the world for what it is. That is a realistic way of approaching love. We women must not be left in the dark, as many so often wish us to be. If we are, we come to a match incomplete and ill-matched to the man. Why some spouses want that of us, I will never understand."

"I don't either. Maybe that's why I fell in love with her so easily as well. In Portsmouth, if a woman doesn't speak up, then how can anyone hear her?" His eyes turned gentler. "You all need to be heard, don't you?"

"Yes. Be a good listener, Mr. Price. That is the only advice that I can give."

Mr. Price stood up and was about to leave, but I was curious about one other thing.

"There is something else that I have been wondering about," I asserted.

"And what may that be, pray tell?"

"Well, Sir Thomas Bertram is the main one who does not support this match of yours, correct?"

"Yes."

"But he also helped you along, somewhat, by inviting you to Mansfield Park and taking in your sister. But on the opposing side of things, Mr. Henry Crawford had his uncle help you along in your career and gave you advancement. That means, that you are torn between both sides."

He sighed.

"Yes, I am. Believe me, Miss Bennet, I have considered this conflict within myself time and time again."

"So, what is that like for you? To know that you are in both men's debt, but then to not know which one to feel more obliged to."

"It is pure agony. To owe both sides of two parties that are against each other is never delightful. Faith, I had never desired my life to ever get this complicated. After all, how could I? I was born to a lowly family to a port city and became a sailor. I am accustomed to things being simple."

"And then you fell into the path of rich individuals, and now life is complicated?"

"Yes, it is. It makes one wonder if wealth creates more

crises. But that philosophy belongs to a better person than myself. But I will tell you this, when the time came to make it a decision, no matter how agonizing it was, the choice was simple to make."

"Why?"

He chuckled.

"I thought it was obvious. I was naturally on the side that my dear Miss Crawford is on."

"Oh," I said, smiling, "I feel like quite a dunce."

"No, you are not. When the time came to decide who I should stand by, it was her. It will always be her."

"Well, those are very pretty words, and I trust that you will mean them. You seem like the sort."

"I hope that I am."

"You are, of that I am certain. Like you said, wealth brings problems. Since you have had to make a life for yourself, rearing from commonality to a career, you know how to appreciate things. Therefore, this is the only advice that I will give. You have your love, so cherish it. If any events that follow after this do not bring about the happy reunion with your family that you wished, do not let it sour your affection for Miss Crawford. The world has a way of killing true love. I have seen matches where both sides lost respect and affection for each other. I don't want that to happen to either of you."

"You talk by way of someone who has had much experience with witnessing marriages that ended in discord."

I thought of my parents.

"I confess that I have."

"I promise you this... I will not do such. Time has taught me to appreciate good fortune when it comes my way. I will not shy from it, and I stopped being afraid of the world long ago. A byproduct of being on a ship and facing enemy vessels every now and again. The world gets less frightening after that."

"Yes, I suppose that it might. Forgive me if I was presumptuous for offering you advice."

"Not at all. I like a woman with a voice. When you have something wise or compassionate to say, don't be afraid."

We were interrupted by Colonel Fitzwilliam, who entered, wiping down his hands.

～

When seeing Mr. Price, Colonel Fitzwilliam greeted him evenly. Having a notion that his company might not be a most comfortable addition—I think he sensed the bond between Colonel Fitzwilliam and me and didn't wish to feel intrusive—he excused himself and continued to walk about the grounds.

When we were alone, Colonel Fitzwilliam turned to me.

"What did he have to say?" he asked.

"He was told that it would suit him to visit the stables and so he went about it," I said, taking out a brush to tend to Horace's mane.

"And you were alone with him?"

"Yes, but how can one be fully so when in stables when there are plenty of stablemen about?"

I looked at Colonel Fitzwilliam and saw that he looked unnerved.

"And what could that look possibly be about? Why do you look angry?"

"Well, I just think it was something he overlooked. When you are engaged to another lady, it is best not to be alone with another woman, no matter how innocent. It can easily lead to vicious gossip that can prove to be injurious to both parties."

"Well, yes, but..." I was no fool. There was more to his words than simple consideration. "Richard, are you becoming irrationally jealous?"

"No!" He blurted out.

I didn't believe him, by a wide margin. Unable to control myself, I began to laugh hysterically.

"Kitty, this is not funny."

"Yes, it is! You just are from the receiving end of this situation and cannot see the humor of it!"

"Well, I..."

"Yes?"

"I..."

"Yes?"

He leaned against the wall.

"Oh, lord, I am a fool."

"If it will help, do you want to know what we spoke of? You cannot repeat it, but I am willing to share with you. Besides, I would like to talk about it."

"It will help me, if you would be so kind."

"Very well, o' irrational one!"

I told him everything and we spent an hour talking of the matter. Thank goodness for the complicated lives of others; they always give us observers something to talk about.

Chapter Seventeen

KITTY'S TALE: FAMILY

After writing down the events of the day in my journal, the sun was setting. After supper, I asked to retire early, for the sake of working more on my journal entries.

I was allowed this, bathed when done, put my hair in curling paper, and sat down at my desk in my nightgown. When I finished writing down my conversations with Finlay and Fitzwilliam, I had a sudden thought.

Uncle Philips!

He had warned me about receiving the attentions of both men before, and here I was, in the same predicament that he had foretold that I would be in.

I hadn't written to him and Aunt Philips for three weeks, and that felt like an eternity.

Sitting down, I began to write to them both, explaining the events that took place there—with the exception of Henry Crawford's history.

When I got to the part where I wrote to Uncle Philips, I wrote most expressly about my situation:

> You shall recall, good uncle, the discussion that we had earlier of the dilemma that I was undergoing. Unable to resist such amiable company, I decided to befriend both parties.
> This has altogether left me to a place that, at first, I was satisfied

with. But now, I wonder, do I do more harm than good by being in both of their lives? For so long, I only thought of how my torn heart made me appear, but now I wonder if it was done out of selfishness. I didn't want to lose their company, for they are part of the highlights of my life. I feel my character developing even more than ever, but not out of a deranged dependence on either gentleman—it is the experiences that have augmented my view of life. When my views expand, so do I.

But now I wonder if I distract them from moving on. It is to the point where I cannot help but wonder if the true antagonist to this story is myself? However, where would I go? To remove myself from their company, I would have to return to Longbourn.

Yet you, Aunt Philips and I know the truth: if I return, mama will want to marry me off. And when she cannot do that, I will only be sent back to Pemberley anyway, so that I can be married off again.

In truth, I have nowhere to go to remove myself from their company. Also, would it make me look weak to run away in such a manner? I would look painfully delicate. Outside of a cough and occasional runny nose, I don't like appearing as being so very fragile. That is one of the chief problems with the predicament of being a lady: we cannot go anywhere that we like...and therefore, we cannot help any situation, because we cannot run to it or run from it.

Now, I find that to be monstrously unfair.

But what should I do? My attention to them is provocative, insofar that it leads them to put their lives on hold. I don't have the right. But I cannot hurt them by abandoning them. Such fortitude is beyond me.

Knock, knock, knock!

I jumped at the sound of it.

"Come in, Lizzy," I said, wrapping my shawl around myself.

The door opened and Elizabeth entered.

"I just came to see how you were," she said, closing the door behind her.

"Thought my cough returned?" I joked.

"Nonsense. Your cough *always* returns, therefore, I learned not to inquire after that."

When she approached me, she sat down uneasily, and I helped her into the chair.

"Is it the baby?" I asked.

"Yes, it is. Our gowns hide it, but I am beginning to show. Jane is as well. I'm not used to having a stomach of this size, feeling disconcerted and imbalanced, or suffering from morning sickness."

"Oh, you have had to purge in the mornings?"

"Yes."

I looked at her stomach.

"You and Jane are going to be mothers," I said, "I cannot believe that. Well, with Jane I can, for she has had to be motherly since she was old enough to tend to us. After all, mama needed Jane to accept the maternal role sometimes. Do you think raising us drove mama to distraction?"

"No, we are not to blame ourselves on that score. Mama is mama, papa is papa, and that is beyond our influence. I am glad that Jane and Bingley are staying before settling in at Godfrey Park. My new situation has led me to appreciating my family being around me more."

I grinned.

"You like me being here. Admit it!"

She rolled her eyes.

"When did I say that I didn't?"

"You didn't say it, but you also never did say it either. Elizabeth, verbal encouragement is nice to hear every now and again."

"Well, hopefully it will help where I have bruised your pride. I came to inquire after you. I was worried."

Seeing that she was serious, I let my jesting tone fall away and I chewed the inside of my cheek.

"Worried about me?"

"Well, these days have proven to be very interesting."

"You think I cannot swallow such serious subject matter as what we are living through? On the contrary, I am very interested to see how this all turns out."

"Oh, I know that all too well. You seem to be just as interested in this all as I am."

"Are you ever worried that the excitement or the provocative experiences that lay ahead might be too much for you... and for the baby?"

"Kitty, you know very well, that my courage rises with every attempt to intimidate me. Any tumultuous events that lay ahead will not overwhelm me." She touched her stomach. "I promise, I am thinking of the child. Nothing will hurt it, but the illnesses that affect the child when it is born." She looked ahead. "I hope that nothing goes wrong with it. And that, if it's a boy, it looks like Darcy."

"What if he looks like you?"

She gave me a faux dramatic look.

"Good lord, let us hope not. I would love him but never forgive myself."

Elizabeth turned to me, and the candle augmented her looks.

"Do you know," I said, "with that look in your eye, and with that maternal glow about you, you are lovelier than Jane now."

"You tease me."

"Indeed, I do not tease you. It is true."

"Well, I thank you. Now, I keep being deterred from my purpose. When I said that I came here to discuss stressful situations, I wasn't talking of the Crawfords or Mr. Price. I was referring to your situation with Lieutenant Finlay and Colonel Fitzwilliam."

~

How startling as well as unnerving.

When it came to my dilemma and difficulties in my love life, I was aware that Lizzy was fully aware of it. However, she was never the main one that I spoke about it to. Rather than speak to others about it, I always talked directly to the men whom it concerned, or mostly with Georgiana. Therefore, to have Eliza come and inquire after me brought on another experience to something that forever haunted me.

"Actually," I said, "you visit me at the precise time that I was mulling over the matter."

I raised up the letter.

"I was writing to Uncle Philips about it."

Elizabeth's expression was dubious.

"You write to our uncle about the two gentlemen?"

"Of course, I do. I have always been closer to him than father. Often, he has given me advice about the men that I have met."

"Well, I suppose that it does make sense. After all, him being a man does give him more experience on the matter than ourselves."

"Precisely."

"But Kitty, I would have thought that the nearest gentlemen in your acquaintance would be the first ones that you go to? Mr. Darcy is very wise when it comes to dissembling the characters in his own sex. Why not ever ask him anything?"

"You think that I don't care for Mr. Darcy's opinion?" I questioned, surprised.

"Nonsense, I know that you respect him. I just wonder if you have achieved the proper comfort around him. He would like it if you did."

Well, this was a rum business! How easy it is to cause offense where no offense was intended, nor even bestowed. I had no idea that I was not being attentive to the one who took me into his home.

"I never knew that I was showing a callous disregard for him," I said. "Have I hurt Mr. Darcy? You must understand that it is hard to even notice such a thing."

"He knows not to take it personally."

"Eliza, it is just that...he is so visually overpowering and impressive. I never even noticed that my not speaking to him about my stressful situation was trying to him."

"At first, he was happy with how you dealt with this all, and he is proud of you. But, when it comes to the master of the house, we have often talked about your situation. I think he merely wishes for you to tell him what you are feeling or which man that you are leaning towards."

"Would it help if I were to tell you, for this one time, and you can relay what I have been thinking?"

"It will. It's actually a nice start, and he might even prefer it that way."

"Then," I said, mischief in my eyes, "you are his spy?"

"You may call me that," Elizabeth replied, sparkling, "if that gives you comfort."

"Very well. Here is where my heart and mind stand."

Elizabeth turned to me, alert and eager.

"First," I began, "when I write to Uncle Philips, I should inform you that I have specifically written to ask for our uncle's help in understanding how I am feeling. I have not written about Henry Crawford's true history, and I would prefer if none of us told anyone in Hertfordshire about that."

"You are proposing that we avoid the truth?"

"No, I do not do it for a cowardly desire to hide reality," I said, "but because it's in the past. It cannot be changed now, altered, or undone. But what is a more recent history is that the Crawfords did come to our assistance when we needed a family to make us look more respectable, under the shadow of Lydia's scandal. We had the right to rise above the disaster that Lydia caused, therefore..."

"Why can't they?" Elizabeth finished my sentence.

"Precisely."

Elizabeth looked away from me and at the other wall.

"Because it is in the past," Elizabeth repeated my words, "it cannot be changed now, altered or undone..."

"Why are you being like Echo right now?" I asked, referring to the Greek legendary character who spent her immortality repeating everyone's words.

She blinked, coming out of her own musings.

"Oh, sorry. It's nothing. Pray, continue."

"But it all goes back to that," I said. "Their time coming to see us, at Longbourn, when all seemed lost. Recalling when Mary and Mr. Crawford visited us, just to assist us, still endeared me to the notion that it would be best if Hertfordshire was ignorant of his history. I preferred it to be better known that ignorance could be bliss, in this case. But either way, you must understand, Lizzy, Uncle Philips is family. He's always been there for me, and I will not forget it. Therefore, I value his advice about what I am undergoing now."

"Well, you were quite close to him. I found that I never could feel any sort of attachment to him."

"It was the same with Aunt Philips as well."

"They naturally endeared themselves to you and Lydia, in either case. And not myself."

"Well, it is only natural, because they preferred bubbling company. You sparkle, but you never flitted about the way that Lydia and I did. They like spirited natures, while you and Jane were more serious and sedate. And in their defense, you often do not indicate any sign of missing them."

"I suppose that I did not find their company to be the sort to fit at Pemberley."

"And you call me the offensive one?" I asked. "They are family, Elizabeth. Well, I can see how inviting them might be trying to Mr. Darcy, but I cannot remove myself from my family's company just because they are not exceedingly dull and speak only of the weather. Our family is a set of people with open tempers. If people can't suffer others, because they cannot bear to be acquainted with a little absurdity, then they are too squeamish for my tastes. So yes, I do miss them."

"Very well. It is natural to do so. Besides, I am no different. Often, I do miss the Gardiners."

"Oh, the Gardiners!" I cried. "It has been too long since we have seen them!"

"It has. I miss them terribly. I had hopes of inviting them to Pemberley for this festive season, but Lady Catherine had no choice but to take precedence." She looked glum, and for good reason. "Therefore, all the comforts of home must be abandoned, to bear a company of people to an estate where I will have to suffer the strictures and dominance of a woman who still hasn't forgiven me for marrying her nephew."

"Well... Merry Christmas, eh?"

"Yes. Whether it be merry is another matter entirely." Elizabeth smiled gently and her eyes relaxed. "I am such a hypocrite."

"How so?"

"Well, I cast aspersions at Aunt and Uncle Philips, but then I visit a woman whose behavior is worse. And who I had to suffer once feeling the inferiority of my connections when it came to my husband. Did you know that, when the Gardiners and I first toured Pemberley, I almost regretted not accepting Mr. Darcy's initial proposal, until I had one thought?"

"And what was that?"

"That if I accepted his hand, I would not be able to invite the Gardiners to Pemberley. Because my uncle was a tradesman, they were regarded as beneath my husband's family, and I would not have been able to invite them. They would have been lost to me. That led to me regretting nothing."

"Until Mr. Darcy appeared on the grounds and surprised you three."

"Yes."

Elizabeth went on to reminisce, and she told me a story that I had known before. Yet, the mixture of being in the throes of maternity made her add more details that she did not tell before. And I just sat there, listening happily, for how she and Mr. Darcy finally fell in love always seemed like a good story to hear. And her original reason for coming, to talk about my heart being torn in two, fell to the wayside and was all but forgotten.

I was not upset at all.

Since she had been wrapped up in her own tellings, Elizabeth didn't know that she had spent such a long time sitting up with me.

The hour grew late, and Sarah and Betsy came in, supplying all the huff and hullabaloo that they always exerted whenever they entered a room.

"Mrs. Darcy!" Betsy cried. "What are you doing up this late?"

"Aye, you little minx," Sarah added, "you ought to be in bed, resting. If your mother was here, she would censure us and call us bad nurses."

"We are not nurses, and don't call her a minx."

"Oh, she knows what I mean. Stop being so puritanical."

"Who are you to call me puritanical?" Betsy declared, taking

Lizzy's arm, and helping her up. "You, who still won't allow a man to kiss you under an overcast of mistletoe."

"I don't like it when men bully me by way of a plant," Sarah responded, "even if it is a holy one. I prefer to have the choice. Now, come Mrs. Darcy. Ignore the gorgon who holds your other arm."

"Who are you calling gorgon, you minotaur!"

"If I am a minotaur, then you are a kraken!"

"Ladies, please," Elizabeth chided them as they escorted her out. "This is Pemberley. If you are going to war with each other, remember yourselves... and quarrel in the kitchens. There is a time and place for everything. Do it behind closed doors."

Ah, Sarah and Betsy. When they would go to live at Godfrey Park, to tend to Jane, they would be sorely missed.

Chapter Eighteen

KITTY'S TALE: FRIENDS & DEPARTURES

Once more, I woke up well before sunrise.

This time, the dream had lasted a little longer. The fairytale world had returned in my subconscious, and I found myself walking through the same land that I had invented before.

Yet, this time, I was not alone.

Every time that I turned a corner, moved past a tree, along a stream, or past a boulder, I saw the flitting of a figure. Sometimes it was a petticoat. Other times it was a man's leg. It was always just close enough to see most of their figure, and I was able to dissemble the identity of which.

Sometimes, it was Elizabeth I saw, moving away from me.

Other times, it was Mr. Darcy.

Then it was Jane, my parents, Lydia, and the Philipses.

Afterwards, I saw the backs of Diana Long and Maria Lucas. Their hair wasn't pulled up but fell down to their backs as they always seemed to be outracing me.

I ran around a tree and bush, trying to catch up with them, then at last I came to a clearing.

There, on the other side of the glade, I saw Georgiana's back.

"Georgie," I uttered to myself.

Soon, she ran through the holly trees, finding her way down an invisible path that eluded me.

Dashing along the branches, I followed her.

What were they all running to? What did they see that I didn't?

Georgiana's figure was the most prominent when it came to disappearing just ahead of me, behind a thick set of elms.

"Come," I heard her say, "why can't you see it?"

I ran faster.

And still, I could not catch up to her swift foot.

To my left, I saw Mr. Darcy's figure, as he was following Lizzy.

Afterwards, I saw the side of Jane and Bingley as they disappeared behind a set of rocks that framed a small waterfall.

And Enara and Arthur as they were behind me. But each time I turned, I only saw their hands, clasped in each other's, as they moved behind some trees.

Afterwards, I saw Mary's and Mr. Atkins's legs as they dashed along a thick set of redwoods. The leaves fell around them, obscuring their faces.

Everyone was clear and both unclear. I knew that they were there, but I could not see them. But they moved along, heedless of the distance that was placed between us.

But I still followed Georgiana, wondering how far she would get before she would forget me, or not care that I had fallen behind.

Until I heard her voice again.

"Come," I heard her words along the air. "Come and find it."

Find what? What was I missing?

Then I woke up again. Rolling over, I dug my face in my pillow, trying to cling to the dream once more. This time, the details were no longer hazy. I had remembered every moment of it.

After breakfast, all of us ladies were sitting in the parlor while the men went hunting along the grounds, in hopes of bagging many birds.

"What is Godfrey Park like?" Mrs. Grant asked Jane, who must have told her about it.

"Oh, it is not as grand as Pemberley," Jane said, "but it is a very comfortable home."

"Indeed, it is," Miss Crawford said, "it is a handsome house, truly. The Granvilles loss is your gain. And it cannot be in better hands than Mr. Bingley's."

"You've been to Godfrey Park?" Jane asked, interested.

"Yes, I have. For a time, I was friends with Sir Thomas Granville's daughter and visited the estate a couple of times. Time drew distance between us. The grounds were lovely, but I recall the house having a tense way about its look. When the time comes, you might take an interest in changing some of the rooms that would suit the look of a family with children."

"It did lack a feeling of comfort," Georgiana noted. "When we visited, it obviously did lack a cheery disposition to it."

"Bingley will like to add his hand to it," Jane said, "while I might be too exhausted," she said, placing her hand over her stomach, "I still am far from objecting to trying my hand at decorating. What suggestions would any of you have?"

"Oh, I am not the best judge on the matter," Miss Crawford said, "when it comes to decorations, I always defer to the judgement of my betters. However, there is one idea I have always had, but it is not fashionable."

"What is that?" Jane asked.

"Color schemes should be particular to each room. What I mean is that one room's main color scheme should be blues. The next room should be green. Then the room afterwards could be yellows, and then it continues that way, to oranges/browns, then red, and then purples."

"Oh, the color scheme concept," Enara said, excited. "That is a splendid idea. In New South Wales, there is one family who has a blue room, where the entire room has blue chinaware and cushions. She is praised for that room in the whole of the village. But for a whole house to be that way... now that is unique."

"I like it," Jane said, becoming animated as she clapped her hands together. "Oh, I think I find that idea to be so very interesting. I must ask Mr. Bingley. I think he would also be interested. Also, it is a very different sort of idea."

"Yes, it is novel," Elizabeth said, "I wouldn't be surprised if the fashion gazettes catch wind of the idea and soon, we see rooms in the ton composed of the same style."

"Then that means," Miss Crawford said, "that I actually had a good idea when it came to interior design. Who would have known?"

"Why do you sound so surprised?" Jane asked. "You are clever."

"I make it a habit of being clever in word use, but I have never been a ready wit in upholstery. I have often been heard saying that if I ever were to have a house redecorated, I would hire someone and wouldn't look at it again until it was done."

"You changed without even knowing it," Elizabeth said. "Oh well, there is nothing for it now. You must have to accept that about yourself."

"Yes, I suppose that I must."

~

To entertain us, Georgiana played a bit of music. Next, she and Elizabeth performed a duet.

Jane, Miss Crawford, and Mrs. Grant sat down together and began to go over ideas for the interior designs for Godfrey Park.

Enara and Elizabeth, wishing to sew, sat together, and discussed Rosings Park.

That left Georgiana and I to sit down to a game of backgammon. This suited me well, because it gave me a chance to get my mind away from thinking about the dreams that I had been having.

Left to our own devices, Georgiana and I were enjoying the simple game, when Lucy entered.

"Miss Darcy," Lucy said, "I come bearing a letter for you."

"Oh, thank you, Lucy."

Lucy handed the letter to Georgiana and looked at the game.

"Who is winning?" she asked.

"Georgiana is." I grunted. "She always is."

"Never fear, Miss Bennet. You will win one, one day."

"Thank you, Lucy. But I'm used to defeat, at this point."

She left us as Georgiana read the sender's name on the front of the envelope.

"Who is it from?" I asked.

"It's from Emma Watson."

~

When hearing the name, Georgiana looked at me apprehensively.

"No need to worry on my account," I assured her. "I have stopped being possessive when it comes to our friendship. I am happy that you and she are reconnecting."

"I will finish the game and read the letter later."

"Nonsense. Letters can easily be urgent and sometimes they ought to be read as soon as possible. We can resume the game when you are finished."

"Thank you," Georgiana said. She opened the envelope eagerly and began to read its contents while I played with my bracelets. Sometimes I wondered if I wore too many of them.

"Oh," Georgiana said, "actually, the letter's contents are general. I'll read it to you."

"It might be in confidence."

"Not at all. It's a letter that speaks of journeys and pursuits. That's something that you and I know much about."

She raised up the letter and began to read:

> Dear Georgiana,
>
> I trust that you are well, dear friend. The more that we write, the more that I cherish the past that we share. I suppose that it has to do with a matter of familiarity. You represent the past and better times. I think the memory of it all warms my heart because of the upcoming journey that draws near.
>
> Soon into the new year, I shall undertake a lengthy journey back home, to Australia. I fear the expectations of returning home and feeling as if I am sojourning to the unknown. What if my family does

not feel any kindred spirit toward me? After all, I return home penni-
less and with no prospects. But when gone for so long, it is not as much
to do with a lack of economy as it is a lack of binding ties. I was raised
by my aunt, and therefore, that is where my heart is. I wonder that,
when going back home, I will mean anything to them but merely be a
burden.

But I am determined to make the most of this experience. When I
do return home, I shall endeavor to make myself as indispensable as
possible. I was not raised to be so fine a creature that I never learned
anything of value. I was taught to be of use, so hopefully that will be
enough.

On January 12th, I book passage on The Lilia, but I do not travel
alone. It turns out that Mr. Howard and Mr. Osbourne also have
booked passage, due to some land that the Osbournes have purchased
in Sydney. Therefore, I will have company.

I also confess to being somewhat curious in one regard. The Lilia's
crew are said to be legendary. They are the most popular commercial
ship along the seas, and are a legend both in Britain, Australia, and
America. Even the French allow them entry into their country, no
matter what conflict we have with them. I don't know what about
this crew makes them special, but we shall see.

Soon, we will be parted by many oceans. Pray that my journey
back home proves to not be fraught with danger.

I will miss you, dear friend. Your correspondence has been one of
the better highlights of my return to this part of the country.

Yours etc.
EW

When Georgiana closed the letter, she looked at me.

"Travels along the high seas," I said, "a perilous journey."

"Yes, it is. But her family is there, and it is her best chance."

"Yes. Now that I have more time to reflect on her situation, it
must be very hard indeed. To be raised by a doting aunt and
uncle, only to be torn from them by a second marriage and was
given no fortune to help her on. Then she goes to visit the
Edwards, to find that everything has changed utterly, and just

when she was getting used to her changed life, now things have to change again. And then for her to be separated from you by oceans. You probably became one of the few stable elements in her life."

"Well," Georgiana said, "I am glad to have helped. To be of use...have you ever had that feeling? Being of use."

"Yes, I have."

Suddenly, a thought came to me. I squinted.

"I just had a thought," I said, then I turned to Enara. "Mrs. Philips?"

"Yes, Kitty," Enara said, lowering her sewing.

"What ship are you taking back to Australia?"

"The Lilia."

Georgiana and I looked in between each other, amazed at the coincidence.

"The Lilia," I echoed.

"Is there something curious about that?" Enara asked.

"It is my friend, Miss Emma Watson," Georgiana said, "she books passage to New South Wales, on The Lilia, on January 12th."

"Yes, that's the ship. The time was changed on us, and it was moved to the 12th. And no wonder, for it is a very popular commercial vessel."

"How so?" Georgiana asked. "Emma writes to me about her ignorance behind The Lilia's fame. It has sparked my interest."

"Well, you may write to your friend about the real reason, for that's one of the few things that I am an expert on. The Lilia is regarded as the most exotic ship along the seas, due to its crew."

"What about the crew?" I asked.

"The crew comes from everywhere. And ladies are a part of it."

"Ladies are a part of the crew?" Georgiana asked, curiously. "How is that possible?"

"From what I have been told," Enara said, "it all started simply enough. Men worked as sailors on the ship. Then the captain allowed a couple of them to bring their wives aboard. This led to them proving to be resourceful, and soon, they became a part of the crew. That eventually led to a trend of just accepting female crew members, in the general sense."

"And they come from all parts of the world?" I asked, interested in her other point.

"Yes. The captain is said to be Canadian American and was born in Quebec. His second in command, is from the United States. Two of the ship-hands are also Indians from some tribes, or some place or the other in the states. Then there are other parts of the crew that are from Wales, Mexico, Spain, India, France, Australia, Germany, and Japan."

"Japan?" Georgiana and I echoed.

"Yes. That's the rumor at least. But since those rumors align with many others, I suppose that it must be true. The Lilia is also said to be one of the largest ships that has ever been seen. I suppose that it would have to be to store sailors with their wives, as well as being able to transport a certain amount of boarders."

"How many boarders?" I asked.

"They prefer to take on no more than twenty," Enara answered, "The reason for such is because the Lilia makes berth at other countries before its final destination to Australia. For example, it stops off at France first, collects more travelers. Sometimes they also arrive in Portugal, then Spain, then Greece, then Italy. This time, they are said to also make berth in Egypt. I suppose that some amateur explorers must be wishing to stop there. Afterwards, we sail between Egypt and Asia, and out into the open Indian Ocean. That's where the journey becomes more overpowering. You won't see land for weeks. But you do get to see some occasional aquatic life. For example, on my way to Britain, I saw a family of whales."

We all lit up.

"Truly?" Mary Crawford asked.

"Yes. I did. It was one of the most impressive things that I ever saw in my entire life. I could try to explain it, but it would not do the scene justice. All that I can say is that the ocean is part of the reason that I could imagine the Greeks thought there were sea monsters who were brought up by the gods to overpower them. In my eyes, the ocean is the one part of the world that humanity can never have any control over. While the water is the most impressive thing in the world, there is something daunting about the experience."

"Yes, there is. That is another reason why it was never a favorite profession of mine for so long. It is such a dangerous path for a man to take. The sea has a way of swallowing men up. When I expressed this to Mr. Price, he understood my apprehensions on the matter, but he said something that led to me understanding his point of view."

"What did he say?" Jane asked.

"He said that the sea calls out to man for a few reasons. We all think that it's because the sea helps us protect our lands, and it does. Britain's naval strength is vital to our country's influence. But that's not why we go to it, despite all its perils. The sea cries out to us because it offers new horizons and other worlds. Worlds we have the right to walk upon, for better or worse. But the walk, the searching of it, is the main thing. Because many of us are not wishing to always sit still and do nothing. Difference calls out to us, and the sea takes us there. Well, I no longer was able to despise a profession that had an attitude that was similar to mine."

We all looked at each other but was not certain how we could say anything as profound as that.

Thankfully, we were spared the trouble when suddenly, the door opened, and Colonel Fitzwilliam entered.

Despite all the delights that can come from members of the same sex interacting, when the opposite gender enters, it cannot help but stir interest.

Colonel Fitzwilliam's appearance raised our spirits, especially since he brought a natural energy about him.

"Colonel," Elizabeth greeted him, about to stand up.

"No, please," he said, "do not take the pains of troubling yourself on my account. Please remain seated, and rest as much as you can."

"Sir, I am with child, but not infirm," Elizabeth jested.

Colonel Fitzwilliam chuckled.

"Yes, I know. But I still cannot help but sound like a worry-wort."

"Very well. Worry away. You come to join us, or do you come as a messenger."

"A messenger, but I do not convey the news that I would wish. I have received word from the war office, and I am wanted in London immediately. I must leave within a couple hours' time."

I sat there, frozen from shock.

"You are to leave us?" I blurted out, without thinking.

Colonel Fitzwilliam turned to me, heavily.

"Yes, I fear that I must. One of my officers defected and was caught in the process. As a result, I must return and hear out his trial before punishment is executed."

"He will be flogged, won't he?" I asked.

"Yes, he most likely will. But if the conditions prove that he was coerced, then maybe I can do something. Some of my lieutenants are a little old-fashioned in their ways and believe that cruelty toward the lesser ranks is a way of keeping them in order. I must go and access the facts before judgement is carried out without my authority."

"If it turns out that he was unjustly treated," Jane asked, "is there anything you can do? I hope there is."

"And so do I. However, sometimes the law is not interested in proper justice as much as maintaining order. It's the age-old philo-sophical debate of it being better to be feared than adored. But I am rambling to stall and delay my time here. I must prepare for depar-ture. Mrs. Darcy, can you do me the honor of telling my cousin that I am arranging for all my luggage to be packed away and could he be so kind as to prepare a carriage to convey me to London forthwith?"

"Yes, I can have Mrs. Reynolds arrange everything."

"Thank you."

Colonel Fitzwilliam gave me one last and longing look.

What do you say when a departure is so abrupt, and you were not given the time that was needed to sort out your farewells? Then again, when are goodbyes ever properly phrased? Only in fairytales do people know how to say farewell. Only in the happiest of books, and the most fantastic. But reality is not of the fantastical sort.

Reality is awkward.

It is inconvenient.

So, all that I could do was stare back.

Our eyes locked and we knew that we could say nothing, because we were not in the proper place, at the proper time, to say anything. Nothing could be said.

All that we had was that look. That all too brief look, while also being a long and lingering one. When it came to him and me, time was relative. It seemed to exist in another dimension entirely.

He was sad.

He was hopeful.

He was a man in love.

I was sad.

I was hopeful.

I was a woman's heart that had been torn in two, by love.

We had one thing that unified us, besides our consistent affection: we knew the heart and soul of each other.

He knew that I would miss him.

Also, he knew that he would miss me.

This cemented my suspicions even more, that my company soon would be the last thing that he needed.

Having no choice, he took his eyes off me, excused himself, and went to pack his belongings.

When the door closed behind him, I breathed in heavily, with my eyes closed.

When I opened them again, I saw everyone looking at me. To conceal this, they all looked at their laps and pretended to either become very occupied with their sewing or their fingernails.

Never one to ignore the obvious, I rested my head on my palm, closing my eyes in frustration.

"Yes, I know," I said, "I know, I know, I know."

"You said it," Elizabeth pointed out, "not us."

"Well," Mrs. Grant said. "We were thinking it though."

"Yes," Mary Crawford chuckled. "I know that I was."

~

Elizabeth called for Mrs. Reynolds, who informed Mr. Darcy and arranged for the carriage to be prepared.

While Colonel Fitzwilliam's luggage was being placed into the coach, we all emerged to offer him our sincerest farewells.

"Well, what more can be said?" Colonel Fitzwilliam acknowledged, "I came and exited your lives with all the abruptness of a jumping rabbit."

We all laughed at that, and the dear Colonel did not spend one moment making his farewell uncomfortable, so he moved down our line, to say something unique to us.

First, he approached Mr. Darcy and Elizabeth.

"I promise I shall return before the baby is born," Colonel Fitzwilliam said. "But until then," he turned to Darcy. "I know that you will protect our ladies and always keep them safe."

"I will," Darcy said. "Come back when you can."

"I know. And give my regards to our aunt. Tell her that I wished to be there for Christmas. My life is simply not my own to rule over. And do your best to weather her lectures."

"I will," Elizabeth said.

Next, he approached Jane and Bingley.

"Godfrey Park is a great estate. You are the proper tenants for it."

"You are too kind," Mr. Bingley said. "Good luck, Colonel."

Then he moved to Arthur Philips and Enara.

"I will not see you both again for some years, will I?"

"No," Arthur said, "Colonel, this is a parting that will not be remedied for quite some time."

"I hope that your journey is safe, you are happy, and that you come back to see us one day."

"May the winds and the waves be with us," Enara said. "If so, we will return, for you all have welcomed us so very much. I thank you, Colonel, for helping me feel like family."

Next, he turned to the Crawfords, Mrs. Grant and Mr. Price.

"Mr. Price, we are men of action and belong to King and

country," Colonel Fitzwilliam said. "True love is hard to find. Be a good husband."

"I will, sir."

He turned to Mary Crawford.

"Miss Crawford, I believe that all will turn out well, for marriage brings about olive branches more than it brings breaches. I believe that you will be very happy. But remember, when we servants to our service come home, we are exhausted." He smirked. "Don't immediately bombard Mr. Price with household questions as soon as he gets into the doorway. Give him an hour to breathe, bathe, and then he will remember how to be a gentleman again."

"Dear Colonel," Miss Crawford said, taking his hand as he kissed her palm. "That is advice that I know how to keep. You are one of the few people that I have ever met that I could bear to receive a lecture from. What a rare gift."

"I miss you already," Mrs. Grant said.

"Mrs. Grant, would that all older sisters were like you."

Then the Colonel turned to Henry Crawford.

"Mr. Crawford, these next few days will be trying for you, but you and I both know that it's something you need to experience."

"There is much that can be said about me," Mr. Crawford said, "self-awareness was usually not one of them. But I daresay, that an old dog can learn new tricks."

"Especially since you are not very old."

"Yes, I suppose I am not."

"Well, for what it is worth, I believe that you are very much improved from the man that you once were. But this is the advice I give, and you will take heed to it: you have your goodness now. Keep it. My family's reputation depends upon it. I am very protective of my family's reputation."

Both men looked on each other and they spoke the same language.

The message was received.

"I understand," Mr. Crawford said.

"I'm certain that you do."

At last, Colonel Fitzwilliam reached me.

Now was the time to know what to say.

"I—" I said.

"I—" Colonel Fitzwilliam said at the same time.

"Oh, you can speak first."

"Nay, you can speak first."

"Oh."

"Oh. Yes. Yes."

Well, this was a disaster, wasn't it?

"Mr. Darcy," Mr. Crawford said, in a way that caught all our attention. "Might I say that I have never seen a better coach and matching horses in the set before? This is a most handsome gig."

"Thank you," Mr. Darcy said, not understanding what Mr. Crawford was attempting to do. However, Lizzy was better at picking up on such cues.

"To show it to best advantage," Elizabeth suggested, "Everyone, come around to this side of the carriage. This is the best way to see the true good breeding of the horses. This one, Phillipa, is one of our sincerest pride and joy."

All obeyed her and moved to the other side of the carriage. Once they were a short distance away, Colonel Fitzwilliam and I looked at each other, amused.

"Well, that helps somewhat," I noted.

"It helps a great deal."

"Yes, I suppose it does."

"We were making a right mess of this farewell, weren't we?"

"It's not our fault."

"This is complicated. I come into your life, then I fall out of it, then I rush in again, and then leave before I said that I would. I have not been fair to you, have I, my Kitty?"

"I am no better," I said.

"How so?"

"I linger."

"You do not linger," he stressed, "And I want this to be rightly understood. I always know where you are. I know how to find you. And I am *the one* who seeks you out. So does Finlay. It is just our way, and we cannot help ourselves. We thank you for forgiving us. We know that it is not easy."

213

"Thank you. I would like it if you had stayed for the holidays, but yes, your life is not your own. Neither is mine for that matter. I shall tell your cousin how I am through it all, and he can convey my situation in his letters to you. After all, we cannot write to each other."

His eyes shifted back and forth when he came upon a happy thought.

"Actually, why can't we?"

"You know why! A lady cannot write to a gentleman."

"Yes, a lady cannot. But that's not what we are now, in theory. For now, we are, through marriage, cousins. What is so very improper about cousins writing to each other?"

I thought about this, and it did make sense. I had to ask Mr. Darcy about it, because I didn't want to do anything false under his nose, but it made all the sense in the world.

"Yes," I agreed, "what is improper about that? We are family now, and family can always write to the other. I shall tell Darcy and Lizzy, and you ought to write to them to let them know that you will do the same. But I should like to write to you. I want you to know how I am always feeling."

"And I want you to know that I am not in the way of forgetting you."

"Colonel Fitzwilliam would not be who he is if he did that."

"If things had been different, Kitty. If I was rich, and you had not met Finlay first, would you have chosen me?"

My stomach had turned to lead, and my arms hung about me as if they were branches bearing dead fruit. I felt so helpless, so empathetic to his poor state, that I could not bear to hurt him. But even by helping him, I hurt him, because of leading him on.

"If I tell you this now," I insisted, "you must carry it with you as a pleasant memory, and not as one that will drag down your chances in life. You must go out and live, right to the fullest."

"I will."

"Yes," I answered, "Once my wandering feet would have been prepared to be a wife, I would have married you. And I would have been the better for it."

His eyes grew misty from the emotion that was stirring up with them.

"That was all that I needed to hear."

At last, he had to leave. Therefore, he climbed into the carriage, it took off and we watched him as it drove down the lane.

When it disappeared from sight, we all entered the house, and removed our outerwear.

As I handed my shawl to Mrs. Reynolds, Georgiana came up to me.

"You look broken," she whispered.

"It's because I am," I said, my voice equally as low.

"Do as I say now."

"What?"

"Do not go to Lambton today and see Finlay. Please, give Richard one day before you go somewhere, and swing from one heartstring to another."

"Don't worry," I said, "I know the right way to act now."

"I know that you do. I just had to check. Go upstairs and rest. Soon, you may have a headache, or you will want to be alone, at the very least. I will make the excuse for you."

I looked at her, grateful.

"You are one of the best friends I have ever had. Is that not funny?"

"It makes sense, in the grand scheme of life."

Doing as she bid, I went upstairs, went to my room, wrote my feelings down and laid down in my bed. Eventually, Lucy came to my room to check on me and she had some water brought up for me to drink.

When she set the pitcher down, she looked at me.

"How are you?" she asked.

"Ever feel like, no matter what happens in life, you will always be chasing down something and it will be just out of your reach?"

"I'm a servant. Of course, I have."

She walked to the door.

"Emotionally, that's precisely where I live, to be honest."

She closed the door behind her.

And I did get a headache.

~

Walking through a wonderland...

Walking through a dreamworld...

Walking amongst the fairytale...

I had found my way to the woods, hills, and trees, that the sun never stopped shining on.

This time, my eyes opened to me looking down and being wet from my thighs downward. All around me, water was flowing along as I found myself in the midst of a pleasant stream.

How refreshing and exhilarating it felt to have the water flowing all around my legs, wetting my gown. Though, it was no nuisance at all. Rather, the water was warm, and it rallied my spirits, as opposed to making them freeze.

Looking down, I saw an occasional school of fish swimming along in the direction that the stream was flowing. Following their progression, I looked around and saw, from my placement on higher ground, that further along, the stream met with a winding river that escaped over the horizon.

Letting out a laugh, I threw caution to the winds.

All was safe here.

There was no chance for society to press its faces upon me and dare cry out 'impropriety'. There was no room, in the vastness of this world, for ugly words and limited views. The stuffiness of a drawing room had no place here, among true nature. True nature at its finest and fullest.

Thus, who was here to judge me? Not a soul.

Raising my arms out, I dove into the drink and began to swim downstream. All around me, was the underwater life, from the fish to the frogs and even occasional bird swooping down to catch its prey.

I let it all unfold, only rising up to breathe in air before I dove down again, and let the current take me downstream.

At last, I reached very shallow waters, where standing was all one could do. Just as I was about to place my feet on the ground, my eyes opened. From under the current, I saw the obscured image of my family.

On the water's edge, along the grassy bank, I saw Georgiana. Behind her were Lizzy, Jane, Mary, and Lydia. Behind them were Darcy, Bingley, Uncle Philips, father, Mr. Atkins, and Arthur.

They had been waiting for me. For how long, I did not know.

Once more, their presence eluded me. What drove them to come to such a place?

When I burst through the surface, making a start toward them, once more, they rushed into the woods and the chase began.

Through the trees, I ran, spotting a set of legs in breeches in one place, then hair falling down the ladies' shoulders, then a petticoat that flapped against the wind.

As I moved behind a tree, I peeked around it. There, on the other side of a set of evergreens, was Georgiana's back. She moved her hand along the tree trunk before she walked leisurely away from me.

"What is your greatest fear?" I heard her ask. "What is decision to you?"

Slowly, I followed her as she turned a corner. This time, no one would abandon me. I would see my family again. When I turned a corner I was standing in a clearing.

All the magic of the trees seemed to evaporate, and I was blinded by the sunlight shining down solely for me.

When I could finally look, I beheld three paths.

To the left, I saw Colonel Fitzwilliam's shape.

In the path to the right, I saw Finlay's outline. I couldn't see their full features—the light was so blinding!

And there, in the middle, was an empty path. It had dead trees, thorny bushes, and was a wave of unknown elements.

What could I do? I had my wandering mind, and I had to choose a path. What would it be? All I knew was, I wanted to be right. So much I wanted to be.

Then suddenly, I felt a teardrop on my cheek. When touching it, I realized that it was a raindrop instead. It was rain! Even the skies were not satisfied with what I was feeling...

I woke up once more. This time, I did not remain in bed. Rather, I pushed the blankets off my person, jumped out of the bed, and lit my candle in the dark. Carrying the candleholder to the desk, I found my journal and wrote down the entire experience. When I finished, I only had a few words to sum up my feelings on the matter:

Dreams are just that: dreams. They are not there to depict a hidden reality but are only a collection of images that the mind jumbles up and produces to us. They do not signify truth, or dilemmas. Until this point, surely that's all there is.

That was what I thought—but never before have I had the same dream, with its progression unfolding before me, and getting longer each time. The dream won't stop but has now become like a haunting.

I know why I have it. But what does it want from me? What can I do?

But a dream is a dream, nevertheless. I was turning into a romantic by searching for meaning as opposed to chaos. I knew that Finlay and Fitzwilliam presented opposing paths. But what of the third path? What of the thorns? What of the uncertainty?

Where did that road lead?

Chapter Nineteen

JANE BENNET'S TALE: SPEECHLESS

I woke up that morning, having experienced the most spell-binding dream. I had dreamt of being in a magical wood, where I was faced with quite a few paths, but I knew not what they signified. Where did each road lead?

But when I opened my eyes, I was still in my guestroom, at my aunt and uncle Gardiner's home.

Eager to greet the day, I dressed, had breakfast with the family, and was blessed with good news. At last, I received a letter from Longbourn and one from Lizzy in particular. The first one gave me a list of news, and mama's complaints about Mr. Collins's wedding. Her grief resonated from off the page.

When finished reading that, I took ahold of Lizzy's letter, and knew very well that she would write nothing that gave me pain.

> Dear Jane,
>
> We are happy that you are safely at Gracechurch Street and AWAY from it all. Or rather, should I say, safe from news that would be trying to anyone's nerves.
>
> And yes, at last, it has occurred.
>
> The wedding has taken place! Mr. Collins and Charlotte married at the church, and in all preparations, they were complete: with profound stupidity on his side, and cold prudence on hers. And in

Charlotte, marrying with the sole design of obtaining her future and escaping spinsterhood, she has triumphed, and in keeping his pride intact, Mr. Collins also has succeeded.

The bride and bridegroom set off for Kent from the church door, and everybody had as much to say, or to hear, on the subject as usual.

Charlotte has promised to write to me often and has made me swear to write to her. I am also fully committed to visiting her in March, along with her father and Maria. Now I shall know the truth! And if Lady Catherine and her daughter are as Mr. Collins describes. However, I still place my faith in Mr. Wickham's report and believe him to be the one with the most truth.

While I hoped that Lizzy was inaccurate and that Lady Catherine and her daughter were delightful and charming, even I believed that perhaps Mr. Wickham's portrait was more accurate in this case. I don't know why... especially since I was dubious of him in other ways.

But even I marveled at Charlotte Lucas. For I knew that I could never marry without affection in the case. Always, and forever, I wished to marry for love. How too often that was considered a strange idea!

~

Happy that I brought two of my best gowns, I was prepared for the wedding and ball that would take place afterwards. With Isabella, Isaac, Ruth, and Daniel tended to by their governess, we proceeded to the church, with our cloaks on (for the sake of modesty), and we saw Miss Caldwell and Captain Thorpe stand in front of the vicar and perform their nuptials. In truth, I was watching a couple wed who I had not become acquainted with. And yet, I was still happy for them.

Miss Diana Caldwell entered in a gown that clearly was specially made for the occasion. I thought she looked very lovely, and Thorpe smiled when she walked down the aisle on her father's arm.

How much the mind delivers itself into an obligatory purgatory! As she walked down the aisle, to her smiling groom, I saw myself walking down the aisle instead and seeing Mr. Bingley at the end of it.

There he was, in the eye of my mind. As if he was beside me now, I felt his influence in the room, and it was as if it was a shadow that would perpetually linger. He was there, in my heart, still.

Biting my lip, I looked away from the bride and groom as they met each other and cast my eye around the rest of the attendees. Amongst them, I saw Mary Crawford with a woman who I could only assume was her sister, Mrs. Grant.

When seeing me, her eyes lit up and she nodded to me. I returned the gesture and immediately felt lighter and sturdier. I was amongst friends and family; therefore, I was not alone. And that counted for so much.

Vows were exchanged, Thorpe placed his ring on Miss Caldwell's finger, the vicar pronounced them husband and wife, and their bond was sealed. They were now one and were meant to walk through life with each other at their side.

We all cheered for them and truly, they looked so happy arm and arm, that I was certain more than ever, that it was a love match.

Before you all now, I vow this: I shall never do anything less. I shall always marry for love!

~

We all exited the church, with rice in our hands, the happy couple exited, and we threw it at them for good luck. They laughed and their expressions seemed to be the exact opposite of what Charlotte and Mr. Collins must have been feeling when they married. On their side, there was flattery of being chosen, but mostly it was a marriage made out of duty and prudence, while this alliance was clearly made out of passion.

They entered the carriage and said they expected us all at their homes in no more than twenty minutes.

We all traveled to their home as well, were met so enthusiastically by the bride and groom and that's when I first met them both. Thorpe and his new bride appeared to be lovely, and I hoped to get to know them better. Soon after I moved amongst the rest, I turned and saw Miss Crawford. Laughing, she ran up to me, with her arms outstretched. Smiling, I reached out and took her hands in mine.

"We see each other again," Mary Crawford laughed.

"Yes, we do. And you and the bride are the two loveliest women in London."

"How can any woman in this room count for anything when you are present?" She turned to my aunt and uncle. "Am I not correct, Mr. and Mrs. Gardiner?"

"I do not know whether to agree or disagree," Uncle Gardiner responded, "for a proper uncle should always favor his niece, and I do. But I cannot deny that you, Mrs. Thorpe, and many other women in the room are some of the prettiest women in the town."

"I cannot help but agree, I fear," Aunt Gardiner said. "Miss Crawford, it is a delight to see you again."

"And I with you. But might I be so bold as to introduce my sister to you, Mrs. Grant. She is dear to me, and I believe you will like her."

"We would be delighted," I assured her. "I am inclined to like her already."

Mrs. Grant was introduced to us, and she was as pleasant as we expected her to be. She had been a widow for a couple years, and therefore, acknowledged that she could stand in front of a newly married couple and not cry.

"No, I shall not cry," she said, while beginning to weep as we cheered for the couple as they walked amongst us. "No, I shall not cry at all. Oh, but this does remind me of when my poor Mr. Grant and I did get married."

"Does it?" Mary Crawford asked, "How so?"

"Oh, Mr. Grant was very gallant on our wedding day."

"He didn't complain of the dinner you both had that day, did he?" Miss Crawford smirked, with a satirical eye.

"Well, I do recall that he found the mutton a little burnt," she said, "but other than that, he was positively splendid."

Mary gave me a look and whispered in my ear.

"My late brother-in-law had a custom of getting upset whenever food was not to his particular taste. If dinner was not as he wished, he would rail about it for an entire day. My sister was too good for him."

"I propose a toast!" Uncle Gardiner said, raising his glass of wine that the servants were passing around on trays. "To Captain and Mrs. Thorpe! A delightful couple who found each other in this world and clearly were destined to make each other happy! May your lives be long, your home comfortable, and feel as if your path together is like going on a lovely adventure that will never end. To Captain and Mrs. Thorpe!"

We all took a glass and raised it.

"To Captain and Mrs. Thorpe!" We all said.

And that was the day that I had first met Mrs. Grant. I liked her immediately.

∾

At the ball, I had the good and equally intimidating fortune of not being in want of a partner. I had danced every dance, and one dance proved to be equally as significant.

Just as I finished a set, my dance partner led me off the dance floor and drew near to Mary Crawford. Before we could say anything to each other, there was another arrival.

"Mr. William Price," the servant declared. A man, wearing a naval uniform, entered. He appeared to be a young and pleasant-looking man.

"Captain and Mrs. Thorpe!" Mr. Price announced, greeting the happy couple. "Sorry for my terrible time in coming, but when you are chained to a ship, business calls you away too often and you realized just how much you are not your own master."

Captain and Mrs. Thorpe greeted him warmly.

"And that is another dear friend of mine," my dance partner,

Mr. Ashburn, said. He walked away from me to fetch Mr. Price. Since I was close to Miss Crawford, I walked up to her, so her company could give me courage, but it turned out that I was not the only one to suffer a shock.

When accosting her, I saw her look equally horrified. I looked where she was staring and I saw her gaping directly at Mr. William Price, the new arrival. Her cheeks had become flushed, her eyes were filled with trepidation, and she was frozen.

Seeing that she was blatantly staring and not wishing for anyone to notice, I walked up to her and took her hand. This made her stir and tear her eyes away from this lieutenant.

"Mary?" I questioned, "are you unwell?"

Biting her lips, she looked back at Mr. Price and then back at me.

"Jane," she insisted, "please do not leave me until the next dance begins."

Her voice lost all charm and elegance and gave way to a very subtle sort of panic. The contrast of it to her usual manner was most alarming.

"Mary?" I asked. "I can see that you know him."

"From another time. And from another life. From the life that I choose not to remember. I shall tell you everything tomorrow. But not today. No! Not today. Today I refuse to be anything else, but happy."

"Yes, we should be happy, shouldn't we?" I encouraged. "We shouldn't let anyone deter us."

Mr. Ashburn also approached Mr. Price, and we heard him mention that he had two lovely women to introduce Mr. Price to.

"He is bringing him over to meet us," Mary gasped.

"Move away toward my aunt and uncle," I instructed her, "I'll speak to them both, and then tell Mr. Ashburn where you are, so he can claim his dance."

"Thank you," she said, breathing in heavily. "But no. I cannot, and should not, spend the entire ball running from my reality. You had the courage to face your past tragedy, therefore, I need to have the strength to face this situation. Even if I am to be despised for another person's shame, I shall not let my courage desert me."

Therefore, we both stood, with two men accosting us.

When they neared us, Mr. William Price's face distorted when he recognized Miss Crawford.

"William," Mr. Ashburn said, "you may come late, but not so much that you missed out on the dancing. And I bring you the two best dancers in the set. This is Miss Jane Bennet." I curtsied. "And this is Miss Mary Crawford."

"Thank you for my side of the introduction, Mr. Ashburn," Mary said, looking bravely at Lieutenant Price, "but Mr. Price and I are already well-acquainted."

"Oh, is this true then?"

"Yes—yes," Mr. Price stuttered. "We have. It was done through my relations. You know of my aunt, Ashburn, the honorable Lady Bertram of Mansfield Park. Well not only did her husband help me along in my line of work, but did I also tell you that they took one of my sisters in as their ward?"

"Yes, you did. You are referring to Fanny, aren't you?"

"Yes. Well, when I was granted leave to visit the estate to see Fanny, it was there that I had the good fortune to meet Miss Crawford."

"You came with great stories of your nautical experiences," Mary continued, "and you brought life to our dull lot." Mary turned to me to explain. "It was when I was staying with my sister at the parsonage on Mansfield's estate. Mr. Price came to visit at the time, and we found happiness with his tales along the seas."

Mr. Price chuckled nervously.

"I am happy that I amused you all. When I first arrived, I felt nervous, afraid of how small I must have appeared in your presence."

"I spent a great deal of my life around men who are in the navy; I was never one to consider such men as being small in the whole course of my life. Even when I struggled with my feelings about the profession."

Mr. Price—blushed. Rather than appearing vindictive at all, instead he looked uncertain, and worried we would not like him.

"So, you are in the navy, Mr. Price," I said.

"Yes. I am a lieutenant who serves on the ship called The Valiant."

"A ship with that name suits you," Mary offered.

"Thank you for your kind words. You are precisely as I remembered you, Miss Crawford."

"Whether that is a good or bad thing, only time will tell," she determined.

"And that is enough talking," Mr. Ashburn said, "for the dance is about to commence. Miss Crawford, I hope you did not forget me."

"No, I did not," she laughed, taking his hand.

"And what of you, Miss Bennet?" Mr. Price asked. "Are you secured for this dance?"

"I have no partners," I answered.

"Then would you do me the honor of dancing with a poor sailor?"

"It would be a pleasure."

Taking my hand, I went to the dance floor again and began to dance with this new acquaintance.

~

"Your dress is very lovely," William Price complimented me.

"Thank you," I responded. "You and Mr. Ashburn appear to be great friends."

"He is like another brother to me."

"Oh. So, you have brothers?"

"Oh yes!" He laughed, "my mother and father gave me many siblings. I am closest with my sister, Fanny, however. Has Miss Crawford mentioned my sister to you before?"

"No, but I assure you that it's not out of negligence, but time. I only met Miss Crawford around a week ago, and we've only had time to call on each other a couple of times. Therefore, I never learned about the Mansfield Park occupants very well at all. But if you favor your sister, then she must be a very special sort of woman."

"She is. Rarely do you come across such good women as my sister. I believe that you would like her."

"What is good, kind and admirable, are always worth meeting."

"Thank you, Miss Bennet."

As we danced, he looked past me and cast his eyes on Mary Crawford as she was dancing with Mr. Ashburn.

"Did Miss Crawford ever tell you that she had a brother?" he asked.

"Yes, she did. If I am not mistaken, he is Mr. Henry Crawford of Everingham?"

"Yes, he is. Judging by your words, I can assume that you have never made his acquaintance."

"No, I have not. Have you?"

"Yes, I have."

"What sort of man is he?"

"He is...a complicated matter. My history with that family is complicated to say the least, and I assume that you know little of it."

I gathered the sense that he was about to say something that would implicate Mary, and I would not allow that.

"On the contrary," I corrected him, "for fear of appearing deceptive, she informed me of her brother's history and nature soon after we met. She did not want to make it appear as if she would ever hide anything from me. Not only did I find it admirable of her, but I felt that it took courage of her to have me decide how I felt about it. After all, only a weak inclination would judge the sister due to the brother's actions. Therefore, I thought no different of her than how I had before."

"Yes," he rushed out, "that is precisely how I feel. Her brother helped me in many ways and then hurt me in others. Or rather, the hurt comes from another quarter, one that is attached to me. He never directly hurt me, and I see how imprudent I have been for speaking on the subject. But I am happy that we did speak on this matter. I have never been of the belief that a sibling is guilty for what the other sibling has done. It is simply nice to hear another person support the idea."

"Well," I blushed, "I am glad that I could be of assistance."

Looking down at me, he rolled his eyes.

"I see that I have been a terrible dance partner! Here I am, dancing with one of the loveliest women I have been acquainted with and I am talking of another woman. That's the tragedy of being a navy man; you are not always given time to practice your manners."

"I very well understand why you were curious. I am a new acquaintance, while she is an old friend to you. You would naturally feel inclined to talk of her."

"But it still will not do," he continued, "you are very agreeable and a wonderful dance partner. And it's time I respected it."

He continued to ask me about my life and then told me stories about being in the navy.

The dance came to an end. Mary and I quickly got something to eat and drink before she was called away to dance with Mr. Price.

"Wish me luck," she whispered.

"I believe that you shall find him very agreeable," I assured her. And I really believed it.

Mr. Price was all smiles when he took Mary's hand for the next dance.

As he did so, I focused upon them both. Yet never would I see what was soon to come. For if you were to tell me that those two people would eventually find their way to reach the other, and fall in love, I never would have known.

But either way, it was such, and I had been there to witness when Mary Crawford and William Price first made steps toward each other. That was something, in many ways than you would wonder.

Of course, more happened at the ball than these two, who had quite the road ahead of them, with many twisted pathways that they had to tread, with thorns on each side. But walk it, they did.

No. There was something else that happened at this ball. Something that shook the very foundations of my resolve and my life.

Eventually the ball came to an end, and another chapter of my life began there.

Yet I shall not tell you now. For that is a story for another day, for when I am ready to unburden my soul to you. Until then, however...

After all, there was an old saying: 'never wash your dirty linens in the street'...

Chapter Twenty

KITTY'S TALE: WIVES & WASHERWOMEN

"That's the spirit, Kitty," Samantha said as I helped her iron the laundry. "You always have to consider to avoid getting any creases in the cloth."

The next day, I had gone to visit the regiment at Lambton. I was helping Samantha iron some of the laundry that she was cleaning for the officers, while telling her about events that had taken place at Pemberley.

"So," she said, "these Crawfords that you are friends with... would one of them be Mr. Henry Crawford, of Everingham?"

"Yes. Has he visited Lambton and made his appearance known?"

"He's ridden through it, but I have not seen him. I merely know about him because of the local village gossip that haunts provincial life. But if this is *that* Mr. Henry Crawford, then there is something that I have to tell you. Kitty, that family is not all that they seem."

I pretended to be alarmed, but I was pretty certain that she was going to tell me nothing of novelty, so I let her gossip unfold.

"I heard that he ran off with another man's wife a few years back. A Mr. Rushworth of Wimpole Street. Far be it from me to tell you all the history of any new favorites that might be in your company, but I want you to know who they really are—and I do this only out of concern."

I smiled.

"Maria Bertram," I said.

"Who?"

"Mr. Rushworth's ex-wife's name is Miss Maria Bertram, of Mansfield Park, Northampton. She was in love with Mr. Crawford, but when feeling spurned, she wed Mr. Rushworth out of haste, threw herself into a loveless match, then ran after Mr. Crawford when he entered her life again. Soon, he chose not to marry her, she hated him, and they separated. I believe I have covered most of the tale."

When I finished, Samantha looked at me—to the point where she began to accidentally pour too much starch onto the laundry.

"Samantha...starch."

This woke her from her blank stare, and she began to wipe the starch away from where she dropped too much.

"You knew?" she exclaimed.

"Yes, I have known. In truth, Samantha, we all know about his history, at Pemberley. You sound a little unsettled because we associate with him."

"Well, I never thought that was the sort that you preferred to associate with."

"If the entire world would exile everyday sinners, then we'd all be sequestered in our own prisons, never being allowed to come out for any day in our lives. It is too harsh of a reaction. Besides, we are trying to help him repent his life and progress onward. That's all you can do when you've made such a dreadful mistake."

"Oh, well, I do see some sense in that. But has he improved?"

"We believe so. That being said, while he has toyed with women's hearts, as well as not regarded Mr. Rushworth's feelings, he ultimately was unattached. Whereas Miss Maria Bertram was the one who performed the ultimate betrayal. He should not have done what he did, but he has the right to recover. Perhaps, over time, so does she."

"You talk in a very liberal way. I never would have expected that of you."

"Me? Why not?"

"Well, being confined to life in the countryside, I thought

that you would have lent such scandal to the wayside and accepted the puritanical doctrines that choke the very life out of all of us."

"If I have disappointed you, then I am glad."

"You haven't disappointed me. I am surprised, that is all."

"But Samantha, did you learn of this through a wide rumor that has spread throughout Lambton, or no? Does everyone know about the scandal?"

"Actually, I have heard nothing about it from anyone here. Lambton seems so far removed from most of England that much can occur without none of these people knowing about it. Also, it did occur years ago, so it stopped being of note to many people."

"Then how did you come to learn of it?" I asked, then I stopped myself. "Wait! Let me see if I can figure this out. You are related to someone who knew of the events, because they are connected to some household or another."

"Finally, you are understanding me in full. It was my cousin's wife's uncle's friend. He is a servant at Wimpole Street and was there when it all occurred. Naturally, he told the uncle, the uncle told my cousin's wife, and my cousin told me. I never saw what any of those rich and fancy people looked like, but for some reason, I remembered Mr. Crawford's name."

"Samantha, I need a favor."

"You need me to conceal this all, don't you?"

I blinked.

"You are one step ahead of me."

"I'm a washerwoman; dirty laundry is everywhere, and we are always the ones who are given it."

I knew that I could trust her, for she was a very true sort of woman. But she was also smart. She knew that she had more to gain by remaining quiet. A servant who understands discretion will always have a place in the world.

"But," I finalized, "if somehow, people do learn the truth, please explain that we are helping the family to recover and improve themselves in society's eyes. People don't understand forgiving repentant sinners, for some reason, but they understand charity."

"True words. Very well, I give you my word and promise."

"Kitty!"

I looked behind me and saw Mrs. Warrens, Mrs. Barrett, Mrs. Hawkins, and Mrs. O'Connor approaching us.

The ladies greeted me warmly and insisted me to come up and sit with them for a while. Samantha excused me, I went with the ladies and sat down with them for coffee and biscuits.

When we were alone, the four knowing women immediately went to the heart of the matter.

"I hope that Samantha didn't tell you first," Mrs. Warrens began.

"We were hoping that you wouldn't know about it yet," Mrs. O'Connor said.

"But servants have a way of getting to the gossip quicker," Mrs. Barrett said.

"It's enough to make one jealous," Mrs. Hawkins interjected. "Very jealous."

"Yes, jealous indeed, for one sometimes prides themselves on being the first in the know."

"But I didn't tell Samantha," Mrs. Warrens added. "Did you?" she asked Mrs. O'Connor.

"No," Mrs. O'Connor answered, turning to Mrs. Hawkins. "Did you?"

"No." Mrs. Hawkins turned to Mrs. Barrett. "Did you?"

"Of course not. Honestly!"

I waited for them to arrive at the subject when they would. After all, Samantha had told me that no one knew about the Crawfords, but herself, therefore, obviously they were going to tell me about something else.

"But no matter how others tell it," Mrs. Warrens said, "I daresay that we tell it better."

"Yes, we do," Mrs. Hawkins said.

"Then tell me at once," I encouraged, "and may the gods of storytelling be with you."

All four of them suddenly grew silent.

"No," I laughed. "This will not do. You cannot tease me about what you have to say and then not tell me the truth about it."

"We just are afraid that the news might be too much for you," Mrs. O'Connor said.

"But it's too late. You have already done everything in your power to draw me in."

"Well, it has to do with your sister," Mrs. Barrett said.

"Yes," Mrs. Warrens extolled, rolling her eyes, "she has many of those. We must be specific."

"Well, my dear," Mrs. Hawkins said, "my dear husband, Mr. Hawkins, is actually good friends with Colonel Forster, and so sometimes we get invited to special dinners."

"It must be nice to be a favorite," I inferred.

"Yes, it is delightful. Anyway, Colonel Forster never fully recovered from Wickham's plight. He really was angry over it, and I think it still weighs on him."

When hearing Mr. Wickham's name, I became alert immediately. I leaned forward, flabbergasted for anything that I might hear. How had that weasel found his way back into our lives? Truly, I was hoping that the North would swallow him up and then spit him out into a river. Honestly! Can't some problems just go away forever? But no. Because that would make life too convenient!

"Has he received news about Mr. Wickham?" I asked.

"Well," Mrs. Warrens continued, "yes, he has. Colonel Forster has kept in contact with Mr. Wickham's dealings in Newcastle. Though Mr. Wickham is still married to your sister, he still feels that Wickham is not to be trusted. And he was right."

"And you know how Colonel Forster tells Mrs. Forster everything," Mrs. Barrett added, "well, when we were at a dinner, she told us that Colonel Forster was a little out of sorts, because he received some distressing news."

"What sort of news?"

"Mr. Wickham...has taken a mistress."

～

Shock!

That was my state of mind.

However, why was I shocked? I knew, very well, that Wickham had married Lydia because he was paid to. Therefore, it would only be natural that he would soon sink into utter indifference and eventually seek pleasures elsewhere.

"A mistress," I groaned. "Already?"

"Oh," Mrs. O'Connor said, relieved, "you accepted that this was inevitable. Good, that will make this easier."

"Yes," I said, "I was pretty aware that anything nefarious could arrive from that union. But I did not suspect that it would arise so soon. Wickham has already taken another woman into his life. And then...well, if you all know of it, then that means that Lydia might know about it as well."

"Yes, she does," Mrs. Warrens said, "from what I hear, she has. She and Wickham were even known to publicly argue about it."

"How publicly?"

"Other officers were present."

"With Lydia, I can see how that could occur. She does not believe in choosing her words and temper carefully, but Wickham is the sort that values discretion. Why would he get himself in the way of a public scene when he likes people to regard him as the victim?"

"I do not know, but with him, there is no limit to what he is capable of," Mrs. Barrett added. "Mrs. Forster now regrets her friendship with Lydia even more."

"So," I said, standing up, "Wickham has shown himself even more. He's still the worst."

"You haven't even heard the worst of it."

"There's more?"

"Yes. Your sister hinted at him making another woman with child. I don't know if there is much else to the story, but your sister was in the street, telling her version of the tale. Therefore, I can imagine that this must be true."

"The only reason that we are here to tell you this is to make you aware."

"This is despicable," I said, "she loved being Mr. Wickham's wife, and now she must feel so betrayed. I would say that she will get used to it because she has no choice."

"No, she doesn't."

The door suddenly opened, and Mr. Hawkins entered. I stood up and curtsied to him.

"Nice to see you, Miss Bennet," Mr. Hawkins turned to me.

"Thank you, sir," I replied, "it is a delight to see you once more."

"Yes, and..."

He looked between us four and saw our cheeks redden, and we looked on him in anticipation of what he was going to say.

He grunted.

"You all share a secret, but of course, it is between ladies, and you do not talk of it to me. Unbelievable." He left the room, damning us. "You should have asked me. But we husbands must always be left out. Always."

Now *that* is how you leave a room.

Chapter Twenty-One

JANE BENNET'S TALE: ANOTHER CHAPTER TO HER TALE

We mortals are always being left out of some sort of information. But when a woman's name is Mary Crawford, I was not left waiting for too long.

Two days after the wedding and ball, Mary Crawford visited me again and she looked lovelier than ever. For within her eyes was a gaiety and liveliness that put me at ease.

"Well," she said to my aunt and I, "this has been the longest two days of my life. For I could not wait to talk about the ball, and I am resolved to speak of it till I become blue in the face."

"Oh, do talk about it," Ruth cried out to her, "because I always like hearing about how dances go."

"Do you?" Mary replied, pinching her cheek, "when I was your age, I considered we older people as the most boring sorts! Toys were infinitely preferable to me than hearing about gowns and dances. You are ahead of me, in every way, Miss Ruth. And where is little Isaac?"

"He is not feeling well," Aunt Gardiner informed her, "and he will be very sorry to miss you. But that gives you and Jane time to enjoy all the talk in the world together. Come, Ruth, to your lessons!"

"Oh, I cannot stay?" Ruth asked.

"You have to practice your geography."

"Yes, Mama."

"Miss Crawford," Aunt Gardiner informed her, "very soon, the tea will be brought in."

"Thank you, Mrs. Gardiner," Mary responded, "the cakes your cook makes are ones that I actually like."

Aunt Gardiner smiled and left us alone. When she did so, Mary sat down beside me.

"Before we begin talking, which we have much to do, I must first say that my sister loved making your acquaintance. She also found your aunt and uncle to be very charming people."

"We adored her as well," I offered.

"She really wants you to come and visit us one day."

"I would love to," I said, "the *only* reason I have not called is because I have been waiting for a friend to call on me. And she never gave a particular date, and I am afraid of leaving any morning, for fear of missing her. But once she does, I promise that I will call on you and your sister as soon as I can."

"Oh! And who is the other friend of yours?"

"Her name is Miss Caroline Bingley. Her brother is Mr. Charles Bingley, of Netherfield Park."

"Miss Caroline Bingley?" Mary repeated, her brow arching.

"Yes. Have you heard of her before?"

"Sister to Mrs. Louisa Hurst?"

"Yes! So, you do know her."

"I have had the *interesting* fortune to have made her acquaintance. I am not very well acquainted with her but have met her only a couple of times."

"They are a lovely set of sisters."

"I suppose they can be viewed as such."

I squinted, seeing unease spread over her face.

"What do you mean?" I asked.

"Well, I confess, that I did not receive the same impression as you. I found them to be not to my liking."

"You did?"

"Yes. You are better acquainted with her, so perhaps you have seen a different element of their characters. I shall admit to that, but I cannot help but still take my first, second and third impressions of them into account. Now, all humans, in some form or another, have some sort of façade every now and again, or something artificial about us, but with them, well, I could not place my finger fully upon it, but—I found their superficiality to be the harmful sort. They had a refusal to acknowledge anyone outside of their sphere and just felt as if everything they did was simply for their own advantage, and that was all. I have my snobbish imperfections, to be sure, but theirs felt extreme. But I suppose that you saw another side of them."

"I have," I augmented, "and if I am fortunate to have you both visit at the same time, I will show you how much better they are once you become better acquainted. That being said, your speech just now made me think I was talking to my sister, Elizabeth. She feels the same as you do and still does."

"Well, I want to believe that she and I have some wisdom to us. But if you believe Miss Caroline Bingley is a good sort of a woman, I concede that maybe there is something to her character that I have not seen. That being said, I shall still determine things from my own perspective. Oh, but we have been thrown off our original point. The ball!"

"Yes, I laughed, "the ball!"

~

"First, it was overall, very wonderful," Mary said. "The best wedding that I ever attended."

"Yes, it was a lovely wedding," I concurred.

"Often weddings or not ever made much ado about. But that wedding was such a surprise. And for Mr. Price to be pleasant was the other added delight."

"I am happy that he made it comfortable for you to see him again."

"And I did promise that I'd tell you about the history behind my fears with him."

"Yes, you did. If it is anything serious, then I can assure you that I shall never utter it after this moment."

"Thank you, Jane. That is of great comfort, and I will rely upon your discretion. Promise you shall not tell a living soul."

"I promise," I swore sincerely.

With my promise, Mary felt enlivened.

"I knew that you were a kind woman," she said, "when I first saw you, I believed you to be better than so many others. I am happy to be correct."

She smoothed out her dress and began her narration.

"Well, it all begins with my time at Mansfield Park. Oh, good lord! I begin and end so many discussions with that estate, don't I? You are perhaps sick of hearing about it."

"On the contrary, I am not vexed by it. In fact, I am very interested."

"Then I shall continue. Well, when I was at Mansfield's Parsonage, staying with my sister and brother-in-law, my sister was eager to see me married."

"To whom?"

"To the oldest son and heir of Mansfield Park, Mr. Thomas Bertram. I was perfectly happy to adhere to this plan. Faith, I believe everyone should get married as soon as they can, if they can marry to advantage."

"Advantage? Now you sound like my mother."

"Oh, I would never wish to do that."

"But do you believe that there should be some affection in the case? I admit, with marriage, I do believe that it is best for both sides to at least like the other one."

"And that was the occurrence that I did not prepare for. Mr. Thomas Bertram was the primary one that I focused on, but I didn't take matters of the heart into account. But believe me, it took *me into* account. Rather than find affection for him, I developed feelings for Mr. Edmund Bertram, his younger brother. Besides, Mr. Thomas Bertram would leave for gaps of time, and he showed no inclination of caring for me when he was gone, therefore, I refused to care for him."

This last remark made me feel less alone, more than I had ever before. Mary knew how it felt to be forgotten when a man left the county and was absent from her. Perhaps if I told her about Mr. Bingley, she would understand.

"So, you fell in love with Mr. Edmund Bertram?" I continued.

"Yes. Life apparently loves irony, because, to my surprise, I felt very deeply for him. He possessed finer qualities that his older brother lacked. First, he had a genuine sincerity, he was handsome, kind, and there was always something pleasing about his mouth when he spoke. Also, he liked me. When developing feelings for someone, I am the sort to not waste my time on a man who feels nothing for me. Therefore, him having an affection for me is a requirement for me ever considering him handsome or worthy of interest. Do I sound nonsensical now?"

"Not at all. I find it perfectly logical to consider a man if he finds your worth considering as well. Affection is something that works best when it is mutual. Of course, unrequited love often occurs, and that is no one's fault either. Yet, what happened between you and Mr. Bertram? For, judging by your behavior, you are no longer in each other's lives. Did he sever connections with you because of your brother's actions? Because if he did so, then I fear to say it, his inclination is something that it is best for you to not have. I mean no disrespect to the gentleman, but would you not prefer a man who would remain steadfast, even when times were difficult?"

"Your counsel helps me now, sweet Jane, but it was more than that. A rift had grown between us even before then. And it was I who began it."

I took her hand in mine.

"Mary," I assured her, "whatever you did, I am prepared to hear. And if what you did was morally offensive, as long as you feel sorry for what you did, then I will never think less of you."

"Thank you. In truth, I am heartily ashamed of myself, and I feel as if I took a step too far somewhere. But I know the woman that I am. And I feel as if, if I could go back in time and do it all over, perhaps I would have done the same thing. Well, it first began when we all were visiting Mr. Rushworth's home, Sother-ton. You remember Mr. Rushworth?"

"Yes. He was the man that was married to Maria Bertram, and then your brother..."

"Precisely. I just wanted to make sure that you were not getting confused with all the names. Well, many of the Mansfield Park family, my brother, and I were visiting Mr. Rushworth's estate. This was all before Maria and Mr. Rushworth got married. While there, we were in a chapel that was in the home. I made some sneering remarks about how it was unnecessary and tedious to drag all the servants to the chapel every day just to force them to pray. Mr. Edmund objected to my statements, but I was resolute, finding the activity of consistently praying to be odious. Then I commented on the many clergymen that I have seen that had either foolish tendencies or spent much of their time either being taciturn or not doing much at all and being paid for it. Yes, I know that my views are scandalous."

"I prefer to think every clergyman is different and should not be judged for what others in his profession have done," I retorted, "but I cannot deny that my sister, Elizabeth, has noted and seen some vicars and reverends who have some of the qualities that you have mentioned."

"My observations were generalities at the time, I admit that now," she persisted. "But you must understand the effects of my education. Too oft I had seen many clergymen who spent their days lax, out of spirits, drear, and only exerting themselves on Sunday to give a few services and give very dull sermons. This has been my experience. It is hard to unlearn something that you have seen all your life."

"It would be difficult to undo so many experiences. But what does this have to do with Mr. Bertram and you?"

"It turns out... that he was preparing to take holy orders himself. He was to become a clergyman."

The surprise of the previous statement was a bit disarming. Mary Crawford had offended the very profession that belonged to the man that she was falling in love with.

"Of course, once I found out, I apologized for all the words that I said," Mary insisted, "I did. I did not want there to be bad feelings between us. And he accepted my apology."

"Oh. But Mary, I am sorry. After all, once you found out that he was a clergyman, that was when you lost all hope, due to it not suiting your lifestyle."

Mary turned to me and looked at me directly.

"Wait, then...you knew that I would consider that to be an impediment?"

"Was I wrong? Sorry if I assumed such."

"Yes, you assumed—but your assumption was correct in many ways. When hearing his choice of career, I felt disappointed immediately. For him and I had been so right for each other in many ways, only for us to be so unlike each other in the most crucial way of all, was a substantial setback. I could never see myself marrying a clergyman. But you seemed to know that about me already."

"I did not mean to make assumptions," I insisted, "but it was from my general observation of your character. You have never appeared to me to be the sort of woman who would be happy being a clergyman's wife."

"Precisely. And forgive me, but I still know that I can never be one, even though I still think of him often. Despite that a part of me is still in love with him."

"You are?"

"Oh, of course. Men are allowed to go out in the world, and that gives them diversions. But we women are doomed to remain at home, where our emotions prey on us. My heart has not been given enough liberty and action for it to become filled with affection somewhere else. Besides, it is not always easy to relinquish your love for someone, just because they no longer love you."

This last sentence surprised me.

"What do you mean that they no longer love you? By that, are you implying that he was the one to ultimately sever the ties that bound you both?"

"Alas, he really was. Initially, the rift between us was due to my refusal to love anyone who was going to be a clergyman. I even suggested that he change professions. Be it from going into parliament or law."

"Mary," I corrected her. "I adore you, truly, but it is no more correct for you to insist him to change professions that he chooses, than it is for him to believe you should change your mindset and become a clergyman's wife. Both of you had desires that were taking you in opposite directions, and neither of you were wrong for it."

"I know it now. It was positively wicked of me to assume he should become something else, just to suit my happiness. But I was heartbroken. For you see me for what I am. I am not meant to be a clergyman's wife. I was not meant for cold prudence and to sit still and just...be there. A lump of passivity and at perpetual rest. Resting fatigues me! I must move, act, be as I am—be the woman that I want to be."

"You are not evil," I assured her. "Nor wicked. You simply are a woman who knows who she is and what she wants in life. Besides, there are sisters of mine who would never want to marry a clergyman, and I refuse to view them as evil or wrong because of it. Not every woman or man is meant for every lifestyle. Faith, the more I think of it, the more I am certain that only my sister, Mary, is meant for a clergyman. The rest of us are not right for it. Like you, something else stirs within them. And it is not evil."

"You understand me so well!" She smiled, overjoyed. "And then there's my education; I was raised to believe it only right to marry well, and to a man who has considerable wealth to him. And then I got criticized for learning that lesson."

"Ah," I empathized, "yes, I have often seen the confusion there. One moment, we are being told that we all ought to marry well. My mother has a habit of always wishing to throw us daughters into the path of rich men. Then the next moment, we are called mercenary for doing so."

"Yes," Mary laughed, "for truly! Where does prudence end and avarice begin?"

"Elizabeth said the same thing once!" I remarked, amazed by the similarity.

"Once more, her mind and mine align. How amusing. Either way, this is why I refuse to let the world label me. Because the world never knows what it wants. All it knows is what it doesn't want. It doesn't want people who are poor, so we are told to shun that possibility and marry considering the wealth of our spouse. But it also doesn't want people who marry in consideration of the person's wealth. Each time you think that you know the world, it does something to show that you never knew it at all. Well, this ever-increasing irony did cause a rift between Mr. Bertram and myself, but it reached its climax when my brother ran away with Mr. Rushworth's wife, Maria."

"Mr. Bertram didn't hate you for that, did he? His moral belief was not to reject you for that, surely."

"No, he did not fully forsake me. After all, it was both our siblings that had run off together. We both were in the same situation. No, the full breakaway began afterward. That was when we saw each other for the last time."

~

At this point, I was sitting with my back straight and my ears alert. This had been such a fascinating story. Pray, it seemed like a story that could only happen in a novel! Yet, if there was one thing that life taught me, was that reality can easily be more fantastical than fiction.

Suddenly, Mary stood up and began to pace.

"I'm trying to see if I can remember the exact wording, so you can best understand what happened," she clarified. Suddenly, her eyes widened, remembering. "I remember exactly how it was that day." Then she began to narrate...

"My friend, Lady Stornaway, had sent word that I wanted to see Mr. Bertram, and he duly arrived. I saw him from the window. When he entered the house and we first saw each other, I went to him immediately. Due to the state of events, Jane, you must believe me, that I was quite aggravated, my spirits were roused, my worries were immense, and I had every intention of solving the problem at hand.

Mr. Edmund Bertram met me, and I confronted the matter immediately. I recall being agitated when I said that I heard he was in town, and that I wanted to see me, so that we could talk over the sad business about the equal folly of our two relations.

But he did not answer. He only looked at me in shock, disapproving of me mentioning it so quickly."

This part of the story shocked me, and I couldn't help but interrupt her narration.

"Why would he be upset at you for mentioning it immediately?" I asked. "Of course, you wanted to talk about the sad business, since you both equally were in distress over it."

"That's what I felt. But he was upset with me, finding it indelicate of me to approach the matter in the way that I had."

I did not understand this at all. What could Mr. Bertram have to be upset over? At this point, Mary said nothing that anyone else would have said if their brother ran off with the other person's married sister.

"Sorry for interrupting," I apologized. "You may continue."

"He indicated that he was upset with how I approached the subject," she continued, "so I spoke graver and said that I did not mean to defend Henry at his sister's expense."

Mary continued for a while in a way that I did not approve of. I felt that her behavior was an attempt to apologize to Mr. Bertram... but I did not believe that he deserved any sort of an apology.

"I reprobated my brother's folly in being drawn on by a woman whom he had never cared for, to do what must lose him the woman he adored—for he had been courting another woman at the time. Then I stressed the folly of his sister, poor Maria, in sacrificing such a situation, plunging into such difficulties, under the idea of being really loved by a man who had long ago made his indifference clear. And it was here, Jane, that Mr. Bertram looked thoroughly shocked at my speech again."

"Why?" I asked, confused.

"He later elaborated that he was shocked at my labelling their behavior as being merely a folly, and that I was not horrified over it; he was repulsed by my lack of having any feminine and modest loathing on the matter. And what's more, he was upset that my chief anxiety was on how both did things in a way that allowed public exposure as well."

Since I had never met this Mr. Bertram, I did not have the

right to fully censor him, nor judge him. But if Mary was telling me the truth, I did not think his mindset to be a kindred one.

"Well," Mary continued, "I admit that, not only was I upset at Henry and Maria's actions, but I was upset that Henry went to see her, that she put herself in the power of a servant, and that they exposed their mistakes in such a public way. Then I went on to speak my anger at my brother not respecting the woman who he was courting at the time. I thought she would have made my brother happy! And she would have. But no! Maria Bertram ran to him, and with him being a sort of creature who was not used to any sort of personal restraint, gave into temptation, they caused a scandal, and so the woman he was courting would never have him now. Everything would have been perfect, Jane! If my brother and Maria had not done what they had done."

I found that I could not agree with Mary in that moment, but I thought to hold my tongue until she finished her story.

"But that was when I got angry. The woman that he was courting was his second attempt at winning her heart. He had proposed to her before, but she had refused him."

"Did she?" I asked, surprised.

"Yes, she did. In that moment, I was upset that she hadn't accepted him. For if she had accepted him, then my brother never would have cared about any other woman and would have been too busy to want any other object. I admit that I felt that I could not forgive her in that moment. The woman knew this, for when she had first rejected my brother, I told her this myself." Mary turned to me. "I know that you think I sound evil now, but I was upset at the time."

"Mary," I persisted, "I shall tell you all that I feel at the end, but I am listening, and I am still very much your friend."

She smiled sadly.

"You give me the courage to continue. So, here is the tragic ending. Naturally, this shocked Mr. Bertram as well, but I didn't stop to care, because I had more pressing matters at hand. I still had to solve our crisis. So, then I said that I thought it best to bring about a marriage between my brother and his sister. Because if they married, and were properly supported by her own family, people of respectability as they are, then Maria might have recovered her footing in society to a certain degree. In some circles, I knew, she would never be admitted, but with good dinners, and large parties, there would always be those who would have been glad of her acquaintance. And there is, undoubtedly, more liberality and candor on those points than how things used to be. After all, this is not the 1700s anymore; people are less severe. Therefore, I encouraged that their father, Sir Thomas Bertram, not remove Maria from my brother's company. Because if he did, then Maria and my brother would never get married, and her reputation would be wholly spoiled."

After narrating this, she moved to the window and looked out of it. I could tell that she was greatly affected, but I didn't know if it was time to speak. So, I thought it best to help her on.

"And what happened next?" I asked.

"That was when Mr. Edmund Bertram found his voice and the lecture came. You must understand that I do not like a lecture. Give me plagues, misfortune, or bad news, but I despise a lecture! He didn't like anything that I said, nor did he even mention the plan I had come up with to save them all. Instead, his response was prudence, cold prudence! He said that he had not supposed it possible, coming in such a state of mind into that house as he had done, that anything could occur to make him suffer more, but that I had been inflicting deeper wounds in almost every sentence. That though he had, in the course of our acquaintance, been often sensible of some difference in our opinions, on points, too, of some moment, it had not entered his imagination to conceive the difference could be such as I had now proved it. That the manner in which I treated the dreadful crime committed by my brother and his sister, but the manner in which I spoke of the crime itself, giving it every reproach but the right —considering its ill consequences only as they were to be braved or overborne by a defiance of decency and impudence in wrong; and last of all, and above all, recommending to him a compliance, a compromise, an acquiescence in the continuance of the sin, on the chance of a marriage which, thinking as he now thought of my brother, should rather be prevented than sought... all this

together most grievously convinced him that he had never understood me before, and that, as far as related his mind, I had been
the creature of his own imagination. I was not the woman that he
thought I was. And so, he had less regret in sacrificing a friendship, feelings, hopes which must, at any rate, have been torn from
him."

I felt my mouth drop open. It must have been so horrible for
her to hear this from the man that she was in love with.

"Well," Mary concluded, still looking out of the window. "His
words shocked me. I was astonished and I felt my body grow
cold. It was as if I was an animal whose defenses rose, and
emotions died. In that moment, I had only one thought: protect
myself. An instinct for survival, and to maintain my pride, I felt
my cheeks redden and I lashed back at him. I smirked and said 'A
pretty good lecture, upon my word. Was it part of your last
sermon? At this rate you will soon reform everybody at Mansfield
and Thornton Lacey; and when I hear of you next, it may be as a
celebrated preacher in some great society of Methodists, or as a
missionary into foreign parts.' I tried to speak casually and care-
lessly, but I had been affected by his chastisement. Like I told
you, I hate to be lectured. But in that moment, I saw it. That was
when he relinquished my company. He said he wished me well,
and that he earnestly hoped that I might soon learn to think
more justly and immediately left the room. But I didn't want our
acquaintance to end that way. I was determined for us to think
well of each other. So, I ran after him. I called to him. He turned
around and I smiled. But he only turned back around and left.
And that was the last time that I saw him."

∾

Now that she was finished, she turned back around to me.

"Now, you know the history of my past heartbreak with Mr.
Edmund Bertram. Before you despise me at all, please understand, I meant well."

I poured her another cup of tea and handed it to her. She took
it and then sat back down.

"What does this tea mean?" she asked. "Does it bode well or no?"

"I do not despise you," I assured her. "And I am happy that you told me all of this. First, I must acknowledge that time has taught me to hear all perspectives before I determine anything. I have heard your perspective, but I have not heard Mr. Bertram's account of things. So first, I shall say that I shall never know all the particulars and can never fully judge him. But...you have never lied to me, even about your nature. Therefore, I am inclined to believe you and the events that you say occurred. Now, if what you say is true, then not only do I not despise you, but verily... I am so glad that you and he are not married. Mary, you seem to deserve better than how part of his nature is."

Mary's eyes widened and she sat down.

"You think so?"

"I do not judge him fully," I persisted, "because, again, I do not know him. But of what you have told me, you were not the only one who was questionable in that situation. First, I neither understand nor like how he reacted to what you said when he entered. When you mentioned the foolishness of your siblings, why was he affronted about it? He was upset that you spoke the truth, and you were unafraid to approach the subject. Also, he immediately disregarded and objected with your desire to solve the problem. While I also do not agree with your brother marrying Maria Rushworth, I see why you thought of it. Having people marry, after they have run off with each other, is a popular remedy. You were trying to save your brother and Mr. Bertram's sister. And what solution did he have? And what behavior did he expect of you, except to play the creature of feminine delicacy where you simply cried and did not offer any substantial advice? I mean no disrespect to him, but do you want to marry a man who always makes you doubt the words that you say and chastises you for speaking your mind? Mary, that is no way to live."

"You understand me," she smiled, "you really understand me."

"But I do not agree that the woman your brother was courting should have married him. I believe that whoever she is, was right to reject him, because clearly, he was not the best suitor. He doesn't seem like he would have been a good man for any woman, and you must see the damage of his behavior and confront it. You must see the wrong in it, and do not belittle its magnitude. And please, Mary, I do not mean to disrespect your brother now."

"Nay, I understand, and perhaps I spoke hastily when I said that I would never forgive her."

"Yes, you did but therein lays the other problem that I lay at Mr. Bertram's feet: he does not seem to take human nature and human frailty into account. You were speaking as a woman who was in distress, saddened by the fact that your brother and his sister caused such a scandal, and you were in an emotional state. When we humans are upset, we can sometimes speak irrationally and give way to sensibility. And then we must apologize for our mistake. You were speaking from a place of sensibility. That is no crime, Mary. You were just human, and accommodations must be made for human frailty sometimes. In moments such as that, we humans must exercise forgiveness."

Affectionately, Mary took my hand.

"This is better than any reaction I expected to get," she smiled happily.

"What sort of reaction did you expect?" I gurgled.

"I worried that you might not be able to stand the sight of me, after all, I am such a lesser creature than you, who are all goodness, while I must appear wicked by comparison."

My tone turned serious, without me even knowing.

"Mary," I insisted, "first, there is something that I will ask you to promise me by the end. I shall tell you of that later. But for now, remember this: you are not Jane Bennet, and so you do not have to act like me. Only I am Jane Bennet, and my actions are my own, but must never be used as a template to oppress other women with. No one should ever feel like they must base themselves off of other people when their natures are so verily different. Therefore, promise me this: accept my nature, do not find me dull, understand that sometimes I will advise you if I think you are acting incorrectly, but never try and turn yourself into me. I was not drawn to you because you were like me; I found you amicable because you were *not* like me."

"Be careful, Jane," Mary chuckled, "you are getting danger-ously close to being too wise to live amongst."

"You had best be joking," I teased.

"I am, believe me."

"And now, back to your 'flaws'. You have them because we all have them. But I could never despise you for them because your flaws belong to people that I love and admire. You talk like my sister, Elizabeth. Faith, she says many things in a similar fashion that you do. But I do not condemn her for her spirted ways. In fact, I think she is the bravest woman that I know. My two youngest sisters, Kitty and Lydia, despise the idea of marrying a clergyman. Are they evil? No. Like you, they simply understand their nature, and that is that they are not meant to be clergymen's wives. Sometimes, I wonder if perhaps even I would not be up for that sort of task. And then there is my mother and Aunt Gardiner, who often encourage us to marry prudently, considering the man's pocketbook as well as our passions. We are educated on the idea of marrying well. And I love my mother and aunt, despite their advice. Therefore, if I love Elizabeth, who sounds like you, love my aunt and mother, who encourage advantageous marriages, like you do, and love Kitty and Lydia, who also do not want to marry clergymen, then I would be a hypocrite for treating you in a lesser fashion. And hypocrisy is not a flaw that I wish to entertain this day."

"Then, if you promise to always accept me, I give you leave to always correct me when I am in the wrong."

"But you were not in the wrong then," I added. "Because as you showed, Mr. Bertram was angry with you because you were unafraid to confront the situation. You did not sit there and cry like a helpless creature, and because you speak your mind. Some of the things you said were insensitive, but your attitude and intention were logical and necessary to confront. Mary, even if you were amenable to the idea of marrying a clergyman—which you never were—would you really have wanted to marry someone who was *always* making you feel guilt for not saying exactly what he wants to always hear...and who makes you hesitate with every-thing you say, because he's trained you to doubt yourself?"

Mary tilted her head to the side, considering this as I continued.

"You would not be happy with such a person. And, as I said, you came up with a solution to save your brother and his sister. He came up with no solution at all and seems to lack a certain degree of forgiveness over small matters that deserve such. Both your brother and his sister showed great defects of character, but you were the one whose first instinct was not to cast them out. That's what family is meant to do—be there for each other. You were there for them...while he seemed to only want you to despair. And lastly, he claimed that the person he adored was a figment of his imagination. Mary, he was never fully seeing you; he saw an image. But you always tell the truth, be that truth right or bad. Therefore, you never lied to Mr. Bertram; he lied to himself."

I could not believe how naturally I was speaking, and truly, there was something very liberating about it.

"A marriage cannot work when both husband and wife cannot admire and respect each other. With Mr. Edmund Bertram only wishing to love you if he could project his mind and thoughts onto you, he only was still loving himself. Therefore, rejoice those things ended where they did. If he is the man that you say, he needs a woman who is just like him and enjoys being guided by him, and you need a husband who accepts you for who you are, and not for who you *could be* after he had melded you in his own image."

"I cannot change all of me," she augmented, "I can only be Mary Crawford. And you know what? I do not want to be anyone else. Sometimes, I will be thoroughly in the wrong, but I will learn from it, in my own way. In this moment, I think you are one of the few people who see me for who and what I am, rather than what I am not, or what I can do for them."

"Us women, in life, are expected to give so much, I suppose, and expect little in return. But perhaps men are similar, and they suffer under that same weight, and I never got the chance to figure that out."

"What does the world want from us, Jane? I cannot tell."

"Neither can I."

~

But part of the narrative was still not fulfilled. Mary still had not told me about what Mr. William Price had to do with all of this. Therefore, I reminded her of him.

"Oh," Mary sighed, "now that is less painful to speak of. You recall that I said that my brother was courting another woman before he ran off with Maria."

"Yes. The woman who rejected his first marriage proposal."

"Yes. She also was a resident at Mansfield Park. She was a ward there. Her name was Fanny Price, and she is Mr. Edmund Bertram's and Maria's cousin."

"Fanny Price?" I repeated. "Price?"

"Yes. She is Mr. William Price's younger sister. Due to their parents having many children and low income, she was sent to live at Mansfield Park. She grew up there, and every now and again, Mr. William Price would visit her."

"So," I repeated, to help clarify it all in my mind, "Mr. William Price is the brother of a woman who lived at Mansfield Park. And she is cousin to the man that you once were in love with."

"Yes."

"And your brother fell in love with her but then ran off with Miss Maria Bertram."

"Yes. And there is more."

I felt my eyes widen in shock.

"There is more to this drama?"

"Yes. One day, I heard that Mr. Edmund Bertram did get married eventually...to Fanny Price."

This was altogether too much for me to comprehend.

"The man you loved married his cousin, who he grew up with, and this was the same woman that your brother once was in love with."

"Yes, I can see that you are shocked."

"I might be beyond shock," I admitted, "this is indeed quite complex."

"Reality, Jane. Reality will always be more fantastical than fiction."

"So that was why you were scared when you first saw Mr. William Price. Was it because you worried that he knew all of this?"

"Yes. I feared that Fanny had told him everything and he would have judged me. But either he was never told the particulars, or he did not care to take on other people's prejudices. Whatever the reason, I thank providence for chivalrous discretion. I quite love it when things like this happen."

"I do not believe that he is the sort to despise you for actions that are not your own. I think he will be kind to you."

"I am happy for it, because I prefer to have friends that I care about, over enemies that I *once* cared about. But whatever the outcome tomorrow, today I can say this. Jane, you have given me one of the most satisfying days that I have felt in a long time. I cannot thank you enough."

Suddenly, the clock struck the hour.

"Oh!" Mary gasped, "is that the time? I told my sister that I would have left before now. She will be worried."

"Will you come again soon?" I asked.

"Of course, I will. You think little of me for not knowing the answer to that already. Gracechurch Street is better than any castle or abbey."

She moved to leave, but then she turned back to me.

"But wait! There is that one thing you said in the very beginning. You said it was about your character, and that you would tell me later. So, I must ask. What did you mean?"

I smiled.

"Mary, you had said that I was perfect. I need you to promise me something."

"What?"

"Never think I am perfect. It is a small thing to ask, so I hope that you can keep it. I will do my best to always be guided by reason, rationality, and serenity... but I am not perfect. I will try to be, but I am human. And no one allows me to be just that...

human. So please, Mary, look at me as a human. And forgive me when I am not perfect."

Mary took my hands in hers.

"Jane Bennet," she smiled, "just for you."

And with that she left, with us each feeling happier.

Caroline Bingley did not come again, I made excuses for her, but I felt no pain over it. For a friend had already come that day. Yes, a friend did. And I learned another chapter to her *tale*.

Chapter Twenty-Two
KITTY'S TALE: SERVANTS IN THE KNOW

Once more, I learned another chapter of my younger sister's *tale*!

When I returned to Pemberley, I immediately sought out Lizzy and Jane and told them the news. They were horrified, to say the least, but only Jane was surprised.

"Poor Lydia!" Jane cried. "I had no idea that Mr. Wickham was capable of such behavior."

"I am upset," Elizabeth added, "but am not surprised in the slightest. For truly, how can a match, so uneven and brought about because two people's lack of control, have led to anything else but such a fate for our sister? It was an imprudent match that we all had no choice but to bring about, and therefore, there was never really much hope."

"But a mistress? And to parade it around Lydia in such a manner. Well, it is downright sinful. It is horrible. It is—"

"What Mary Crawford and Henry had to witness their uncle do to their aunt," I said, connecting it all together.

Both sisters looked at me and they considered the parallels so horribly.

"Oh, good god," Jane said, "this is really happening to our family?"

"And this has shown that we're not the first family for this to happen to," Elizabeth said, resigned. "And I daresay that it won't be the last. And if Lydia and Wickham were to ever have any children, they would have to undergo and experience the discord between their parents, in the same manner that the Crawfords did. Then they will not stand a chance at achieving any sense of morality and good conduct. They will be ruined from the very beginning. Well, I daresay that it does present the idea of when does influence end and responsibility for one's own actions begin? In moments like these, I am sure that I still do not know."

~

"...because," Georgiana said, "maybe, there is no real answer."

Once I had talked with my sisters about Lydia's poor situation, I told Georgiana about it. When I told her about Elizabeth's point, she augmented an answer that I foresaw, because I had been thinking the same thing.

"I know," I said, "one does not know precisely what to think. Jane is planning on inviting Lydia to come to Godfrey Park to stay with her for a time, but she has no notion of how to do it without having to invite Mr. Wickham along."

"The idea of seeing him again would be dreadful, Kitty," Georgiana inferred. "I may no longer be in love with him, but it still would hurt to see him."

"As it naturally would and should. It is good to forget him but never forget how he behaved. There is nothing wrong with carrying that memory with you, so that none of us be duped by him again. He does not deserve your attention or company. Don't worry, Georgie, he will never be admitted to Pemberley. At least, I pray that he will not. And if we ever have no choice but to invite him here, don't be afraid to avoid him. I trust that you both will be doing each other a service by that."

Georgiana looked at me.

"I forgot to ask," she said, "how does this all make you feel? Lydia is your sister, and you both were very good friends."

"We were," I said, simply. "And this is where I feel the effects of growing up and feeling the pain as innocence dies."

"It hurts you to know that your sister is being treated as such."

"That's the problem. Georgie, I don't care what Lydia is going through. That's what frightens me. I don't care."

Georgiana's eyes widened.

"Oh."

"I know that I must sound like a terrible person, but I am..."

"Tired," she answered for me. "You are tired of caring for a sister who put herself in the situation she is in. You tried to reach her before, to show her what she put you through, and she couldn't care. You are tired that she cannot see, and maybe never will see how her actions affected you. You are tired that she was the favorite, and you were cast to the wayside incorrectly. You are tired of all the times that you both spoke, but she was the only voice that some people heard, and yours might as well had never happened. But above all, you are tired of trying to help her, and she never appreciated it. Never appreciating whenever anyone tries to help her."

"That's it," I sighed, closing my eyes. "I am tired, Georgie. I have nothing left in me to care—no sympathy. No nothing. I am not saying that I welcome her always being banished somewhere else. But I am somewhat happy that she is undergoing this."

"You are?" she asked, frightened.

"Yes, but you need not be alarmed, because it is not what you think. As horrible as her present circumstances are, I think... this will help her wake up. This will help her see the life that she walked into, and it will, ironically, help her develop more."

Georgiana did not respond, but only looked at me, and this gave me the confidence to continue.

"If Lydia did marry Wickham, and he proved to be an exemplary husband, cherishing, and doting on her, then it would lead to her never changing. She would be as she always was. But no. He proved to be precisely as we knew he would be. The worst. Sometimes the bloom from our false realities needs to die, for us to see the reality for what it is. There was a dream that was my life, and I lived in it, in full. Then something happened that humbled me and forced me to wake up. It hurt, Georgie. It hurt so much. But it was all worth it in the end."

"Oh. I suppose the same happened with Wickham and me. My love for him was a dream, the dream burst and fell into a nightmare. I cried myself to sleep for days. And nights. It was pure agony. But then I rose out of it, and when I did, I saw the world differently. It was even as if the whole color of the world changed."

"You were a child who woke up and became a woman. Not all of us can say that, because we weren't given a reality that punctured the dream. Lydia does not need to live in a dream forever. She needs that same lesson. As terrible as this is, perhaps, this is her lesson. As hard as it is, I admit. However, as I said before, I do not want her to spend her life away from us."

"Good. Because if you did, that would make you just like the Bertrams."

"And we cannot have that, now can we?"

"No, we cannot."

"Either way, Jane will eventually invite Lydia to come to her home. That will give Lydia the serenity and sense of security from being around her family. There is but one thing I am sure of."

"What?" Georgiana asked.

"Lydia and I will never be the friends that we used to be. Somehow, a river has come between us, and I don't think either of us knows how to cross that great divide."

As we talked on a little more, there was a knock on the door.

"Come in," Georgiana said.

The door opened and Sarah and Betsy entered.

"Oh, there is news," Sarah cried.

"Yes, the time has come. I am just as interested as anyone," Betsy said.

"Not more interesting than me," Sarah said.

"Sarah, everything is more interesting than you. Don't talk nonsense so early in the day."

"It's not even early, you numpty!"

"Ladies," Georgiana said, "what is the news? Bicker after you have enlightened us."

"There has been a letter," Betsy said. "It's addressed to the entire Pemberley household."

"Mrs. Reynolds delivered it into Mr. Darcy's hand himself," Sarah added, "and he's gone to read it."

"Who sent the letter?" I asked, but I pretty much already knew the answer.

"Mansfield Park," Betsy answered.

Georgiana and I felt the magnitude of the answer. We finally were going to get a response from the family that we had no choice but to offend by every possible method. The reply back would not be sanguine or penitent.

Pride would exchange blows with more pride.

"Did they ask for us?" I asked. Then I turned to Georgiana. "Can we not go to your brother and ask him about the contents of the letter? He can only tell us no once."

"I don't see why not. 'No' is not the easiest word to hear, but it won't knock us backward."

We both stood up and Betsy and Sarah breathed in, prepared to follow us.

"No, no," I said, "you both must stay here. We'll tell you what is going to happen when we return. We don't want you getting into trouble for being too intrusive."

"Oh, balderdash," Betsy groaned. "Thwarted by aristocratic propriety."

"This is the only thing I miss about Longbourn," Sarah said, "there, the news was always spoken for the whole household to hear."

"I agree," Betsy said, as they left the room, "no being shifted to a corner and left in the dark."

When they disappeared, I was astounded.

"I think that must be the first, and only time, that I ever saw them agree so peacefully on anything," I uttered.

"Yes, it does seem to be so very novel, and I have only known them for a matter of months."

"Your brother must despise them."

"He does, outwardly, but internally, he adores them."

"Really?" I was surprised by this.

"Yes. They give him something to complain about. We all need something to complain about every now and again."

"Yes, it does sometimes bring animation to our cheeks."

Coming to a decision, we both stood up.

"Oh well, it's time to see what your brother has to say."

We went to Mr. Darcy's study.

When we reached the door, we just stood there.

"These doors are so intimidating," I said.

"Yes, they are. When I was a child, I was always afraid to knock on them and speak to Father."

"Why? Was he cross whenever he was in here?"

"No. He was often very amiable. It is merely that these doors are so...so..."

"Intimidating."

"Yes."

We both breathed out and in.

"Oh well," I said, knocking. "Nothing for it."

"Come in," we heard Darcy call.

We opened the door and stood there, facing Mr. Darcy, Mr. Bingley, Lizzy, and Jane. My nervousness immediately changed to anger.

"Wait," I began, "were you all discussing the letter *without* us?"

"Kitty," Mr. Darcy said, "that is nothing of the sort. The letter arrived and we thought it best to read the letter in the privacy of my library."

"You read it without us," Georgiana echoed, but with more force than mine.

"Georgiana," Mr. Darcy stated, "why do you take that tone with me? That is uncouth, for you are both aware that I have just as much a right to open my own letters. And you both are being very presumptuous, don't you think?"

We both accepted that, *maybe*, we were being very forward and vulgar.

"Sorry, Mr. Darcy," I apologized.

"Yes. Sorry, brother," Georgiana said.

"They were perhaps merely being eager," Jane excused, "and forgot themselves."

"Yes," Mr. Bingley supported, "it was probably a result of the excitement that comes from hearing of the matter."

"I accept that, for it is natural," Mr. Darcy said, "but that does not give you the right to lack propriety. Georgiana and Kitty, I expect better from you, this day forth."

"Yes, sir."

"Yes, brother."

"Very good. Well, since you already are aware, yes, I have received a letter back from Sir Thomas Bertram, Mansfield Park, and the letter is as I expected."

Georgiana and I gave each other a look, worried that it was all that he had to say.

"And?" I could not help but prompt.

"Oh, he is very evidently angry with us," Elizabeth explained, "and is offended by our presumptuous manner."

"And as a result, he feels that it is only necessary," Mr. Darcy explained, "to visit Pemberley in a week, to explain why we are erroneous to address him in such an undignified manner."

"That is my favorite part," Elizabeth asserted.

"Sir Thomas Bertram is coming to Pemberley to argue his case?" Georgiana augmented.

"Yes, he is," Mr. Darcy stated. "More likely to assume that I am the sort to roll over and bend to his will just because of his knighthood."

"He has never seen you at all," I realized, "and probably has never even heard a report of what you look like."

"No, he has not."

Sir Thomas Bertram accidentally had walked into his own doom. It was altogether of comical proportions. The poor man probably expected to arrive to see a little man of feeble convictions that could easily be shaken about like an ant against some heavy winds. What he didn't know was that he would soon be facing an oak who had weathered tempests.

"And he does not intend to come alone," Elizabeth added. "He shall arrive with his two sons, and his daughter-in-law, Mr. Edmund Bertram's wife."

"Fanny Bertram," I clarified. "Mr. Price's sister."

"Yes. Apparently, longing to see her brother, she pleaded to be brought along. Sir Thomas made it very evident that while Mrs. Fanny Bertram does love her brother, she is very apprehensive about him choosing Miss Crawford. And Sir Thomas remains steadfast in his belief that he thinks his nephew is making one of the largest mistakes in his life."

"And we will have to see this family in seven days," I said, "knowing that they still do not support the match, we have angered them, and it might lead to a full debate."

"Well," Elizabeth finalized, "the earth was created in six days, wasn't it?"

"True," Mr. Bingley agreed.

"Yes," Georgiana said.

"If we believe what we read," I said.

"In a manner of speaking," Jane said.

"It was," Mr. Darcy said.

"Well then," Elizabeth said, "we can't really complain about our problems, now can we?"

"You always used that excuse when I had to clean up my room and put my dolls away!" I declared.

"Did it work?"

"Yes."

"Well then, what are you complaining about?"

A plague upon her relentless sense and logic!

Chapter Twenty-Three

KITTY'S TALE: THE WAITING

After the Crawfords company was notified of this new event on the rise, there was a natural wave of anxiety that swept over them, unless your name was Henry or Mary.

"Well," Miss Crawford said, "quite frankly, I am glad to finally be able to confront the matter."

"As am I, sister," Mr. Crawford said.

"You all are not worried that you might not find success at the end of this scenario?" Arthur Philips asked.

"That's the humor of it all," Mr. Crawford said, "if you can apply humor to this situation. Sometimes, when you have made your mistakes, fallen in many ways, you understand that success might not be the end of your adventure. Nor will you ever become the white knight that you wished yourself to be. But you must try anyway. It's the climb. The climb is all that matters, in the end. Did you ever try to rise above the hole you put yourself in? I aim to try. But one thing is certain."

He looked to all of us.

"You all tried to help my family. You listened. You forgave. I will never forget this day, nor will I allow you all to be mistreated when the Bertrams arrive. I will do what I can to regulate their behavior, though I confess to being a poor influence."

"You need to hold fast to your courage, sir," Mr. Darcy said, "for the life you save might very well be more than just your own."

Mr. Darcy turned to me.

"Kitty?"

"Yes, Mr. Darcy?"

"I require your services."

My chest swelled with pride. I felt the flattery of his request and as if I had a specialness to me.

"Yes, sir. How may I be of service, for surely, I would like to help if I can."

"I am sending a letter to Colonel Forster to grant Lieutenant Finlay a day of reprieve in six days so that he is here when the Bertrams arrive. I would like you to hand deliver it to Colonel Forster specifically. Then, if he permits, speak to Finlay yourself so that he is aware of what is in store for him. Georgiana will accompany you."

"Yes," I said.

Once all was settled, a carriage was drawn, and Georgiana and I were riding to Lambton. When we arrived, we immediately called on Mrs. Forster, who saw us both eagerly.

"To have the ladies of Pemberley visit me," Mrs. Forster cried merrily, "now it is a great honor, indeed. When the village hears that I have had such illustrious visitors, I will be the talk of Lambton. How do you both do?"

"Very well, thank you, Mrs. Forster," Georgiana said as we sat down and had to follow the express strictures of paying a social call. In life, it is best to always be direct, but that is not the way it is with us ladies. You must meet, sit down, take a cup of tea or coffee, and then after pleasantries are exchanged, then you may finally get to the point for your coming.

"When I last was at Pemberley," Mrs. Forster began as she served us a cup of coffee and some cakes, "I was so amazed at the splendor that I was not certain on where to look. It was like looking on real elegance, in a way that I had never known."

"Since it was a formal dinner," Georgiana explained, "I fear that you did not get the chance to see a tour of the entire house."

"No, I did not. It must all be very fine, wouldn't it? Yet, I know that you all must be terribly busy, and being granted a tour would be a tedious business for you."

"Oh, I know that tone," I said, reading between the lines of what she said.

"What do you mean, Kitty?" Mrs. Forster asked.

"Come, old friend," I said, "I know you as well as you know yourself. That last sentence really meant that you want a tour of the place but are too bashful to ask."

Mrs. Forster's expression morphed into sheepishness.

"I was doing my best to appear delicate."

"And you did a fine job of it. But I was too much wishing for the truth, that I couldn't wait for us to procrastinate the matter any longer."

"If you would like an invitation to tour Pemberley," Georgiana said to Mrs. Forster, while drinking her coffee, "then I would be delighted."

"Oh," Mrs. Forster cried, "that would be the most splendid thing in the world. Thank you, Miss Darcy."

"See?" I questioned. "The joys of having a tactless friend."

"Oh, Kitty, you are not tactless. You just didn't feel like beating around the bush."

"No, I did not."

"Now," Mrs. Forster said, "I can write to my family. Oh, they will be wild with envy when they read that I am to visit Pemberley again, but this time get to see the rooms. This is too much of an honor."

Now that we, to our surprise, had the advantage of having Mrs. Forster feel like she was in our debt, it was easy to mention that we had a letter of great import. We requested that she send an officer to retrieve Colonel Forster, because he had an express letter sent to him, from Pemberley.

Feeling even more important because she felt that she was a part of something interesting, she had a servant retrieve Captain Carter and go and return with Colonel Forster.

While we were waiting, Mrs. Forster asked me about my family. I told her that they were all well, and that my sister, Mary, and Mr. Atkins had returned to Meryton.

Then, with an apprehensive look in her eye, she asked me if I had received word from Lydia. Of course, I knew about what had transpired, from her own report. I decided that there was no point in ignoring the reality that she herself had to confront.

"No, I have not," I said, "but if you are worried about telling me anything grave or disturbing, then you may set your mind at rest. I am aware of Lydia's predicament, and our household has been notified."

When hearing this, she breathed a sigh of relief.

"Oh, that is good. I was worried about being the one who had to tell you such news. While I knew that it was necessary, I admit that it was a task that I did not enjoy."

"Who would? I'm sure that I would not. Thank you for doing your duty and wishing to keep me informed. Also, steps have been taken in hopes of improving Lydia's situation."

"Oh, that is very good. Sometimes, I look back on that whole fiasco and wonder where it all began to go wrong. Truly, I never expected life to take that turn."

"You mustn't blame yourself, Mrs. Forster."

"One cannot help but do so. After all, if we all spent our lives blaming others and never ourselves, there would be no room for revelations to occur, now would there be?"

"That is true," I said, feeling a little humbled.

"Yes," Georgiana said, "very true."

Mrs. Forster continued to speak more animatedly about when Lydia and she had gone to Brighton together. She found very apt listeners in us. First, it seemed like she needed to talk about it. As if, talking about it helped purge her of the grime and grit that comes from bad memories. Secondly, it seemed like her life might be a little dull now, and her memories were the most interesting thing to talk about. That is often the case with things. And thirdly, she was interesting. In truth, our sordid pasts (which we ought to regret) can be the most compelling things to narrate, because we listeners love to hear such things. Perfection does not, a good story, make.

Therefore, there was never a quiet or dull moment passed between us until Colonel Forster arrived.

When he did, he was animated, and eager to see us. For my part, it was a nostalgic feeling, for I reminded him of better times in Meryton.

With Miss Darcy, it was the feeling of flattery that comes when a great lady comes to visit. Both sides of his happiness were satisfied.

We handed him the letter, he read it, and the change of his disposition was very swift. It transitioned from a look of ease to one of alertness and professionalism.

When he finished reading it, he turned to Georgiana and me.

"Lieutenant Finlay is training the troops. I shall have Captain Carter take you to him. Inform him that he can be spared from his duties while you visit and return to them when you leave."

"Thank you, Colonel," I said, grateful.

"My pleasure, dear ladies."

≈

Captain Carter was very amiable when he came to escort us to the training grounds. Perhaps it was because it freed him from his duties for a while, and I could understand that desire. Therefore, he was very talkative as he walked alongside us, even going so far as to slow down his footsteps, for the sake of drawing out his time with us.

The regiment was not going anywhere anytime soon, therefore, Georgiana and I were in no great hurry. Therefore, we humored him, and the time passed pleasantly.

When we reached the training grounds, I saw Lieutenant Finlay as he was arranging marches for the troops.

I watched him as he barked orders, and the ranks fell into proper lines. I marveled at his vocal prowess and at the fine figures that our officers cut when they marched in such an efficient way. The red, white, and gold on their regimentals were seen to impressive advantage.

However, upon closer inspection, I paid more attention to the soldiers' uniforms. Their redcoats looked dashing as ever, but I was not as dazed with them as I once was. It was amazing at how a redcoat lost much appeal to me. There was a time where I ran quite wild over seeing a regimental out of the corner of my eye. But now...they were handsome, but no more than any other man in Britain. I suppose that the outfit no longer mattered.

Even more so, I found myself inspecting the man's uniforms more closely. A redcoat will always be a striking thing and cut a very fine figure on a man. That, complemented against his white breeches and waistcoat, is also very fine. But the more that I looked at the white breeches, I began to notice that, while they looked clean, there was something powdery about them. When I commented on this to Georgiana and Captain Carter, Carter had a proper explanation.

"An officer must always look his best, unless he is mid-battle. As a result, his uniform must be clean to the upmost degree."

"I never wondered how you all could manage to maintain them, until now," I said.

"It's not something that is often thought of, despite that it is very important to us. Naturally, we have them cleaned as much as possible by either our wives or the washerwomen. However, sometimes an officer can be far away from either lady, or simply he didn't manage his income properly and couldn't employ a washerwoman. If that be the case, and his clothes are dirty, he can sometimes suppress the sordid look, by the way of a musical instrument."

"What do you mean?"

"One of the musical instruments that we play while we march is a flute. Often, it exudes a white-powdered residue on it. If we officers are ever desperate, we put the flute's residue on where the stain is, it blanches out the spot, and while we look a little powdered, the stain no longer is there. It has been whited-out."

"Really?" I asked, amazed. "That is quite ingenious actually."

"I always wonder who the first person was to make that discovery," Carter said, humorous, "if he did, I would like to shake his hand. He's saved me from a few blunders in my day."

We respectfully waited till Finlay was done his exercise, which wasn't long. For no more than a couple minutes into being there, he spied us. Upon seeing us, I waved to him. Smiling he nodded, noticing me. Captain Carter took this as the perfect sign to approach him, deliver Colonel Forster's news that he was relieved, and Lieutenant Finlay approached us.

"You speak well," I said when he approached us.

"You tease me," he said, "I speak terribly."

"You would only say that if you really were confident in your vocal skills."

"We shall see." He bowed to us both. "Ladies, it is a pleasure and a privilege. To what do I owe the honor?"

"Would you be upset if we didn't just come for leisure, but because we had a purpose?" I asked.

"Not at all. Not everything in life are things spoken by way of leisure. Has something happened?"

"We received a reply from Mansfield Park, Lieutenant," Georgiana informed him. When hearing this news, his eyes swelled with interest.

"Ah, I see. Might I have the honor of walking with you along that small bit of wilderness over there? It's more picturesque than training grounds and there are some evergreens that the winter cannot defeat."

We accepted, he offered us his arms, we placed ours in his and we walked along, with him in the middle. We exchanged pleasantries all along the way, until we reached the trees.

Once we did, he turned to us.

"What news does the letter bring? For I doubt that Sir Thomas Bertram would immediately feel humbled. On the contrary, I suspect that his pride was wounded, and he would have replied about the offense taken."

"And you would be right," Georgiana said.

"There is no act of contrition on his part," I said, "and he is to come to Pemberley in six days' time."

"Mr. Darcy sent us to request your presence on that day. He has already written to Colonel Forster to give you leave of your duties. He hopes you may oblige him."

"I had wished to be a part of the meeting, therefore, yes, I shall attend. What time does he expect my visit?"

"He has hopes of you arriving soon at 11 o'clock in the morning. You will have supper with us, whether the Bertrams arrive, as planned, or not."

"Then I shall be at Pemberley for most of the day?" He said, looking at me fondly.

"Yes," I laughed gently, "no matter how the day goes in or out, you shall."

"I would like some more particulars on the matter," he said, "would you prefer to walk along with me for a little longer so that my curiosity can be satisfied?"

"Who are we to argue?"

We walked along a little more, and conveniently, we came upon Denny.

"Miss Bennet and Miss Darcy," he said, approaching us as he removed his hat and bowed his head. "How very fortunate, while also being a complete surprise."

"The surprise belongs to us as well," Georgiana said, "you came out of nowhere."

"Oh," Denny said, "I can explain very easily. My unit was dismissed since we completed our training for the day. I was returning to my quarters to sit in front of the fireplace and ponder about my life when I suddenly saw your fresh and handsome faces. Might I take this turn with you, or would I be an intrusion?"

"Not at all."

He offered Georgiana his arm, and they walked ahead while Finlay and I dawdled behind.

"Tell me truly," Finlay said, "Mr. Darcy did not ask me, did he?"

"No. It was more like an order than anything."

"I had a feeling."

"You mustn't be angry with him," I defended Mr. Darcy, "giving instruction is just his way. And even that's not his fault. He's been trained that way by habit."

"Yes. Being the master of a great house gives a man no choice but to be authoritative. I am not offending him at all, for I know a little bit about that myself. When you are a lieutenant, even when you are at leisure, you still carry that leading tone in your voice."

"Yes, I heard, a moment ago. You sounded impressive."

"Thank you," he said, rolling his head backwards and looking up at the sky.

"No," I said, "I meant that. I was amazed by you."

He looked down at me fondly.

"You were?"

"Yes. You had a natural way of controlling the officers. Also, another thing is evident. They respect you. Your men respect you."

"I had the luxury of *not* being a man of luxury. I was not born to wealth and therefore couldn't buy my commission. I had to rise through the ranks. I was worried that this would stir the men to despise me. After all, I was from no great house, but a commoner. Therefore, they would be angry with me rising through the ranks when they still remained at their present station. And then, the best thing happened."

"What?"

"I was transferred. Therefore, all the men who despised me were gone from my company, and I was able to start all over with a new batch of officers, who were quick to impress, moderate in learning of my history, and very slow at developing any prejudice toward me. Nothing is scarier than jealousy."

"Oh, I know that all too well, believe me. Jealousy creates all sorts of mischief because it is often masked behind a just cause. Many an injustice has been committed because someone accused someone else of being nefarious, when all the while, they simply were jealous of the other person."

"Yes, that happens a lot."

"I'm sorry if it has ever happened to you. It's not a delightful experience."

"Thank you, Kitty, and you are right. It's bloody agony."

He looked at me, a little annoyed with himself.

"Blast it!"

"What?" I asked, surprised. Why was he angry? I thought we had been getting along charmingly.

"Here I am, at the perfect time to woo you. It may be terribly cold, but there is a romance to the scene. Especially with gray clouds silhouetted against the thick trees...and I do not say anything charming. I do not take advantage of this opportunity at all."

"Oh, must everything be pretty words all the time?" I groaned. "I love romance, and I love charm, but surely that cannot be the beginning and end of every discussion that we have. There would be no room for anything else. I was happy with what we were discussing. It can't be flattering all the time. Sometimes, we must be practical. Besides, you were telling me more about your history. Don't you think that I want to know you?"

"Yes, I suppose that you are right."

"Besides. Our bond did not begin in a conventional way, therefore, I never expected it to fall into that direction either."

"Yes, you did know me, even when I did not let you know me, didn't you?"

"Oh, at first, I was confused as a chicken in a horse stable. But time helped me."

"Colonel Fitzwilliam left for London."

"Yes, he did. How does that make you feel?"

"He and I both know that we are glad to be away from each other's company. It doesn't matter that I admire him, and he respects me. We can never be more than rivals to each other."

"You admire him?" I asked. "Oh, Finlay, I am proud of you. Ever so proud."

"You are?"

"Yes. I daresay that I cannot think of any other time in my life that I was prouder of a man. Your situation is not easy. But to admire the Colonel, despite all rivalries."

"Well, we know what the other one is entirely about. Besides, he is a good man. I understand why you grew to feel fondly for him, after I had left you in Hertfordshire. He offered you tenderness, didn't he?"

"Will my confession hurt you?"

"No. I am prepared."

"Yes, he did. You both offered different things."

"What did I offer?"

"You offered love at its hardest, at its most pure and bold. He offered love at its softest. Would you believe that you both found the proper proscription for making a woman fall madly in love with you?"

"Yes, I can."

He lowered his hand from my arm and touched part of my gown. It did not reach my skin, but slowly, he wrapped his hand around the cloth of my garment and held it fast.

He was living in his dreams.

And perhaps, so was I.

We walked on longer, in such a state. Neither of us were saying anything because the silence was just so sweet.

He continued to hold a piece of my gown in his clutches, and we walked even slower.

"I make you give yourself away, don't I?" he asked.

"You do not do anything that I do not allow. Be not alarmed, Lieutenant, for there is no taking in on your part. However, this will be the furthest that I go. I do not want to make my family ashamed of me."

"Why?" He spat. "I do not show frustration with you, or your family. My complaint is a general one. We are full grown. You are a woman, and I am a man. Why must our actions shame others? Why can't our actions only be a shame to ourselves? Why can't we stand alone in front of the goddess of humility and prudence and face her as individuals?"

"Sadly, that is not how our society works," I said, sighing wistfully, "we are all anchored down, aren't we?"

"Yes. I tire of it."

There was a small boulder nearby. I walked to it and sat down on it.

"Then ignore it, for now," I assured him. "We are as close to one can get when they are alone. We have nothing to be ashamed of now. Therefore, we must not be."

"Kitty," he said, laughing, "you are braver than I."

"I've never been on a battlefield."

"I think that you would brave it better than anyone. I suppose..."

"Yes?"

"That I am so terribly proud of you."

My smile widened.

"You are?"

"Of course, I am. When I first met you, you were Lydia's older sister. But over time, you are so much your own woman now. Such a natural change indicates an ability to adapt very well. And you have."

He raised his hand to my face and held my chin in his hand.

To feel the touch of his fingers on my skin was so calming, so affectionate, that I closed my eyes.

"I love this," I said, "but we must not remain this way for long. I will not cause a scandal for Pemberley."

"Kitty, you are not Lydia."

"No, I am not. And I must keep it that way." I looked at him with a smile in my eyes. "No matter how sorely I am tempted."

"I would know how to please you. I swear it."

"I know. No matter where I go in life, no matter how far, you will always be in my heart."

"I better be."

~

Soon, it was time for Georgiana and me to depart. Finlay and Denny escorted us to our carriage, helped us inside, we bade them farewell, and were off.

Looking through the glass I saw both gentlemen watch us as we left.

When I turned back to Georgiana, she was blushing.

"What?" I asked her.

"It's Denny. He seems genuinely kind."

"He is. He just wants the little things in life."

"He just feels safe to be around. He was not trying to charm me at all. He just wanted to talk."

"That's his way. And..." then I realized what she was feeling. Oh dear! That would be too inconvenient. "Georgiana, no!"

"Oh," she chuckled, "of course not! I'm just saying that it's nice to have a simple and easy conversation from a man who wants no more or less from me. My wealth draws too much attention. It's just nice to have someone who does not care about that."

"Oh, alright then. That makes a great deal of sense."

We rode home, and when we got there, we applied to Mr. Darcy immediately. We told him and Elizabeth that Finlay would be available to visit in six days.

Darcy showed his happiness in the usual manner that he did: stoically. But we knew that he was happy.

"Well," Mary Crawford said to us when we told her company the news. "This all can either end very well, or very badly. There is no in-between."

"And there is no going backwards," Henry Crawford said, "everything is going to change."

"Yes, it is."

"Well, then we shall meet it, head on."

Those next six days were both the shortest and the longest days of our lives. Each moment felt like we were walking into a social battle that would take place in a drawing room, with only a visit and tour from the Forsters, to break the eye of the storm.

But finally, the six days came to an end.

And I woke up the next morning, knowing what we were in store for...

Chapter Twenty-Four

JANE BENNET'S TALE: THE SADDENING SOCIAL CALL

E very day that I wake up, I almost never know what I am in store for.

The next day, Aunt Gardiner had no engagements, so we were in the sitting room together, where she had recently learned to knit, and thought perhaps that it was best to teach me. The yarn and needles fascinated me, and she was preparing to teach me how to make a shawl, when I saw a carriage arrived in front of the house.

"There's a carriage," I informed her, and then I went to the window. Caroline Bingley emerged from out of it and my heart warmed immediately. "It's Miss Bingley. She has come."

"Oh!" Aunt Gardiner remarked, looking at the knitting. "Then we must hurry."

Very quickly, we rushed around the room, putting everything away so that the sitting room looked neat.

At the ringing of the bell, I went to the hall, a servant opened the door, and I made sure that my face was the first Caroline saw.

"Miss Bingley." I smiled and added, "I am delighted to see you."

Caroline entered, and immediately, her face looked disdainful of everything that she saw. She looked over the room and did not appear to like it. At last, her eyes fell on me.

"Jane," she said, and I noted that her voice had no warmth, "it is a pleasure to see you again."

Her tone gave no indication of her actually being happy, but I supposed that she simply needed a little time to get used to her surroundings.

"My apologies for not coming sooner," she said, equally cold again, while removing her pelisse and handing it to Julia. "But I have been much preoccupied with friends of mine."

Hearing her spending time with friends over me was something that I quickly attempted to not be offended by.

"That is what I find delightful about you," I observed, "you always make sure to keep your engagements."

"Thank you."

"And I would like to introduce you to my Aunt Gardiner. Aunt Gardiner, this is my friend, Miss Caroline Bingley."

Aunt Gardiner came forward, introduced herself and warmly welcomed Caroline to her home.

Caroline followed us into the sitting room, and Aunt Gardiner ordered tea to be brought. Caroline looked all around her, and once more, I detected a disapproving look.

"Well," she began, "Mrs. Gardiner, your house is very... comfortable."

"Thank you," Aunt Gardiner replied, a little downcast, for Miss Bingley's remark was very indelicate and false. It was obvious that she did not like the house at all and found it simple and unappealing.

The tea came and we all poured a cup and drank. Cakes were offered to Miss Bingley, and she took one look at them before she rejected them.

"The cakes are quite delicious," I tried to persuade her.

"Jane, let me be the best judge of what I eat," she stated flatly.

"Oh," I replied, feeling the slight. "Well, your gown is lovely, and you look like you are in the best of looks."

"Thank you. I am so happy to be back in town. The fashions here shall *always* be superior to anything in the country. In truth, I found town the superior in everything, including the company. I felt so lost being anywhere else."

This talk was so alarming that I couldn't help but feel hurt.

"Well, I am happy that you are returned to your friends," I responded. "I know how it feels to be separated from people that you care about. The only thing that helps me endure being away from my sisters is my aunt and uncle. And to speak of matters of similarity, my aunt was just telling me that she was raised in a village called Lambton, which is no more than five miles from Pemberley, Mr. Darcy's seat."

"Ah," Caroline's eyebrow raised slightly, "were you, Mrs. Gardiner?"

"Yes, I had the good fortune to have been raised in that lovely village," Aunt Gardiner said. "Of course, I have not had that pleasure of ever being acquainted with the Darcy family, but seeing the elegance of such a home in the distance always had a magical feel."

"You would love the inside of it," Caroline remarked, "for I have been there often myself. And the interior is even more impressive than the exterior. My brother is invited there even more often than I am."

"Then Mr. Bingley is well?" I asked. "I hope that he is in good health."

Caroline's disposition became even more distant and removed. Next, with a strange sort of subtle contempt, she opened her mouth and formed her reply...

～

Caroline's visit was almost as short as the last time that we saw each other. After having informed me, most decidedly (and pointedly!) that Mr. Bingley knew of my being in town, but he was much engaged with Mr. Darcy. Yet each time that she spoke of it, it appeared as if she was attempting to convince herself of her brother's partiality to Miss Darcy, more than she was trying to convince me.

After this point was made very clear, and Caroline made no wish to see me again, her carriage was drawn, and even I felt too glad for her to be gone. She offended my aunt and that hurt to see.

Yet, as coincidence would have it, as Caroline was going to her carriage, another carriage pulled up and Mary Crawford's head poked out of it.

"Happy to see me, I dare say!" she called as the carriage door was opened for her. "You clearly are not upset with me for being an hour earlier than I said I would be."

"Mary," I smiled, equally happy to see her—and even more overjoyed for Caroline to see that I was not forsaken by other friends. Going up to her carriage, I met her eagerly as she stepped down.

"I came out with two tasks," I said, "to see you and to bid farewell to Miss Bingley, who is about to depart."

Miss Crawford looked to her left and her eyes fell on Miss Bingley. Both women looked into each other's eyes, and I was reminded that they had met before. This encounter reminded me more of Elizabeth. For the way that Mary Crawford and Caroline looked at each other, was the same fashion that Elizabeth and Caroline would interact: with subtle antipathy.

"Miss Bingley," Mary Crawford said, curtsying, "came to visit our dear friend."

"Dear indeed," Caroline replied, curtsying as well. "Miss Crawford, I never thought to find you in a neighborhood such as this."

"Whether it is because you overestimate me or underestimate me, I shall never know."

Miss Bingley's eyes turned to slits.

"How is your brother?" she asked.

The meaning was evident. I felt so ashamed for Mary Crawford, and I felt like such a coward for not defending her. But I did not know what to say.

"He does very well," Mary answered, "and is far enough away for me not to be accountable for any of his actions. I daresay that I am different than you in that respect. For how is your brother? And has he done the correct thing of coming to Gracechurch Street to pay his respects? For if he has not come, he better do it.

For a lack of a visit is equally as incorrect as taking too long to visit."

My heart swelled at Mary's saucy words to her, and her willingness to make an enemy on my account.

I was not blind; both women did not like each other. And, judging from what Caroline had shown me, I was inclined to think Mary was the truer one of them both. She admitted to her flaws and virtues, as well as her bad memories of herself, mingled with her good memories. In this brief encounter, I felt as if I knew Mary, but I never had actually known Caroline. For better or worse, Mary always told me the truth about herself, and so I knew where I stood with her. An imperfect friend, who would never deceive or hurt me, is infinitely preferable to the Caroline Bingleys of the world.

As such, I was more inclined, then more than ever, that Mary was the sincere one, even in the matter of Mr. Edmund Bertram.

"Good day, Miss Bingley," I finalized. Both women looked at me. Without knowing it, I had put an end to their verbal confrontation. And I was glad of it; I did not want Caroline to say anything back to Mary, and I didn't want Mary to be ridiculed for protecting me. I could only think of what Caroline would say about her behind her back.

Caroline got in her carriage and drove off.

"Come inside," I smiled at Mary. "Aunt Gardiner will be most happy to see you!"

And so was I.

~

When we entered, Aunt Gardiner was lively, and we were both happy that Mary had come again.

Removing her bonnet and pelisse, Mary had no fear of remarking on what just occurred.

"So," she began, "I suppose I was mean to your friend, but I can never help but be mean to her. Are you going to chastise me for being impertinent to Miss Bingley? Is Jane Bennet about to be upset with me?"

It was altogether strange! The entire time Caroline was here, I kept my composure, and never let my feelings pour forth. But in front of Mary, my courage escaped me.

Suddenly, I began to weep.

"Oh, Mary!"

Covering my face, I sat down.

"Jane..."

Mary rushed to me and held me as I began to weep.

"Jane, dear," Aunt Gardiner rushed to me as well.

"Mrs. Gardiner," Mary said, still embracing me. "Do you have a cold compress?"

"I'll return with it presently." Aunt Gardiner left us alone.

"There, there," Mary coaxed me, "never fear, the dragon is gone back to her den, and she will not return again. Take heart, at least you are free of her now."

"You knew?" I whispered. "You knew what she really was."

"Time taught me that one."

"But you knew...you know about Mr. Bingley?"

"I was never going to say anything before...but one time I overheard Miss Bingley and her sister boasting about saving their brother from a most imprudent match with a woman they knew in Hertfordshire. I did not want it to be you that they were referring to, but upon this encounter, I see that I was correct."

I was overwhelmed and aghast.

"Do not forsake me," I begged her, "do not forsake me."

"I will not."

"Yes, I am the woman. But Mary, I came to London to forget about him and recover. So please, if you care for me at all, let us never speak Mr. Bingley's name again."

"On considering my disdain for the sisters, that is something that I am happy to oblige."

Aunt Gardiner came back in with the cold compress so that I could place it upon my head.

"Forgive me," I rushed out.

"Jane, there is nothing to apologize for," Aunt Gardiner assured me.

"I echo those sentiments," Mary supported.

"I shall be cheery again very soon," I intoned, "but please, can we never speak of this moment again...once it is over?"

They assured me that they would do so, and I believed them both.

Aunt Gardiner was called away, because Ruth cut her finger, but Mary sat with me a little longer.

"So," she finalized, "this is the last thing that I will say on the matter. You received heartbreak in the country, and then you ran into an older heartbreak here in town. There is good news from this."

"And what is that?"

"Things could not get any worse, and therefore happiness is most likely to be around the corner. There! Now we shall be silent on the matter forever."

She sat with me like that for an hour before she had to return home. And I did believe that I became myself again.

The rest of the day was spent with a weather of intense cloudiness. However, I now could see things clearer. Now, I knew what would happen.

Chapter Twenty-Five

KITTY'S TALE: THE BERTRAMS COME TO PEMBERLEY

M y eyes opened to a day of intense cloudiness. However, I knew what would happen. It would have a foggy hue for a significant portion of the day, but it would not rain.

This ambiguity of mother nature sat deep within me as Lucy helped me get dressed for the day. It felt as if the sky was saying 'anything can happen, and anything *will* happen'.

And anything did happen.

First, Lucy had a hard time arranging my hair.

Second, the gown I wished to wear for the occasion had a hole in it. So, I wore a newer blue gown that I had made.

Thirdly, my shoe's heel broke.

Of course, I had quick replacements for what was broken, and Lucy knew a quick way of doing my hair with it still looking very presentable. But I still couldn't help but feel as if this was a bad omen of sorts.

I kept my worries to myself and met everyone for breakfast.

When we sat down to eat, the anxiety, apprehensions, nervousness, and inner sense of chaos was palpable. Truly, it hung in the air, creating a wall between all of us.

We could all see each other, but we never looked up from our plates.

We could all hear each other, but it was as if no one had a voice.

We all sensed each other, but we felt isolated, and as if we were in our own worlds.

"For goodness sakes," Mr. Bingley said at last, "someone tell a joke already."

We all chuckled at this but still could not think of anything to say.

Finally, we finished eating, and we all were able to sit in the drawing room, each committed to some sort of meaningless task.

Us ladies sewed. The men read books or the gazette. I noticed that Georgiana wore her white muslin gown that was multi-layered and had a sheerness underneath. Our gowns accidentally complemented each other's.

When the door opened, we all jumped, and only relaxed when Lieutenant Finlay was announced.

We all stood, received him warmly, but there was such a life-lessness to our party, that we all made such an awkward business of the matter. Truly, we didn't have anything to say.

Before Finlay could regret his ever coming here, I nodded my head, gesturing for him to sit by me. This reminded me of the time when mama had been winking at me, so that she could get Mr. Bingley and Jane alone to talk with each other.

Well, I could only hope that Finlay was quick to read my expression.

He did so, approached me, complimented my appearance, and then sat down beside me.

"You catch us in a very dull state this morning," I said. "This has nothing to do with you at all."

"Thank you for the reassurance. But in truth, I suspected as much. In life, many people have grown lax, fearing any sort of confrontation that may come their way. And to be sure, waiting on the edge of a battle is just like this."

"It is?"

"Oh, yes. The waiting is as hard as the actual battle itself sometimes. The battle is the possibility of doom, death, destruc-tion, and disturbance. However, waiting for the battle to occur is doubly terrifying. For you are not in the thick of it yet, but instead it's the time where you have no choice but to let the dread wash over you. That is what everyone is going through right now. You are waiting on the edge of a battle that might occur. You all are nervous."

"Does the eve of battle ever frighten you?" I asked.

"Every time."

I felt the heaviness of his answer.

"Finlay," I implored him, "how can you bear it? How can you bear this feeling so very often?"

"Because it's all that I know. People call us fighters to be savages, but that is very untrue. We think, we feel, and even theorize. We wonder what life has in store for us if we were to survive this battle. That's what stirs us on and helps us remember our courage. We remember that there is a morning after."

"There's a morning after," I chanted, whispering to myself, "there's a morning after."

~

Finlay's arrival precipitated the arrival that we all both dreaded and looked forward to.

Very soon, we heard a carriage coming down the lane.

Instinctively, Georgiana and I rushed to the window to look out of it.

It was a handsome coach, fitting for a knighted gentleman— whatever knighted meant anymore. Honestly, how many men had that title, and they actually earned it? I'm certain that I do not know.

"Well," I announced, "they are here."

"Everyone," Arthur Philips said, "gird your loins. This is about to get fiery."

"Once more, dearest," Enara said, "I appreciate your use of imagery."

"Thank you. Wait, was that an insult?"

Enara rolled her eyes, amused.

We all arranged ourselves in different places throughout the drawing room. Finlay stood by where I sat, and Mr. Darcy and Elizabeth arranged themselves so that they were in the center of the room.

We all waited.

Eventually, we heard Mrs. Reynolds greet some people. Whoever our visitors were, they used their words sparingly.

Or perhaps they were nervous.

Good. I wanted them to be such.

When people are nervous, they say all the wrong things.

I wanted them to say all the wrong things.

I wished for it.

Our drawing room door opened, Mrs. Reynolds entered, and she made the announcement.

"Sir Thomas Bertram, Mr. Bertram, Mr. Edmund Bertram, and Miss Fanny Bertram."

"Fanny!" I heard William Price utter, excited as well as scared.

One by one, the four of them entered.

The first was Sir Thomas Bertram. He was an elderly man, with gray hair, with a touch of white along his sideburns. He was of medium height, was a little heavy in his expressions and his face was undefinable.

The second was his sons, Mr. Bertram, and Mr. Edmund Bertram. Both were a little taller than their father. Both were men of handsome build and had dark brown long hair that they tied in the back.

All three of them were impeccably dressed, with clothing that was refined and suited their persons, but was not ostentatious or too flamboyant for them. Their appearance had a natural elegance.

The only thing that marred this image of aristocratic allure was the lady who stood next to Mr. Edmund Bertram. From her dress down to her air, she had a diminished feel. Perhaps I am not describing it very well. Her clothing was neat, clean, her dress was simple but suited her well. She had chestnut brown hair that she styled appropriately, and it flattered her face. Her features were not grotesque at all but were lovely in a simple sort of way.

That was it! Everything about her was simple and did not

possess any striking quality. Even plain women can have a strik-ingness to them, or a natural grace that makes you admire them.

With this woman, who I figured to be Mrs. Fanny Bertram, William Price's little sister, there was something about her air and manner of walking—and in her whole demeanor. She reminded me of a mouse that was trying to retreat into its hole, after having seen how large the world was.

She was meek. But then again, we have often been told that they shall inherit the earth. All I can say is that, if Mr. Edmund Bertram transferred his affections from Miss Crawford to this woman, then he never should have fallen in love with Mary to begin with. Everything about Miss Crawford was the complete opposite to this woman.

And when watching Mrs. Fanny Bertram, when seeing how she leaned toward Mr. Edmund Bertram, looking up at him with a look of total dependence on him, I wondered how could a man have such different taste so very quickly?

Mary Crawford never looked to anyone with a sense of blind adoration. Her mind was always at work. Then again, Miss Craw-ford was much lovelier than Mrs. Fanny Bertram. Miss Craw-ford's looks blinded Mr. Edmund Bertram, perhaps, and he fell in love quicker than he knew it.

All these reflections, I had within the blink of three seconds.

And judging from the way that Sir Thomas Bertram looked on us, he had done the same thing. He looked as if he had smelled something awful, and his eye had a very damning look.

Little did he know, Darcy was known for having that SAME look.

But Mr. Darcy had perfected it.

When seeing his sister, William Price was unable to contain himself.

"Fanny!" he cried.

"William!" Fanny Bertram declared, equally as overjoyed to see him. Leaving her husband's side, Fanny rushed up to William Price and William hugged her, showing all the powers of sibling adoration.

"How I missed you," William Price professed.

"I missed you as well."

All we could do was sit there and look on them. Their happy embrace did have an immediate effect on us. In truth, we wondered how we could go on after that, about to undergo a debate, when familial affection had laid itself out before us. For a moment, all discord seemed pathetic.

When they released each other, they looked deeply into each other's eyes.

"I am sorry that I must cause you pain, sister," William Price said.

"I know that you do. Oh, brother, I worried that this would end up in such a way. I wished that none of this conflict had to happen."

"I know that you don't, gentle Fanny. Nor do I, but some things are important to me, and they are worth fighting for. Miss Crawford is such, and therefore, I must commit to this. Some things need to be resolved, and righted."

He held her hands fondly.

"I love you," he said.

Over William's shoulder, Fanny Bertram looked at Mary Crawford.

"Good day, Fanny," Mary Crawford said, "Or, should I say, Mrs. Bertram?"

"Good day, Miss Crawford," Fanny said, looking at the floor. "I confess, I never expected us to meet as such. You often talked of your disdain for the Navy as a profession."

"And people have been known to change," Miss Crawford replied. "It is part of the pains of growing up."

"Well, yes, I suppose."

To smooth things over from the very beginning, Miss Crawford turned to Mr. Edmund Bertram.

"Mr. Edmund Bertram, I congratulate you on your bride. I trust you both make each other very happy."

Mr. Edmund Bertram looked at her, with a coldness.

"Thank you," he finally managed to reply, "for I managed to find the greatest woman in England. A woman of superior virtue."

We all flinched. His words were meant to praise his wife, but it was not done out of such goodness. Rather, he was insulting Miss Crawford, and that was the moment that broke any respect I could have had for him. He dared to call himself a clergyman? I disliked him enormously.

"There are many forms of perfection, Mr. Edmund," William Price said, wholly aware of Edmund Bertram's true intent, "My sister possesses many of those qualities, yes. But so do all the ladies in this room...with no exception. And I beg you not to debase yourself by ever hinting otherwise."

Edmund looked at William Price, a little unnerved, but still resolute. Despite that William Price was Miss Crawford's fiancé, Mr. Edmund Bertram assumed that he would not defend her. What was Mr. Edmund Bertram thinking? What man would idly stand by and let his beloved fiancée be insulted?

Meanwhile, I looked at Fanny throughout all this. She looked between her husband and her brother with equal amounts of empathy. And how could she not? She was evidently torn between her love for both men. I was glad not to be in her shoes.

Then I saw her have a passing expression. It was directed at Mary Crawford. Within the blink of an eye, it was gone again. But I had seen it, and I could not forget it. There was something in Fanny Bertram's eye that made me lay down the events that I knew about Mansfield Park.

Of when Mary Crawford had gone to Mansfield Park.

Of how Mr. Edmund Bertram immediately fell in love with her.

Of how he continued to feel for her, even when they disagreed and debated.

Of how, the only way that he broke off any attachment to Miss Crawford was when they disagreed entirely about having Maria and Mr. Crawford marry—and the cold manner he felt she had spoken.

Only then did he release her, but it was not because his heart grew cold from her, but because his mind did.

And Fanny Price—nee Bertram, was there to pick up the remainder of his heart.

But for him to have ever married Fanny to begin with meant

that Fanny must have felt for him. She had to have! Or else she would not have accepted him unless he was her only prospect. But that was not the case. I saw the way that she looked at Edmund Bertram. She obviously loved him.

Which led me to believe that Fanny Bertram had to have been feeling for Edmund for quite some time, while he had been feeling for Mary Crawford.

Now I knew what that look was about.

No one is *perfect*; perspective just makes it appear as such. And I had found it out.

Of course, all my inner musing was by the work of a moment, because our minds can transfer a few seconds into an eternity.

Therefore, soon after William Price returned Edmund Bertram's insult, Mr. Darcy began to make introductions.

Without any sense of shame or nervousness, Mr. Darcy faced Sir Thomas Bertram.

"Sir Thomas," Mr. Darcy began, "I welcome you and your family to Pemberley. Mrs. Grant, will you be so kind as to give the introductions?"

"Most readily, sir," Mrs. Grant said. Since she was the only one who could introduce everyone in the set, while also being the most neutral one in the lot. She introduced the Bertrams to us, then introduced us to the Bertrams.

Once we all bowed and curtsied to each other, Elizabeth turned to the group.

"Please, do be seated," she instructed. The Bertrams were hesitant, but eventually, they took their appropriate seats.

This was quickly overturned when Sir Thomas, who had sat down for only three seconds, jumped back up again, heavily disturbed.

"No," he instructed, "pray forgive me, but this will not inherit."

"What, pray tell?" Mr. Darcy asked, unmoved.

"This whole charade. I find it highly offensive, since I came here to make my point of view known, especially at the offenses that have been charged against me. To sit down and indulge all the niceties and pleasantries that come from a visit don't seem to be proper, in this case. I would like to get to the heart of the matter immediately."

Mr. Darcy smiled. For some reason, that made him more intimidating.

"I was hoping that was what you wished. For it saved me the trouble of having to introduce the matter myself."

When hearing that he had played directly into Mr. Darcy's hands, Sir Thomas did not answer immediately. He had played his first move, and it turned out that he had merely offered the first play to his rival debater. Now, within his eyes, was a desperation to find the next best move to make aboard this game of proverbial chess.

Mr. Darcy stood up.

"Company, Sir Thomas Bertram has requested to forego the traditional habits that is owed to a guest, and I am happy to oblige him. The matter is pertaining to the rights of Mr. Price's and Miss Crawford's marriage to be recognized and carried out by their families. It is also for them to be given the honor and respect that a newly married couple deserves. Also, if there is a potential hope already, then you all can discuss an end to the breach between both of your families."

"That will never occur," Sir Thomas Bertram said. "For I shall never forget the conflict that the Crawfords have caused by their entrance into our society."

"From what I heard," Mr. Darcy said, "it was your daughter, was it not, who ran away from her husband?"

"Because she was seduced by that rake!" Sir Thomas declared, pointing to Mr. Crawford.

"Whatever I am," Mr. Crawford declared, "I am sure that I deserve the name."

"However," Miss Crawford countered, "Miss Maria Bertram is a full-grown woman, responsible for her own actions. I sympathize with her pain, but she cannot be enticed unless she preferred it. To exempt her from this equation is not sound."

"You be quiet, madam."

"How dare you silence her, sir?" William Price said, enraged. "I never would have thought that of you."

"I will make it very clear, Sir Thomas," Mr. Darcy said, his eye stern and overpowering, "you will not disrespect any lady in this house. You claim to be a gentleman, then you shall act like it."

"I beg your pardon, only in that regard," Sir Thomas said, "but I come to this house, under the express regard to not, nor my sons, be hailed as the villains in this case. The Crawfords entered my household and toyed with the hearts of my children."

"Toying?" Jane voiced. "What toying has Miss Crawford committed?"

Sir Thomas didn't speak but was a little uncertain about what to say. Instead, instinctively, his eyes shifted to Mr. Edmund Bertram, who remained by his wife. Seeing his father in distress, Mr. Edmund stepped forward.

"My father speaks congenially out of love of a family member."

"Then I will make a suggestion," Elizabeth said. "That any grown man, who willingly gives his heart away, cannot blame the woman. His soul made the choice himself, and the woman is not to blame if he did anything foolish on his part. No woman can be blamed for whoever chooses to favor her, and it should not be set down that she is guilty for his emotions. Just as the same can be said for a woman who chooses to give her heart to a man. Heart-break is painful, but it is up to the woman if she chooses to let it ruin her life forever and never tries to rally from it. What you propose is that others ought to be blamed for a perpetrator's behavior, merely due to influence. If that be the case, how can a person take responsibility for their own actions? And what you must consider is that one of your daughters ran off to Gretna Green to wed, and your other daughter ran off, and left her husband. If, by your definition, others are responsible for whisking your children into a world of wickedness, you must ask yourself what influence they have had from home?"

This acknowledgment set all the men back for a moment, but eventually, Mr. Thomas Bertram came to his father's defense.

"That is not fair to lay at my father's feet," he defended, "for my father has always been a man of piety and purity."

"Piety and purity?" Finlay echoed, spouting the words with a cold bitterness. "That is a very interesting way of putting the current situation."

"Two words which we are happy that you spoke of," Mr. Darcy added, "and we shall lay at your feet, by and by. Until then, you are Mr. Thomas Bertram? The Thomas Bertram who, between gaming and horse-racing, were known to ring up a significant debt, even to the point where it endangered the finances of Mansfield Park's estate?"

Mr. Thomas Bertram blinked, utterly perplexed that Mr. Darcy was so enlightened about his activities. Come to think of it, we all were.

"Sir, where did you hear such erroneous reports?" Mr. Edmund Bertram challenged.

"By your brother's own voice," Mr. Darcy said, "Over the last few days, I've had my valet send inquiries out to my friends in the ton, and Mr. Bertram, I must say that you went through a phase where you loved to implicate yourself. You often boasted of your extravagancy, even priding yourself of not being nearly as in debt as your friends. It is quite common knowledge, and that forced you, Mr. Edmund, to not take up your post at the parsonage as soon as was expected."

We all looked at the Bertrams, to see how they would receive such reports. They were so overwhelmed by Darcy's thoroughness in researching their history, that they didn't think of a reply.

"Mr. Bertram," Mr. Darcy stated, "there is a saying that we have here in Derbyshire: 'don't wash your dirty linens in the street'."

In the game of chess, this would be equivalent to the knight taking out a pawn.

Since Mr. Bertram had been silent for too long, he seemed to be aware that there was no point in lying. Therefore, all that he could do was accept the matter and stage his defense.

"I was younger back then, I do not deny," Mr. Bertram explained, "but time has humbled me, and I have learned."

"Precisely," Sir Thomas said, "my son's folly was the product of youth, and therefore, he has the right to be judged on his current actions. Not his past ones."

Mr. Edmund looked at his father, and it seemed like he was the only one that was aware of the hypocrisy of his family's words.

"Very well put, sir," Mr. Bingley stated, "would you please repeat that?"

Sir Thomas opened his mouth and then closed it again.

"The product of youth," Mr. Darcy repeated for him, "and therefore, he has the right to be judged on his current actions. Not his past ones. Yes, sir, very wise. Very wise indeed."

"Therefore," I said, "should that philosophy apply to anyone else in the world, or just those who are Bertrams? We are all young, and foolish, at one time or another. Therefore, if your son is given the luxury of being forgiven over time, then shouldn't that philosophy extend to others?"

"And moreover," Mr. Darcy added, "it is the Christian thing to do. Forgiveness for those who wish to repent and indicate a desire to improve themselves, of course."

I looked at Mr. Edmund Bertram. He looked down at his feet, only to look next at his wife.

Fanny Bertram was looking between him and William Price. She was at a loss of understanding what to do. Since our debate began, she had said not one word.

But what was certain was that the men in her life had just had their words served back to them.

Bitter, Sir Thomas Bertram turned to Mr. Crawford.

"Still having others fight your battles for you, will you, sir?"

"I let no one fight for me," Mr. Crawford said, "they do this to convince you that my sister is worthy to wed Mr. Price, and that she deserves all the respect of a lovely bride. And, also, to look kindly on my other sister, Mrs. Grant. I want to see them be accepted in your company, as they deserve to be. Whatever flaws you lay at their feet, it is imaginary or exaggerated. I entreat you to allow the Darcys and their company to help you see reason. They are a worthy family. I will be the only person who defends myself. No more and no less. But as you say, Sir Thomas, youth can attribute to many mistakes occurring, and time helps a person develop. If my sisters have any flaws—which are but small ones that all of us possess—I think they should have the same chance of redemption as Mr. Bertram."

"I do not want to hear you speak, sir," Sir Thomas said to Mr. Crawford, "you ruined everyone's lives."

"So did your daughter," Mr. Crawford retaliated, "the sins of your child are the same as mine."

"First, I have properly punished my daughter for her crimes."

"Yes, perpetual banishment, I know."

"I had no choice, for you seduced her, then did not marry her."

"I had no intention of her following after me, but I was weak, and I gave into my worst sides. However, I never expected our separation to be met with her being forever marred from her own home. I thought, whatever punishment she received would occur, but eventually would be forgiven. She is your daughter, man, and you must answer for the neglect in her education and for her actions. Where were you to help teach her the right way of things? She was left to a pampered and spoiled education by her Aunt Norris, who indulged her to the point where Miss Maria Bertram never learned self-control."

"Mrs. Norris has also been removed from Mansfield Park, therefore, I have also corrected that mistake."

"Forgive me," Jane asked, "but is that your solution to every-thing? If someone makes a mistake in error, you perpetually banish them from your life? When it comes to cases of betrayal, I can understand that. But for everything else, isn't that extreme?"

"When Maria did as she did, she might as well have betrayed me. What most of you are ignorant of is that before my daughter married Mr. Rushworth, I offered her a chance to break off the engagement."

"You did?" I asked.

"Yes. I was aware of her indifference to him. I tried to spare her from a life of being ill-suited with her husband, but she would have none of it. She would marry him anyway, and do you know why, sir?" He said, turning to Mr. Crawford. "She did it to be strong on you. To show you that she wasn't going to sit around and pause her life, waiting around for you. It was her idea of triumph."

"What?" Mr. Crawford asked, a little disturbed.

"Oh," Sir Thomas said, "you did not know that, did you?"

"No. She told you this when she wed Rushworth?"

"No. She told Mrs. Norris, who told me."

"She never told me, and I wish she had. For, now, that has lessened my guilt."

"It *lessens* your guilt?"

"Of course, it does," I interrupted. "Mr. Crawford was wrong to ever attempt to engage Miss Bertram's affections, at both times that he did it. But we have determined that. However, you gave your daughter a chance to escape a life of misery, she did not listen, underwent a ceremony where she hated the man she was marrying, and then all this happened. Don't you see? All of this happened because she made the ultimate wrong decision. She chose to marry a man, sheerly out of spite for the previous man who spurned her. And you saw it happening before your very eyes."

"Precisely," Miss Crawford added, "you could have prevented this if you had just tried to talk with Miss Maria in the right sort of way."

"I did."

"No, you didn't. You never spoke with her in a fatherly way of a man trying to understand and coax his daughter. You always spoke by way of authority. That was why she did everything to avoid you and why Miss Julia eloped. They were afraid of you. And don't tell me that I am ignorant of the matter. I know what I know because I heard it from Maria's own lips. The sisters were terrified of your strictness, your wrath, and your gaze. You never were a proper father to them. You never developed an affectionate relationship but was always tyrannical. I am tired of fathers not knowing how to talk to us little girls that live in their homes."

"Miss Crawford, that is unfair, and I will not have that," Mr. Edmund Bertram declared, "and you will unsay it in the next instance."

"Our father has always been attentive to us," Mr. Bertram added.

"Attentive to you both, perhaps. You are his sons, and often more attention is given. But what of us? What of us daughters? We need a father's love and kind words as much as his steady hand to guide us. What parents did Maria and Julia have to guide them into being shining examples of womanhood? Truly, think? What were they given?"

In chess, this was the moment where a knight and a bishop stared down each other.

~

Mr. Edmund Bertram was no longer on the offensive with Mary Crawford. Between remembering his religious affiliations, or that the men in the company would not allow rudeness to occur, his tone turned to one of quiet sincerity.

"Our father is not your uncle," Mr. Edmund Bertram said, "I ask you to not confuse them."

"Your father?" Mr. Darcy said. "That is the part that I was hoping to appeal to, in one chief manner, at least."

"What manner is that?"

"Sir Thomas, Mr. Bertram, and Mr. Edmund Bertram, once more I remind you both that the main request that we have here is that you offer Miss Crawford and Mr. Price your blessing to be married and do everything to welcome them into your family circle. Do you accept this condition or not?"

"We still have reservations on the matter," Mr. Bertram stated.

"Good, then we may proceed, because so do I. For, Sir Thomas, you have me at a disadvantage when it comes to morality and balancing out such matters. For, help me understand how a sailor marrying a woman who happens to be the sister of the man your daughter ran off with, is committing a worse sin than a master of a plantation, who owns over a hundred enslaved people, and makes them work against their will and without pay?"

When hearing this, I looked at the Bertrams and Fanny. Both

had turned red in the face, unable to deny that, in the eyes of life, there might be a sort of imbalance there.

"You see," Mr. Darcy began, "I have a great distaste for people who hold up a virtue for some, and do not do it themselves. I also have no qualms debating, all day, with three men and a lady, who condemn others for crimes that are not nearly as severe as their own. I find that unfair."

"I do not have to stand trial for my way of receiving income," Sir Thomas declared. "What I do is legal."

"Because over two hundred years ago, the English monarchy deemed it proper to make England wealthy off the backs of enslaved people that they dragged from their own homeland. That's a little after the same time that an English monarch beheaded two of his wives for false accusations of adultery. Does the excuse, 'well that person committed an offense' justify your own? If that be the case, then we are returned to the same dilemma that you brought up before: the dilemma of a person having suffered from a bad influence, or them having to finally become responsible for their actions. The abolition is making more inroads, day by day. William Wilberforce and many others have passed anti-slavery acts here in Britain. And the reason for our country's slow progression toward liberation is done primarily from the popular notion of 'out of sight and out of mind'."

"Your evil dealings are not done on English soil," Lieutenant Finlay stated, "therefore they are hidden. And what is hidden beyond people's vision, are impossible to correct. But more and more pamphlets are circulating throughout England, showing the real treatment that these enslaved people undergo on these islands. The truth is getting out, and soon, everyone will see the horrid picture. And Britain will suffer for people like you, perpetuating a practice that should have ended soon after it was despicably begun. You are not the shining character of England's future, sir. You are the darker elements of a generation that is going to end."

"How dare you?" Mr. Darcy added, to support Finlay. "How dare you accuse anyone of moral lapses, of crimes committed, when you have committed one of the worst crimes, in the eyes of

God, and grace?" Then he turned to Mr. Edmund Bertram. "And how your offspring turn a blind eye, standing in a pulpit, breaching about the sanctity of their faith, of love for all man, and they turn around and ignore this? Such characters have no right to step inside of a church, let alone speak for one."

"I am true to my belief," Mr. Edmund said.

"Yes," Fanny finally managed to utter. "My husband is true in his love for god's divinity."

"Thank you, Mrs. Bertram," Edmund replied, happy that his wife defended him. However, her innocence displayed the naiveté of blind obedience. I did not hate her, but I wanted her to see how her point was not connected to what we were speaking of.

"And what of a reverend's duty to mankind?" I retaliated. "For, does it not show that, if a man adores God on Sunday, but then censures others for their missteps while his family commit the worst crimes for all other six days of the week, then what is the point of that faith? By showing love for our fellow man, no matter their appearance or station in life, we are showing our love for God. Both are connected. Don't you both agree?"

Edmund and Fanny looked at each other.

"Yes," Edmund Bertram replied, resigned. "I confess there is truth to that."

Sir Thomas and Mr. Bertram looked at the other brother.

"But you can forgive you family's history," Mary Crawford said to Mr. Edmund Bertram. "Why is that? Could it be because they are your family, and you love them? Therefore, your love carries you to the point of forgiving your father. If your love for family extends that far, then can you not see that my love for my brother extends so far as well? And that Mr. Price's love for me extends also far enough that he forgives my philosophical viewpoints on certain matters? Why is your love more important than mine?"

Mr. Edmund Bertram did not know how to reply. This is what it was like to see the bishop buckle under the gaze of the knight.

Seeing that his brother was losing ground, Mr. Bertram decided to press the matter.

"Whatever you think of my father's way of earning revenue, he is a knight, and he is worthy of respect."

"And are not the slaves who serve under him so unworthy of that respect?" Finlay augmented. "As I understand it, you, Mr. Bertram, even visited Antigua with your father. Am I correct?"

Mr. Bertram's expression drooped. I leaned forward, determined to scrutinize. I think I saw a quick flash of pain slice across his face. He was scared, in some way.

"Yes," Mr. Bertram responded, "I did."

"Then you saw what I saw," Finlay said. "The occupants living in terrible housing conditions. Their state of life poor. Their downtrodden backs as they enter the estate, hands bound as they enter their new life of bondage. Of every freedom and right as a man and woman being stripped away from them, little by little. Of the men and women getting a lashing across their backs whenever the taskmaster deems their work unsatisfactory. Of the women—and how they are really mistreated...by those taskmasters. And what is done to them."

"Sir," Mr. Edmund Bertram hissed, looking at his wife, "we have ladies present!"

"Only a weak woman is afraid to hear this," Elizabeth declared, looking at Mrs. Fanny Bertram. "We've all been told the truth here and are not afraid. For so long, we have not been told the truth about what happens in such places, for fear that you all believe our feminine delicacy will not be able to withstand it. But it's important for us to know. It's important for us to know why all the female abolitionist societies are so angry in London. Now, we know what they are angry about and why they will never stop." Once more, she looked at Fanny, empathetic. "Ignorance is bliss. I know that. But we must not be afraid of being told the truth about such matters."

Fanny Bertram, overcome by the reports that Finlay had given, was already wilting under the image that was placed before her. But Elizabeth's admonishment made her feel that she would appear as pathetic if she were to begin weeping. Therefore, all her eyes were left to do was be filled with a sense of dread of reality, forcing her to wake up, and she looked at the floor, avoiding our gaze.

"You know what I speak is true," Finlay said to Mr. Bertram.

"You saw it all. And probably told yourself it was a nightmare that you could wake up from once you returned to England. You perhaps even lied to yourself and told yourself that the ends justified the means. But in your heart, you knew what you were seeing was awful. You know that you had seen hell, and it was Antigua."

Mr. Bertram was silenced, his eyes filled with horror as he remembered memories that he perhaps had suppressed.

"Whatever your moral qualms of my estate and how I run it, sir," Sir Thomas said, "there is no legal bonds on me. What I did is still according to the law."

"And your moral duty? What of that?"

"What I did by way of a father providing for his wife, servants, and children. I will not apologize for being a sound businessman."

"And we return to the original matter," Mr. Darcy added, "and it's the matter of your children. That is how you defend your actions? Love of children, am I correct?"

"Of course, it is. For what father do you know who will not do anything for their children?"

"Including not forgive them so much that you perpetually banish them from your home and never see them," Mr. Crawford responded, considering Maria Bertram. "Is that a father's love?"

"You have four children, do you not, Sir Thomas?" Mr. Darcy asked.

"Yes, of course, I do."

"You swear to this, even in the face of the Lieutenant Finlay, who has been to Antigua?"

Sir Thomas looked at Finlay, whose expression did not cower. Finlay looked firmly at this knight and was unmoved.

Sir Thomas did not respond. At first. Rather, his eyes changed a strange hue as the light from the candle hit them and he finally responded after a distinct pause.

"Yes, of course, I have four."

"Whatever your flaws," Finlay said, "you had honesty to your name. Lying does not become you. And in your eye, I can see that it is not. Just like I can see, as plainly as you, that Mr. Thomas Bertram is not your first son."

Mr. Bertram looked confused.

"What the devil are you talking about?"

"I'm talking about the fact that Sir Thomas Bertram has eight children, but only four does he count. His eldest son's name is Ajax, a child he conceived with one of his slaves, named Isobel. You are not the eldest Bertram son. Because you were born with skin such as mine, you were simply the one that counted."

In the game of chess, this was the primary move: check!

When Finlay dropped this fact, naturally it produced an outpour of sensations.

Excepting Darcy, we were wholly ignorant of the matter. Therefore, our company was met with shock. The same could be said of the Bertrams.

"That is a lie!" Sir Thomas declared. "I have suffered great indignities in this house, and I will hear no more. Sons, we leave this accursed place."

"Precisely!" Mr. Bertram declared, moving past his father to make one final plea to be the one to get the last word in. "It cannot be true in the slightest. I was at Antigua and there was no Ajax to speak of."

"Of course, there wasn't," Finlay determined, "because your father probably was aware of the family resemblance. Ajax is a mulatto who was known for bearing a remarkable resemblance to your father. I would know, for I saw Ajax before, and when your father entered, it confirmed my memories. Before you went with your father, he rented Ajax to another master, to keep him away from your discerning eyes."

"And then," Mr. Darcy added, "when you left Antigua, the first thing that he did was get Ajax back. After all, despite everything, it's hard to sell your child when he looks precisely like you. You *can't* tear yourself apart." Darcy turned to Sir Thomas. "You oversaw his return yourself." Next, Darcy turned back to Mr. Bertram. "Why do you think he was not upset for you returning to Mansfield Park while he remained behind? Why did he not return to Mansfield Park with you?"

He turned to Sir Thomas Bertram.

"Now, you may be wondering how I know this?" he asked.

"You cannot know it," Sir Thomas said, grief-stricken. "You cannot know this."

"But he does know of it," Finlay responded. "Through me. You see, many ships pass through Antigua, breaking their journey there for one reason or another. Sailors cannot help but see what they see and become familiar with where they take shore leave or bring cargo aboard. News travels. I already was aware of Ajax's existence, but once I had Colonel Forster make inquiries among his fellow officers in the navy who travel there, they reported back to him accurately. I learned about your visit to Antigua from the Crawfords, and I just reasoned it out. But that look of horror on your face confirms it and says it all. Ajax is your son. Your other children were easy to pass off as being mulattos who were spawned from the horrible acts inflicted on the poor women from your taskmasters. But not dear Ajax. No. He's your firstborn, when you were a young man, and you were filled with great feeling. When you perhaps even loved his mother—in the only way that a master could think what love was. Isobel bore Ajax even before you met your wife. And that's why you can't deny it. Because you love the mulatto son of yours."

Despite himself, tears escaped Sir Thomas's eyes.

And this is what, in chess, they call Checkmate!

It was over. Any defense that the Bertrams could concoct for defending their hypocrisy or their ignorance, was at an end.

There was nothing more to hide behind. There was no false morality that could shield them.

Sir Thomas was weeping, despite himself.

Mr. Bertram, his eldest son, was looking away from his family, clutching the table that was nearest him.

Mr. Edmund Bertram just stood there, frozen. Everything but his eyes, which were not blank and expressionless. Rather, they were filled with the subtle terror that comes with being so thoroughly wrong:

He watched his father condemn Maria Bertram to a life away from them.

While his father was condemning many people to a life of free, hard, and oppressive labor, with no hope of freedom on his part.

He, Mr. Edmund, had turned his back on Miss Crawford for her 'base ways'.

And when all the while he was never condemning his father for this horrible act.

He preached the word of God from the pulpit of his parish.

When all the while, he was allowing a savage system to flourish under his very nose.

It was like watching a man fall apart, while he also remained composed.

At last, Edmund Bertram spoke. He didn't move, but his words came through his barely-opened mouth.

"It's true, isn't it?" he asked. "Isn't it, father?"

Sir Thomas moved away from us, went toward the nearest window, and leaned against it.

That was all the answer that was needed.

And during all of this, what was Fanny doing?

At first, she had begun to weep and was holding herself under the weight of these horrors being presented to her. She began to shake. At last, she leaned against her husband, who moved for the first time. Looking down at his wife, he placed his arm around her, letting her collapse into him as he pressed his head against her hair. Both were mortified.

Instinctively, I looked at Miss Crawford, to see how she viewed this scene. After all, she once favored Mr. Edmund Bertram. She had no look of superiority, but mere interest as she whispered something to William Price.

I would be shown what it was, for soon after she had spoken, William Price stood up, walked over to his sister, and touched her arm.

Fanny looked up at her brother.

"Who is without sin, Fanny?" he asked. "Who, with the beam in their eye, can remove the speck in another?"

"Forgive me," Fanny said, lunging into her brother's arms, "I should have been stronger. I should have stuck by you, brother. I just wanted what was best for you."

"This is what is best for me," William said, holding her, "this is what is best. And even if not, this is my life. I cannot have others dictate it for me, nor whom I love. I will love where I love, and no one can order me to do otherwise. I have my freedom, Fanny, and therefore, I know no other way. I love Miss Crawford, and I always will. Please, be happy for me."

Fanny looked between them both.

"If you are happy, brother, then so must I be." Fanny offered her hand to Mary Crawford, who walked up to Fanny and took it. "Well, this is love then?"

"It is," Mary Crawford said.

"Miss Crawford, whatever our past and difficulties, please, I beg you. Love my brother unconditionally. Be loyal, loving, and never leave. Stand by him, and he shall stand by you."

"I promise," Mary stated. "When it comes to my heart, I never lie."

"Well then," Fanny Bertram said, placing Mary Crawford's hand in her brother's. "Go to it. And be merry."

Now we all looked at Mr. Edmund Bertram, who was the next person that this affected. Standing there, watching his wife accept the circumstances, Edmund Bertram had no choice but to submit to the high principles that our faith proscribed. He did not go near the Crawfords, but his face showed that he had fully given in.

"Welcome to our family," Mr. Edmund said, "I suppose, at the end, I have no right to judge anyone."

"Mr. Edmund, that is all that we could wish," Mrs. Grant said.

"Then I find that I am converted. I wish you both all the joy in the world."

Next, we looked at Mr. Tom Bertram, the eldest son.

At this point he had sat down, and it was obvious that he was careworn and looked as if he had been knocked about by the tides of controversy. When he saw us looking at him, he returned our look, but it was neither defiant nor disgusted. He just looked heartbroken.

"You all look at me, do you?" Mr. Tom Bertram noted. "Everyone looks at Tom and awaits his well-wishes."

"We should like to have it, Mr. Bertram," William Price said.

"Yes, and you deserve it. I am quite the selfish mule, you know. I cannot help but think of myself from time to time. I wish that I could stand and wish you two all the joy in the world, and accept that your mistake, Mr. Crawford, is no better or worse than the mistakes of many of us men in the room—we are just better at hiding it. I should say all these things, but I... I am not the firstborn. I have a brother. An older one. And now...what am I? What am I then?"

We all looked down, seeing that he was truly unsettled.

"You are my firstborn," Sir Thomas insisted. "You always will be."

"No. I am not. I am merely the firstborn that matters to you, in the eyes of society. I am the acceptable one. That is the only difference."

"It doesn't matter," Mr. Crawford advised, "if you will listen to me at all, a son is still a son. The order doesn't matter, nor does it change anything at all. Just be aware, that somewhere out there, is a man named Ajax, and you could meet him one day."

The only one that was silent: Sir Thomas Bertram.

He knew that it was his cue, therefore, we prepared ourselves for what he had to say back...

Chapter Twenty-Six

KITTY'S TALE: THE SOLUTION

S ir Thomas's eyes were now red from a combination of guilt and subtle vexation.

"Oh, you all cry out with your purity," Sir Thomas bellowed, "are you proud of your work? Now my firstborn is beside himself and doesn't feel his worth. My second son and his wife had to hear a sordid tale. Are you proud?"

"Exceedingly," Mr. Darcy stated, with no hint of apology in his voice, "because would you rather remain in the dark forever, making wrong decision after wrong decision? We all did the best we could to bring you into a light of self-reflection. I am not about to apologize for it."

"How easy it is for you," Sir Thomas announced, forlorn and saddened, "to speak from a place where you inherited your fortune with no immoral ties attached to it. I cannot tell you what it's like, but I will try, so that you better understand me. I inherited my estate. All that was at Antigua was given to me, and I had to uphold it, to maintain my house, wife, and children. How can I untie myself from something that saves my family? Can you not understand me at all?"

"I do, but I cannot condone it. It is too far away from all that I have been taught."

"And neither can I. I have been taught the same level of resilience as you. Can you not respect your elders?"

"Even an old dog can learn new tricks."

"But I cannot," Sir Thomas said, "my plantation has helped me support my wife, children, and maintaining Mansfield Park. I cannot release my property of flesh in Antigua, or I will go bankrupt. I will lose everything. I cannot do that to my family. I cannot! My loyalty is to them first, no matter how some of them have turned out." He looked at us all. "I cannot tell you what it is like...to be in a state where the only way that you can do right by your family is if you do wrong everywhere else. You are all spared from having to make those decisions."

"Oh," Mr. Darcy sighed, "is this where you shout out that you are a victim of circumstances? That you have this difficult decision to make. I will not let you. I'm tired of gentlemen and ladies always making an excuse, but they condemn others. Therefore, this is the choice that I give you: make amends with your daughter. Teach her right and wrong, and welcome her back into your home—if she would wish it. Happily, accept Miss Crawford's marriage to your nephew, welcome them into your family, allow them to even marry on Mansfield Park, or we will weigh the scales of your actions, and your sons' longstanding indifference to your actions. The choice is yours. Mercy for mercy. What say you?"

Sir Thomas was still silent.

"I know that admitting you were wrong is not easy," Mr. Darcy added, "I have been in your predicament myself. But believe me, once you acknowledge your error, you are not a lesser man, sir. You actually become more complete."

"I just want to be understood," Sir Thomas bellowed.

"We do understand you," Finlay finalized, "but can you understand us? Do you see the disconnect?"

"I have never been thus treated in my entire life."

"Tell that to the people who you own. Believe me, their grievances are worse."

Mr. Edmund Bertram turned to his father.

"Father," he said, "we must accept that maybe, we took a wrong turn somewhere. Maybe, in our desire for a purer life, we ignored the impurity in our own. We cannot complain about those who ruined our lives, when maybe it was us who ruined ourselves, the entire time."

Sir Thomas sighed and turned to Mary Crawford and William Price.

The air felt heavy.

Because our actions were.

"Welcome to our family," Sir Thomas said to them both.

~

"Good lord for alliance!" Mary Crawford said, quoting Shakespeare.

"Well, I confess that it is about time, don't you think!" William Price said, smiling eagerly. "I did truly want you happy for me, uncle. I just have to follow my heart. That's all that I wanted."

Sir Thomas walked up to William Price and shook his hand.

"You must forgive this old fool. I just wanted, so much, for everything to be just right."

"I know, uncle. I know that you did. That is the one thing that has made this whole conflict acceptable. I know that you cared, underneath it all. You just needed time to see what the right thing was to care for."

"I just want—"

"Your life to be perfect," Elizabeth finalized.

"Yes."

"Sir Thomas," Jane advised, "seek that perfection, but also understand that perfection does not exist. It never has. Chase it, but don't choke everyone with it. When you do that, you inevitably choke yourself."

Sir Thomas looked at Mr. Darcy.

"I know that you regard me as the end of England's great lie. I represent a generation of old ideas and stuffy ways. But this is all that I know. It's what I inherited. It's *all* that I know."

"But it doesn't have to be," I stated, having come to a realization, for quite some time. "I know someone who can help you."

"Help me?"

"Yes. Your main crime is not only the doubleness of standards that you hold against others, but your own actions. You inherited a plantation, and you continued its mission, even when the rest of Britain was leaving you behind. In fact, Scotland abolished slavery in 1778, so part of this country has already left many of us behind. You don't need to do this alone, nor lose money by liberating your slaves. Rather, I know someone who can easily help you transition from slaveowner to employer, without losing your profits."

"My father!" Arthur Philips declared.

"Yes. Sir Thomas, his father is my Uncle Philips. He's an attorney in Meryton, and he specialized in situations like these. Not only did he represent masters in court, but he spent a great deal of his life speaking with accountants and finding a definite plan where you could pay your slaves, and soon transform them into your tenants, who work your lands."

"But if I pay them, I lose income," Sir Thomas stated.

"Father, let's listen to them first," Mr. Bertram said.

"And it's quite the humane concept," Mary Crawford added.

"And not necessarily lose your income," Arthur continued, "my father knew that an immediate falloff could occur if a master were to start handing out salaries. Therefore, he met with accountants in London, to see how a master could distribute a base salary for a month of work, with a promise of a higher salary if the slaves produced a steady amount of work per day. But mind you, the amount of work must be realistic, and not exorbitant, making it possible for the slave to earn that raise. Trustworthy people must oversee this venture, to ensure that the new employees are now being treated fairly. If you always promise them a slight raise with each outpour of successful product, until they earn the traditional wages as any other average fieldhand, they will work. But you must *uphold this promise*. Work up to a place of equality, and believe it or not, you will not only make up for any money that you have distributed to them, but you actually can increase your profit."

"Slaves who have a knowing income to strive for," Finlay concluded, "are always more productive than those who are being tortured."

"This is what your father did throughout his career?" Mr. Bingley asked Arthur.

"Yes. You could argue that *that* is the main reason why I am an only child. My father spent so much time traveling around to accountants in London, then traveling to the West Indies to make certain that the distribution was properly settled, and that the enslaved were not being cheated in any way, nor swindled."

"Yes," I said, "one time, he had to leave early, due to a yellow fever outbreak."

"Your Uncle Philips has been to the Indies?" Mr. Bingley asked Jane.

"It's bizarre," Jane said, "he has, but he never told us the reason for why he did." Jane turned to me. "Why did he tell you?"

"Because I always wished to know him, so I asked him," I said, so innocently, that Jane and Lizzy felt a little ashamed. I suppose it then occurred to them that they never took the time to really get to know Uncle Philips. And it made sense. Lizzy and Jane favored the Gardiners, and it was Lydia and I who often went to visit the Philipses. Whenever Jane and Lizzy went, their appearance was transient, almost as if they went there and saw our aunt and uncle, while not *actually* seeing them. But I loved Uncle Philips and found him and Aunt Philips to be the most fascinating parts of our family. So, naturally, I would ask Uncle Philips about his life, and he was eager that someone cared to be interested. Men and women are different creatures, but we're the same in another crucial way: we all need attention every now and again, especially from our families. Uncle Philips was no different.

"My father's plan is a guarantee," Arthur Philips continued. "He has succeeded at helping at least six masters transform their plantations into farmlands with paid workers. And then, after a three-year plan, most of the masters were so successful that they could even spend their money to improve their ex-slaves' living quarters. It is possible, with the right management. If you would but let me write to my father on your behalf, Sir Thomas, I am certain that he would be able to act as your intermediary between the proper accountants who can help you not only liberate your labor force, but increase your profits at the same time."

"That is a wonderful idea," Mr. Edmund Bertram said, "isn't it, Fanny?"

"Yes, it is, my dear," Fanny Bertram said, looking excited for the first time since she came here. "A good idea, indeed."

"Father, please consider it."

"And I could be the one to go to Antigua and facilitate it all," Mr. Bertram said, eagerly wishing to show that he was of any worth, "I can do it."

Sir Thomas still stood there, frozen.

Mr. Darcy decided to take pity on him.

"Sir Thomas," Mr. Darcy said, "just because I disagree with you, I do respect your rank and peerage. But the fact of the matter is that a lot of Britain is wishing to disentangle themselves from the Trade and want nothing more to do with it. The abolition will win, and it's because we respect you that we are giving you a chance to extract yourself from a dying failure and emerge into a better future. If you help your plantation transition to a place where all your 'workers' are paid and earn raises based on their productivity—within reason—then you will set the trend. And others will follow. You will live the rest of your life, and eventually die, a hero of England."

～

When hearing this last appeal, Sir Thomas's face couldn't help but alter. It displayed a glimmer of light that radiated from a man who, feeling like he had lost every ground that he came to gain, now saw a light at the end of the metaphorical tunnel.

Sir Thomas was a strong man, but his sons weren't. They didn't know how to stage a defense against the natural power of Darcy and Finlay put together. It also didn't help that Darcy and Finlay both looked stronger than those three, put together.

Thus, it was only a matter of time before he had no choice but to bow down to Finlay's superior logic, and mine and Arthur's offer.

However, it was vanity, sweet vanity, that won the order of the day! Darcy knew, better than anyone, to appeal to the side where appearances mattered the most. If Sir Thomas were to liberate his slaves, then begin paying them a base wage that increased with every new outpour of successful product, then he could boast about it. Even other slaveowners wouldn't feel as if he was betraying their way of life but would soon want to follow his example. Sir Thomas could be the one to set the scene, as it were. And who wouldn't want that?

Sir Thomas turned to Arthur Philips.

"He has a certain way of knowing how to transform a planta-tion to an estate of hired-hands, without any financial loss?"

"Yes, my father does."

"Mr. Philips...write to your father, posthaste. Inform him that your letter shall soon be followed by one of my own."

Finally, a solution was reached.

"And Mr. Price's wedding?" Elizabeth asked.

"It will be at Mansfield Park's parish."

That was the second step.

However, he turned to Mr. Henry Crawford.

"I know that my daughter had the choice not to marry Mr. Rushworth. I know that she is responsible for her own actions, and I know that she chose to come to you. But it doesn't change that you toyed with my daughters' hearts, as well as another lady who you claimed to care for, while being a libertine at the same time."

"I know what I am," Mr. Crawford said, "and I understand your apprehension toward how to receive me. Therefore, I do not impose myself upon your company. I only ask to be allowed to see my sister on her wedding day. Then I shall leave from the church immediately. Also, when you are ready to accept your eldest daughter back into the family and household, please tell her that I am sorry. Much of her mistakes were manifested through my own. I apologize that it took me so long to see it. I do not have you act as an intermediary for me out of cowardice. But rather, I know that the last thing that Miss Bertram needs is to impose my presence on her. My lack of appearance in her life is the only apology that I can give her. And if it helps, you may tell people that I lured her away with the promise of marrying her, twice."

We all looked at him, surprised.

"What?" Mrs. Grant asked. "Henry, you did that?"

"No, he didn't," Mary Crawford said for her brother. "He's giving Miss Maria her best chance." She deduced what he was intending. "If it circulates that Henry offered to marry her before she married Mr. Rushworth, but did not hold to his promise, it places Maria Bertram into the role of victimhood. Then, if he made her the offer again while she was married to Mr. Rushworth, it places the blame entirely on his side. Playing the martyr, brother?"

"Perhaps I am," Mr. Crawford said, "I'm already villainous, so what is the worst that can happen by being the sole villain? And who knows? Maybe I might turn out all the better for it by the end."

"Thank you for the offer," Sir Thomas said, "but my daughter needs to remember what she did."

"Maybe she does know," Mrs. Grant said, "you'll never know until you see her again."

"And if you would do so well as to let me offer any advice," Jane requested, "but talk to her gently. Being cold and stern will only make her turn away from you more. Ask her why she did what she did, what made her react in such a way, and what spurred her to turn her back on her entire life. I have had such talks with women who have committed intense mistakes before. The source behind them, one discovers, is deep, and it turns out that the lady just needed someone to talk with her and understand her. Put simply, your daughter needs a loving father. Not a judge."

Sir Thomas sighed.

"It's been so long since I have seen her. I wouldn't know how."

"I'll go and see her."

This was not spoken by any of the Bertram men. Rather, it came from one of the most unlikely of places. It was spoken by Fanny Bertram.

When we all turned to her, she felt intimidated under our gaze. She drew near her husband again, who took her protectively by leaning into her, indicating his support.

"Uncle and father," Fanny said to her father-in-law/uncle (I don't know why, but I found that dual title to be a little off-putting), "I can see why this task is so cumbersome for you. It is difficult and it can be overwhelming. Of course, I understand why it must be. You have done everything you could to be a great father, and I appreciate all that you have done for taking me in and caring for my brother. Therefore, let me help you. I shall go to see Maria, and see how she feels about her past, learn what prompted it, and see if she wants to return home."

Mr. Edmund Bertram couldn't have looked prouder.

"My wife's chief defect," he said, "She makes herself indispensable. Fanny and I will go and visit Maria together. Whenever you are ready to receive her, we can begin the process of reconciliation."

"Yes," Finlay finalized, "for that is the religiously moral thing to do."

"Very well," Sir Thomas said, "you may go to her."

Everyone breathed a sigh of relief, internally. Now all points had been achieved.

"Good," Mr. Darcy stated, "if your family would be so kind as to stay for dinner, it would do us a great honor. Sir Thomas, everything said and done so far today has been done out of necessity and not contempt for your house or your name. However, everyone here has a great desire to respect your family. Please spend the dinner proving that we are right to have that desire."

"Well, I would prefer to end this day having gained someone's high esteem," Sir Thomas said, "therefore, let us see the table that Pemberley sets. If the dinner is delightful, then that is where we may begin."

Mr. Tom Bertram was so relieved that he collapsed into a chair and rubbed his face down.

"Thank God for the ending of this all. This afternoon was so uncomfortable that I worried it would never end."

Chapter Twenty-Seven

KITTY'S TALE: THE OTHER SIDE OF FANNY PRICE

How admirably things turn out when the conflict is over and both sides are so desperate to get along, that only nice things are said.

The dinner passed charmingly, and I had the good fortune to be seated next to Finlay the entire time.

While we ate, I caught him smiling at me so intensely that I had to ask him why he was so happy.

"Because I am proud of you," he replied.

"Me? How so? You were the real savior. If it weren't for you, we never would have learned the truth that saved everyone."

"Yes, and you brought on a solution, no matter how others ignore it." He looked at Sir Thomas, while still whispering to me. "I can tell you what's going to happen. Your uncle is going to give him the best advice in the world, an accountant will sort out everything, Sir Thomas will make those proper changes, then he can boast to everyone of how he has reformed. He will be a hero, and you will never be mentioned."

He was right. I would never be mentioned. Oh well, such is life!

"The product of being a single lady with no influence," I said, resigned.

"Well," he said, "yes, your voice will go unnoticed for now. But Kitty, that doesn't mean that you have to like it." He looked at me, shrewdly. "A person is only as small as they allow others to make them. You want to be seen and heard, make a bold impression and don't be afraid to make a loud noise, when there's a time that you ought to. Those are the first women that our world despises, but those are also the women that history loves to remember."

I looked at him, ashamed.

"And what if I'm not that strong?" I asked. "What if I let you down?"

"If that happens, I'll love you anyway. I'm a man in love: I'm giving encouragement, *not* an order."

Under the table, he dared risk everything. Slowly, he placed his hands gently on my thigh and closed his fingers around my gown. Falling to the wayside of propriety again—it's not easy rejecting someone you love, and I am no saint, but merely a woman—I placed my hand over his and held it.

When I did so, his body tensed up and then relaxed.

"But that's not the real reason that I am proud of you," he continued.

"What then?"

"It was because we were unified. It wasn't me speaking for myself. You were speaking with me, supporting me, and being by my side. When you are a soldier, you cannot fight a battle on your own. You rely upon the man who is to your left and to your right. You were the soldier to my left and my right, all at once. You were there for me. That's what I'm proud of. You were there for me."

"Thank you for knowing that's what you should have been proud of."

"Of course."

The rest of the dinner ended well. Soon, it came time to depart. Before they all left, the Mansfield Park company needed to refresh themselves. From wishing to check their appearance first, to needing to use the Necessary Room, they were attended to.

Eager to know something that had been eating away at my curiosity for quite some time, I offered to assist Miss Fanny Bertram. Leading her from the Necessary Room, I escorted her to my room to refresh herself and check her appearance in the mirror.

As she took her hair down to rearrange it, since a few strands had fallen, I sat down on the other side of the room.

"Oh pray, do not trouble yourself on my account," Fanny said, "you do not have to wait for me."

"I do not mind," I assured her, "do as you do." When she wrapped her hair into a knot, I decided that now was as good of a time as any. "You must be happy that your brother is marrying a woman who can assist him in his career as well as brings a fortune with her, while also being perfect for him."

"Yes, I am," Fanny rushed out. "I love my brother and want the best for him."

Her words were hollow, and I knew that she didn't believe a word that she had said.

"Even when that woman is someone that your husband once loved, and you were jealous over?"

Fanny halted in the mirror and her face turned white with shock. She barely moved, but only turned her head toward me, very alarmed.

"If you are attempting to tell me that I am wrong," I continued, "lies don't become you very well. This you probably know." Still, she said nothing. "You probably never told yourself that you were jealous. But I know the look of a woman who is jealous of another woman, because she was the man's first choice. If it helps, you did not give very much away. Also, I am aware of your history with the Crawford family."

"Surely my history with the Crawfords does not indicate so much."

"I know that Mr. Crawford courted you, and you rejected him. Mr. Crawford is alluring and is known to draw in any woman eventually. Either that is so because you are naturally immune to his charms, or you were immune because you already had feelings for someone else. And the way that you look at your husband indicates a woman who has been in love with him for quite a long time."

I took a step toward her, and she began to shake.

"I am not here to hurt you, Mrs. Bertram, but merely wished to ask if you wished to talk about it. It must've hurt you to be so wonderfully in love, when the object of your affections liked another. You don't have to speak. If you like, I can take your silence as a yes. It did hurt, seeing Mr. Edmund Bertram in love with Mary Crawford, didn't it?"

Fanny did not respond.

"And, unless I am mistaken, Mary Crawford had no notion that you were in love with your cousin, was she? Again, you can be silent, and I will take it as a yes."

She looked at the floor, and once more did not respond.

"Well, it wasn't Mary Crawford's fault that Mr. Bertram fell in love with her. It's very easy to blame the woman for when the man falls in love with her. But I tell you this now, jealousy is as dangerous a sin as any other. No matter how right you think you are, at the end of the day, nothing is more terrifying to a woman than when another woman is jealous of her. It leads to you thinking ill of the other woman, in a very inappropriate manner. It also leads to a woman greatly exaggerating the flaws of the object of her jealousy. It can ruin a life. It's the same with men. Again, I don't know how far your envy went, or if you ever were able to consider that it was envy that you were feeling. All I'm saying is that no one is perfect. Mary Crawford is not perfect. Neither am I. And deep down, when you battle with your own consciousness, neither are you. Therefore, be happy for your brother. And are you willing to accept Miss Crawford as your new sister?"

"It is so difficult," Fanny said to me, wistful and on the verge of tears. "It is so difficult. My brother is marrying the woman who my husband once liked."

"But your husband never married her. He married you."

"What if he regrets marrying me, whenever he sees her?"

I took her hands in mine.

"Mrs. Bertram—Fanny—listen to me. If you ever are afraid of that, then talk to your husband about that."

"No, I cannot do that."

"Why not?" I asked, confused. It seemed like he would be the right person for her to talk with.

"The last thing he needs is my irrational thoughts."

"Fanny," I said, "I'm doing this for your own good and to help you. Brace yourself."

I slapped her.

~

It was neither a vicious slap nor a harmful one. It would only leave a sting on her face that lasted for a minute and then would disappear entirely.

But it did the trick. She went from a Weeping Wendy to an alert and highly offended face.

"Of course, you can talk to your husband about your feelings!" I declared. "He's your husband. He's the main one that you ought to unfold your emotions to. If you cannot do that, who can you do it to?"

"I don't want him to think me as such."

"You will find that he might need to talk about it. And it doesn't always have to be about him. The discussion can be about you. You will find, deep down, that he probably did want to have this talk all along. However, if you ever do wish to talk and fear it, if you have a sister, don't be afraid to confide in her. Believe me, it is the greatest thing."

"I will feel so embarrassed if I tell them all that I had been feeling envy."

"There is no reason to feel such. That is what family is for. And believe me, that is the first step to recovery. But Mary Crawford is not your enemy. She just happened to be the one that your husband chose, before he realized that you were the perfect woman the entire time. You have the man you love. You can let this all go now. However, if you feel that you have no one to confide in, then never fear to write to Jane, Lizzy, or myself. We can help you recover and will keep your secret. Never believe that your husband will turn away from you. He loves you, and he made the perfect choice. Cherish that. And let your own jealousies die."

She did not respond but only nodded. Finally, she established her composure.

"Thank you," she said, "I know that it was kindly meant. Perhaps I did need to say it out loud. I do feel differently now."

"It's called catharsis. Soon, you will feel purged."

"I do."

While she said this, it was difficult for me to cultivate any sort of compassion for her. Her tone was too dispassionate and serene, that I could not warm to her entirely. In fact, I could not fully tell what she was feeling. No wonder Edmund Bertram might have taken so long to get to the point of it. Her disposition did not lend itself to discerning what she was really feeling. He probably had no idea that she was in love with him for the longest time.

At last, Fanny went to the door, and I stood up to escort her downstairs, but she halted as she placed her hand on the doorknob.

"Miss Bennet?" she asked me.

"Yes?" I said, equally as still as her.

"Do you know how it feels to love someone who loved another before you?" she asked.

"Yes, I do."

"Was it difficult as well?"

"Our situations are different. You grew up with your cousin. With my situation, I had just met the man."

She looked at me and I realized that I gave a very unsatisfying answer.

"No," I said, "I didn't feel much jealousy at all, but quickly moved on. Then again, I had something else going for me."

"What was that?"

"The other woman was one of my sisters."

When hearing that, Fanny immediately looked interested.

"She was?"

"Yes. She was. And I had to ask myself: what was more important? This man, or my sister. Naturally, my sister was the one I chose. So, I let the man go and released him from my affections. I count myself lucky. I don't know why I have always had the resolve to not love a man who doesn't love me in return. I cannot ever fully understand the turmoil that your heart has been through, but I can understand somewhat."

"It was like my heart was forever being ripped out of my chest. I felt in pain and so terribly alone."

"You were never alone, Fanny. Find those in your family, confide in them, and let them know what's in your heart. Suffering in silence can sometimes be unhealthy. Remember, Edmund chose you and obviously appreciates your worth and knows that you are the best choice for him. Let Miss Crawford's ghost go and see her in a new way."

She smiled at me.

"Thank you. I think I can."

Finally, she gave me an emotion that I could work with. At the end of it all, I found something to connect to.

We rejoined the company, and it was time for the Bertrams to depart, to journey back to Mansfield Park.

We saw them off. Kind words were offered, but we perhaps were all eager to part ways with each other. We both were two families who could be friendly with the other, but never be close.

As their carriage departed down the lane, I stood next to Mr. Crawford and Jane.

"Well, Mr. Crawford," Jane said, "you have your goodness now. I will hold you to it, sir."

"Mrs. Bingley...just for you."

"No, not for me. For yourself. For yourself."

Chapter Twenty-Eight

KITTY'S TALE: ONWARD TO ROSINGS PARK!

The days till our departure quickly wound down to when we were to travel to Rosings Park for the holidays.

As was customary for that time of the year, there was a bit of frenzy in the air. This was also added to the weather...the cold, bleak, and chilling weather. Snow fell occasionally, we had two ladies who were in the throes of pregnancy—and for all that we knew, Enara could be as well, and she simply wasn't aware—and we had to prepare for arrivals and departures.

Now that the Crawfords had the joys of knowing that they had a family that would meet them, arrangements had been made. They had received an express invitation to Mansfield Park, so that they could have a wedding at the parish during the twelve days of Christmas.

Seeing them leave closed the chapter on another part of our lives. One that we had hoped would remain closed forever. We knew that we very well might see the Crawfords and Bertrams again, but it was the strife and conflicts between their families that we hoped we had put an end to.

Therefore, when we saw the Crawford's carriage off, headed to Northampton, we felt that we had earned the holiday...until we recalled that we would be going to visit Lady Catherine de Bourgh. That was enough to dampen our outlook on the situation.

All these events gave me no choice but to put my domestic lessons on hold. I couldn't take the time to learn to cook more, clean, or tend to horses. Oh well, sometimes a person has a right to be leisurely.

We were also inundated with a siege of letters. From our parents, from the Fitzwilliams, the Gardiners, etc. We also had to mail our letters of Christmas cheer and goodwill as well.

On our last day at Pemberley, when Lucy and I were packing my things in my trunk for travel, Betsy entered.

"Miss," she said.

"Yes, Betsy," I said, as I sorted out my ribbons.

"Sorry to disturb your packing, but you have a visitor."

My heart livened and I knew who had come.

"Is he in the front parlor?"

"Yes, he is, miss."

"Thank you. Lucy, just pick my best gowns and all other necessities."

"Very good, miss," Lucy said as I picked up a parcel and rushed out of the room. I ran down the hallway, rushed into Georgiana's room, and yanked her by the hand.

"Where are we going?" Georgiana asked frantically as I pulled her out of the room.

"Finlay is here, and I need a chaperone."

"Ah. I should have known."

We moved around the servants who were arranging everything for our journey.

We walked down the steps quickly and dashed into the front parlor.

"Enjoying the view?" I said to Finlay's back as he was looking out of the window.

"It does not compare to what stands behind me."

He turned around and he had a small-wrapped box in his hand. When he saw what was in my hands, he was surprised. He was even more surprised when he saw Georgiana. His last comment was not proper, so his cheeks reddened. Georgiana greeted him, then quickly excused herself, moved to the other side of the room, and sat down at the pianoforte.

"You brought me something?" he asked me.

"Why should I not? Forgive my lack of imagination, but I never bought a man a present before. All the maids in the household told me: 'buy a man something that is practical, that he will use very often'."

"I have the good fortune to not ask for advice. Women are easier to shop for because there is so much more made for you all."

We both sat down together, said 'Happy Christmas' to each other, and exchanged presents.

He opened his first, and his eyes widened.

"My word!" he exclaimed, laughing, "these are beautiful."

It was a nice pair of black boots.

"I had to get Mrs. Forster to secretly find out your shoe size," I said.

"Ah, you used a spy, did you?" he asked, with a glint in his eye.

"I've decided to always use every tool that is left to me."

I opened my gift, and it was a lovely necklace.

"Oh, Finlay!" I cried. "It is beautiful!"

Standing up, I rushed to the nearest mirror, put on my necklace, and looked at it.

"Finlay, I cannot believe it!"

"You thought I could have you go to Kent and not do something to make you remember me by?"

"We're both very scheming people, aren't we?"

"Yes, we are."

We stood there, staring at each other. We didn't have much time. We sensed that we didn't.

"On Christmas Day," I said, "will you think of me?"

"Will you think of me?"

"Yes, I will."

"And I will think of you."

"Don't die before I return."

"And you do the same," he replied, laughing.

"Good. Because I have mastered my cough, and I aim to be healthy when I return. You will have a woman in control of her breathing."

"Your cough is enjoyable."

"A cough is a cough. But thank you for seeing the light in it."

I looked at him, wistfully.

"I don't know why I look at you in a way where I feel as if I will never see you again."

"I feel the same. But we will, Kitty. We will."

"I know. Pemberley is where all roads lead to. Live and be merry, Lieutenant."

"Don't forget me here, Kitty. Return as soon as you are able."

~

Finlay could not stay long, because he had to return to his duties.

Georgiana and I saw him off to his horse.

Walking up to his horse, I touched its mane and looked at Finlay in the saddle.

"Good journey," he said to me fondly.

"Good holiday."

In our eyes was all the affection in the world. Having no choice, he tore his eyes from me, rode down the lane and Georgiana and I watched him as he departed.

"I know that you still are not ready to marry," Georgiana said, "but do you think you will soon?"

"I do not know," I admitted, "but if I were ready to marry, I might know which man I would choose."

Georgiana's eyes widened.

"Which man?"

For the first time, I was about to do something that I never did with her; I was about to withhold a secret.

"Georgiana, I love you. But this is the one truth that I must keep to myself. For my decision could change, with the whiff of time. When I am ready to talk of it, you will be the first one to know. I promise."

"I'll hold you to that."

We went back in from the cold.

~

The next day, it was time to depart for Rosings. Since we had all arranged everything properly before, there was no frenzy when we arranged to set out right after breakfast. It was early in the morning, so that we could reach Rosings Park by the late afternoon.

Since our company was large in number, it required three carriages, and we were all conveyed into them, chilly, but determined to do it.

"Kitty!" Elizabeth said, approaching me as I put on my cloak, bonnet, and comforter.

"Yes," I said, "what is it, Lizzy?"

"Yesterday, the post came, and the letters were improperly arranged. One letter arrived for you. It's from Uncle Philips."

"Oh," I said, taking the letter that was in her hand. She gave me a quizzical look. "This has nothing to do with the Bertrams at all, I assure you. It's pertaining to the letter I wrote when you and I talked. No more than that."

"Oh, pity. I was ever so curious."

"Lizzy, you know what they say curiosity does to cats."

"I've seen many cats walk away from their curiosities, so I find that phrase to be terribly inaccurate."

I put the letter in my reticule.

Mrs. Reynolds saw us off for departure. Sarah, Betsy, and Lucy were to come with us, to tend to the ladies. One valet was needed to look after the men.

Soon, we were on our way to Kent.

I was in the carriage with Georgiana, Bingley, and Jane.

Now that we were underway, I unfolded the letter and began to read it. At first, it was him wishing us all a good holiday, but then he got to the heart of the matter.

> *Kitty, you know my reservations on these two men who have decided to choose you, while not choosing you at all. I remain steadfast in my belief that their desire to remain in your life is not good for you, because you will always be torn in two.*
>
> *Even if you were to choose one, you will feel the pain of hurting the other.*

There is a time to run from things. Sometimes running away is the proper response, and there is no shame in it. In fact, it can often be the right thing to do.

But then I remember that you are young. I know that I can trust you to not do anything foolish, disreputable, or hurtful to your family. And you are only young once. Rather than be frightened by the duality of your circumstances, I will tell you this: enjoy your life. Try as the world will to make you feel otherwise, there is no sin in being happy. There is no crime in wishing to feel more alive than ever. If these men's company make you happy, then let time be your guide and perhaps everything shall work out in the end. That's usually what happens here in Hertfordshire, especially if your last name is Bennet.

But I do not want you to put your life on hold. If single life still calls out to you, and you still feel the need for a journey of some sort, keep your eyes open. If there is a path you wish to walk down before committing to a ceremony, then walk down it.

Find your own way.

Find your journey.

And then you might find your answer.

Either way, I will be proud of you.

And so will your aunt.

Be safe, be well, and be respectful and loyal to those around you.

Your stuffy uncle,

GP

When I closed the letter, I held it to my chest, feeling the beauty of his words.

Fatherly affection! Thy name is Uncle Philips. I wanted to cry with how he understood me. I wanted to roar out that somewhere, out there in the world, was someone who knew what swelled within me. Who accepted that my path was not going to be a customary one.

And he was right. There was a journey ahead for me. And it would prove to be much larger than anything I would have suspected. I would go on to face strife, danger, death, loss, passions, love lost, love gained, friendship tested, find courage, and my life would change completely. But this was a road that I had to walk down, and fate willed it.

But in the meantime, onward to Rosings we go!

End of Book 7

Afterword

Hello, Readers! This one, naturally, had a different shift than the books before it and the one that will take place after it. When I first plotted out the book, it was to have a different sort of confrontation between the Bertrams and the residents at Pemberley.

However, due to a recent set of events, things took a little turn and the situation altered. It actually had to do with an article that was recommended by a person on the Jane Austen Fan Club. It was an article on Dailymail.com UK. It is called:

Jane Austen's brother was an anti-slave Activist, it emerges in boost to the family's name after their father's infamous links to the Trade.

This naturally caught my interest, because the only connections I ever heard of the family being associated with different cultures was Cassandra Austen's late fiancé. According to history, he was a parson who joined a military expedition to the Caribbean and died of yellow fever. Cassandra Austen never remarried. That was the extent of my education when it came to the family having such encounters.

Then this article produced (and is still available to find online if the reader types the title in), about how the Austens had connections to the slave trade and that Jane Austen's avoidance of the issue has been long in question. It starts with stating:

> 'Jane Austen's brother Henry was publicly involved in anti-slavery activism despite their own father's role in the dehumanising trade as a plantation trustee, academics discover.
>
> The author's 'silence' on the slave trade that her father George Austen is believed to have played a part in has long been a topic of debate among literary scholars.
>
> Now records unearthed by Devoney Looser, Regents Professor of English at Arizona State University, show that Austen's own brother Henry had been an outspoken abolitionist.'

The article talks of Jane Austen's father being a trustee to a sugar plantation in Antigua. Since Jane Austen was known for commenting on the world around her, being a great study of character, and also including her observations in her books, I cannot help but assume that is where Jane got the idea of the Bertrams gaining their fortune from the sugar on Antigua. Also, evidence of Jane Austen using her family for inspiration was apparent throughout her works. Her brothers were in the Navy. There was even a letter where her brothers commented on which one of them was most like the naval officers in <u>Persuasion</u>.

But since we are in a world where all historical figures are being scrutinized for any affiliations, they might have had to nefarious organizations, I guess I should not have been terribly surprised that this might have been a subject that scholars mulled over. It also is augmented that Jane Austen was very silent on such matters, suggesting that we shall never know about what she really thought.

In many ways, that was her genius. Since Jane Austen's opinion is not well known, and her sister did right by destroying many of Jane Austen's letters (something that has vexed many historians over the decades) we know very little about many of Miss Austen's viewpoints. This has added to her mystery, but also her ability to be very generally well-loved around the world. As a result, her works never become dated, and no one ever has to fully worry about liking an author whose' ideas proved to not age well. In the world we are living in now, we want to know everything about the authors we love, but I think this was the right thing for Cassandra Austen to do.

Even if that were the reverse, I often say that we must always not fully judge historical characters by 21st century standards. We must take into account the time they were living in; did they do the best they could in that time, weigh out the good they have done and the bad, and see if they changed their opinions and habits to become better over time.

With Jane Austen, she often was not verbose about the matter. This leads to people having no choice but to assume that Jane Austen had no opinion on the matter, or that maybe she was conflicted. If we were to assume such, her confusion is understandable.

First, Jane Austen was born and raised in a world where the Trade was still acceptable. This was a part of life.

Secondly, her father was a loving father who brought her paper, at a time where paper was expensive. He believed in her talents. It might be as hard to reconcile love with one's father, with knowledge of him having connections to a plantation. Whatever he was entrusted to, Jane can't forget that he supported her chief passion: writing. Nor could she forget her love for him. Besides, since her father was a trustee only, the historian also points out that Jane's father could have always signed his name as a trustee just to help a friend or to help the estate be passed over to the right hands. If this is true, her father was not really connected to the Trade. But if it were not the case, he still is her loving father, and she would not forget that. Family ties are complicated.

Thirdly, Jane was not witness to the events that happened on Antigua. The Trade was kept very much out of sight in Britain, as opposed to America, where slavery was more obvious, and inescapable to witness. It's not like the Grimke Sisters, who were two sisters who left their home and became abolitionists, in protest of the horrors they saw on their father's plantation. They were present every day to see what the horrors of the Trade was like. If a heinous act is left out of sight, then it's harder to fight. After all, one cannot always know what to feel about something that they did not see. Some people can and they have a great empathy to their nature. With others it can be harder, and sadly, it takes a long time to see the errors of their oversight.

But with Jane Austen herself, whatever her father might have been entrusted with, it ought not to reflect on Jane, because we do not know all the true details. Also, in such circumstances, even if Jane Austen ever was confused on how she felt about the subject, a progression is shown in her writing. Her juvenilia and her first three complete works, *Northanger Abbey, Sense and Sensibility*, and *Pride & Prejudice* are devoid of any such subject matter. But once we get to *Mansfield Park*, Jane Austen makes a reference to it, as the means through which the family earns their income. And also, the family is very tightlipped about mentioning anything about the matter in its entirety. Jane Austen does not indicate anything positive or negative about this, but it is merely a fact. Thus, this shows a potential indecision or ambiguity on the matter.

Then, in *Emma,* Jane Austen 'shifts gears' as it were and makes a direct reference to the Slave Trade, has a character be in support of the abolition, and the character, Jane Fairfax, calls it the 'the sale of human flesh'. The publication of *Emma* took place very much after it became evident that her favorite brother, Henry Austen, was strongly opposed to slavery, and had become an outspoken abolitionist. This was also well after when Jane's other brother, Francis, believed that slavery in Britain was 'much to be regretted'.

When Jane Austen died, she was unable to finish *Sanditon*, but for those of us who have read it, we know that Miss Austen introduced a half-mulatto character to the tale. Another term for a half-mulatto was quadroon. This all indicates a shift in Jane

Austen's view of what she was willing to do in a subject matter where there was so much confusion about the world she was in.

This led me to have the Darcys and the Bertrams engulfed in the dilemmas that the Austens would have gone through. It was so much to the point where I basically inserted the Austens into those two families, played out the scenarios that they were facing, and maybe Jane Austen would have had that debate herself, in the recesses of her mind.

That's why this book was different than how I had initially planned for it to be. And the same reason that I had the Darcys help to improve the Bertrams' circumstances than have them cast out.

Britain, like both Americas, Australia, Asia, Africa, and every other land, was undergoing a growth process where they had to start making up their minds of the old ways and practices that they had to leave behind. Change is not easy, especially in a world where we are always being torn between one viewpoint and the next—much like today. Especially when change, if correct, is met by opposition from the old guard.

In the article, a museum has noted that it will do more study on the connection, stating:

'The museum said it would look for potential connections to slavery through her (Jane's) behaviour such as the use of sugar in tea and wearing of cotton clothing - which experts say are all 'products of empire' brought back to Britain from colonies in Africa.

If that's what the museum wishes to do, then they may do as they wish.

And if it is done to shed more light on that time period in a general sense and show the truth behind how Britain functioned and how it got its imports, then I can see the importance of it.

Yet, when it comes to Jane Austen herself...in these cases, I view her as a real-life version of Catherine Morland from NA. Like Jane Austen, Catherine goes to Bath and is immersed in all these new sets of individuals, and she is being torn left and right on what to do. On one hand, you have the Allens, then the Thorpes, and then the Tilneys. In each circumstance, Catherine has to tread between them all, suffering under deceptions from the Thorpes and General Tilney. Then they also are drawing her in for the worst reasons, under the guise of them helping her. And she has to wade through them all, trying to sift out who she ought to listen to, who not to, and how to overcome her own self-deceptions.

That's how one should view Jane Austen in her own time, as her own version of Catherine, trying to make her way through a metaphorical 'Bath', wherever she went. What I can say is that wherever Jane Austen ended up, it was always undoubtedly attempted to end in the right place.

At the end, no matter what you feel, we ought to all return to the same place: that no matter what, we love her writing and her, because she is Jane Austen. And she deserves it.

If you read the article, think as you choose. The Trade was also used in this book as a metaphor. Many of the characters in this story have commented on the concept of their own personal freedom.

Kitty dreams about finding a path that helps her rise above the everyday trappings that she feels she is often falling into.

Georgiana wants the freedom of not being chased after for her money.

Finlay and Colonel Fitzwilliam want the freedom of being able to enjoy Kitty's company without being shamed by society.

William Price wants the freedom to marry the woman he wants.

Mary Crawford and Mrs. Grant want the freedom of not being rejected for their brother's actions.

Mrs. Forster and Colonel Forster want the freedom from suffering under Wickham's past and Lydia's plight.

Fanny Price wants freedom from the weight of her history with Mary Crawford.

All are looking for liberty, in some form or another.

Thus, the Bertrams' confrontation of their 'true means of income', and their rising above it, proves to be a catharsis and journey for many of the characters. At the end of it all, they come out with a stronger completion of themselves.

Thank you for reading this next installment in the series. The next book will have a more festive tone.

Until then...later days!

Ney Mitch

THANK YOU FOR READING

Did you enjoy this book?

We invite you to leave a review at your favorite book site, such as Goodreads, Amazon, Barnes & Noble, etc.

DID YOU KNOW THAT LEAVING A REVIEW...

- Helps other readers find books they may enjoy.
- Gives you a chance to let your voice be heard.
- Gives authors recognition for their hard work.
- Doesn't have to be long. A sentence or two about why you liked the book will do.

Also by Ney Mitch

WITH SATIN ROMANCE

Austen Gaskell Series

Curiosities & Contemplation

Resolved & Resigned

Triumph & Tragedy

Woes & Worries (Coming soon!)

~

Kitty Bennet Adventure Series

Vanities and Vexations

Forms & Fashions

Romance & Recklessness

Nuance & Novelty

Doubts & Difficulties

Follies & Forgiveness

Joys & Judgements

~

Romance & Revolution Saga

The First Impression

~

The Memory Series

Moments of Moments Past

Moments of Moments Present

Moments of Moments Future

Moments of Moments Infinite

~

Pride & Prejudice Reimaginings

Rapture & Rebellion

Fortune & Misfortune

Desire & Destiny

Pride & Peace

Resolve & Revelations

Hope & Hopelessness

Faith & Family

~

Chances Series

Chances Are

Chances Come

Chances Fade

Chances End

~

Seasonal Situations

Considearations Near Christmastime

Curiosities at Christmastime

~

Novels

The Tale of Mr. & Mrs. Bennet: A Pride & Prejudice Christmas Tale

Considerations Near Christmastime